# Sleigh Bells and Second Chances

## Love in Mission City Book 3

### Gabbi Grey

# R yan

The moment I landed in that war zone, I knew I'd made a big mistake. I wasn't a soldier, and my good intentions almost got me killed. Being wounded and shipped back home to Canada was both a blessing and a curse. I'm safe now, but I can't stop thinking of the men I left behind. My therapist claims Healing Horses Ranch will help heal my wounds—physical and mental—but I'm not sure how much tranquility and wholesome fresh air I can take. But then I meet a beautiful, shy man who makes moving forward seem almost possible. Can I let go of the past and reach for a future with Simeon?

Simeon

I've made peace with being different from the folks around me. I love my home in Mission City, and if anyone needs something fixed, I'm the guy they call. When the owner of the therapy ranch hires me for a big project, I'm excited to get started. I always work alone, but one of the patients keeps hanging around, and I can't bear to send him on his way. I can see how much he's hurting. If helping me helps him, that's a win for us both. As we share the work, something about that wounded man draws me deeper and deeper in. I'm no therapist, and I have my own issues, so am I a fool to be thinking about a future with a guy who's likely to leave once he's healed?

*Sleigh Bells and Second Chances* is a slow-burn, age-gap, hurt/comfort, mid-angst, gay romance novel with a shy handyman, a reckless former gamer, a precocious borrowed kid, and a therapy dog named Tiffany.

multimedia, audio, or other medium. We support the right of humans to control their artistic works.

No generative AI was used in the creation of this book.

Edits by ELF

Cover by Jo Clement

# Dedication

Kaje
Renae
ELF
Wendy
Jeanine
Stacey
Michael Dean

# Contents

1. Chapter One     1

2. Chapter Two     8

3. Chapter Three     16

4. Chapter Four     26

5. Chapter Five     35

6. Chapter Six     45

7. Chapter Seven     55

8. Chapter Eight     61

9. Chapter Nine     70

10. Chapter Ten     78

11. Chapter Eleven     87

12. Chapter Twelve     97

13. Chapter Thirteen     107

14. Chapter Fourteen     116

| 15. | Chapter Fifteen | 126 |
| 16. | Chapter Sixteen | 137 |
| 17. | Chapter Seventeen | 148 |
| 18. | Chapter Eighteen | 158 |
| 19. | Chapter Nineteen | 166 |
| 20. | Chapter Twenty | 176 |
| 21. | Chapter Twenty-One | 184 |
| 22. | Chapter Twenty-Two | 198 |
| 23. | Chapter Twenty-Three | 209 |
| 24. | Chapter Twenty-Four | 221 |
| 25. | Chapter Twenty-Five | 232 |
| 26. | Chapter Twenty-Six | 241 |
| 27. | Chapter Twenty-Seven | 252 |
| 28. | Chapter Twenty-Eight | 262 |
| 29. | Chapter Twenty-Nine | 273 |
| 30. | Chapter Thirty | 285 |
| 31. | Chapter Thirty-One | 293 |
| 32. | Chapter Thirty-Two | 305 |
| 33. | Chapter Thirty-Three | 314 |
| 34. | Chapter Thirty-Four | 324 |
| 35. | Chapter Thirty-Five | 335 |
| 36. | Chapter Thirty-Six | 344 |
| 37. | Chapter Thirty-Seven | 358 |
| 38. | Chapter Thirty-Eight | 365 |

39. Epilogue      373

40. Interested in knowing more about Gabbi?      384

# Chapter One

Simeon

I'd nearly finished attaching the ceiling fan to the socket when the front door of the prefab I was working on burst open.

Naturally, I dropped the fan.

It narrowly missed my head...but then crashed down to the floor.

Damn thing shattered.

"Oh shit." Rainbow's truly contrite voice carried across the small space.

With a knot in my chest, I descended the ladder. Mindful of the remains of the fan—along with the shattered lightbulb, I made it to the kitchen floor. The crunching under my work boots had me wincing.

"Damn, Simeon, I'm so sorry."

Out my peripheral vision, I spotted her advancing.

I held up a hand. "S-stop. Don't c-come closer."

To my relief, she halted. "What can I do?"

"There's a b-broom and dustpan in the bedroom. C-can you get them?"

"Of course. Let me just shut the door. Tiffany and I were out for a stroll, and—"

"Go t-take care of Tiff." I winced that, in my moment of current distress, I couldn't say the therapy dog's full name without risking another stutter. Having one this severe was bad enough—but stuttering on a name, even a dog's, made my stress worse.

Rainbow left the house.

Grimacing as I went, I headed to the bedroom in search of the broom and dustpan. Locating them was easy—I was always diligent with all of my tools. Sweeping up the mess was something else entirely.

*At least I had a reason for being clumsy. Cousin Suzette was always bumping into walls. Until—*

Nope. Wasn't going to go there. Thinking of her never led to a good place.

As I swept, I realized I didn't even know what Rainbow had wanted. As the manager at Healing Horses Ranch, she was my boss. Well, her sister Kennedy owned the ranch and was technically my real boss. But the psychologist was busy most of the time, so Rainbow had the day-to-day management of the therapy center. Add in the four retired show horses as well as two therapy dogs—one official and one not—this place was busy.

Rainbow was supervising me as I put the finishing touches on this prefab house she and Kennedy were building for their parents so the couple could stay whenever they wanted to visit.

I finished sweeping up the last of the glass, but made a mental note to bring my shop vac tomorrow just in case any little bits remained. I snagged the destroyed ceiling fan and dumped it into the large garbage can I'd brought for this job. Prefabs were supposed to be mostly finished, but this one required more work than I anticipated. That didn't bother me. Rainbow and Kennedy were two of the nicest people in Mission City, so I didn't mind spending time here.

A knock at the door drew my attention and I headed that way.

Rainbow stood on the outside and waved.

I opened the door, checking to ensure she was alone. When I confirmed she was, I beckoned her in.

She entered with a wince. "Okay, Tiffany is with Kennedy and Justin for their next appointment. We've got a new patient coming early this morning. He's meeting with both Kennedy and Justin."

I cocked my head. I couldn't remember ever hearing of a client meeting with two therapists. Did that mean they needed extra help, or was something else going on?

Rainbow flicked her hand back and forth in front of her face. "I've probably said too much. Just...he's a special guy and we want to make certain he's getting the proper level of care. Personally, I think Justin's amazing, but he still holds himself back because he doesn't *officially* have his PhD." She said the word in air quotes.

I didn't have any degree and so was in awe of everyone around here.

"I've c-cleaned up. I should v-vacuum, though."

She snapped her fingers. "Be right back."

And she was gone again.

I shrugged. Then I eyed the pile of laminate flooring as well as my kneepads resting innocuously next to them. I sighed. *You're just thirty-eight. Get on with it.*

Still, when Rainbow returned with a vacuum, I offered a wide smile.

She pointed to the kitchen. "Least I can do."

"I'll m-move some of the laminate to the b-bedroom. Thank you."

She rolled her stunningly pale blue eyes. With her blue/black long hair and memorable eyes, she was an attractive woman. And single.

I snagged a pile of flooring. *And I'm not the least bit interested.* I was gay. I knew I was gay. That was that.

As I returned to the main room, she shut off the vacuum and pulled her phone from her back pocket. "Oh, it's Adam." She tapped her screen. "Hey, Adam." She tapped her finger on the kitchen counter. "Not busy. Just here with Simeon." She held my gaze. "Sure, I can put you on speaker." She tapped the screen as I moved closer.

"Great. This is perfect."

I cocked my head, silently asking Rainbow if she had any clue why my friend was calling.

She shrugged.

"So Dean proposed last night." He paused. "Well, I sort of proposed. I mean..." He sighed. "We're getting married."

Rainbow squealed. Actually squealed. "You know I'm taking all the credit."

Adam chuckled. "We didn't even meet at the ranch."

She eyed me. "Some of your most important moments have been here."

I nodded. I knew Adam had been in therapy here, so she wasn't sharing anything new.

"Oh, so have you talked venues?"

Adam cleared his throat. "It's barely been twelve hours. Dean left me with a long list of people to call while he's out tromping in the woods."

Dean was a forester who'd come all the way to southern British Columbia from Australia to learn about vegetation management. He just happened to meet a wonderful Canadian guy, and apparently, they were getting married.

"Venues, Adam."

He laughed. "Right. No."

"Well, I think you should have it here. When were you thinking?"

A long silence ensued. Finally, Adam spoke. "We're thinking a short engagement. He's got his work permit and permanent residence papers, so he can stay in Canada. But..."

"You don't want him changing his mind?" Rainbow grinned.

"Or me chickening out."

Even as Adam said the words, though, they didn't ring true. He *loved* Dean. I'd never seen two men more suited. Then I flashed to several other gay couples I'd met recently who would also fit the perfect category.

"How about a Christmas wedding?" Rainbow beamed.

I eyed the sunny weather outside. The unseasonably nice weather wouldn't last. We were already into the second week of November, and the rains had already come. They'd only be more intense by Christmas. Of course, we might have a white Christmas. Odds were against it, but anything was possible.

"Uh...you really don't mind? Don't you need to, I don't know, consult with Kennedy?"

Rainbow laughed. "She might own this place, but it's also my home. She'll be thrilled, Adam."

I had no doubt she was right.

"Well, great. Oh, and Simeon, you're invited, okay?"

My jaw dropped.

"He'll be there with bells on," Rainbow assured Adam.

My ears roared as she said her goodbyes.

"N-no." I winced. Crowds. People. Noise. Me...stuttering. No thanks.

"Well, we singletons will be sticking together. Oh, do you think they'll invite other single people? I hear hooking up at a wedding is a thing." The woman had seven sisters, and yet only one had been married. Twice. I still couldn't fathom the lot of them were all single—except maybe their sister's two disastrous marriages had turned them off the institution.

"I b-bet they'll invite Everett." The handsome man was a friend. And I was pretty sure my friends had tried to set me up with him. I had little in common with the smart lawyer, but somehow we'd become friends. Two single gay guys as all our friends hooked up.

"Oh, I bet they will. Everett will be coming solo as well, don't you think? Unless he's seeing someone? Do you know?"

"D-don't think so."

"Okay." She drew in a deep breath and let it out slowly. "I need to confirm Kennedy doesn't have a problem with this—which I'm sure she won't." She gazed around. "Anything else I can do to help?" She tapped the vacuum cleaner. "I think maybe I've done enough damage for the day..."

I managed a grin, still obsessing about how many people would be coming to the wedding. "I'm g-good. Thank you."

She snagged the vacuum cleaner and headed out.

I headed into the bedroom where I secured my kneepads over my jeans, took another sip of coffee from my thermal mug, and tackled the task of installing the flooring.

A wedding. Crap. I was okay one-on-one with folks, or even in a small group when I knew people. But a wedding meant everyone. I could use up all the fingers on both hands and still not count just the folks Adam and I knew in common. And then there'd be Dean's friends, total strangers. Sweat ran down my back. *Maybe I can pretend to be sick.*

Except Adam was a good friend. What kind of wuss would I be to do that? And I wanted to see him and Dean declare their love. It made me a little jealous after all these years alone, but mostly I was happy for them. I needed to share that moment. So I'd soldier on. Maybe I could ask to be Tiffany's handler for the event. I wasn't a guy who needed therapy, but anyone would find a furry dog at their side a comfort...

An hour later, I surveyed my accomplishment. The first bit of the bedroom was looking good.

My knees ached, sweat dripped down my brow, and thirst overwhelmed me. My coffee was a long-distant memory, and lunch was still several hours off. Even when I started early, I ate my lunch at precisely noon. Routine worked best for me, and sticking to a schedule, whenever possible, calmed my mind.

After dusting off my hands, I started up again.

# Chapter Two

Ryan

As I sat in Justin Bridges's office, I glanced out the window. The lush forest beyond the parking lot called to me. Through his other window, the riding ring stood in contrast to the forest just beyond that. I'd spotted the barn and stables before Dr. Kennedy Dixon had ushered me from my car into the ranch house.

The massive great room we'd come through had soaring wood beams that stretched two stories, with a wall of windows facing out over the back deck and to the riding area beyond. To one side of that big room lay a corridor I was told led to three other therapists' offices. To the right was a bright and cheery kitchen, and I'd been ushered beyond that to Kennedy and Justin's offices.

Now I sat on a couch facing the two therapists who sat on high-backed chairs and watched me with what I could only term only term *sympathetic* looks.

I was so sick and fucking tired of people's sympathies.

*Whatever. Get over yourself. You're one of the lucky ones.* The phrase I'd used thousands of times since I'd come home. Like, dozens of times each day. Usually when I was grinding through physiotherapy and wishing I'd died. *And how many* did *die?*

*Wrong thought.*

I rubbed my hands on my thighs to keep from rubbing my chest. "Yeah, so I'm here."

Kennedy smiled.

A genuine smile—which I appreciated.

"Your father's worried about you."

I rolled my eyes.

The psychologist tilted her head. Her stunning looks didn't fool me for a moment. Chestnut-brown hair, luminous brown eyes, and a killer body. She wore her jeans and chambray shirt like a real cowgirl. A cowgirl with a PhD and a stack of accolades.

"You question your father's concern?"

"Uh..." *How to put this?* "My father's concerned about his reputation. Bad enough his son went off to fight in some far-flung war that has nothing to do with him...but to come home badly injured? With ugly physical wounds as well as some potential psychological trauma? Yeah. He needs me fixed up right quick so I don't cause a ripple in his country club set."

Kennedy exchanged a look with Justin.

Wow, he was also a looker. Red-gold hair and beard, stunning blue eyes, and also a genuine smile. Sincerity radiated off them in waves.

Too bad they couldn't break through the ice around my heart.

I had no doubt they'd try.

And fail.

I scratched my nose, holding in the wince that radiated through my chest at the movement. "Look, Marcus Branigan says you're the best." My physiotherapist had offered several suggestions, but Healing Horses had been at the top of his list. "And my dad's willing to fork over the dough." This place wasn't exorbitantly expensive—but it wasn't cheap either. I'd heard something about a sliding scale. Or had that been funding to help people who didn't have the means? Regardless, Daddy Dearest could pay for the Cadillac version of therapy. He'd written a huge check and told me to do my best.

"Your father paying for your treatments in advance was unnecessary." Kennedy smiled. "Appreciated, but unnecessary."

"Yeah, but I might've flaked or something." I hadn't in two years—not since leaving Canada and going to Ukraine—but my father didn't know that. All he saw was a son who'd managed to be injured in visible and embarrassing ways. I hadn't even had the decency to die.

"No one's forcing you to be here." Justin straightened a bit. He wasn't a small guy. Taller and broader than me, that was for sure.

Not that I was puny...just not solidly built. Plus, between the months on the front line, where provisions were scarce, and my injury that brought me home, I wasn't in great shape. Had lost a lot of weight in that time. I'd had the weight to lose, though. I'd always been...heavy. That version of me was unreachable. I barely remembered what it'd been like to be large and glued to my couch. Playing video games.

*Don't go there.*

"I know you're not *forcing* me to be here. That my father isn't either." I scrunched my nose. "Hell, my physiotherapist isn't *forcing* me to be here."

"But he recommended it." Kennedy crossed her hands casually in her lap.

Neither therapist had a notepad, and neither had asked to record the session.

I assumed that meant they had excellent recall. Or they weren't expecting me to say anything profound.

Could've gone either way.

"Yeah. He recommended it." Because my physical exertions during the nightmares were proving bad for my recovery. In his physio office, he could ensure I was doing the exercises properly. Was protecting my chest wall. As I thrashed in my bed at night, all bets were off and, more often than not, I was sustaining additional damage. Damage my body couldn't afford to endure. "He thinks if I, like, talk to you, the nightmares will stop."

"It sounds like they're frequent." Justin held my gaze.

I'd read Marcus's referral. I'd asked to...so I would know exactly what the two therapists did and didn't know. That wasn't to say they hadn't spoken to Marcus informally. Hell, they probably had. My physiotherapist admitted he didn't make many personal referrals. He could've just handed me a list of clinicians. Almost had, apparently. But he'd wanted my permission to speak to whomever took my case. *So he can confirm how batshit crazy I am? Oops. Not supposed to use the 'c' word about myself.* The psychiatrist who'd interviewed me after I'd landed back in Canada had given me some literature. She'd wanted to see me regularly, but I was only spending as much time in Toronto as it took to make me stable enough to get back to Vancouver. My medical team in Vancouver wanted me to stay in a rehab clinic.

I'd threatened to yank out my IV and walk out the front door.

Given I couldn't take two steps without losing my breath, that'd been an empty threat.

But they'd gotten the message. They patched me up as best they could and urged me to seek rehabilitation services—if only on an outpatient basis.

I'd thrown a dart at British Columbia and landed on Mission City.

Well, not quite. I'd looked for the farthest I could get from Vancouver while still being within transit range. That meant Mission City. The commuter train ran into the big city in the morning and returned in the evening. I could get to higher-level medical care if I needed it, but I managed to find a small studio apartment I could call my own. I still needed my father's help, though. Any potential disability payments hadn't kicked in yet. The Canadian government didn't know what to do with me. Canada hadn't sent troops to Ukraine. They were completely in opposition to Russia's invasion, but sending soldiers wasn't possible.

Whatever.

I'd gone.

A few of us went over together.

More than half of our little group had come home in pine boxes.

I was one of the lucky ones. I blinked. "Sorry."

The counselors exchanged another look.

Kennedy leaned toward me. "We can help you, Ryan. Both Justin and I have experience helping people who've suffered trauma."

I nearly snickered. I wanted to say no one had been through what I had. Which was arrogant. Trauma didn't differentiate. Plenty of Canadian soldiers had returned from overseas assignments with issues. And civilians could face trauma of all kinds. Just…I felt like no one could understand what I'd been through. Still, I managed a smile. "I'm quite certain I don't need to keep seeing both of you. There must be other people in need of your services."

For an instant, it looked like Kennedy was going to speak.

Justin beat her to it. "I'm a PhD student. I have six years of clinical counseling under my belt, but I wanted you to know I haven't completed my degree."

Understanding dawned. "My father said he wanted the best, and he assumed that meant the person with the most degrees."

Kennedy's smile was rueful. "He was...specific." She met my gaze. "And I'm happy to take you on as a patient. No hesitation. I'm busy, but if you're flexible, I can make this work." She glanced over at Justin. "But there are things you might not wish to discuss with me."

I snickered. "You heard my pecker's not working."

Where I expected she might blush, she instead held my stare. "Your father was...very forthcoming."

Well, at least that hadn't come from Marcus. I'd asked him to keep that part to himself. Honestly, I didn't care who knew. But my father had a reputation to uphold. Dead heroic sons were best. He could still spin me as being brave. The physical flaws, however, didn't sit well with him. Another reason I'd happily left Vancouver as soon as I was well enough to cope on my own. I now lived in a small ground-floor studio apartment in a massive apartment complex. Tiny. But I had a bathroom of my own and a small living space.

I was golden. No one bothered me. No one nagged me. No one looked down at me.

"Listen." I took a deep breath. "I can talk to a female therapist just as readily as a male therapist. Heck, I'd be happy with an enby counselor. I can talk about my lack of action downstairs or not. It doesn't matter. I mean..." I leaned forward. Not so much that doing so caused physical pain, but enough to get my point across. "I wasn't getting a lot of action before I crossed the ocean. So if I don't get much now, I think I'll survive."

An overweight gamer who never left his father's basement didn't tend to get lucky very often. The occasional hookup barely counted.

"So if Kennedy's busy and Justin can make room, then I see Justin. Look, my father might be paying for this—for which I'm grateful but not enough to admit that to him—but I won't feel beholden to him. He's doing this because I'm not right in the head. He cares about shit like that. Me? I'm happy to hole up in my apartment, go to physio, and generally move on with my life."

"What do you do when you're in your apartment?" Justin tilted his head.

*Does he know? If so, why ask? If not, do I want to reveal my secrets?* "I read." I patted my messenger bag. "I'm always reading. Good for the soul."

"No television? I mean you likely avoid the news—"

"I read. Ever been to the library? Lovely place. Great librarians—Marnie, Loriana, and Johanna. Great ladies. Loving the purple hair Johanna rocks..." *Jesus, shut the hell up.*

"Do you have an eReader? Then you're not confined to just what's in the library."

"Did you know that Cedar Valley has seventeen libraries? And that Marnie can order me books from all of them? They even have a reciprocal relationship with Vancouver. Takes months, but I can get books from there too. Hell, I even still have my library card from when I lived in the city—so I could drive in and take out books, and then the Mission City library can arrange to return them if I don't want to drive back." *And they needed to know none of that.*

"Do you listen to audiobooks? A local author has her entire trilogy on audio—"

"R.D. Watt? The Zaragosa Chronicles? Marnie recommended that first. Read and loved it." I offered a sheepish grin. "The owner of The Owl's Nest bookstore ordered me a copy and got it autographed by R.D. So yeah, I'm good."

"My son has a signed copy." Justin appeared to consider.

*Do therapists talk about their families? Because that would be a good way to go.* "How old?"

He shook his head. "Not why we're here."

*Ah, so that's where he's going. Fair.* "I'm private too. But I can see you're trying to provoke me. Trying to poke the bear—"

"Oh no." Kennedy shook her head. "We'd never—"

"I'll save you the trouble. My car is twenty-five years old. Still in good shape...but old. I even drive a stick. No technology—of any kind. I don't even own a microwave. No television, no e-Readers, no MP3 players, no computers..." I floundered. "Just a hard no. It's not open for debate. Electricity to power my stove and my heater? Sure. I don't mind some creature comforts." *Better than I had during most of my time in Ukraine.* "The rest? Marnie looks on the computer to find me real books. I let real people check out whatever I buy. Although if I can have it delivered after I've placed an order on my flip phone, that's even better. I don't do tech and, for the most part, I don't do people. As long as you don't try to change my mind on those things, we'll be fine." *Jesus. Word vomit much?* Still, I focused my attention on Justin. "We clear?"

Slowly, he nodded. "Yeah, we're clear."

"Great...when do you want me to come back?"

# Chapter Three

Simeon

Tuesday was unexpectedly both mild and sunny. For mid-November in southern British Columbia, this felt like winning the lottery. Then I reminded myself that this warmth might be a result of climate change. We'd had a good rainy period for most of late-October and well up until now. We'd needed it. After the parched and wild-fire-filled summer, the reprieve was appreciated. I never complained about rain and snow.

Well, that wasn't strictly true. If I had an outside job to do and couldn't because of the weather, I'd become slightly irritated. Mildly. I'd find something inside to do and just move along.

"Hey Simeon." Kennedy waved as I stepped out of the prefab house and into the sunshine.

I waved back. My boss was good with few words from me. She looked so different from Rainbow and their other six sisters. While Rainbow and the rest of the Dixon crew had blue/black hair and pale-blue eyes, Kennedy had dark-brown hair and deep-brown eyes. I'd witnessed her taking some ribbing, as the firstborn, from her sisters. The joke was she was the mailman's kid. Not true, of course. Her parents were devoted to each other. And while her seven younger siblings were dead ringers for their mother, Moonshine, Kennedy truly favored their father, Brian.

"I'm wondering if you can check something out in the house." She rubbed her temple. "Rainbow's tried to fix this bathroom tile repeatedly, and it just...won't fix. I can hire someone—"

"I'm h-here. I work f-for you." I pointed to the ranch house.

She grinned and led the way. I toed off my boots and followed her upstairs—to the private family quarters. Somewhere I'd never been and somewhere I now felt uncomfortable.

As if sensing my discomfort, she gently laid a hand on my arm.

That gesture calmed me. On my first day on the ranch, Rainbow asked if I was okay with small touches. I'd been surprised.

As if sensing that surprise, she tried to back away from her request. Of course they never touched patients without consent. Just that, touch was important, and so, when the moment was right, sometimes they offered support.

Totally fine if I was uncomfortable...she wanted to explain in case I saw other people doing it.

Her words stuck with me and, three days later, I sought her out and said it'd be okay. She didn't touch me often, but a pat on the back or a squeeze of my forearm often went a long way to soothing. And, in the end, I realized I was touch-starved. My grandparents were too frail—and too old-fashioned—to reach for me often. Even when I was distressed, a regular occurrence, they didn't tend to initiate contact.

And I was too scared of rejection to try on my own.

"You okay?"

Kennedy's words penetrated my memories. "Yeah." I smiled. "I l-like how casual everyone is on the ranch."

"With each other? For sure." She squeezed my forearm where her hand lay, and then gently led me to the bathroom.

Instantly, I recognized the problem. "Uh, these subway tiles are cute..."

"But also from the seventies."

"Uh... Yep."

"How much would it take to replace them all? With something that'll last fifty years again?"

"T-that's a long time."

She grinned. "I'll almost be ninety. That works for me—assuming I can still do stairs." She cocked her head. "Or I might wind up selling the place to a younger generation of counselors. Or gifting it."

"This is your l-legacy." I had to protest. I'd only been here a handful of times, but clearly this place was part of Kennedy and Rainbow.

Kennedy smile shone in its brilliance. "I'm so glad we hired you." She turned back to the black-and-white tiles. "Do you think you can fit this in?"

"Of c-course. You decide whether you w-want this first, or you want the prefab done first."

"Prefab. But I know you book out in advance, and I don't know if you'll have time to do the bathroom."

I eyed the peeling vinyl floor. "I suggest a t-total do-over." I winced. "I mean, if that's in the b-budget."

"It is." She smiled. "My parents have sold their property. A massive acreage that a developer is planning to subdivide. That makes me sad in some senses—so many memories of tromping around the property—but we need more housing. The developer's keeping part of the wilderness as a sort of park, so that's something. Somewhere we can take our kids." She smiled ruefully. "Not that any of us are matched up and planning families."

She waved her hand in the air as if swatting away the idea. "What I'm trying to say is my parents made a fortune on the sale. Their new house up in 100 Mile House is lovely, but cost just a fraction of what they profited. Between Dad's airline pension and the time Mom put in with the school board, they're truly well-off. So they split some of the proceeds between the eight of us. I have enough to pay for the renovation of this bathroom. I don't know what Rainbow is going to do with her share. I should have you look at her bathroom as well."

"S-sure."

"Then I'm feeding you lunch. Rainbow made a massive pot of chili that'll feed all of us for a week. I love leftovers, but even I'll get tired of it. If you help..."

"I w-won't turn down chili." From the little I knew of the women, that would've been an insult. Although Kennedy and I were the same age, I hadn't gone to school in Mission City. I'd heard stories of the Dixon sisters and all the mischief they got up to. Caring about Kennedy and Rainbow was easy. "Uh..." I named a price for the reno.

Kennedy shook her head. "No way."

My heart fell.

"I looked into what a remodel will cost. It's more than double your price. I'm not willing to cheat you."

I blew out a breath, trying to center myself. I couldn't believe I was about to argue about offering a lower price. "I get a d-discount on the materials. I'll be doing m-most of the work myself. Gio, a guy I hire, will h-help me with the bathtub install and t-the floor—"

"That sounds great. Except either Rainbow or I would like a shower installed instead of another two bathtubs. We're thinking long-term."

"You want a s-seat? A g-grab bar?" Those were things for older people—or the disabled—but both women were still young.

"Yes, that." She nodded. "My parents might want to use them when they're here. We did a bathtub in the prefab because my dad loves them. Mom's a shower person... and that was way more information than you needed." She countered with an astronomical price and ended her quote with, "That's for both bathrooms and the least amount I'd wind up paying someone else. If Gio needs the work, I'm happy to pay him as well."

I cocked my head.

She shrugged. "I assume you know his history. Well, I've heard it as well. You're giving him a fresh start. You're a good man."

Gio had spent time in prison in east Asia when he got caught with weed. He'd completed his prison sentence and returned to Mission City. His new boyfriend—and high school crush—Mercer, hooked him up with me. Mercer ran the paint store and I spent a lot of time there. When he asked if I could throw work Gio's way, I was happy to do it. Strong guys willing to do menial labor were in short supply some days.

"Gio's a g-good man."

"Great, so we're in agreement." She gestured for me to leave the bathroom.

Which I did.

"The p-price—"

"Is what we just agreed on, and if things are more complicated, then I pay more. Let's go eat that chili."

Sometimes the logical thing to do was not to argue. If I took this money from her, then I might be able to lowball a bid for someone who didn't have the money. Plenty of low-income people needed help. Just...Kennedy didn't need to know if I shared the wealth.

I was happy to follow her downstairs to where the scent of chili filled the great room. My stomach growled as we headed into the kitchen. I gently brushed Kennedy's arm.

She turned with a smile.

"C-can I put my sandwich in your fridge for t-tomorrow?"

"Of course."

I nodded.

Rainbow clapped her hands when Kennedy and I entered the kitchen. "Oh, yay."

I couldn't help myself—I grinned. She was such a happy woman, but I felt like her greeting for me was extra special. I got a warm glow in my chest when she directed her enthusiasm toward me.

She gestured to the table where three counselors sat, eating.

Justin was a cute ginger with red hair and beard. He was happily married to Stanley. I adored both them and their kids.

Avery Stinson was an addiction-and-trauma-counselor. Denise Lang was the resident child psychologist. Both women were blonde, although Avery was a bit taller. They were also two of the kindest people I knew.

Rex, the cream lab, sat placidly at Avery's feet. Not an official therapy dog, but he still did plenty around the ranch. His secret power was keeping kids occupied. He never tired of them.

"W-where's Tiffany?" I asked. She was the ranch's official comfort dog, but rarely left Kennedy or Rainbow's side.

"She's, uh, busy." Justin met my gaze, then shifted his focus to Kennedy. "He hasn't left the property. I mean, his car's still here and Tiffany took off after him. I've checked repeatedly, and she hasn't come back."

Rainbow placed a bowl of chili at the table and gestured for me to sit.

I did as bade.

Kennedy sat next to Justin and placed her hand over his. "Don't worry. One, she'll bark when she's back and wants in. Or she'll just trail along with the next client."

"Yeah."

"Two...if she went, then she thinks she can help. If she's still gone later, then searching her out will help us find him." She turned to Rainbow. "Let one of us know immediately if he comes back."

"Disturb you?" Rainbow set her bowl at her place and sat.

The four counselors exchanged looks.

"I've got an easy workload this afternoon." Avery waved her spoon in the air. "Mostly caretaking clients—all of whom would be understanding. All of whom were in tough spots at various times themselves. If he's willing to stay and talk it out, show him to Max's office and come and get me. I'll let you bring Rex with you and take care of my client, and I'll help him." She glanced between Justin and Kennedy. "Then Rainbow will nab either of you as soon as you're available."

"Not ideal, but workable." Kennedy frowned. "I've got a...rough afternoon."

"Mine's not much better." Justin eyed his food. "I feel like I should be looking for him." He winced. "I don't even know..." He glanced at me.

I'd sort of been tactfully trying not to pay attention while eating as quickly as I could so leaving would be logical. "I c-can leave."

"I was just going to say what might trigger him." He smiled. "We trust you. You're not getting any great secrets here."

Which was what I figured. The ranch had a reputation as the best counseling center in Mission City and they wouldn't be careless with confidentiality. "Max?" That name was new to me, and I thought I knew everyone who worked on the ranch.

"Oh, Max Crawford. He's the psychiatrist who mainly works out of the hospital. He has a few clients he sees up here. People who would be traumatized or just have problems if they had to meet him in a clinical setting. He mostly rides horses with them."

"L-lovely day today."

"Yes." Rainbow grinned. "I have plans to do some outdoor work."

"N-need help?" I was a bit ahead of my own work, and if she needed—

She shook her head. "Nah. Just little things like taking the horses out for a stretch. I'll..." She cleared her throat. "Be able to keep my eye out without being obtrusive."

Impressed. I was damn impressed. She'd confided early on that she didn't have a counseling degree—or inclination—but her empathy made her a great addition to the ranch. And she was a generous boss.

"Oh." Kennedy tapped the table with her index finger. "Rainbow? Simeon's going to renovate both our bathrooms."

"Yay." Rainbow fist pumped the air. "Best investment ever. What a great way to spend my inheritance. I'm loving the idea of a walk-in shower."

"Hey." Kennedy frowned. "I thought I was getting the walk-in shower. We agreed one of us had to have a bathtub. Although it'll be a nice, new one. Simeon is going to help us pick one out."

*Oh I am, am I?* Well, I'd done it before.

Thus begun a friendly and lively discussion between the sisters over who would get the shower and who would have the bathtub.

Avery caught my gaze and winked.

Yeah. The food wasn't the only thing warming me.

The sun still shone as I walked the short distance from the ranch house back to the prefab. *Wish Rainbow could've used my help. What a beautiful day to be outside.* I eyed the new structure, trying to determine if there was anything to be done on the exterior. Alas, I had crown molding to install inside, and that needed to be completed. At least in the bedroom where Gio had painted last week. He was working on a different project today and needed neither help nor supervision. I planned to swing by there after work to check out the final result and to settle the bill with the owner. She'd had initial doubts, but now was more than willing to let Gio do the work. His reputation around town was solidifying as a good guy who made a mistake as a young man. Plenty of people around Mission City needed second chances. Needed redemption. Just as many folks willing to give it.

I entered the prefab and gazed around. I'd cut the molding yesterday. I should've been finishing the flooring first, but my knees protested at even the thought. What I loved about working for myself was I could go with what my body wanted. Standing on a ladder to do crown molding now. Flooring again tomorrow morning while Gio painted.

*See? You're really good at this.* I needed that affirmation sometimes. My clients said it. My grandparents said it. My parents...had not. My dad had been embarrassed by my stutter. By my low grades in subjects I couldn't wrap my mind around. A shop teacher saw my talent for working with my hands and taught me everything she knew—often staying after school to give me extra lessons. Her support practically saved my life, when I was drowning in how useless Dad said I was. Without her, I wouldn't be here today, working at a job I loved on a bright fall day.

I positioned the ladder, took a moment to confirm Gio's paint job was flawless, then grabbed my nail gun and the piece of molding I'd cut yesterday.

Only to realize I really needed help holding it in place. I'd forgotten how long the wall was.

*Damn. Should I grab Rainbow? She'd be happy to help...* Nah. If I got a few center nails in perfectly, then I'd be able to do the rest no problem. I positioned myself, said a little prayer to the universe, and depressed the gun to shoot the nail, and did a little happy dance inside when it worked. I did several more in quick succession to secure the molding before barking somewhere inside the house nearly had me falling off the ladder.

*What the hell?*

# Chapter Four

Ryan

I screamed.

The noise stopped.

A dog barked.

I curled into a ball.

*Why did you think the bathroom would be safe? Bathrooms aren't safe when the bombs are dropping. A bit of ceramic won't prevent a drone from blowing everyone into pieces. Oh God, the blood.*

The dog woofed again.

A hulking figure appeared in the door.

*Oh God, they've found me. I can't even find a good hiding spot. Nowhere is safe.*

"H-hey." Slowly he stepped into the room. He was a giant in this small space. "L-let me get Rainbow."

*Rainbow? What does a rainbow have to do with...?*

*Oh.*

I fought for breath. "No!"

Golden furry Tiffany stepped to the guy, nuzzled his hand, then came back to me and wormed her way under my arm. *See? You remember the dog's name. Rainbow works with the horses. Kennedy owns the ranch. Justin is your counselor. What are five things you can see?* Oh, Jesus, the exercise that had so often been taught to me. How to ground myself after a panic attack. I didn't feel ready to come back from the sheer panic—the abject horror. Wasn't in any shape to deal with people.

"Sorry. N-n-nail gun..." The hulking figure slowly sank to the floor.

Whether he understood I didn't want him to find Rainbow, or whether he realized I wasn't fit to be left alone, I couldn't be certain. But I wanted to be left alone. That's why I'd come to this empty house.

Right?

I just didn't know.

He pointed to himself. "S-Simeon."

God, poor guy couldn't even say his own name without stuttering. Although maybe he didn't have a stutter? Maybe he was just nervous? I'd screamed. I was certain I'd screamed. So why had this guy come *into* the bathroom? Why not run the other way when he had the chance to get away?

I drew in a breath. "Ryan." *Fucking hell*. The word had barely come out as a whisper.

He cocked his head, held still for a moment, then spoke. "Ryan." He repeated the name. Not quite a statement. Not quite a question.

I nodded.

He gestured to the spot next to me on the floor. "Can I s-sit there?" That would allow him to lean against the tub like I was. He'd be close to the wall while I was smooshed against the toilet. *This sure is a small bathroom.* Well, a small bathroom for a small house.

I eyed the nail gun he'd lain on the ground. Pretty innocuous in the technology department. But the noise... I was back in Toretsk all over again. I shook violently. *Because I'm cold. Not terrified, not anymore.* Although the BC sun was out, we were well entrenched in November. The heat also clearly wasn't on in this space. Hell, I wasn't even certain if the electricity was hooked up.

*And you left your coat back in Justin's office. Fucking hell.* I supposed I could ask Simeon to get it, but I didn't know what his role on the ranch was. Chances were *coat fetcher* wasn't one of them. His paint-speckled jeans and chambray shirt over a henley suggested laborer, not counselor. Of course, around here, things blurred. Kennedy wore jeans and a chambray shirt as well. And she had a PhD.

Most importantly though—more than the fact the cold of the bathtub I rested against was seeping into my bones—was I didn't want to be left alone.

Tiffany had tucked herself under my arm near the toilet.

Simeon very slowly sat on the other side.

He adjusted his position—likely because sitting on the cold floor was uncomfortable as fuck—and our thighs brushed.

"S-sorry."

I snorted. "Buddy, if anyone should be apologizing, that would be me. You don't have to stay. I'll be out of your hair any minute."

He turned his head so our gazes met. His stunning hazel eyes mesmerized me, some of my panic fading as I stared at him. His blond hair sort of flopped. A little scruff adorned his chin. Like he'd shaved yesterday but not today. He took a breath. "D-do you want me to g-go?"

*Truth time.* "No." I quickly added, "I mean if you have to go or if you feel obligated to get Rainbow or, you know, you're on the clock or something—"

Slowly, he raised his arm next to me. He casually draped it on the bathtub behind me, almost a hug, but a safe respectful distance off.

Respect wasn't what I needed in this heart-racing, still shaky moment. I curled into him.

*Fucking hell, you don't even know this guy.*

*Yeah, but he's offering comfort. You either accept it from him, or go back to Justin and ask for what you need, or you leave, alone and badly fucked up.*

Since talking to Justin and being alone both sounded as unappealing as eating four-day-old moldy bread—which I'd done several times—I continued to tuck myself against Simeon.

He wrapped his arm around me.

Okay, well this confirmed he was likely not a therapist. I'd done my research—the rules about touch were pretty strict.

A slight smell of sweat was mostly overwhelmed by wood. He'd been nailing something with that nail gun. So...wood? I couldn't remember what I'd seen when I'd arrived. I'd just been hellbent on finding a place for myself. And I had.

To a point.

*Should've run into the forest.* Justin had explained the size of the property—as well as the fact it was fenced off. He said the fence mostly kept out the local bears and coyotes, but not always. *Maybe this bathroom actually was smarter.*

I'd been more interested in meeting the horses. I liked the idea of equine therapy. Of Justin and me out riding horses while we discussed the shit my life had descended into. Of not having to look him in the eye as I either bared my soul or lied through my teeth. Either was possible on any given day.

Simeon clasped my shoulder with his arm, slowly bringing me closer.

Probably because I kept shaking. Kept shivering.

Tiffany snorted and put her snout on my lap. She gazed at me with the most compassionate dark-brown eyes. Like she understood.

"Sweet girl. She's needed at the ranch, though, right?" Panic settled at the thought of giving her up before my heart stopped trying to climb out my throat.

"They've g-got Rex." Simeon continued to grip me. "He's n-not a formal therapy dog, but he does a damn g-good imitation most of the time." He rubbed his hand up and down my arm, creating some friction. "If they need Tiffany, I'm s-sure Rainbow will come and get her. You n-need her right now, so she'll stay." With his other hand, he scratched the top of her head. "She's a s-super good dog."

I sniffled. "She's the best dog."

He sighed. "I always wanted a d-dog. My d-dad was allergic, and then…" He sighed again. "My grandparents are t-too old to have a dog underfoot. M-might trip them or something and they might fall and break a hip. I could keep the d-dog in my room, but that's not f-fair to the dog, and…"

"You, uh…" *Jesus, this isn't any of your business.* Still, asking the question would keep me in the present. I got the feeling he was okay with that. Well, he still held me like a child in need of comfort…that spoke to a kindness of spirit I rarely saw. "You live with your grand-parents?"

He scratched his jaw. "Yeah. They're o-old. Older. Need help. I can help." He ran his hand along his thigh. "Then I'm, uh, n-not lonely."

*Is he worried I'd judge? God, that's the last thing I'd do.* "I think that's sweet. All my grandparents are gone. Well, not in my life. My mom's family is from Manitoba. When she divorced my dad, she went back there. She—" I swallowed hard. "—told him she never wanted to see him or me again." *Move on.* "My dad was much older than a normal dad might be when I was born, so his parents are dead."

"That s-sucks." Simeon held fast. "My parents d-died in a f-freak t-train accident." He sighed. "I d-don't talk."

Yet he was with me. And struggling. Guilt ate away at my gut. "We don't have to talk. In fact, I should be letting you get back to work." I pointed to the offending object that had triggered the panic attack.

"Yeah. W-would you like to help?"

"Help?" I squinted as I gazed over at him.

"If y-you're okay."

*Am I okay? How do I feel? Five things I can see...* I named them off quickly—all very bathroomy things. "Sure, I can help."

"You need a c-coat."

I snickered. "I have a coat. Sitting in Justin's office." As close as I was going to get to admitting how bad things had become for me to get up and walk out without stopping for it. I couldn't run, of course. Most of the time when I moved, I also struggled for breath. Here, though? While sitting still? I didn't struggle as much.

"You c-can have mine or..." He met my gaze with those mesmerizing eyes. I'd thought they were brown, but now I saw more moss green. "or I t-text Rainbow to bring yours. S-she won't ask q-questions."

Since Simeon was way broader and taller than me, I could only imagine how swamped I'd be in his jacket. "Why don't I start by helping you? I might work up a sweat." I tried to smile.

He did smile. "Okay. B-but I have to t-text Rainbow. Missing Tiff."

The dog raised her snout.

"Yeah. I should take her back."

He shook his head. "Not n-necessary. I'll open the d-door and let her go. Quick t-text and all good."

That sounded deceptively easy, but he knew everyone who worked here. Or I assumed he did. If he thought that would be enough, then I'd accept that. Slowly, I shifted, getting balanced to stand up.

Tiffany rose, stretched, and headed toward the door.

Simeon stood next. He held his hand out for me.

I grasped it and, levering myself against the bathtub, slowly rose. And gasped when pain ripped through my chest.

In an instant, a hand pressed under my ribcage on my left side. That hand was so close to the wound that it should've hurt. But his touch was so gentle that I barely felt it. He stabilized me, though, and as I breathed through the pain, my center of balance returned. My vision stopped swimming. The breath returned to my lungs.

He sighed. "You c-can't reach up."

I winced. "I thought we'd be nailing something to the wall or, hopefully, the floor."

"You shouldn't be d-doing anything."

"Don't fucking tell me what I should and shouldn't be doing. I've had enough of people telling me what to do."

His face remained a mask.

*I've hurt him. The last person I should be yelling at.*

He blinked. "We can d-do the floor in the bedroom. You can hand me the p-pieces of laminate."

"I'm sure you can grab them yourself."

"Goes f-faster with help."

God, he was still speaking to me. Even though he was clearly uncomfortable. And I was snapping at him. I squinted. "I'd really be helping?"

He nodded furiously.

"Well, yeah." I eyed Tiffany. "Maybe you can take her back first?" That would give me time to get my shit together. "And save Rainbow the trip with my coat, let her know I'm okay? Or Justin…if you see him." I owed them an apology, but I was way too raw for that.

"Sure. You w-want chili? Or a cheese s-sandwich?"

"A chili sounds like a lot of work." And I didn't want anyone to fuss over me.

"There's a big p-pot made up. No work at all. I'll b-bring you some."

"I'm not sure my stomach can handle chili right now."

Simeon nodded and headed into the main living area.

Curious—and wary—I followed. And spotted the lunch bag I'd missed earlier.

He opened it and retrieved a plastic container. He returned and handed it to me. "N-Nanny made it." He blushed. "That s-sounds bad."

I grasped his hand before he could pull it back. After our encounter in the bathroom, I didn't figure this familiarity would bother him.

He didn't try to get away.

His rough hands scraped my soft fingers. For all I'd been to war, my hands were still baby smooth. "I think it's great your grandmother makes you a sandwich. That tells me that she loves you. That—" I swallowed hard. "—that's the sweetest thing."

He nodded, slowly removed his hand from my grasp, and stepped back.

"Uh… Don't tell anyone I freaked out. I'm okay."

He held my gaze for a long moment before he whistled.

Tiffany came to his side.

I lowered my hand to her snout.

She sniffed and then licked.

"Thank you."

She woofed.

Then the dog that saved my sanity followed the most enigmatic and intriguing man I'd ever met out of the house.

# Chapter Five

Simeon

"He's o-okay."

Rainbow clutched Ryan's coat against her chest and eyed me suspiciously.

Well, suspiciously was the wrong word.

Worriedly.

Finally, she handed me the jacket. "Will you talk to Justin before leaving tonight? Or Kennedy?"

I frowned. Ryan specifically asked me not to tell anyone. So either I broke his confidence and spoke to Justin or I held my silence and maybe put my job in jeopardy.

*Kennedy's not going to fire me.*

*I hope.*

Slowly, I shook my head.

She cocked her head. "If he asked you not to, then of course you should respect that." She shrugged. "If you need Tiffany or Rex, just come back."

"Tiff was g-great."

The dog had drunk a bowlful of water then wandered down to Kennedy's office where she'd gained admittance. Whether she'd get a rest or whether she was helping the next patient, I didn't know.

Rainbow smiled. "Tiffany's the best. Why don't you take a couple of sodas back with you? You might be thirsty—"

Even as she spoke, the sound of an engine starting carried through to where we stood by the sliding glass door facing the riding ring.

She met my gaze. "I guess he didn't want his coat."

I darted to the parking lot. I'd assumed if Ryan wanted to leave, that he'd take the direct route through the building that would bring him right by me.

Nope.

He'd gone around the long way—to the seldom-used front yard. Obviously he had his keys in his jeans pocket, because he was driving away.

Instinctively, I checked his jacket pockets. A toonie and a wad of scrunched tissue. Slowly, I returned to Rainbow. She's stood on the back deck, her face pointed toward the sun. From this angle, I saw her eyes were closed behind her sunglasses. When my boots hit the deck, she turned. "Gone?"

"Y-yes."

"I'll let Justin know. You sure you shouldn't talk to Justin?"

Slowly I shook my head. "S-should I r-return this to Ryan?" I clutched the jacket.

She winced. "I can't tell you where he lives. Even if the information's public, which I'm sure it's not, it's not really appropriate for some virtual stranger to turn up on his doorstep ..." She bit her lower lip. Then shook her head. "Thanks for the offer. I'm going to say *no*. He knows where to come back for it and he's not too broke to replace it."

I nodded. I completely understood. Pointing back to the prefab, I nodded again.

"Yeah, for sure. Do you need help?"

Thinking of the crown molding, reluctantly I nodded for a third time.

She clapped her hands together. "Yay. I can do the horses later. I feel like, I don't know, sawing some...stuff." She didn't swear. I'd never heard anyone here say an expletive. But clearly she'd wanted to say *shit*.

Slowly, I handed her the jacket. She tucked it inside the house, then joined me. "Ready?"

I nodded. Then laughed at myself. *So eloquent.*

She grinned. She was okay with me not speaking as much.

I appreciated that because it meant I didn't have to struggle. For her, though, I would've done it.

For Ryan, I had.

Which was something to think about as I drove home that night. I'd enjoyed the afternoon with Rainbow chattering on about anything and everything. The woman never ran out of things to say. Then she'd pointed out she was known as one of the quieter of the sisters.

I'd withhold judgement until I'd actually met all eight. The likelihood of that happening was pretty slim. Which might be a good thing because chatter from a friend could be fun, as long as they let me just listen, but chatter from a stranger wore me out.

I'd also gotten an earful from Torah—the second oldest Dixon sister and the dog trainer—who'd shown up just before I'd quit for the day. She'd introduced herself as well as her dogs King and Bishop.

She hadn't talked my ear off at quite Rainbow's level. Just had needed to tell someone about the search-and-rescue work she'd done earlier in the day up on one of the local mountains.

Appropriately, I'd been impressed.

Fortunately, she hadn't required me to say much. Whether that was because she knew about my stutter or because she'd been on such an adrenaline high after the rescue, I couldn't be certain. But the Dixon sisters were a lot for a guy like me.

Eventually Kennedy had come out to liberate me. She'd smiled, thanked me for my work during the day, and asked me if I'd stay for dinner.

I'd managed to say Nanny was cooking. I didn't even care how pathetic that might make me sound. Anything was better than joining the assembled crew and worrying I might slip up and say something about Ryan that he didn't want them to know. I was ninety-nine percent certain I wouldn't...but that one percent worried me.

Humming, I drove through the back roads north of Mission City. My grandparents owned a place in the Mission City hills—just on the opposite side from Healing Horses. In fact, they weren't far from the street where all my friends lived.

Where Justin also lived.

Until today, that hadn't meant much. When my friends got together and included both of us, Justin and I had never discussed his work. Heck, we hadn't discussed mine either. Mine was boring as hell. No one wanted to hear about drywall, leaky roofs, installing laminate floor, or chasing bats out of rafters. Yet I'd done all of those things. I loved being a jack-of-all trades. I hadn't yet been asked to get a cat out of a tree, but that might happen. Especially since the local firefighters didn't generally do that.

Justin.

I passed the street where he lived as I continued on my way.

Hopefully Ryan would talk to Justin, explain what happened, and everything would be okay.

Except...what had happened? Something clearly triggered him into a panic attack. I hoped it wasn't something I'd done, but I had to suspect the loud sounds of my nail gun. Which super sucked.

I made the left turn onto Ferrars Street. I'd made this journey with my parents only monthly for the first nineteen years of my life.

Then my life changed in an instant. My parents had been on a train headed from Vancouver to San Fransisco for their twentieth anniversary when the train derailed. Four people died, my parents among them.

I'd flown down to Portland and arranged, with the help of the Canadian government, to get them repatriated, but I was a mess, shaken, wavering between conflicting emotions—what I thought I should feel, and what I actually felt—and unable to get words out when I needed them. Nanny and Bops pretty much took care of the remaining details, choosing a cemetery in Mission City, where my mother grew up with them, for a final resting place.

My father's parents, instead of supporting me, picked up stakes and moved to Costa Rica. I hadn't heard from them since. My own grandparents. Of course, I didn't really miss them. Their idea of support would probably have been more yelling and demeaning me. They'd encouraged my father to criticize me continuously—as if they could harangue the stutter out of me.

*Like that hadn't failed for nineteen years.*

I'd never received so much as a postcard since. Which was absolutely fine. My mother had loved me unconditionally. Her parents, my maternal grandparents, loved me unconditionally. So what if I could rarely get out an entire sentence without stuttering? Most people figured out what I was trying to say. Most people didn't run out of patience. And I was very careful to keep those who did out of my orbit. Good riddance to them.

My phone rang through the Bluetooth.

"Simeon." It'd taken years, but I could get my name out without stuttering. Unless under extreme duress.

"Hey, it's Gio."

"Hi." I eyed the community mailboxes as I drove by. *I can go tomorrow.* "I w-was going to text."

"Thought I'd save you the trouble. We good for tomorrow?"

"Y-yep."

"Mercer doesn't need his SUV, so I'm going to drive it up. That way you don't have to come all the way into town to get me."

"Don't m-mind." I signaled to pull into my driveway even though there wasn't another car for miles.

"Yeah, but that way you're not tied to me. And it's a pain for you to come to town."

I almost repeated I didn't mind—because I didn't. I enjoyed grabbing a Starbucks latté as a treat and then sitting back and letting Giovani talk for the entire trip. Apparently he'd been surrounded by guys who didn't speak English while in prison. He'd tried to learn their language, but didn't have a knack.

Gio maintained that after all those years of enforced silence, if he found someone willing to listen, he was willing to talk.

I would've thought the opposite. If I'd spent all those years in prison, I wouldn't have wanted to share anything. I would've been too ashamed.

My employee—and now friend—was more philosophical. If someone heard his story and stayed away from breaking the law, that wasn't a bad thing. Marijuana might be legal in Canada, but other drugs weren't. And although he'd only been caught with a couple of joints, he'd actually been more of a dealer—helping the local tourists get high. If he'd been caught with his entire stash, he would've likely been sentenced to death.

Philosophical.

"Okay." I stopped before the garage, engaged the parking brake, and was about to turn off the engine. "You all right?"

"I'm awesome." He chuckled. "I have news."

"I c-can't wait to hear it."

"Tell you tomorrow." He cut the line.

I killed the engine, grabbed my empty lunch bag, and exited the truck, using the remote to lock it. The alarm engaged, and I headed into the house. Often I was exhausted after a day's work, but today I had a pep in my step.

Our four-bedroom rancher sat on several acres. My grandparents' property was pie-shaped at the end of a cul-de-sac. Very narrow by the street and wide at the back in the wilderness area they let grow wild. The property sloped down, so we had a walkout basement. That was my space. Neither grandparent could make it down the stairs easily anymore, making me super grateful the main part was one story. I was sad that Nanny couldn't wander down with cookies anymore, but glad I could help them stay in their familiar home.

After an epic debate, they allowed me to hire a young woman to clean the house once a week. I made it seem like they were doing her a favor and she needed the money, which was only half true. She did—badly. She worked at the seniors' home five days a week and cleaned houses on her two 'days off'. She had six siblings to support back in Honduras. Although she was paid well as a nurse—now here on a work visa—living in Mission City wasn't cheap, and she still needed to send every penny home. But she could've found a different client so I was glad she'd taken my grandparents on.

I used my key to gain admittance to the house. The scent of garlic wafted through the air. And tomato sauce.

*Nanny's had a good day.* She was having fewer of those, which hurt my heart. *Need to cook up some meals this weekend so she'll have something to heat up next week on the bad days.* I told Nanny that I needed to practice for when I got married. Which was a joke, but one I didn't share with her. I was never getting married. However, one day she wouldn't be here, and knowing how to cook would be a good thing. Under her tutelage for the past seventeen years, I did okay.

I removed my coat and boots in the main hall. I really should go downstairs and change into clean clothes, but I didn't want to make my grandparents wait for me if I didn't need to. Tonight, I'd managed to get most of the sawdust off my clothes. I stepped into the family room.

Bops sat in his recliner watching the local five o'clock news. "Some stabbing in Surrey. So glad you don't live there anymore."

I nodded. I was too...but not for the reason he thought. Bad memories. Odds of me getting stabbed these days would be pretty slim. That many people on the streets and in the stores? I shivered. I didn't *do* people. Not my thing. "Me t-too."

He grinned. "Nanny cooked up lasagna. Made three batches. You'll need to take one down to the freezer. She'll freeze one up here, and tonight we feast." He met my gaze.

The message went unsaid. *She's had a very good day.*

Guilt still swamped me, thinking about how much work went into making lasagna. My favorite. If I'd known how hard it was, I would've picked something much simpler when she asked me. Like grilled cheese sandwiches. Which were a close second. I stepped into the kitchen.

"Perfect timing." Nanny sat at the table, chopping carrots. "These are for your lunch tomorrow. With a slice of lasagna. Will they let you use the microwave?"

The prefab didn't have one yet, but the answer came easily. "Rainbow will l-let me heat up the slice in the m-main house." I kissed my grandmother on her cheek.

Her skin was cool against my lips. She wore a turtleneck under a crew-neck sweater and a cardigan, with wool pants, thick socks, and sturdy faux fur-lined slippers. And she was still always cold.

"This is g-great."

"We can eat at the table." She pointed to the seat next to her.

The seating arrangements were always a dance. Bops liked to sit in the living room and watch his news, but he could be pressed upon to join us. Nanny wanted to hear all about my day—which proved annoying to Bops if we sat in the family room while he tried to watch television. We ate on TV trays no less, when we gave in to his preference. True relics of the sixties.

"I d-don't have much to say…"

"Well, then, let's make Bops happy tonight, and you can say it during commercials."

Which meant two hours of news and then Wheel of Fortune. I could usually escape by the time Jeopardy came on—but not always. Nanny thought I needed my education expanded. Half the time, I didn't even understand the categories. Just…the trivia show didn't hold my interest. Neither did Wheel with the odd expressions that people used.

Still, I could use advice. "I m-met someone at w-work today."

"Oh?" Nanny perked up.

I grabbed the carrot peelings from the sink and put them into the compost container. *Enough to run it out later. Have to remember.* Our bear-proof container did a good job of making compost I would use come summer. I didn't have much time to spend in the garden, but I planted various hearty fruits and vegetables so Nanny would have fresh ingredients to work with.

"N-not a girl." I grinned as she pursed her lips. I gave her another kiss. "N-not romantic. Sorry. B-but I could use your advice." I wasn't ever going to see Ryan again, but some sage words from my grandparents would help soothe my jangled nerves.

And they loved being useful. They couldn't help on advice about renovations. My grandmother had been a secretary at Mission Collegiate and my grandfather an accountant. He knew a hammer from a hacksaw—he'd cared for this place for more than sixty years—but I'd long ago learned all he could teach me about tools. They were in their early nineties and wouldn't be around much longer. A miracle they still were. They didn't go out anymore. Thanks to me, they had everything they needed here at home. Most of their friends were gone as well. That made me sad.

When I drove them to a funeral, I was reminded one day I'd be doing that for them.

"T-television it is." I helped Nanny up. While she made her way to the family room, I organized three plates of lasagna—all apportioned with the amount each of us ate. I stuck the carrots in a container and loaded them into the fridge.

Finally, I poured three glasses of milk. The sounds of the TV carried from the living room in a familiar background. I heard Bops greet Nanny and tell her to take a load off her feet.

*Yeah, we're going to be okay.*

# Chapter Six

Ryan

"Yeah. Sorry again. Just wanted to tell you that I'm okay. And it was really cool you didn't think I was a weirdo." I'd stepped into the prefab, found Simeon standing in the middle of the room, and blurted that out.

He appeared startled to see me.

*Oh shit. Should have knocked.* Except the door had been open. Which, in retrospect, didn't necessarily mean I should just walk in.

"N-not a weirdo." He scratched his chin. "I d-don't talk m-much."

I winced. Here I was, forcing him to communicate again. "Right, so I should just—"

"Y-you don't have to leave."

Remaining rooted to the spot, I met his gaze. *Why is that so hard? Right—maybe because you don't look people in the face anymore?*

Anymore? I hadn't before much either. Too busy playing my games, thinking about playing my games, or obsessing about which new game I was going to try. People just didn't factor into my life.

In war, all that had changed.

Simeon tilted his head.

Right, he'd spoken. I was supposed to respond. "I, uh, just had a session with Justin. He had to come in early to fit me in...which made me feel all kinds of guilty and—"

"He w-wouldn't mind." Simeon said the words with absolute certainty. "He c-cares."

I rubbed my hands over my eyes. "Yeah, he really does. They all do. Which just makes me feel more guilty."

"Why?"

I stopped what I was doing and met his gaze. My eyes still blurred. "Because they don't need to be cleaning up my shitty life, you know?"

"What's s-shitty about it?" He appeared genuinely curious.

*Do I tell him about the tech phobia? Do I tell him about the war? What the fuck? Of course I shouldn't tell him about the war.*

Still, I drew in a breath. "So, like—"

"Hey, Simeon, this is the last can of—" A gorgeous man with jet-black hair and lightly tanned skin stopped as soon as he spotted me. "Uh, I was going to say I think we have enough to finish the trim, but—"

I waved. "I was just going."

"No." The guy spoke up. "I'm just doing trim in the bathroom. Gio, by the way. Well, Giovani. But everyone calls me Gio."

"You work with, uh, Simeon?" *Could you ask any dumber question? They're both here...working...*

He grinned. "Simeon's my boss."

Simeon made a noise low in his throat.

Gio grinned. "He hates when I call him *boss*. Sometimes I do it just to irritate him."

The *boss* sighed.

"But today I'm feeling giddy with good news and so I figured I wouldn't annoy him."

Simeon's cheeks turned ruddier.

"Uh, what good news? I love good news." And I should've been leaving, but couldn't help myself. Clearly this man wanted to share.

"I bought rings. I'm going to propose to my boyfriend." His grin split his face. "I'm waiting until the right moment, you know? We already live together, so that's not such a big deal. But his younger siblings sort of come and go and..." He paused. "The first snow, right? That's romantic. I can take him out, and we'll be bundled up and—" He scrunched his nose. "We'll just be wet and cold. Oh, but we could do it by the fireplace. I mean, we'd have to make sure we weren't too hot. But a night when the wind's howling and the snow's falling...?"

"Might his siblings interrupt?"

"I'll plan it on a night when they're not there. Although..." He considered. "Maybe I should get them involved? They're a really tight-knit family. Their parents died in a head-on collision with a drunk driver, and—" He stopped abruptly, gazing over at Simeon.

"M-my parents' train derailed and they d-died. N-not the same thing." He offered Gio a tiny smile. "I'm h-happy for you. M-Mercer is a lucky man."

"Mercer is the best." Gio whispered the words with reverence.

I liked that he talked openly and casually about his gay relationship, and that Simeon didn't seem the least bit bothered. I hated to stereotype, but I usually thought guys in construction would lean more toward homophobic. A few of my online gamer friends had been as well—which bugged the shit out of me. I never spoke up, though. I was ashamed of that now.

"T-this is Ryan." Simeon grinned. "He's going to help me sort the f-flooring in the bedroom."

Gio grinned. "Oh, maybe he could help me paint this room once I'm finished with the bathroom."

"I would…" I considered. "I could probably do the baseboards." I leaned closer. "But I've never held a paintbrush in my life."

He placed a hand to his chest in clear mock distress. "Never painted? I do declare, you are missing out on one of the greatest adventures in life."

Simeon glared. "He's h-helping me."

I wasn't certain how coming in to apologize led to me helping…but I loved the idea. The book Marnie the librarian recommended was good—but not enough to hold my attention for the entire day. I tried to schedule my appointments to see Justin midday so I would have something to break up the monotony, but this morning was extra. I was lucky he'd been able to fit me in at all. I hadn't, however, been totally honest with him.

*Water under the bridge.*

*Or whatever the dumb expression is.*

I smiled at Simeon. "Happy to help."

Gio saluted and headed back into the bathroom.

Simeon made his way to the bedroom, and I followed. For the next two hours, I helped him install tile flooring. And he hadn't really needed my help—but things went a bit faster with the two of us working. I eyed the kneepads. "Is this a tough job?"

He sighed. "S-sometimes my knees ache. N-nothing I can't handle."

I didn't quite believe his dismissive words. Given how much my chest ached sometimes, I admired he could do the work.

After that, we didn't speak. I expected that to feel awkward...but it didn't. He had a quiet presence about him. He was almost like a gentle giant. Not hulking, by any means. Just a solid guy. About half a foot taller than my own five-nine. That blond hair falling over his eyes was adorable. Those eyes, when they met my gaze, were as stunning today as they'd been yesterday. In the morning light that spilled into this room, they had flecks of gold.

"Coffee!" A woman's voice carried from the main room.

Simeon met my gaze and grinned. "R-Rainbow."

"Okay. Well, I don't have to—"

He gestured for me to get up. When I didn't, he nodded. He rose—with a wince—then he held out his hand.

*Damn. He gets it. Standing from a sitting position on the floor is hard.*

Not only did he grasp my hand, he bent and supported my left side as he guided me up.

I barely felt a twinge. I managed a smile. "I need to keep you around all the time."

His eyes flashed with something I couldn't identify. I wanted to grab onto it. To ask what he was thinking.

The moment passed, though, and he smiled. "C-coffee."

"Yeah."

We made our way to the main room. The design of the house offered a small bar from the east wall—dividing the kitchen from the living space. A couple of barstools would fit nicely, and whomever was in the kitchen would still be able to see everything going on.

Rainbow stood with Gio near the bar as they sorted four insulated mugs.

She spotted Simeon and me and grinned. "One strong latté for my hard-working friend, and what I have left is a tea for..." She cocked her head as she looked at me.

"Your o-other hard-working f-friend." Simeon grinned. "He's h-helping me. And doing great."

"Oh." She met my gaze. "I noticed your car in the parking lot and wondered if you might be here. If not, I would've found a home for the tea." She held up six colored packets. "If there isn't a flavor you want, I can easily hustle back to the house. I think we've got...about thirty flavors."

"Do they make that many?" Gio sipped his coffee. "You are my hero."

Rainbow grinned. "You're so easy to please. Sunshine has nice things to say about you. I think she had a crush on you in high school."

"I love mint, thank you." I advanced as she handed me the packet and pointed to a mug on the bar. "Sunshine?"

"My older sister." She gestured to Gio. "He was between Sunshine and me at Mission Collegiate."

"Sandwiched in." Gio raised his coffee in salute. "A rarity—I didn't have a Dixon sister in my class."

I glanced at Rainbow.

She placed her mug on the bar and yanked her phone out of her back pocket. She swiped a few times, then handed it to me.

I stared. And quickly counted. Seven raven-haired beautiful women with varying shades of blue eyes.

Then Kennedy, my almost-therapist. With her brown hair and brown eyes. After a moment, I realized the significance of what I saw. "Eight of you?" I might've croaked that.

"Yep. Kennedy's the eldest. Then Torah the dog trainer, Zephyra the vet, Sunshine the..." She frowned.

"Is she the one who works at The Owl's Nest?" I hadn't made the connection between the very helpful sales clerk and the woman before me who'd greeted me when I arrived. In reality, though, they could be twins. The seven non-Kennedy sisters were nearly identical.

"Yes." Rainbow grinned. "I just...she's also..." She furrowed her brow.

"Nosy." Gio offered that up. With another grin.

I read that as teasing.

Rainbow cocked her head. "I was going to say intuitive. She reads people better than any of us, even Kennedy."

Something coalesced in my mind. When I'd first stepped into the store, she'd been bright, cheerful, and—to me—irritating. Almost immediately, she'd backed down. I figured that was because of the frown I gave her. And possibly it had been. But it might also have been her intuition that I needed to be left alone. "She's...nice."

"O-overwhelming at t-times." Simeon smiled. "In a g-good way."

"Right." Rainbow grinned. "Then it's me. I'm sort of the middle child. Then Spring who is working at the Mission City Gazette as a reporter. Finally the twins, Autumn and Summer. They're starting university soon."

"M-my friend Dean, from Australia, told me a-about Spring's column in the n-newspaper. She writes a-amazing human interest s-stories."

Rainbow beamed. "We're proud of her. But she wants scoops and exposés and stuff she'll never find in Mission City. Personally, I think she should move to a larger market—like Vancouver. Or even Surrey. That city's growing so—"

"N-not Surrey." Simeon spoke firmly. "N-no."

I gazed between Gio, Rainbow, and then him—as if to divine where his vehemence came from. I'd never lived in Surrey, but I knew it to be a vibrant multicultural growing city. A bit of a gang problem, but nothing too serious. I couldn't think of a reason why Spring couldn't move there. Or, hell, she could even commute. It'd be brutal, but it'd be just over an hour each way in rush hour traffic.

"Okay." Rainbow laid a hand on Simeon's forearm.

He breathed again.

"She's not going to go, so you don't need to worry. I think she'd move to Calgary or Toronto before she chose Surrey. We just...I like the idea of keeping her close. Not on the other side of the country. But that's big-sister protectiveness. I also want what's best for her, and if that means leaving and spreading her wings, I'll support that too."

"You're a good big sister." I still couldn't fathom. "Only child, here."

"I have a twin. I'm the better-looking one, though." Gio thumped his chest.

Rainbow laughed. "I believe you're identical. Like my sisters Autumn and Summer."

"Yeah, but I style my hair better."

We all laughed at that.

After a moment, Simeon pointed to himself.

"You're an only child as well?" Rainbow asked the question casually.

I hadn't been certain whether Simeon was drawing attention to himself or if he was trying to say something. I was grateful for Rainbow's intuition. Maybe Sunshine wasn't the only sister who saw things. I gently nudged Simeon's biceps with my own. "We solo kids have to stick together."

Rainbow laughed. "There were days, in my childhood, when I very much wished to be an only child." She pressed her hand to her heart.

"But not a single regret." She dusted off her sleeve. "I didn't mean to interrupt—"

"Yeah, you did." Gio grinned. "You just wanted to see the three handsomest men in Mission City."

"Uh..." Simeon grinned. "M-Mercer...?"

Gio's eyes widened. "Uh...oh shit. Right...three *of* the handsomest men in Mission City. Because clearly my soon-to-be fiancé is the best looking of all of us."

I managed a smile. About the sixth one this morning. I had no idea what Mercer looked like. He could be the ugliest, but Gio's love shone through and I'd lay odds he didn't care what his future fiancé looked like.

"Soon-to-be...?" Rainbow cocked an eyebrow.

Gio's eyes went wide again. "Oh, God, please don't say anything. Especially to Sunshine."

"One of the biggest gossips in Mission City?" She appeared to be considering.

Simeon laughed. "Rainbow w-won't say anything."

"No, I won't. But you'll have to share over lunch. With a bunch of therapists who won't say a word. I have enough chili for everyone. Come when you're ready. Oh, and I'm baking fresh rolls."

"I...uh..."

She met my gaze. "Everyone is welcome to our extremely informal lunch."

"I have my l-lasagna," Simeon protested.

"You can heat it up in the microwave."

I flinched.

Rainbow met my gaze as she continued. "Why don't you come a few minutes before Gio and Ryan? We'll get you set up, and then they can join us when lunch is ready."

My heart stuttered as my breathing returned to normal. Just the idea of a microwave set me off. And Rainbow clearly knew that. And I wasn't even bothered that she did.

"All right." Rainbow snagged her mug. "Three of the handsomest men in all of Mission City...although my dad's pretty distinguished with his silver hair and his pilot's uniform. Just have to toss in that older guys are in the running."

"M-Maddox." Simeon grinned. "Or Stanley."

"Oh, good one." Rainbow winked. "Justin will love knowing you think his husband, an older gent, is handsome."

Simeon's cheeks pinkened.

With a laugh, Rainbow left.

Gio waved and headed back to the bathroom.

Simeon turned to me. "You o-okay with this?"

I chuckled. "I'm getting the feeling the Dixon sisters are kind of like steam rollers."

He squinted. "I d-don't know Zephyra or the younger t-three, but yes, the other f-four are a bit... Okay, maybe a lot." He held my gaze. "If you keep putting in the time, I should be p-paying you."

I shook my head. "You're getting me out of my apartment. I should be paying you." I sipped my tea. "Let's get back to work."

And so we did.

# Chapter Seven

Simeon

I wasn't clear why I was hurried into the kitchen to microwave my food before Ryan and Gio were joining us, but Rainbow made some kind of gesture I didn't understand.

She hastily snagged my container, dumped the lasagna on the plate, and two minutes later, my steaming food was before me as I sat at the kitchen table. A very large kitchen table, thank goodness. Not enough to seat the entire Dixon clan...but the dining room table in the great room could accommodate all ten of them. With a seat or two to spare, if memory served.

"You should start." She offered me a smile.

"I c-can wait."

Yet she offered a beaming smile and returned with an empty serving bowl a moment later, which she unceremoniously upended and placed over my plate. Thereby covering the food.

*Well, that works.* My lasagna wouldn't be piping hot, but it wouldn't be cold either.

Avery breezed in next with Rex at her feet.

The pooch scooted under the table and plopped onto my feet. A nice, solid weight...given his size.

"Uh...I hope that's okay." Avery eyed her dog. "He's...not usually so friendly with strangers." She meant strange men. Something in his past had ingrained a fear of men he didn't know. Once he saw someone was friendly and safe, he was fine.

"Gio is c-coming. And R-Ryan."

She nodded. "Well, it's good Rex has got you. Let me know if he becomes a problem. I have him on a leash so he can meet the new people. When he's comfortable, I'll let him off."

I scratched Rex's ears. "Never a p-problem."

"Right." She plopped down next to me, handing me a cloth to wipe my hands. "Rainbow says I have to come out to visit the house."

I didn't really consider the prefab a *house,* but everyone had a different definition.

Rainbow put a basket of heavenly smelling fresh rolls on the table. Directly in front of me.

Avery started to rise. "Oh, I should be—"

"Sit back down." Rainbow glared. "You've been dealing with trauma all morning. I baked and hung out with three of the handsomest men in Mission City." She put the chili on the table as Justin hustled in.

"Oh, was Stanley here? I'm sorry I missed him."

Everyone laughed.

Rainbow pointed to seats as Gio and Ryan arrived.

Ryan clearly took that gesture to mean the seat beside me was available, and he hustled to sit next to me.

Our hostess threw her arm around Gio. "I meant these three." She gestured to Ryan and myself. "I mean, I get the entire rainbow here."

*Huh?* Oh. I was blond, Ryan was a redhead, and Gio had dark hair. At least, I assumed that was what she meant.

"And, of course, Stanley would be up there. Silver fox." She made a cat's claw with her fingers and mimed grabbing.

Kennedy came from behind her and poked her in the ribs. "We're all here, let's eat."

I removed the bowl that had been keeping my lasagna warm. Since Nanny's lasagna was the best I'd never tasted, I would've eaten it stone cold.

Ryan eyed it.

"Have a t-taste." I gestured to his yet unused fork.

"I couldn't—"

"My g-grandmother will be offended if you d-don't." I gave him the look my grandmother always gave me when she wanted me to feel guilty. The look that had worked for thirty-eight years.

He grinned. "Well, I wouldn't want to disappoint your grandmother." He used his knife and fork to cut off a small piece. I wanted to insist he take a bigger one, but everyone was watching us.

I reddened. "I have enough to s-share with everyone." If I cut it into six small pieces, everyone would get a taste.

Rainbow shook her head. "That's super sweet, Simeon. I need the chili finished. If you have room, make sure you have some as well." She pivoted to Kennedy. "Where's Tiffany?"

"Outside. She wanted to stretch her legs. Maybe roll in the grass."

The therapy dog would never wander far from the house, and sometimes I'd see her wandering the yard by herself. Probably recharging after such a stressful job. I loved that Kennedy knew what her dog needed without having to ask.

Ryan moaned. "Okay, best lasagna ever."

"Oh really? Because that Italian place down on—" Justin cut off his words at Ryan's glare. "Just kidding."

"I've had their lasagna. And it's delicious." Ryan pointed to his plate. "This is better. Seriously."

I started to push my plate to him. "H-have mine. I get leftover again t-tonight."

Ryan held up his hand.

And met my gaze.

Clearly he read my pleading—although whether he assumed I was over lasagnaed, or he realized I wanted to do something for him, I wasn't sure. He nodded, took my plate, and handed me his untouched bowl.

Feeling happier than I had in a very long time, I scooped some delicious chili into my bowl, buttered my roll, and sat back to enjoy the most amazing meal.

After lunch, Ryan and I helped with the dishes while the counselors went back to their work and Gio headed back to start painting the main living area of the prefab.

Ryan leaned over to put a plate in the dishwasher, his fingers shaking enough he had to catch the counter and his breath hissed.

Instinctively, I placed my hand just below his ribs on his left side and my other on his back. Slowly, I helped him straighten.

"I'm okay." He might've snapped that.

Rainbow was in the great room brushing the grass and twigs off Tiffany before the dog went back to work, so she couldn't hear us.

"I know." I tried to center my thoughts. "O-overdoing it doesn't help."

"What do you know?"

"B-broken arm in grade four." I winced at the memory. "Broken wrist in g-grade nine." Different school. Different teachers. No one to question why a kid who was so cautious was also so clumsy. Fortunately, I got bigger, and the abuse stopped. But the terror never fully went away until the day the Royal Canadian Mounted Police showed up on my doorstep and told me I was an orphan. I'd never told anyone about the abuse, so the RCMP wouldn't have known I needed help. But, in delivering the news they assumed would devastate me, they essentially set me free.

"Ouch." Ryan clutched his side.

"C-can you tell me—"

He shook his head vehemently.

"O-kay." I eased him so his hip rested against the counter. Then I hustled my ass to get all the dishes into the dishwasher. I was putting the last of the cutlery in when Rainbow returned with a towel.

"She does love to play." Rainbow grinned. "Oh, you've finished everything."

"We're happy t-to help." I moved closer to Ryan, lest there be any confusion about who the *we* was.

"That's great." She gestured to Ryan. "Sounds like he got the best food of all of us."

"Your chili is p-perfection." I smiled. "But Nanny's lasagna is..." I perked up. "Can I b-bring a batch for tomorrow? For everyone?"

"Well, I'd hate to ask—"

"You d-didn't." I nodded my head. "Okay. Oh, she'll b-be so excited."

"That's a lovely gesture." Rainbow eyed her kitchen. "If I make a batch of raisin buns, will you take them home? A trade of sorts?"

Since I loved raisin buns, I wouldn't turn down that offer. "That'd be great. T-thank you."

She grinned. "And I'll have some for you too." She directed her smile at Ryan.

"Thanks." He held up his hand. "I'm heading home now. Lunch was lovely." He met my gaze. "Truly."

Disappointment lanced through me. I'd assumed we'd be working together through the afternoon. Which was crazy because surely the guy had better things to do than hanging around with me. Or maybe he'd overdone it. Maybe I'd pushed too hard. "Uh, o-okay."

"But thanks for the lasagna."

"M-more tomorrow."

"Yeah, right. More tomorrow."

Except he didn't show.

# Chapter Eight

Ryan

I eyed Marcus Branigan.

My very attractive and very straight physiotherapist stared back. Implacable. Unmoving. Most importantly, unmoved. His nearly black hair was a little shaggy, and his piercing dark-brown eyes showed more wisdom than I might have expected from a guy just a couple years older than me. Of course, by life experience, I likely had him beat by a mile, so where was my wisdom?

"I didn't mean to...you know..."

He eyed me. "Whatever you did—which you won't share with me—has exacerbated your injury. You're worse than you were when I saw you Thursday morning. That was less than a week ago, Ryan. What did you do?"

I winced. "Put a dish in a dishwasher."

"Oh. Well, it's great that you're using a dishwasher. Normally I'd say standing and doing dishes is good exercise—especially for balance—but with your—"

"Not my dishwasher."

He snapped his jaw shut. Likely surprised I was using any tech. We'd had that conversation in the first five minutes. No TENS machines, no laptops, no tablets, no nothing. He'd understood. And had respected my wishes. After five sessions, he'd asked if I would consider seeing a counselor.

I admired his restraint in waiting until we had a therapeutic relationship before dropping that little bomb.

*Wrong word. Wrong thought.*

"Okay." He gently probed my ribs. I'd removed my shirt, in this exam room, and he was the only person in the world—other than the doctors and nurses who'd patched me back up—who'd seen the mess. I'd once considered myself good looking. I was overweight and needing to build muscle, but with my golden-red chest hair, I rocked the grown-up look. If I sucked in my stomach, and at just the right angle, I was...decent looking.

Within six months of showing up on the front lines, I'd lost all the excess weight. Now I was nearly gaunt. With scars all over my chest.

Again, he pressed his hand to my side.

I hissed out a breath.

"Okay, well at least you didn't do lasting damage." He muttered, "I hope."

*Was I supposed to hear that? Well, I did.*

"Be right back." He left the room.

I glanced around. Pretty innocuous. The pale-gray walls felt soothing rather than drab. The gentle classical music—barely audible—spoke of elegance and relaxation.

The practice also employed a massage therapist.

Marcus had suggested that might be something to consider. Not for my chest, obviously, but to relax some of the other areas on my body which compensated for the injury. In relieving the strain on one body part, I created strain on another.

Truthfully, that all sounded very complicated.

Moments later, while my mind still wandered, Marcus returned. He held a cold pack in his hand.

I winced.

He frowned back. "I really want you to alternate heat and cold. Cold's easy—"

"Because I can manage a refrigerator."

"—right. Heat, though..." He cocked his head. "Easiest is a compress in the microwave."

"Don't have one."

"Would you consider a heating pad? Yes, you plug it in...but it doesn't use technology."

I bit my lower lip.

He sat on the stool and advanced. He indicated my side.

I nodded.

He wrapped the cold pack in a small towel, then pressed it against my side.

For a moment, only the scratchy fabric of the towel registered. Then the cold seeped through and I drew in a sharp breath.

That my chest and lungs really didn't like. I coughed.

"Sorry." He didn't appear the least bit repentant.

Still, I gave him the benefit of the doubt. "Yeah, thanks." Deep breathing was apparently part of my recovery, and I just had to get used to it. I bit my lower lip again—something I rarely did, but seemed to do often here. "I suppose..."

He met my gaze.

"Yeah, I can do a heating pad."

"Great." He grinned. "I think that'll ease a lot of your discomfort. Broken ribs are serious. You need to keep doing the coughing and deep breathing exercises to prevent pneumonia."

I shook my head. "Pressure on my chest makes me feel like I can't breathe." I offered a rough smile. "Losing half a lung and having one's heart nicked by shrapnel imbedded in one's chest doesn't lend itself to many options." I drew in a breath. "But I can see the exercises are important, and I'll try harder."

He nodded solemnly. "Yeah, I know. Your ribs will heal in time, but that means moving them as little as possible, other than deep breaths. How's the pain at night?"

"Uh…" I squinted. "As long as I sleep on my right side, I'm almost okay. I have a bunch of pillows to prevent me from rolling onto my back or, worse, my left side. Truthfully, I prefer sleeping in the recliner. Then I don't shift at all."

"That's not great for your back."

I just stared.

He chuckled. "I know…bigger problems. I really wish you'd let me use the ultrasound wand on your—"

"No."

"But—"

"No." I glared. "We've talked about this."

"I know." He sort of shrugged. "But I want you to get better. I have a list of things I can use, and most involve some form of technology. Or manipulations that would cause damage—so obviously they're out. I just…am struggling to help you."

I hesitated. "Am I becoming a burden?"

His horrified expression, all wide eyes and raised eyebrows assured me that I'd missed the mark.

"Hell, no. I can slowly do small things to try to make your life easier. We can figure out how and when to increase your range of motion. We've got you driving. You're able to stand longer, and your balance is better."

"Are you selling me on your services? Because obviously I'll keep coming back..."

He offered a small smile. "I just want it so you're in less pain."

""I'm not taking the heavy painkillers anymore." As soon as I could stand the breathing exercises without them, I'd scaled back to over-the-counter drugs.

"That's good. But you had two surgeries where they opened your chest. As you said, your heart got nicked, and you lost half a lung. You have broken ribs that are healing nicely." He drew in a sharp breath. "I don't know what you went through over there. Will never know. But I can see the wounds on your body and, more importantly, I can see them in your soul."

I scoffed.

"Not like that." He met my gaze. "Your body always has a lot of secrets to share. My profession involves interpreting those signals and figuring out how to fix what's broken. To make the patient as whole as I can. Obviously that's not always possible. Crap happens. Some injuries can never be overcome. So I help those patients adapt. When your ribs heal, I think there's a chance you can have close-to-normal function back in your body. Do things you've not been able to do in a long time."

"My cock's still broken."

Marcus sighed. "You always just have to go there. Have you discussed it with Justin?"

Ah...so Marcus was getting reports from Healing Horses. I'd authorized two-way communication. I had nothing to hide and if somehow my healthcare practitioners communicating helped...well, I had nothing to lose either.

"I don't have anyone to get it up for."

Except that wasn't entirely true. A certain tall, muscular, blond-haired, hazel-eyed handyman came to mind.

From an objective standpoint, Gio would've been the more attractive. Strong body, chiseled jaw, hair that flopped in just *that* way. He resembled a European model who might strut down a catwalk in Milan.

Simeon was more...of a hometown boy. Someone comfortable. Easygoing. Happy. Not exotic at all. Not the kind of guy I'd have noticed in the past. If I followed my former patterns, I thought I'd be missing out on someone special. He felt like someone I could be friends with. And I hadn't had many of those in my life.

Marcus waved his hand before me.

I straightened.

And winced.

And rolled my eyes.

He grinned. "Sorry about the pain, but I think you were thinking rather deeply. I asked if you'd mind if we switched to heat."

"Heat's fine."

"Great. I've got a pad I think is just the right size. I'll send you home with it."

"How much does it cost?" A question I never asked before going overseas—because my dad paid off my credit card each month—and one I asked every single time the issue of money came up since I'd gone to Ukraine. Credit cards were useless on the front lines of a war. I'd managed to get my hands on some of the cash my dad sent, but there weren't many places to spend it. We'd needed ammunition. That couldn't be bought with a few dollars.

"I'll add it to the cost of today's session."

Which my father would pay. That knowledge sat well with me. He had access to hundreds of millions of dollars. One of the richest men in Vancouver, in fact. He just didn't advertise that fact. His real estate portfolio was staggering—and that wasn't even how he made the bulk of his money.

"Be right back."

Marcus rose and my gaze followed that fine ass as he left the room. He wore khakis and a pale-blue dress shirt with the clinic's name. A clinic he owned. Pretty impressive, given he was only a few years older than me.

*What have you done in those years?*

*Won a few gaming trophies.*

*Gone to war.*

Neither of those felt particularly impressive. The first because any shmuck with decent reflexes and tons of hours to kill could achieve that. The second because it had almost killed me.

And we weren't winning the war.

Not losing...but not winning.

I itched to be back with my friends on the front lines.

Then a pang of pain reverberated through my chest as I remembered the four men who died when the ordinance had exploded so damn close to us. We hadn't had time to take shelter. One minute we'd been laughing, the next we'd had mere seconds to react. Those friends—to a man—had left behind wives and children. I'd been the only to survive. Me. The only person without any of those obligations.

The one thing I'd successfully managed to guilt my father into doing was sending money to those four families. I might've threatened to go public. To this point, I'd just been a *brave Canadian* who'd defied orders and had gone into a warzone. Canada wasn't at war and couldn't be seen to be sending troops. The handful of us who went were completely on our own. I'd been prepared to die and be buried over there. I might love my country, but she owed me nothing.

My father, upon hearing of my grievous injury, moved heaven and earth to get me from Kyiv to Toronto via Germany and a second round of surgery. I couldn't calculate what it cost him—but I suspected in the millions of dollars.

I was supposed to feel gratitude.

And I did—for the people who risked their lives to get me out. For the doctors and nurses and hospital staff who cared for me. For the transport people who first got me to Toronto and then for the crew who got me safely back home to Vancouver. I'd tracked many of them down and had sent thank-you letters. That had been part of my recovery in Vancouver—finding ways to express gratitude at being alive when so many others had died.

Marcus returned with a box. He sat on his stool, opened the box, and pulled out a large, fluffy, pale-blue thing attached to a cord.

To my relief, I didn't panic at the cord.

He handed me the instructions.

I rolled my eyes.

He shrugged. Then he plugged the thing in and showed me how to adjust the temperature. "Never on high. Not with your injuries. It has an auto shutoff at two hours but, to be safe, turn it off when you're going to sleep—even for a nap." Gently, he placed the heating pad against my side.

I secured it under my arm and wrapped my hand around it. Awkward as fuck.

"This will work better when you're in your recliner. Or on your side. And don't ever lie on it."

I fingered the instructions. Amazingly, I'd never used a heating pad.

"Fifteen minutes and then you can go. Do you need help to put your shirt on?"

"Nah." Since my hands and fingers worked as intended—and I could usually wrestle my arms into obeying—I'd manage.

"Great. Just signal me if you need anything."

I waved him off. "Go heal someone else."

He hesitated.

"Really...I'm going to be okay."

"Yeah, I think you will."

I sat with the heating pad until the fifteen minutes elapsed. I unplugged the thing, but wasn't able to figure out how to get it back into the box. *Fuck it.* I managed to get into my shirt and do the buttons up. I wasn't going to bother trying to tuck it in.

As I left, my gaze swept across the treatment area. I didn't see anyone. The clock read ten past six. Damn. The clinic closed at six. I headed to Marcus's office to apologize for keeping him late.

The door was ajar, and I almost knocked.

Marcus wasn't alone.

Nope.

He was in the arms of someone.

A man.

A lithe man with gorgeous hair and a killer body.

They'd locked lips.

I slipped away with a grin on my face.

Okay, so maybe not so straight after all.

# Chapter Nine

Simeon

For someone accustomed to working alone, I was sure feeling lonely this morning. Gio finished painting the main room yesterday. He'd come back when I was done with everything to do touch-ups, but he was mostly finished. I could've done the touch-ups, but he liked feeling useful. Feeling accomplished. Since he wouldn't take money for those things, I couldn't exactly complain. He claimed the work was part of the entire package.

I'd finished the laminate in the bedroom. Late yesterday, the appliances arrived. The specialist came to hook up the dishwasher, and the over-the-oven microwave, as well as the washer/dryer in the closet.

Not much space to hang clothes, but this prefab was supposed to only ever be a temporary place to stay. A few days or maybe a week. If someone needed to move in, they could always get a wardrobe. Although it would be a tight fit with the dresser, two nightstands, and queen-sized bed in the bedroom.

The sectional couch had a pullout bed as well. Rainbow said that was in case one of her sisters wanted to crash while her parents were visiting. Between the spare rooms and pullout couches in the great room of the ranch house... I did the math in my head. Yep, just about every Dixon sister would have a bed.

*That's a lot of people.*

I eyed the flooring for the main room of the prefab.

*You could hire someone. A kid with good knees...*

Hell, Gio would be happy for the extra work. He'd let me know how much those rings cost. I'd blinked, trying to take that in. No wonder he worked every job he could get.

My phone buzzed with an incoming text.

Maddox.

—So...—

I waited.

—Violet tried to flush her plushie down the toilet. —

I winced.

—In my bathroom. While I was dealing with Victor. —

Uh-oh.

—I didn't realize until the water leaked down the hall. —

Oh dear.

—Could you come? I'll pay double. I'll pay triple. —

I had to answer, holding back the smile.

—I'm not a plumber. —

—I know. It's the floor in the bedroom. Ravi's working an extra shift, and I've got both a deadline and two hellacious toddlers...—

I waited.

Nothing more came. So I sent a text.

—Let me talk to Rainbow and see if I can take a day off. —

My phone buzzed again.

—I'd really appreciate that. —

I smiled. I ensured everything was secure in the prefab and was locking the door when I heard a sigh. I turned.

Ryan stood before me. "Sorry."

"F-for what?"

He cocked his head. "Rainbow said you were expecting me yesterday."

I was pretty sure I hadn't said that to Rainbow. Maybe she'd read my disappointment when I discovered Ryan wouldn't be there to share Nanny's lasagna. That everyone swore was the best they'd ever had. Compliments I'd shared with Nanny.

But I'd missed Ryan.

Which made no sense because I'd only spent a couple of hours for two days with him. I had no right to expect him to return. He was under no obligation to me. "N-no. All good." I pointed to the ranch house. "I have to t-talk to Rainbow."

"Well, I'll leave you to it." He looked miserable.

"C-come with me." On impulse, I beckoned him.

After a moment's hesitation, he followed, looking less unhappy.

Rainbow stood by the riding ring, her cowboy hat shielding her eyes from the drizzle. Damp weather with cold rain was back in full-force. Our three days of reprieve were long over. She spotted me and waved. "Hey Simeon. I see Ryan found you."

Likely her way of saying she'd directed him. Possibly also her way of asking if I was okay with it. After my disappointment yesterday, she'd likely have figured I'd be eager. And I had been.

I stopped just before her. "M-Madox texted."

"Yeah?"

For expediency, I brought up the chat and handed her the phone. I didn't have anything in the chat I was worried about and no way would she snoop.

She giggled, pressing her hand to her mouth. "Oh dear. Poor Maddox."

Ryan cleared his throat.

Rainbow smiled as she handed me my phone back. She met Ryan's gaze. "Our friend, Maddox Baker, has two-year-old twins with his husband Ravi. One of those twins thought she'd flush her...plushie..." She frowned.

I nodded.

"Right. Down the toilet. And apparently Maddox wasn't aware and, uh, the plumber has fixed the clog problem..."

I nodded.

"But there's water damage to the floor. Maddox has a bad knee from an old injury, and Ravi's a pediatric nurse at the Abbotsford Hospital who works insane hours..."

Ryan gently nudged me. "He's asked you to help?"

"Y-yep."

Rainbow handed me the phone back. "Of course you need to go. My God, Simeon, you're weeks ahead of a nonexistent schedule—we don't need the place for months. You've been working flat-out, and don't think I didn't notice you were working on Remembrance Day." She lightly smacked my biceps.

Heat rushed to my cheeks. Hard to miss my truck—but I'd hoped they hadn't noticed. To me, it had just been another Friday. A day to remember our veterans and soldiers, for certain. But staying home and missing a day of work didn't make sense. I'd said a quiet prayer of thanks then settled into doing something that would help others.

"Do you...?" Ryan glanced down at his running shoes. "I mean there's not much I can do, but..."

While his head remained lowered, Rainbow did some weird nod with her head.

Encouragement?

Could I find courage in that?

"P-please."

Ryan gazed up. "Yeah?"

I nodded vigorously.

"Except I don't know where the guy lives."

Rainbow pointed toward the house. "Let me draw you a map."

I frowned, still holding my phone. Why would I just not give him the address and he could look it up with his GPS?

Slowly, Ryan pulled out his flip phone so I could see it. Quickly, he slid it back into his pocket.

*Holy shit...they still make those things?* I'd bought one of the first smart phones on the market and always kept up with the latest one. The more communication I could do on my phone, the easier my life. "M-map."

He nodded as we turned to follow Rainbow. I had a bag of the stuff I'd need, plus I still wore my tool belt.

Only as we got to the house, did it hit me. "Y-you can follow me." Traffic was nonexistent up here. He'd have no trouble. In fact, if it hadn't been far out of my way to return here later, I would've just offered Ryan a ride there and back.

"Better he has a map." Rainbow opened the sliding glass door. "I'll include how to get back to his home so you don't have to lead him."

*Aw crap.* I hadn't thought of that. It would've been a hassle for me to drive down to Ryan's place with him following me when we were done...assuming he lived somewhere in Mission City proper. I would've done it, but I liked not having to. I drove an electric truck, and we got our power through hydro, so I used only clean energy. I still preferred not to drive more than necessary.

For Ryan, though, I'd do it.

Rainbow emerged from the hallway leading to the administrative office—where I'd filled out piles of paperwork—sliding a piece of paper into a clear sleeve. "That's everywhere you might need to go. I hope you don't mind...I snagged your address from your file."

Ryan laughed. "You're helping me out. I don't mind in the least. Am, in fact, grateful." He took the sleeve from her. "This is a great map. Thanks for marking out the route. Saves a lot of squinting at the one I bought. I had to go to the visitor center to find one. They used to sell them at gas stations, right? Everything today, though, is through the phone. It's so impersonal."

I wasn't certain how GPS could be *impersonal*. That being said, Dean helped me find an Aussie voice I liked, and so my GPS spoke in this super sexy accented voice. Dean was delighted by the whole thing—understanding I didn't have a crush on him—just an affinity for the sexy intonation. "I'll m-meet you there." I waved.

"Yeah. I'll follow you out to the car." He nodded to Rainbow. "Thank you. Thank...everyone."

She blinked. "Anytime, okay? We'll see you on Monday. Oh, and Friday's the decorating party."

This time, Ryan blinked. "Decorating party?" His voice had a confused and disbelieving quality.

"Well for Christmas, of course. I'll need you both to help. Four o'clock. We do hors d'oeuvres, eggnog, and we adorn the counseling center and the offices. Oh, and the tree."

"A real tree?"

She shook her head. "Nah. Way too much work. We've got an amazing fake white one that I just love. Nice and tall to fit the space." She eyed me.

"I c-can help." I'd planned to be here anyway. I had about a week's worth of work to finish. Things were moving quickly, but the flooring was going to take a big effort, and I could only do so many hours a day before my knees gave out.

"Oh, Simeon, that would be wonderful. And we need someone to help sort the lights. We're always so careful when we put them away, but they get tangled, and we need an expert to untangle them."

Ryan smirked. "I'm not an expert, but I think even I can manage a string of lights."

If the tree was as high as she suggested, it might be more than one.

"Perfect. I'll mark you both as helpers. Eggnog okay?"

I nodded excitedly and Ryan bit his lower lip. So I quickly added, "He prefers t-tea."

He blinked.

Rainbow grinned. "Perfect. We'll have plenty of that—Kennedy drinks tons of decaffeinated Earl Grey in the afternoon, and I think Avery's going to have her favorite cinnamon and vanilla."

Ryan cocked his head. "I haven't tried that."

"It's some white tea. There's another flavor I can't remember...anyway. Like, thirty varieties to pick from."

"I appreciate that." He met my gaze. "I appreciate people remembering."

I wanted to tell him that I remembered everything about him. That he was important to me. Still, we had to get moving. "Y-you can follow me. But having a m-map to get home is good."

"Great."

We waved to Rainbow and headed to the parking lot. An older Ford sat in the space next to my truck. Older was an understatement. My grandparents had owned the same car. Like, thirty years ago. I remembered riding in the front seat when Bops took me out. I'd been seven. These days, kids weren't allowed to do that because of airbags. I doubted the car even had air bags. I glanced inside.

"No p-power anything?"

"No power steering, braking, or windows. It does have airbags."

Relief flooded me. I couldn't imagine driving without the other three, but they were creature comforts. Well, power braking meant fewer skids...right? I could barely remember. "D-drive safe."

He nodded to my hulking truck. "I think you're safe."

I flinched. "Not necessarily. Size isn't everything."

His face was instantly contrite, with his mouth opening. Then shutting. Then opening again. "Right. Sorry about your folks."

"Sh-shit happens." I winced. "Sh-shouldn't have said that."

"Shit?" He grinned so wide his face nearly split. "I love a fucking good swear word." He gestured to the clinic. "In public I try to keep the swears to a minimum. When I'm with Justin? I get to let'em rip. Like back when..." He trailed off. His face fell—the smile disappeared and his brow knit. "Just...before."

"You c-can talk to me." I longed to reach out and touch him, but I feared he would shatter into a million pieces. "I'm a g-good listener."

"Yeah." He flipped his keys in his hand. "I'll follow you."

Well, I knew a dismissal when I saw one. "G-great." I got into my truck, and soon we were on our way to the Baker household.

*It's really nice to have someone around.*

*Even if he's not staying...*

# Chapter Ten

Ryan

The wood cabin before me was nice enough. Nothing spectacular. Well, the two stories of windows on the left side were pretty cool. *Bet that lets in so much sunlight.* I'd never thought about things like that before. I'd preferred the dark of my dad's basement—better for playing my games.

I parked behind Simeon's pickup truck on one side of the driveway just in front of the two-car garage. I had no idea if anyone else was expected home.

He got out—into the rain that had started falling in earnest halfway here.

I pulled the hood of my coat over my head and exited my vehicle as well. "Is there anything I can carry?" I raised my voice over the rain that pelted his truck, the asphalt of the driveway, and us. Typical west coast rainforest rainfall.

After shaking his head, he grabbed a toolbox and a loaded tool belt. I didn't figure I could've safely carried either. *Thank God he's got more sense than me. So…why am I here?*

The front door opened, and a flash of white barreled toward us. It stopped, examined us, then started barking its head off.

"Princess Sofia!" The man looming in the doorway shouted in a booming voice. "Knock it off."

Said princess did not *knock it off*.

Carefully, I bent to offer my hand to sniff.

Simeon, just as carefully, scooted around me.

*Smart man.*

The pooch eyed me. Then licked my hand. Then launched herself at me.

My chest stung a little when she hit it, but she was just a tiny thing. What I couldn't figure out was how to stand with her in my arms.

*Should've been doing those balance exercises Marcus assigned you.*

*Yeah, yeah, yeah.*

I'd done a few—just not the number he insisted on each day.

*That's going to change.*

"You can put her down. She needs to, uh, go to the bathroom."

Unceremoniously, I dropped the princess. A whole six inches.

She glared…but was clearly fine.

"Princess Sofia, go pee." The exasperated man spoke in clear annoyance.

She continued to watch me. Then she looked over at the man still standing in the doorway. He now appeared to be holding one child and preventing a second one from escaping.

*Oh my God, everyone here is nuts.*

I loved dogs. But I didn't *do* dogs.

Kids were cute. But I didn't *do* kids.

Finally, the pooch moved away. She went to a tree, squatted, and, uh, peed. Then, clearly smart animal she was, she headed for the house, went right through the guy's legs, and apparently kept right on going.

"You're wet, you little sh—" He shut his mouth.

I rose. Very slowly. I made my way over to him. "Shweetheart?"

He grinned. "Ah, welcome to the Baker-Laxamana household. Swearing is supposed to be reserved for when my two angels are asleep. This is Victor." He hefted the child a little higher on his hip. "The one who's vanished back into the house is Violet. Watch her like a hawk. And for God's sake, never leave your phone unattended. Best to keep it in your pocket and be wary of movement when you're least expecting it." The ginger-haired man with the stunning blue eyes smiled. "I'm Maddox. I'd shake your hand..."

I'd been standing under an awning. When he stepped aside, I followed. I might've wondered, for a moment, why he hadn't invited me in first. Clearly he felt all the warnings were necessary—in case I decided this wasn't worth the hassle. I removed my coat and hung it on a rack next to Simeon's.

Who was nowhere to be found.

A little white furball, though, was chasing another child.

Right, Princess Sofia was chasing Violet.

*I can do this.*

Both children had jet-black hair, dark-brown eyes, and tanned skin. So very different from their father whose pale skin resembled my own. He had a mixture of gold and gray in his beard. Gave him a distinguished look. Although he trimmed his beard, the thing was definitely bushier than my own.

Still...between Justin, this Maddox guy, and myself? We had just about every flavor of ginger covered.

I cleared my throat. "Maybe I can, uh, dry off the dog?"

Maddox followed my gaze. "Princess Sofia, off the couch."

The dog, who had been standing there, plopped down and gave the most defiant look I'd ever seen.

A sigh from my host. He asked the child, "Can I put you down, buddy?"

"No, Papa."

Another sigh. "I need to—"

"No."

At least I could be helpful. "Where might I find a towel?"

Maddox gestured to the kitchen. "Through the far door into the laundry room. There's a basket with her name on it."

"Got it." I toed off my running shoes and made my way through the house to the far door. I opened it and found a decent-sized laundry room. On a bench, three huge baskets were labeled. Princess Sofia's was the last one. I snagged the crumpled towel and then headed back. *I seriously need my head examined.*

A streak of toddler nearly knocked me over, but I managed to close the door before she got past me. I was willing to take a wild guess that she wasn't supposed to be in there. Closed door and all.

I returned to the great room with said toddler hot on my heels. As I'd suspected, even on this horrible gray, rainy day, the room had an incredible amount of natural light.

Maddox sat in a recliner with his son on his lap.

"Great light. Not too bright with the sun?"

He shook his head. "I have tinted windows. You can't tell, but it keeps the glare and the radiant heat down when it's sunny. The full east exposure means stunning sunrises. And the bedrooms all face west—so they get the amazing sunsets." He eyed Violet, who'd settled onto the ground with a pile of building blocks. "Which these two are awake for far more than they ever should be..."

Stealthily, I approached the pooch who appeared to be dozing.

*Isn't there a saying about letting sleeping dogs lie? How does that go...?*

"She loves being toweled down." Maddox spoke the words softly.

The pooch, however, must've had super amazing hearing because she leapt up and, I would've sworn, grinned.

I held out the towel.

She appeared like she was going to lunge again.

"Uh, no." My chest ached just thinking about the damage she could do if she leapt the two feet. I moved forward as quickly as my broken body would allow and engulfed her in the towel. I started with the top of her head and slowly made my way down her body—vigorously drying her as I went.

When her snout appeared, she licked my chin, clearly aiming for my mouth.

I snapped my lips shut and rolled them inward.

She persisted.

I pulled my head back. "No licking me."

Her dark-brown eyes examined me.

"No kissing either." Maddox's voice carried from behind me. "You have to be extremely specific with her. She's about as smart as the kids are."

I continued my rubs, keeping a close eye on the tongue that lolled out. "Really?"

He snorted. "In some ways smarter. *She* would never flush her stuffie down the toilet."

"Ouch." I finished the rubdown by squeezing the extra moisture from her tail.

As I pulled back, she swiped my chin.

I glared.

She turned her head as if to say *nothing to see here...just move along.*

I laughed. "She's quite a character."

"And I'll tell you one day about the time she jumped out of my moving truck, and it took me hours to find her."

I pressed a hand to my chest. "She was okay?"

The dog woofed.

Violet's gaze shot up. First to the dog, then to me.

Her stare intimidated me more than the dog's. "I'm just going to put the towel where...?"

"In the washing machine would be amazing. You're Ryan?"

"I assume Simeon told you about me."

"Yep. Said you were his helper and to be gentle with you."

"Gentle?" *Not sure I like the sound of that. He shouldn't be telling people anything about me.*

Maddox cocked his head. "That you were recovering and shouldn't be lifting heavy things. Like stupid pooches." He glared at the princess. The princess who'd resettled and was licking her paw. She didn't even look up.

"Not 'sposed say stoop'd." Victor glared at his father.

Said father sighed. "I told myself they would be the best thing in life. And they are. Don't get me wrong..." He sighed again. "They are also the bane of my existence."

"Fair." I looked around. "Is there anything I can get you? You look like you have your hands full."

"A knee that doesn't act up when the rain's bad?"

I pressed a hand to my chest. "Maybe...a physiotherapist? I know a good one—"

"Wouldn't happen to be Marcus Branigan?"

"Uh..."

"There are some great physiotherapists in Mission City, but he really is the best."

"He's..." I flashed back to the kiss I'd seen. The embrace between him and his lover. "He's good people."

"Right. But the knee's as good as it's going to get. So me working on the soggy flooring isn't going to happen."

"Yeah, I can see that. I should probably go see if Simeon needs help. Since I'm his *helper*." I tried not to put too much derision in the word. I was as useless as teats on a bull. Hell, I wasn't even certain why I was here. But Simeon had asked, and I didn't have the power to say *no*. "Anything you need before I go find him...?"

"A cola. There's a bottle in the fridge. A small one. Could you bring it?"

I grinned. "With pleasure."

"There are enough for you to take one as well. And for Simeon."

"I'm good, but I'll grab one for him. Uh, where is he—"

"Up the stairs, last door at the end of the hall. You really can't miss it." He winced. "The plumber didn't have time to take his boots off."

Slowly, my gaze trailed from the front door to the stairs. Ah...I'd missed the mud trail. "I can clean that up." I wasn't even sure how to use a mop and bucket, but I'd try.

Maddox's relief was palpable as he slowly smiled. "There's a cleaner thing that you attach these magic wet clothes to...also in the laundry room."

Ah, I'd seen a commercial for that. *How hard can this be?*

Twenty minutes later, as I cleaned up the last of it, the answer *fucking difficult* came to mind.

Getting the wet cloth on the moppy thing wasn't too tough. But using the scratchy bit to clean off the dried mud? That was harder. What I really needed to do was get down on my hands and knees and scrub the muck. Something I'd never done in my life.

Even now, in my studio apartment, I had a young woman come by once a week to clean. My dad insisted and Marcus agreed—for now. But I was having her show me how to do things so that when I was healed I could manage myself. I hated being reliant on others. Before the war, I hadn't thought anything of the fact other people did my laundry, cooked my food, and cleaned the house. Now, shame would swamp me when I acknowledged I'd never even thanked them. Or made any effort not to make a mess.

*I will do better.*

"Everything okay?" Maddox's whisper carried across the room. He sat on the recliner with his legs elevated.

And two toddlers curled on him—fast asleep.

I nodded, removing the soggy dirt-covered cloth. I moved to the kitchen and added it to the four others I'd used into the garbage bin under the sink. So much mess. Still, I returned the moppy thing to the laundry room, quietly shut the door, and eyed the dog who'd followed me around but had given me space. "You're being good?"

If dogs could narrow their eyes, she just did.

I moved back to the main room. I caught Maddox's gaze, the pointed at the pooch at my feet.

He shook his head.

She snuffed.

I smiled. Then I indicated the stairs and made it clear I planned to go up.

He nodded.

Just before I went upstairs, I realized I'd forgotten the colas. I nabbed two. I used to mainline soda pop, but now I found the bubbles distressing. Sometimes I didn't recognize the man I'd become.

Maddox offered me a wide smile when I twisted the top off and handed him the bottle and cap.

I figured the less twisting he had to do, the less likelihood of waking the little ones. The motion strained me though.

He cocked his head.

I tried to wave him off.

"You need something? For the pain?"

"I don't take anything."

"That's fair. I've got heating pads and ice packs as well." He hesitated. "Sorry, I'm being intrusive. I see someone in pain and I want to help."

Likely could tell by my wincing and, when things got bad, I lost whatever color I managed to normally have. "I'm okay."

In no way did he look convinced. Instead, his brow knit. "I shouldn't have—"

I held up my hand to stop him.

He snapped his jaw shut.

A smile ghosted across my lips. As much as I could manage. "I wanted to help. I'm so, uh, tired of not being able to help." *Good catching. Saying* fucking, *even when the kids are asleep, would be bad.* Instead, I eyed the pooch. "Will she follow me?"

"Entirely possible." He smiled. "You dried her off. You're her friend for life."

With a nod to him, I turned back to the staircase and headed off to find Simeon.

As I'd predicted, little clacking nails followed me across the hardwood floor.

# Chapter Eleven

Simeon

*Where the hell is Ryan?*

I'd almost assumed he'd left, except I really figured he'd come up to let me know he was leaving. He seemed like a considerate guy that way.

But I'd been up here for almost forty minutes.

I sighed again. Such a mess. The bedroom's hardwood floor had gotten completely soaked, and the water had done enough damage that some boards were already warping. I shot off a text to Maddox.

—*Bad news.* —

—*Hit me.* —

—*Most of the floor has to come up...better if the entire thing.* —

—*Whatever it takes. We have the money.* —

Money had been the very last consideration on my mind.

—*I'll ask Rainbow if I can do this first.* —

—*Ravi and I can stay in the spare room.* —

*—Let me get back to you. —*

Then, a pause. I was about to put my phone away when it buzzed again.

*—Ryan almost finished cleaning floor down here. Great guy. Should be up soon. —*

My heart leapt at the news. *See? He hadn't left. You shouldn't think the worst of yourself.* Because I hadn't been thinking the worst of Ryan. I'd been thinking I wasn't worth remembering if he'd taken off.

Before I forgot, I sent off a quick text to Rainbow.

*—You okay without me for a couple of days? —*

*—Just don't miss the decorating party.—*

With a flurry of smiley emojis. Even in text, her effervescence shone.

*—Wouldn't miss it. Thanks.—*

A thumbs up.

I smiled as I tucked my phone into my back pocket. I snagged the crowbar I'd remembered to bring in and started working on the next board.

"Huh."

Ryan's voice caught me unaware. I nearly let go of the implement and cringed as it could've gone flying and hit something.

Or someone.

I pressed a hand to my chest.

He held out his hands in the universal *I mean no harm* gesture.

I tried to smile while nodding to say I understood.

"Man." He bit his lower lip. "Like huge apologies on that one."

"It's o-okay."

He gazed around. "What can I do?"

I placed the crowbar on the ground. I snagged the desk chair and brought it over so Ryan could sit close to where I was working.

He apparently understood my suggestion, and he sat. Then he handed me a cola. I nodded my thanks, then put it on the nightstand on a coaster. I'd get to it in a moment. I snagged a plank of wood from the floor and proceeded to show him how to remove the nail from hardwood. "Watch you d-don't impale yourself."

He grinned.

I'd loosened the nails, so all he had to do was use the flat bar to gently roll them out. I laid a plastic bag I'd snagged on the ground and indicated he could drop them in.

Then I moved a second chair over and gingerly piled the wood on it. This way he didn't have to reach. He could drop the denailed wood on the floor. No worries.

Once he clearly had a handle on what he was doing, I resumed my work of prying up the boards. Things were going well until I realized the damage extended under the solid wood sleigh bed.

*Shit.*

I popped off a text to Gio.

*— Want to earn extra cash? Manual labor. —*

*— Where and when? —*

*—Now and I'll text you the address. —*

I got a thumbs-up emoji. In return, I sent the address.

Then I popped one off to Maddox letting him know Gio would eventually turn up.

Another thumbs-up.

I dreaded what this would cost, but neither Ryan nor Maddox could help. The latter could wield an axe to cut down trees, but lifting of anything heavier than a large bag of Sofia's dog food or one of his children was out.

While Ryan continued to work, I quickly searched flooring options. If Maddox wanted hardwood again, I'd do it. He'd built this place himself. Well, after his injury, his dad had organized workers to finish it. But Maddox had chosen all the finishing touches.

Apparently he hadn't anticipated a Violet coming into his life. He'd once confided he always wanted children. Just, after Stanley left, he hadn't thought it would happen. But he met Ravi and...after a round of IVF, Ravi's sister had become pregnant. Using Maddox's sperm. Apparently the Laxamana genetics were strong because I never would've pegged the twins as his.

Carefully, I selected sample images of hardwood, laminate, and vinyl floors and sent them off to Maddox for his approval.

—*Which can withstand another torrent of water?* —

—*Vinyl is best. Some look really nice.* —

—*I liked the third vinyl option. I'll text Ravi and get back to you.* —

"How's it g-going?" I eyed the pile of nails Ryan had dropped into the bag.

He shrugged. "Possibly the most boring job ever."

I winced.

"Sorry. There are worse. Much worse." He didn't meet my gaze. "And I could name several off the top of my head, so let's just forget everything I've said."

*Do I push? Sit back and wait for him to come to me?* On an impulse I didn't understand, I knelt before him—gazing up to meet shadowed blue eyes. "Y-you can talk to me." I tried to swallow down the emotion pressing up. Even compassion could trigger the stuttering to get worse. "I'm n-not Justin. B-but I can listen."

He grasped the hand I had placed on his knee.

I wasn't supposed to touch without invitation, but if I didn't balance, then I was liable to land on my ass. Possibly with a nail in it—if I wasn't careful.

He squeezed my hand. "I just...it's too raw."

I nodded. I started to push up but halted when he placed his other hand on my shoulder.

"Maybe...someday..."

"Sure. Whatever w-works for you." I willed him to see the earnestness in my expression. To understand I'd never push. That I'd always hold his secrets—if that was what he wanted.

He squeezed my hand and shoulder once more, then released me.

With extreme care, I pushed off him and back to standing. I hadn't noticed him favoring anything other than his chest, but he might have injuries I knew nothing about. I certainly shouldn't be leaning on him in any way.

I grabbed my crowbar and resumed my work.

The silence wasn't as oppressive as I thought it might be. We'd both said what we'd needed to say. I didn't really have anything to add to that, or any other, topic. Instead, I just worked to a steady rhythm until the bedroom door burst open.

"Help has arrived." Gio stepped into the room with a flourish.

Mercer followed behind and held up his hand. "That would be me."

I grinned. I adored Gio's soon-to-be-fiancé. *Don't say anything about the rings.* I eyed Ryan. *Hope he remembers as well.*

Mercer and Gio were a study in contrasts. I loved how they'd come together so perfectly and were such a study in complementary couplehood.

I pointed to the bed. "If we shift the b-bed, I should be able to pull the f-flooring up."

Gio snagged a piece of warped wood. "This took *how* long?"

"Yeah. T-that's what I thought. Not treated p-properly to start, I think."

"He should ask for his money back." He eyed the bag of nails. "Ryan, you're doing a great job."

Ryan rolled his eyes.

"Don't mind that lug." Mercer playfully smacked Gio on the chest. "My name's Mercer. He belongs to me."

Gio puffed out his chest.

"Sorry, we don't *belong* to people. We're not, you know, pets or anything like—" Mercer pointed to his partner.

Ryan snorted.

Mercer, after a long moment, smiled. "Yeah. It's like that. Boyfriend feels inadequate, though. Which is nuts, right? Because I'd never had one before him, and—"

Gio snorted.

I shot him a warning glare. He might hurt Mercer's feelings. Or he might give Ryan the wrong impression.

*That's not your problem. Ryan's an adult...he can reach his own conclusions.*

Mercer eyed the bed. "Would it be better to take it apart?"

"No." Gio and I said the word at the same time.

Ryan chuckled. And continued pulling nails from the wood.

"Okay." Mercer eyed the bed. "How do we know the frame wasn't damaged by the water either?"

Gio and I met each other's gaze.

Immediately, he dropped to his knees by the bed and poked around. "This is pretty solid construction, and it's barely damp." He popped back up. "We're good to go."

"Should we remove the mattress?" Mercer kept eyeing the bed.

Gio slung his arm around his boyfriend. "You don't *have* to help."

Mercer poked him in the ribs. "I'm just trying to make certain we don't all get hernias."

Hadn't been my biggest worry. Putting my back out was, to me, a worse thing to do.

"I wish I could help." Ryan tossed the next piece of wood onto the discard pile with a bit more force.

"You are." Mercer grinned. "I've heard good things about your chaperoning skills."

Ryan cocked his head.

"Well, I know these two are up to no good when I'm not around to supervise." He pointed between Gio and myself.

Heat crept up my chest and into my cheeks.

Gio guffawed. "Right, Mercer. You shouldn't believe all the stories Rainbow is telling you behind my back. She always was a gossip."

Ryan blinked.

"J-joking." I met, and held, his gaze. "She's n-never gossiped." I glared at Gio.

He winced. "Yeah, sorry...wrong sister. Sunshine's the blabbermouth."

Mercer chuckled. "Nice save. And the absolute truth." He turned to Ryan. "I'm just joking around. Mostly because I know, as attractive as Gio is, that Simeon would never make a move on an employee."

Ryan's gaze shot to mine.

I was ninety-nine percent certain the furrowed brow was because he hadn't known I was gay. Or at least hadn't had it essentially confirmed.

Gio cleared his throat.

Mercer gazed at him. And flushed. "Oh."

I laughed. A little forced, but I managed. "I t-think we've surprised him."

Ryan shook his head. Then sort of moved his head in a weird way. "I... I don't make assumptions. You didn't say anything—and you still haven't—"

"I'm g-gay." *Jesus Fucking Christ. Of all the words to stutter on, it had to be that one?*

"Well…" Ryan gazed around. "That would make four of us."

Gio laughed. "Six if you include Ravi and Maddox."

"That's a lot of gay men." Ryan's gaze didn't leave mine. As if asking if I was okay with someone sort of casually outing me without at all meaning to. "But I'm cool with that. I just…" He swallowed. "I haven't shared that with many people."

By that, I read *virtually no one*.

*Does Justin even know?*

"We w-won't say anything." *Make him understand this is a safe space.*

He squinted. "Actually, I can't say I care." He pressed a hand to his chest. "I've defied death. What's coming out?"

Gio clapped him—gently—on the back. "That's the spirit."

"Right." Mercer surveyed the room. "I think we can manage to shift this thing."

And so we did. Took about forty-five minutes to move the bed out of the way, for me to rip up the flooring, and for us to move the bed back so I could do the rest of the floor. Some of the boards farthest away from the door weren't warped, and I was careful with how I removed them. There was just nowhere else to move the massive bed.

"Some of this might be salvageable."

"That local group that rehabs old spaces to make them livable for people in transitional situations…" Mercer trailed off.

"The people he donates both paint and his time to." Gio grinned. "And mine. They've created about thirty homes—sometimes just rooms, but other times rehabbing old houses or condos in need of love." His eyes darkened for a moment. "If not for Mercer, I might've needed to ask for their help."

Mercer moved quickly, pressing a kiss to Gio's temple. "Well, you didn't, and now we help people who do. That simple."

"Why h-haven't I heard of them?" Hurt lanced through me. I could totally help.

Gio cocked his head. "Simeon, you're already completely booked with work. And you do plenty of stuff at cost or even at a loss for your poorer clients."

Heat raced to my cheeks, and I studiously avoided Ryan's intense gaze.

"W-well…" I blew out a breath. "I can d-do stuff too."

"I'll give the organizer your name." Mercer smiled. "We can always use help. Salvaging this flooring will help. If Maddox doesn't mind—"

"He doesn't." The voice coming from the doorway had us all turning.

Maddox stood in the doorway. "They're watching a show, and I have thirty seconds. Pizza's on the way. I ordered four different types, so hopefully there's something for everyone. I think you were saying something about giving away the flooring. I'd be over the moon. If a donation helps, you can have that too." He met my gaze. "Have you ordered the vinyl?" He snapped his fingers. "I didn't tell you that Ravi gave me the go-ahead. So…do whatever you need to do. If one of you can watch the kids, then I'll grab what Ravi and I need from the closet and dump it in the spare room. Thank God we have a queen-sized bed."

"If you w-wear shoes, you should be able to walk in here. All the n-nails are in the bag."

He scratched his auburn beard with noticeable flecks of silver. He was an older dad for sure. "I just would prefer to close this room off entirely. Safer for everyone."

"Of c-course." I pointed to the desk and large, comfy reading chairs. "I should have the rest of the f-flooring up shortly."

"And we're helping." Gio wrapped an arm around Mercer and put a hand on Ryan's shoulder. "We make a good team."

Ryan's cheeks reddened under his beard. Not as thick as Maddox's. But absolutely adorable.

I'd never say as much, of course.

He rose. "I can watch the kids. I'm not much use here."

Before I could protest, he'd walked out of the room.

Maddox blinked.

I winced.

Still, after a moment, we got to work, and by the time the pizza arrived, the flooring was completely up. We devoured a good portion of the pies, then loaded the warped flooring into the back of my truck, and after a long day, I headed home.

*At least Ryan stayed and seemed to enjoy the pizza.*

*I'll have to find a way to thank him.*

# Chapter Twelve

Ryan

**M**y physio appointment on Friday went fine. I did mention the work I'd done the day before—which had been pretty easy in comparison to what the three other men had accomplished.

Marcus was pleased I'd gotten some exercise without exacerbating my injury.

I did not ask him about the guy I'd seen him kissing earlier in the week.

He assigned me more exercises and sent me on my way.

Marnie, the assistant librarian, had convinced me to try a J.D. Robb book set in the future. She explained about the woman police detective in New York, some criminal she was investigating, and that there were nearly sixty books with two coming out each year. In other words—if I liked book one, I was set practically forever.

I had enjoyed book one, so she found me the next twelve and let me check them out. She casually mentioned the library had eReaders and MP3 players—donated by a generous patron—so people could check out digital material. I thanked her for her consideration, said I wouldn't want to deprive someone else of the opportunity, and headed out with two bags of books.

She said she'd collect the next twelve for me.

I thanked her. Her vibe read cautious, but friendly. Sort of like myself. I was open to being friends with someone—in a superficial way—but I wasn't interested in being someone's best buddy.

*Liar. You would totally be Simeon's best buddy if he wanted.*

As I sat at home in my recliner, I reflected on the past week and all that had happened. The ranch, the little house Simeon was building, as well as Maddox and Ravi's home.

Then I thought about all the people I'd met.

Obviously I'd known Justin, Gio, Mercer, and Maddox were gay. Plus, by logical extension, Justin's husband Stanley and Maddox's husband Ravi. Or at least bi or pan or something. Now I suspected my physiotherapist was gay. Okay, so that was a good number of queer guys in my life. Likely there were more, and certainly there might be lesbians as well.

*Simeon's gay.*

That I hadn't expected. I knew better than to stereotype. One of the buffest, beefiest, and most hardcore soldiers in our unit had been gay.

He died.

Four men dead. Four men I would've given my own life for. Because they had families who cared about them. People who missed them. People who mourned them. If I'd taken any one of their places, no one would miss me.

Trying not to feel sorry for myself was a challenge. A crappy father just really made for a shitty recovery. Who was I doing this for? Him? Yeah, no way. Myself? That was logical, of course.

I eyed the clock on the wall. Seven o'clock on Friday night. I didn't have an appointment on the ranch until Monday morning. *I'm going to go out of my mind.* My gaze wandered to the pile of books Marnie had sought for me. With the promise of more. I hadn't been a big reader before I'd gone overseas. Playing games took up all my time. During my time in the war, we'd been constantly on edge. Reading had been impossible there as well.

Sitting in this chair, as comfortable as I could get, wasn't helping my disposition. Night had long fallen. We were just a month away from the winter solstice.

My flip phone sat on the side table, hooked up to the charger. Which was a bit of a joke since I never called anyone. My power barely went down each day. Still, phones were a lifeline I'd never take for granted.

*Damn.*

I wasn't certain I'd ever felt so alone in my life. So disconnected. So...lonely

*This wasn't how it's supposed to be.*

All the physio in the world was not going to make me well enough to go back to Ukraine. Canada had basically swept my involvement under the rug—as they should. I certainly didn't want Canada drawn into that war. I wanted the Ukrainians to win—but I didn't wish for a world war to accomplish that.

Even I understood geopolitics.

But I didn't know how things were going. I read the Mission City Gazette once a week. If I had a computer, I could check the articles that were only posted there.

Even the library was closed—if I wanted to go down and read the Vancouver Sun or find the courage to sit at a computer.

*Nope. Not doing that.* Just the idea set off a panic within me that I could barely control.

Slowly, I lowered the footrest. After a moment, I rose.

*Hey, no dizziness. That's great.* The head rushes didn't always happen, but when they did, I found them disconcerting. The doctor said eventually they should pass. Like eventually the pain would lessen. Eventually the scars would lighten. Eventually I'd get some—but not all—of my life back.

I liked the doctor I'd secured in Mission City. Dr. Marco Raymond was in his mid-forties with graying brown hair and an infectious smile. I liked him. And I should be listening to him more often.

*A gentle stroll down First Avenue will do the trick.* Surely some businesses would be open. I'd spotted a Greek Restaurant. Subway would be open. Oh, and Timmie's, of course. I couldn't have a coffee, but I could have an herbal tea. Or I could get in the car and drive to The Junction to go to Starbucks—

Nope. Walk. Walking to The Junction was an eventual goal. A healthy person could make the walk in just over twenty minutes. I figured I could, one day, make it in about an hour. And, fortunately, I could take a shuttle bus home. Or a cab. Or I could sit at the White Spot for two hours, get my strength back, and return to this tiny apartment. To what end, I had no idea. To say I'd done it? To feel a sense of accomplishment? That I was human?

*Folly.*

Still, Marcus had asked me to draw up a list of ten goals, and that walk was on it.

I snagged my peacoat and headed for the door.

*Phone.*

I nearly left it behind but, like, shit could happen. Bad things could happen...even in small towns in Southern British Columbia. After I locked the door, I pocketed my keys, took a lungful of air, and headed down to First Avenue. Having an apartment so close to the center of town was nice. Mission City's downtown was nothing like Vancouver's in terms of business and vibrancy. As I passed the little car dealership, though, a sense of rightness settled in me. A sense of peace I hadn't felt in a very long time.

Only a few tables in Timmie's were occupied. I caught sight of a cute guy with his nose buried in a newspaper. Old-fashioned or technophobe? As much as I wanted to ask, I'd never be so bold. Even as a tuft of hair fell across his forehead, I headed toward the counter.

A young woman in a hijab smiled at me.

"Uh, small herbal tea and one chocolate Timbit."

"Great." She rang up my total, and I swiped my card.

Three minutes later, I was heading out of the store after giving the cute guy one final perusal. *A missed opportunity? You were never social before...why might you be now?* Right. Except...he looked lonely. I felt lonely.

I passed Stavros's, but no scent of Greek food reached me. When I reached Subway, though, the smell of fresh bread assailed me. I'd eaten a fresh salad and a hot dog for dinner.

Some bad habits died hard. I figured the healthy salad shit zeroed out the nitrites. I was supposed to see a nutritionist eventually as well. Dad offered to have someone cook meals for me. I'd put my foot down—having a cleaner was one thing. I really would've struggled with housework. I did not, however, need someone preparing my meals. That much, I could handle. I bit into the soft Timbits goodness and a rush of nostalgia hit me. My dad wasn't much for traditions, but he'd allowed me to ride my bike to Tim Hortons once a week to buy a six-pack of Timbits. If they didn't go stale, I might've tried to make them last. Alas, they needed to be consumed in the first day or two.

I'd never offered one to either my father or any of the staff. Nope, like the little selfish brat I'd been, I'd hoarded them for myself.

*Move on.*

After folding the paper wrapper, I tossed it into a recycling container.

Except I couldn't move on. In order to accept what happened to me in the war, I had to reconcile who I'd been, why I'd gone, and what I'd thought I could accomplish. Only then could I accept that I'd failed in my mission.

*Not fail.*

Justin's soft voice carried through my consciousness as I crossed the street.

*Reframe.*

I finished my tea and tossed the cup into another recycling container. Then I passed a gift shop showcasing plenty of lovely things. I had no one to buy something for, but I still stopped to gaze into the window. Such pretty things. Some sturdy. Some delicate. All destined, hopefully, to good homes. I was about to move away when a painting caught my notice. I opened the door and stepped inside.

While outside the weather was misty and chilly, a blast of warm air greeted me.

A woman at the counter glanced over—likely because some bells rang when I entered. She waved. "I'm Lena. Whatever you need, you just let me know."

"Uh, thank you." I made my way over to the painting. "Is this a print?"

She came to my side. "No, that's a Tessa Carlyle original." Lena pointed. "She brings me smaller pieces and gives me a discount. Still, they're...expensive."

I squinted to read the price tag. I whistled. "Is everything in here that expensive?" This wasn't an art gallery by any stretch of the imagination. She did have one display that appeared to be original artwork of various kinds. Scarves, earrings, necklaces, sculptures, and a number of other clearly unique items.

Lena appeared to follow my gaze. "We have a decent-sized Indigenous population in and around Mission City. They're specifically from the Stó:lō people. Several of those items are from a Matsqui artist who lives over in Abbotsford."

"They're amazing." My mind wandered to Kennedy, Rainbow, and Avery. Surely I'd be allowed to give them little gifts, right? They weren't my therapist. Justin was out but maybe something for Simeon?

I'd never bought a gift for anyone before. What did one buy for one's father when the man had everything? His derisive and dismissive treatment of my kindergarten art project ensured I never did that again. I told the teacher that my dad loved my art. Meanwhile, I tossed all my projects into a garbage can on Granville Street so they never even made it into the house.

"For certain I want the painting—it's stunning." And would fill my apartment with something vibrant. The nature scene was of a falcon scooping a salmon out of the river. The motion leapt off the canvas in a way that stunned.

Lena grinned. "She also does risqué paintings as well. Those are way more expensive."

I managed to smile back. "I think one painting is enough for now. Although…" I curled my hand around my phone. "If she replaces that one, could you let me know?"

"Sure." She held my gaze. "Or I can just give you her card and you can email her. She actually answers the damn thing herself. She's not as well-known as she should be outside of the Lower Mainland of Vancouver and Cedar Valley. I think when word gets around, she's going to be in high demand. As it is, she teaches classes at the university. So freaking talented. Let me get her card for—"

"No." I winced when Lena jumped a little at my vehemence. I tried to smile. "I'm happy for you to get the commission. It's only fair…you introduced me to her."

"Sure." She said the word uncertainly.

I pointed to the display of various Indigenous items. "I have several special women in my life…perhaps you could help me select a few things?"

She beamed. "Of course."

Forty minutes later, I left with a woven cloth bag full of various things that I might or might not be able to gift, as well as the painting—wrapped securely against the elements.

Lena's unrelenting smile brought me warmth.

The fact I was charging this to my father's credit card brought only a moment of hesitation. My finances weren't sorted yet. He'd given me the card to use it however I saw fit, with a limit that would've fed a village in Ukraine for more than a week. Since I'd…encouraged…him to make regular contributions to humanitarian causes in the region, I could buy these things for the women who worked at the ranch on my father's dime and not feel guilty. Given how much the man was worth, this was nothing to him. Literally.

I strolled down the street until I arrived at The Owl's Nest.

*Oh good, they're still open. I should've checked. Oh wait, I can't.*

Stupid internet being connected to stupid computers and smart phones.

*Speaking of phones…you have one. The store has an ad in the paper. Put two and two together and you make a phone call to find out their hours of operation.*

The door swung open with Rainbow's nearly identical sister standing there in a billowy royal-purple cotton blouse and a gypsy-style red-and-gold skirt. "Are you coming in?" She met my gaze. "Your hands are full, and so I figured if you were coming in, then I'd open the door, and if you weren't, then I could just wish you a good night and close the door again because all the hot air's being sucked out, and Dickens gets really cranky when he pays the electric bill—"

"Hey!" A disembodied voice came from some direction I couldn't pinpoint.

My gaze met a soft-blue one. She grinned.

I stepped in from the cold and damp.

The bookstore was much as it had been just over a week ago when I'd been here picking up the RD Watts young-adult fantasy novels.

My mouth opened to speak when Sunshine snapped her fingers. "You're Ryan. Dickens got Raven to sign those books for you. I remember. Sorry." She waved her hand in front of her face. "It's been a bit of a crazy week." She pointed around the store.

Aside from the cat who lay atop a cat tree and was cleaning itself—and alternately staring out the window to the street—I noticed the decorations. I grinned. "You have been busy."

She nodded. "We always wait until after Remembrance Day. But soon after, we go nuts because Christmas is, obviously, our busiest season." She eyed my bag and painting. "Would you like me to tuck those behind the counter for you while you browse?"

"Uh, sure."

The gorgeous blond guy appeared from behind a door. "Don't let her bulldoze you."

Apparently undaunted, Sunshine gently took my painting and the bag. "Dickens, you want me to sell books...right?"

"Well...yeah..." He frowned. "But I also want people to feel free to come in and browse without pressure."

"Weren't you heading home for dinner with Spike?"

He pursed his lips. Then he whistled.

The cat leapt down from its perch and sauntered over to him.

To this point, I hadn't noticed how big the cat actually was. Not necessarily fat...but sturdy.

Dickens waved. "Spike and I appreciate you being willing to close up on a Friday night." He turned his attention to me. "Although I always appreciate a purchase, I'm more interested in forming relationships with people living in Mission City. You're new...beware the Dixon sisters." With a wink, he and the cat departed, closing the door behind them.

"Well, I never..." Sunshine pressed a hand against her chest in clear mock offense.

With a smile, I wagged my finger. "Rainbow warned me about you. I'm not sharing any of my secrets." Because this was the gossipy sister.

She arched an eyebrow. "That almost sounds like a challenge. I'm going to find you something special."

And so she did.

# Chapter Thirteen

Simeon

I'd been working away at Maddox's floor for nearly three hours when the bedroom door opened and white running shoes came into view. I barely had time to register them when the scent of fresh-brewed coffee reached my nose. Taking a leap this generous soul had brought me a cup, I eased back onto my heels and offered a smile. "Thank y-you." The words sort of died in my throat as I swallowed.

Ryan stood there, with a sheepish grin on his face. He held up a steaming mug. "Maddox said you might be thirsty. He also said to let you know that lunch is in about an hour and he's making roast beef."

"For m-me?"

"Uh...he said something about sandwiches and leftovers for a week and since the toddlers are out with Ravi at a program called Toddlers and Books at the library that he was taking full advantage. The kitchen is a disaster area, and I think he's running code on a laptop."

"T-that's Maddox. A m-multitasker."

"Ah. Well I'm shit at cooking and code..." He broke off. "Computers just aren't my thing anymore."

*Anymore.* No missing the way his eyes clouded over.

"But I have coffee and am here to help. I swear it's not because I want roast beef." He offered a cheeky grin.

The shadows in his eyes, however, didn't completely go away.

Instead of trying to rise, I organized myself so I was sitting on my butt. Gratefully, I accepted the coffee from Ryan. I cocked my head.

He waved me off as he sat. "I had a tea at the ranch." He met my gaze. "I hope it's okay I'm here. Justin..." He cleared his throat. "I admitted, in my session this morning, that I'd spent a lonely weekend alone." He then managed a small smile. "I might've also asked if you were around. Not..." The wince was subtle—but clear. "Yeah."

"T-that's okay. I would have been at the r-ranch, but..."

"Justin said Maddox had mentioned the flooring was delivered this morning, and how he was so damn grateful the ranch could spare you." Slowly, he sank to the chair by the desk, just a few inches away from me.

Heat flared to my cheeks. That seemed to happen a lot.

"Before I knew what was happening, Justin called Maddox to see if another pair of hands might help. That might've been—"

"O-overbearing...?"

Ryan laughed. "Or considerate. Could be seen either way. And yeah, Maddox invited me over. Even if not to help on the flooring, then just to supposedly keep him company." He frowned. "That man didn't look like he needed company."

"He w-would have made it work."

"You know, I believe you're right. I offered to help, and he smacked his forehead and said how he'd planned to ask you if you needed a hand, and he'd forgotten, and could I run a cup of coffee up, and that if you didn't need my help that he could definitely use some." Ryan shivered—clearly all for show. "I think he was going to recruit me to do dishes."

"That sounds...h-helpful." I grinned.

"If you don't need me, I'll certainly head back down."

Except he'd have to stand to wash dishes. *Is he up for that?* Helping me would be much simpler. I sipped the coffee then swallowed the black liquid gold. "S-stay. If you w-want."

He blinked. "I want."

"G-great." I handed him the coffee mug, which he set on the desk. I was about to resume work when the sunlight suddenly poured into the room.

A shaft of light landed on Ryan, ever so slightly muted by the window panes of frozen glass behind him, with the frost still visible. In the light, he looked like an angel—with his stunning red-gold hair like a halo.

I smiled even as I blinked back tears. The sheer beauty of the man with the incredible depths of pain he endured. I wanted to take away that pain. But I didn't know how. Wasn't qualified.

"Are you okay?"

"Y-yes." I pointed to the pile on the floor. "H-help me?"

"Happy to." Slowly, and with great obvious care, he lowered himself to the ground. He pointed to the pile. "That's vinyl?"

I nodded. "Waterproof vinyl p-plank flooring." I picked up a piece. "L-looks like laminate, but is m-more durable and, as the name says, waterproof."

"So the water...just pools? Goes elsewhere?"

I nodded.

Ryan grinned. "Let's hope no more plushies are flushed."

"The w-water didn't get shut off f-fast enough." I smiled back. "M-Maddox is...p-philosophical." I nearly tripped a second time on that word. Damnit. I wanted to be able to use big words—to impress Ryan. The impact was lost if I couldn't even say them properly.

"Let's get to work." He winked. "I want to earn my keep. Or, in this case, my roast beef."

We worked in companionable silence for the next hour and a bit. Part of me was grateful he didn't require much in the way of socializing from me. Another part of me longed to ask questions. Why had he been so lonely this weekend? No family or friends? I didn't know everyone in Mission City, but I was damn sure I would've remembered him if I'd seen him around. So was he new in town?

"Hey, you two." Maddox's deep voice filled the space.

I'd heard him coming, but apparently Ryan hadn't and he clearly startled, pressing his hand to his chest.

Maddox held up his hands. "Apologies. I thought I was clomping."

"In s-sock feet?" I grinned, all the while watching Ryan.

He managed a strained smile. "My hearing isn't always as good."

I couldn't remember him saying something before. *Is he embarrassed about it? Assure him.* "Y-you're okay here."

His eyes widened. And not, to my reading, as a good thing.

"Roast beef's ready. If you can tolerate two excited toddlers, then you're welcome to join us. If you want to keep your sanity, I'd advise to stay up here. I'll happily bring you—"

"D-downstairs." I gazed at Ryan, willing him to understand. That, for reasons I couldn't explain, I needed him to get along with my friends. This made absolutely no logical sense—and yet its import couldn't be understated.

He smiled. This time, the light reached his eyes. "Toddlers and roast beef sound great."

Maddox shook his head—yet with a smile. "Don't say I didn't warn you."

Fifteen minutes later, as Ryan pulled a piece of corn from his hair, I winced.

"Violet." Ravi glared at his daughter. "We do not throw anything. Least of all food."

The munchkin grinned. Clearly she didn't take the admonishments seriously. And why would she? She was all of two years old.

I didn't know much about child development. *Does she understand consequences? She must be too young for a timeout.*

Ryan, however, grinned back. "I have to say, she has remarkable distance and speed. I didn't see that coming."

"Why would you?" Maddox put another piece of meat on Victor's tray and added the smallest amount of gravy.

As I expected, Victor grabbed it, smooshed the gravy so it went everywhere, then chomped on the meat.

I smiled.

Ravi rolled his eyes. "She's our other Princess."

All the adults glanced over at the pooch who sat, at the ready, willing the toddlers to drop food for her.

As if noticing all of us—and knowing what we were thinking—she lazily licked a paw.

I cleared my throat. "If y-you ever need someone to watch Princess Sofia, I'd be h-happy to."

"That's sweet of you to offer." Ravi beamed.

"You have no idea what you'd be getting into." Maddox cut his husband a look as if to say, *knock it off*.

Ravi's grin grew wider. "In fact, we're going to see my sister in Calgary with her wife. Sofia was going to stay with Justin and Stanley, but they've really got their hands full—"

"Uh..." Maddox cleared his throat. "I thought we talked about Sofia staying with Adam and Dean." He scratched his beard. "We're also worried about the house..."

"Well, they're preparing for the wedding." He tilted his head. "Had you heard? It only just—"

"D-Dean texted me after Adam called Rainbow." I grinned. "He's s-super excited." I turned to Ryan. "Dean's Australian. H-he works in forestry management. He's got a p-permanent job offer which is good because he's fallen in love with a C-Canadian. They're g-getting married. I h-hope you can meet them. They're great g-guys."

Adam had burns on his face and arm from a car accident that killed his twin brother. I hadn't even known him until this year because he was so reclusive. Maddox and Ravi had arranged for Dean to stay with Adam—something about an apartment falling through—and Dean had...coaxed Adam out of his self-imposed exile. I considered the men friends.

*Should you warn Ryan about Adam's scars? Nah. He seems like a pretty chill guy who would just roll with the punches.*

*Wait.*

*When would Ryan and Adam even meet?*

That was a good question.

"Would Sofia stay at your place?" Ravi used his meat to push some corn onto his fork. "You live with your grandparents, right?"

Heat flared to my cheeks. That was happening a lot lately.

"Right." I considered. "I w-would have to leave her alone while I work, and my hours are sometimes long. I don't want Nanny and Bops to feel o-obligated."

Ryan raised his hand. "I can take the dog. I mean, I don't think she's allowed in my studio apartment, but I could stay here. House-sit for you. Would that work?" He gave me a long look. "And Simeon can come over to check on us. Unless his grandparents need him?"

*He understands.*

"They're g-good as long as I check in with them."

Ravi dropped his fork and clapped his hands. "Perfect! We were worried about the house and were going to ask our neighbor Felix to check on the place. He's a teacher in the school district and also newly married." He rubbed his forehead. "We keep meaning to have him and his husband Jacob over for dinner."

"We should have a Christmas party." Maddox grinned. "For the neighborhood. It'll mostly be gay partners."

"And kids." Ravi gazed at his two. "You know the others are going to boss ours around."

"Might put them in their place." Maddox murmured that.

"Opal is Justin and Stanley's f-foster daughter. Along with their s-son, Angus."

"Justin mentioned them." Ryan smiled. "I think the rule is that therapists aren't supposed to talk about their families. But when you're eating lasagna, all bets are off." He gave me a meaningful look.

*Had we discussed personal stuff the day we ate at Rainbow's kitchen table? I should be able to remember, but I can't.* The memory of him enjoying Nanny's lasagna was my main memory of that day. "Oh, I can b-bring some lasagna when you're staying here."

"So it's settled?" Maddox gazed at Ryan. "You really want to stay? Sofia's fine to be left alone for several hours at a time, so you don't need to watch her all the time. You can also take her with you to the ranch. She and Tiffany are best buddies. She came with me for all my appointments."

Said so casually. As if going for therapy at the ranch was no big deal. I loved that about Maddox and Adam. They were open about needing help. Adam had once pointed out that if he shared his experience with successful counseling, perhaps someone might decide to go for themselves. That one never knew what trauma and pain lay just beneath the surface of another person.

Those words struck me as profound. Both he and Maddox had been recluses before meeting their future partners. Both had been coaxed out into the world and had, on their own, seen therapists at the ranch.

*Is Justin helping Ryan? He's here...so that's something. He admitted he was lonely on the weekend...what did that admission cost him?*

"Well, this is perfect." Ravi grinned. "See, thanks to Violet's escapades, we've gotten to spend more time with Simeon, and now Ryan's going to house-sit and pet sit for us. Like I said—perfect."

Maddox didn't quite look convinced. "I feel like we're shoving things at people."

Ryan held up his hand. "I volunteered. I mean, how hard can one dog be?"

Ravi and Maddox gazed at each other. Ravi snickered, Maddox rolled his eyes, and then they both broke into gales of laughter.

Ryan cocked his head at me.

I shrugged.

After a moment, Ravi wiped his eyes. "My first day here, I let Sofia out for a pee. Little sh— Uh, twit, chased a squirrel into the backyard. The wooded backyard that abuts a municipal tree farm that goes for miles. I found her..." He winced. "But couldn't get back."

Maddox's expression sobered for a moment. "And I'm former search and rescue. I was able to locate them." He pointed his fork. "This twit took his jacket off to warm up the dog."

"Hey." Ravi shrugged. "You found a way to warm me up."

"With a mylar blanket."

"I meant later."

Maddox chuckled. "Yeah, you would. One-track mind."

"Hey." Ravi attempted to grouse, but he utterly failed as he broke into a wide grin. "You like my one-track mind."

"Yeah, I kind of do."

Ryan giggled.

The sound warmed my heart.

"S-so she has to g-go out on a leash."

Princess Sofia's daddies smiled fondly.

"Fuck yes." Maddox slapped his hand to his mouth.

"Fu-fu-fu-uck." Victor grinned.

Ravi pointed a fork. "That's on you." He chuckled. "I still like the idea of a get-together before we leave. Are you two available Saturday night? We can have an impromptu celebration of our new bedroom floor."

"You planning to entertain in the room?" Maddox grinned. "I don't know if the other guys are up for that."

"Well, possibly Dean." Ravi winked. "Just kidding. But yeah, I'll see who's available."

"I am." Ryan cleared his throat. "We have the decorating party at the ranch on Friday, but I'm available." He glanced my way. "I wouldn't want to speak for anyone else."

"Well, I h-happen to be available." I beamed. "L-looking forward to it."

# Chapter Fourteen

Ryan

We finished Maddox and Ravi's bedroom floor in two days. Near the end of the second, I had to head for physio.

Marcus was pleased with my progress.

I told him about helping with flooring. Not all that impressive, since I wasn't actually doing the laying. Still something and, clearly to him, more importantly, I was getting out and socializing. Part of the reason he'd encouraged me to go to Healing Horses in the first place—the need to get out. Also, to deal with my problems.

To wit, my cock still had no interest in anything. Even when I imagined peeling Simeon out of those jeans, tearing off his chambray shirt, and yanking his T-shirt over his head...

Nothing.

Nada.

*Nichto.*

Oh. Damn. That was Russian. Better to use *ni*. Or *niet* which was sort of Dutch. Or something.

Regardless, I couldn't get my dick interested.

Dr. Raymond promised me this was likely just a matter of time.

*Likely.*

He also said sorting out the psychological from the physiological would be a challenge. My vascular system worked properly. Nothing in my chest had affected *down there*. So the problem was in my mind?

Marcus didn't know either.

As I sat alone in my apartment on Tuesday night, I reflected on the past two days. They'd been...almost fun. I hadn't faced the negative spiraling thoughts that so often consumed me when I was alone.

I eyed my phone. *Should've asked for Simeon's number. He's good at texting.*

The guy was. His thumbs were amazing, and his dexterity clear.

Yet he was also gentle. He'd helped clean Violet's grubby hands and, to my surprise, the gravy in her hair. In comparison, Victor had been pristine.

And somehow I'd agreed to a cocktail party on Saturday. With extra kids, dogs, and gay guys. More than I'd ever been in a room with, that was for certain.

On that thought, I settled in with my sixth Eve Dallas novel and was asleep shortly thereafter.

Waking to a dreary Wednesday was nothing new. Ever since I'd come home, rain dominated the weather. From a special spot just up the road, I could see Mount Baker—the dormant volcano in Washington State. Which was lovely. But it could only be seen when the sun was out. Which had happened, like, four times. And two of those times, I'd been at the ranch.

*The ranch.*

Yesterday, Simeon had casually mentioned he'd be back at the ranch today and working on flooring.

He hadn't asked. That wasn't his style. He'd left the door open—if I was brave enough to step through.

*Fuck it...I am brave.* Well, not in the ways that counted...but I could be brave when it came to helping lay flooring.

I showered—pointedly ignoring my chest. I had a stool in the shower where I could rest my foot. That meant I didn't have to bend all the way over to wash my legs and feet. And I didn't need to see my cock and balls to wash them. I was grateful the mirror was fogged over when I got out.

*Damn. Forgot to turn on the fan. That's important...I remember that's important.*

Well, nothing to be done about it now. I dried off carefully, then hung the towel on the rack—another thing I never used to do. My new cleaner gently explained to me why I needed to do it. Aside from the fact no one else was going to...practical reasons existed why it had to be done. Like black mold.

So with images of gross things in my mind, I reverted back to army habits and cleaned up after myself. Part of the slothfulness had been doing what I'd always done back home, part was an attempt to obliterate the army from my mind, and part was not being physically capable of doing everything in the early days.

Sufficiently dry, I moved back into the main room and started pawing through my meager clothes. I'd put off buying more—my body still hadn't settled on a comfortable weight. Living rough for several years hadn't leant itself to keeping the weight I'd been before—which was good. But without the bulk of being overweight, I didn't know where I was supposed to land.

*You could ask Marcus. Or Doctor Raymond. Or...wait for it...you could google it when you go to the library.*

Since none of those three options appealed, I snagged my checked flannel shirt, a pair of jeans that fit decently, and added gray knit socks and my sneakers. I tossed on my peacoat, assured myself everything was to rights, then I headed out to my car.

I'd finagled out of Rainbow that Simeon was a sucker for lemon-loaf treats from Starbucks. And drank his coffee black. I pointed my car in that direction and, within just a few minutes had my tea, a coffee, and two lemon loaves. Then I headed up the Cedar Connector toward the ranch.

*Should I have grabbed something for the others?* Ah, they'd be okay. Plus, I didn't know knew what they all wanted, who was working, and whether or not they would even be interested. I had a vague memory of Justin saying he had to go into Simon Fraser University for an in-person something or other to do with his PhD.

A doctorate. In clinical psychology.

I barely had a college diploma in programing. And that was only because my father threatened to take away all my gaming systems if I didn't do *something* with my life. Two years later I had a diploma I never planned to use, and I was back in his basement full-time playing games.

*What a fucking waste of a human being you are.*

Was, I tried to correct myself. Was a waste.

I'd saved lives while in the war. By killing people with the drones I controlled, I'd saved our people from being killed by the soldiers on their side.

But I hadn't been able to save my friends.

Four mangled and broken bodies.

Four families left to mourn.

Me being medevacked out of there and barely surviving. *Pain. Blood. The smell of burning and—*

I pulled onto a road off Cedar Street and struggled to breathe. I managed to get the car into park and cut the engine before the shaking overtook me. Trying to curl into a ball didn't work well with a steering wheel in the way.

And wouldn't be good for my chest anyway, so maybe obstructions were a useful thing.

Pressing my hands to my eyes, I tried to obliterate my memories. The sights. The smells. The taste.

A knock on my window had me startling and pulling my hands away from my face.

Perhaps I should've been scared of the figure looming over me, but I had enough of my wits about me that I could recognize I was in Mission City and not somewhere in a warzone.

Slowly, I rolled the window down.

"Hey." The guy waved. "You okay? I'm a teacher at Cedar Street Elementary, and I saw you and I thought, you know, I'm just going to go say *hi*. My name's Felix, and I'm not usually nosy, but—"

"Do you know Maddox?" *What the fuck?* That's *where your mind's gone?*

He eyed me. "Yeah. I live on Maddox's street. My husband Jacob and I are friends with Maddox and Ravi."

"And Justin?"

Slowly, he nodded. "Would you like me to call one of them?"

"Justin's in school." My voice came out calm, but I had no idea how.

"Right." He offered a measured smile. "But I bet I could call someone else. There are plenty of people—"

"Simeon?"

Felix cocked his head. "Sure. My husband's a contractor, and sometimes he hires Simeon for odd stuff. We're also friends—through Maddox, which you've clearly figured out." He yanked out his phone. "What's your name?"

"Ryan." Even that was a struggle.

"Great. Just one second." The adorable dark-haired man stepped away from my car and held a brief conversation.

A bell rang over at the school. Only did I now realize there were tons of kids running around in the spitting rain.

Felix returned. "Simeon's going to come with Rainbow. He can drive you wherever you need to go—including to the ranch if that works. Or home. Or to Maddox's place, I suspect."

"Your kids—" Ineffectually, I pointed.

"My friend Ben's going to watch my class while I'm out here with you. I've got everything under control." He hunched over. "Would you like to come into the school? You should probably roll up your window—you're getting wet. And how cool is it you have a car with windows that, like, actually roll down?"

"Will you...?" I eyed my car.

"Sure, if you don't mind." Felix, apparently a mind reader, headed over to the passenger side.

I picked up the tray of drinks and food as he slid in.

He offered a smile.

"Do you drink coffee? I have a black one."

"Nah, but thank you. That for Simeon?"

I nodded. "And a tea for me. Would you like the tea? Or a lemon loaf?" This all felt wholly inadequate.

"I'm good. But how about you sip your tea while we wait?"

He rescued the tray from my shaking hands.

I winced.

"It's really okay. I deal with ten-year-olds having meltdowns every day. This is easy."

Somehow, I believed him.

He handed me my thermal mug with the little tab from the tea-bag sticking out.

"Thank you."

"Process of elimination." He poked the paper bag with the food. "Did you eat breakfast?"

I shook my head.

"Do you think you could try to eat this? I find my kids always do better when they've eaten. Oh, my husband as well. He has a habit of working through lunch and then comes home super cranky."

"Fun." Was that the right response?

Felix smiled, his eyes sparkling. "I have his permission to take charge. He's a good man."

"Sounds like it. He hires Simeon?"

"Yeah. I mean, rarely. Simeon's always so busy. Just he's got a couple of skills that Jacob struggles to find guys with. So if he's stuck, he calls Simeon. And he's friends with all the guys on our street, and that makes him friends with me because, as you can see, I just make friends wherever I go." He puffed out his chest.

I snorted.

He glanced at me sideways, then laughed. "Yeah, that's what Jacob would say. I'm actually quite shy. Not with the kids...but with adults. It's why I chose to teach."

"Why me?" I needed to know.

"I saw what I perceived as pain. I mean my first thought was *is he going to hurt the kids?* That's always my first thought. But then...I saw pain. I thought maybe physical pain..." He tapped the drink tray. "Thank you for not telling me to mind my own business."

"That was an option?" I might've croaked that. "I've found Mission City residents are...nosier...than where I come from."

"Where do you come from? I'm not detecting an accent..."

"Vancouver."

He chuckled. "No, we're not Vancouver. I did my teaching degree at Simon Fraser and that was as close to Vancouver as I wanted to get. I'm not a big-city guy. I like...simple. I like knowing my neighbors and being able to say hi to people I see all the time."

"I think I need to try harder."

He tilted his head. "You know Justin, Simeon, and Maddox. That's a start."

I smiled. "And Violet, Victor, Ravi, Rainbow, Kennedy, Avery..." I squinted. "And Sunshine and Dickens and Lena and..." I floundered. "That cute guy who gives me my Starbucks."

"Tristan."

"Right. Him." I sipped my tea. "Marnie, Loriana, and Johanna at the library..."

"And you've been here how long?"

I squinted. "About a month. Oh, I can't forget Dr. Raymond and Marcus." I could've just opened my medical records—I was just vomiting out information.

"Good doctor, good physiotherapist." Felix smiled. "You're already part of the town. Oh, have you eaten at Fifties yet?"

I shook my head.

"Okay, best burgers in Mission City. If Sarabeth's working, tell her Felix says *hi*."

*No way am I going to remember all this.*

"Oh, here's Rainbow."

An SUV pulled onto the side of the road in front of us.

Felix waved. "Felix Stevenson. Just call anytime. We're friends now." He hopped out of the car, put the drink tray back on the seat, and closed the door.

Stunned, I sat for a moment longer as Felix shook hands with Simeon. As Felix hugged Rainbow, Simeon made his way over to me.

I lowered the window.

He dropped to a crouch so we were just about at eye level.

"I'm okay." I forced a laugh. "But your coffee's cold."

"It'll k-keep." He held my gaze with those lovely and compassionate hazel eyes. "What do you need?"

*You.*

But I wouldn't say that. I didn't have the right. He didn't need my shit. He didn't need to be helping a man who could barely help himself.

"I don't know."

Slowly he nodded. "W-well, I think I should drive."

"Yeah."

"W-we can go back to y-your place. We c-can go to the ranch. You can come h-home with me."

I cocked my head.

"W-we can hang out in my room. Well. I live in the b-basement. Huge space."

"Your grandparents would be okay with that?"

Going home with him? It sounded…decadent. I should've been accepting a ride back to my apartment. Or going to the ranch for some counseling or some shit. Even if Justin wasn't there, a plethora of other counselors worked there. Surely one of them could fit me in.

"Why don't you c-come and meet Nanny and Bops? I can ask them to t-turn the television off. W-we can just sit. They're g-good at sitting."

I believed him. But the thought of people made my skin crawl. Well, people other than him. "Your basement?"

He nodded.

"Yeah...okay."

He grinned. "I'll t-tell Rainbow."

I didn't ask how he'd retrieve his truck. I didn't ask how much money he'd lose if he spent the day with me. I didn't even ask if he was certain he could deal with me and my neuroses.

Instead, when he came back, I let Rainbow guide me out of my car and around to the passenger side. She accepted, reluctantly, the coffee and lemon loaves. Well, until she broke into a grin and admitted Avery loved Starbucks coffee and Kennedy was partial to lemon loaves, and if there happened to be a second, Rainbow wasn't going to turn it down.

She made me smile as she ensured I had my seatbelt secure.

Moments later, Simeon was getting into the driver's seat.

And having to push said seat *way* back.

I smiled.

*Maybe this'll be okay.*

Or not.

I just didn't know.

# Chapter Fifteen

Simeon

While Rainbow charmed Ryan, and after I'd thanked Felix for his quick thinking, I shot off a text to my grandmother warning her that I was bringing home a friend. I said we'd go around back so as to not bother her. Well, I specified Ryan needed to be alone right now. I said we might come up for dinner if he was feeling better.

She shot back three thumbs-up. Almost as if she understood brevity was important.

I'd pocketed my phone, thanked Rainbow as she headed to her SUV, and then gotten into Ryan's car.

Ryan's super-compact car.

My head touched the roof.

My knees were nearly in my armpits.

After adjusting the seat back as far as it would go, things were marginally better.

*Marginally.*

Fortunately, my grandfather had taught me how to drive stick as soon as I turned sixteen. My father tried to insist the lessons were a waste of time.

My mother had stood up for me.

Bops won that round.

I'd learned a new skill. One I'd always be pleased to have. Especially today.

Quickly, I figured out the clutch on this car was extremely sensitive. Pleased I only stalled out once, I soon had us heading up into the hills north of Mission City. While Rainbow would head northwest, I'd take us northeast.

Ryan remained silent as we went—just taking occasional sips from his tea.

*I have tea in my living space, right? I have a kettle, so I must have tea.*

Panic started to set in. I'd never had anyone down there before. The cleaner had come yesterday, so that wasn't a huge worry. *But did I put my underwear in the laundry hamper? Oh, better yet, is the door to my bedroom closed? What will he think of my tiny living space?* I had a television as well as a laptop and printer I used for business. All in plain sight. If I didn't use them, would he be okay? Maybe better to go into the bedroom. I didn't have any electronics in there. At Nanny's insistence. Something about proper sleep hygiene and no screen before bedtime.

I scrolled on my phone instead of watching television.

And would never admit that to another living soul—lest they tell my grandmother.

Ryan pointed as we passed a street.

"Y-yes. That's M-Maddox's street. We'll s-see him on Saturday." Whether or not that was true might be an open question. Ryan might not be up to company. Although the cocktail party was two days away. Tomorrow was the decorating party. Another event with lots of people. I just couldn't tell how he'd be. This was the worst I'd seen him since that first day. He was trying, but his knuckles were white and he continued to tremble.

Again, I was so grateful Felix figured out to call me. That being said, I didn't understand how he'd figured out that Ryan and I knew each other. Had Ryan said something? That meant I was important, right? Or had he spouted a bunch of names and I was the first person Felix reached?

*You're overthinking this.*

I flicked my indicator. "F-Ferrars Street."

"Okay." Ryan continued to gaze out the passenger window.

I geared up as I gained speed. I would never go over the limit on my street—but I'd drive pretty close. I knew all the deer-crossing spots as well as which families had young kids.

Now, the time I'd nearly hit a bear...? Yeah, hadn't seen him coming. Or it might've been a female. Huge beast. No cubs following, though. I'd waited for more than five minutes and no other creatures had appeared. *Maybe that's why you thought it was a male bear?*

Oh, right. I wasn't being sexist—I was being logical. Early April. Four years ago. Occasionally I spotted a bear from my back patio. I gave them a wide berth, and they had little interest in me. The deer, though, were more inquisitive. They'd come right up to the house and try to steal my blackberries. I did my best to shoo them away...all the while being super pleased I grew something they liked. Co-existing with nature this far from the city was important.

I flicked the indicator and geared down as we came to my house. I turned, then glided us into the spot I thought as my spare. I parked my truck in the garage most nights. My grandfather's Buick was also in there. Keeping it running was important, and the thing was still insured. I hoped, though, if an emergency arose, that my grandparents would call for help. Neither had a license anymore.

"This is..." Ryan gazed out the windshield. "I don't think I've ever seen a prettier house."

*Pretty? Huh.* He'd told me he came from Vancouver. Since that city had every kind of house available, I wouldn't figure my grandparents' would be anything special. I cleared my throat. "F-four bedrooms. I have a s-space in the basement. P-private."

Ryan met my gaze and blinked. "Yeah, okay." After a long moment, he undid his seatbelt, opened the car door, and slid out.

I did the same, ensuring I didn't whack my head on the frame.

When we met at the hood of the car, I offered him his keys. Reluctantly, he took them. "You still need to get your truck."

"It'll k-keep. I promise." With that, I gestured for him to follow me around to the side of the house. A set of concrete stairs led us down to the backyard. I walked toward the back door and pulled out my key. Locking it seemed silly, but being prudent made sense.

Bears could open unlocked doors.

I entered and shuffled over so Ryan could come in as well. After closing the door, I bent to remove my boots.

He toed off his sneakers. Then he slowly wandered into the space.

The entire wall facing the backyard was glass—with floor-to-ceiling windows. My patio was under my grandparents' back deck, so I never got direct sunlight. What I could see was a modest lawn leading to a slope and then solid wilderness. Our property wasn't fenced in—was really too big for that. Instead, animals could wander around freely. And I could go as far back as I wanted. Eventually, through the forest, I'd come out to the same tree farm Maddox's property backed onto. We'd never done it, but theoretically we could've walked to each other's houses.

I pointed. "P-Princess Sofia got lost in those woods."

Ryan burst out laughing. "Oh God, I can totally see that. Did you see the gleam in her eye? She's a little shit."

"T-twit." I offered the correction with a smile.

Ryan cocked his head. "You don't swear. Does it bother you that I do?"

I shook my head. "I was t-thinking about not swearing around the kids."

He glanced around. "You have rugrats I don't know about?"

That brought a smile to my face. "No. I'm j-just thinking about Saturday. W-well or Friday. Lots of k-kids."

Still, he shifted from foot to foot.

"W-when I swear, my s-stuttering gets worse. S-some brain to mouth c-connection goes haywire. So I d-don't very often." I offered the smile my grandmother always said warmed her insides. "W-when I'm alone? If I h-hit my thumb with a hammer? G-guaranteed f-bomb."

That did make him smile. "Yeah, okay."

"Would you like something to d-drink?"

"I don't drink alcohol."

"G-good. I don't either. None here." I smiled as best I could. "D-different types of soda. Bad for m-me, but whatever."

That made him smile. "We all have our vices." He pressed a hand to his chest. "Do you have root beer?"

"Yep." I gestured to the couch.

"Thanks."

"Oh, c-coat."

I moved to help him out of it. At first, he appeared annoyed, with his brow furrowed. Then, as if sensing I meant no harm, he let me slide his gorgeous coat off him. "L-love this. So soft." I hadn't expected wool to be soft. Had been expecting coarse.

"Thanks. This was...my dad bought it for me. I don't know why..."

"He l-loves you?" I hung the coat on my coat rack as Ryan slowly sat.

The laugh coming from him wasn't happy. "My father sees me as a tool to accomplish goals. If I ever need to present myself in any society, then I must look good. That coat speaks of quiet elegance."

I moved to the fridge. "Oh? Uh...ice?"

"Sure...? I don't want you to go to any trouble."

"No t-trouble."

"Well, thanks, ice would be great."

I nabbed two glass mugs and set about preparing two root beers—also a favorite of mine. "Elegance?" Wow, made it through the word without getting tripped up.

"Right. I must never leave the house without looking a certain way. Without dressing a certain way. He's always on display—investors, employees, the media. I never wanted that life. Fortunately he figured that out pretty quickly and has set up a succession plan that doesn't include me."

"Oh?" I moved to the couch where he sat. Instead of reclining back, he sat slightly bent over. *Is he in pain? Should I offer something? No, surely he has his own stuff.* "I h-hope it's okay."

He offered a brilliant smile. "Simeon, everything is okay."

No missing the meaning in those words.

I put my drink on the coffee table, the moved to the front door where I removed my coat. I'd barely started working, so I wasn't a mess. I wasn't going to think about the fact I was going to be another day behind.

*Ryan is all that matters.*

I grabbed my drink and debated where to sit. "Oh, would you prefer the chair? Sometimes I just sit and w-watch outside." I'd angled it so the television didn't obstruct the view.

"Thank you. I'm settled now."

*Does that mean he's in pain? That moving would cause more?*

I didn't know how to talk to him about what was going on. So I wouldn't. I sat on the couch next to him. Not touching or anything...but close. I fervently wished he might feel my calm.

*Calm? Who are you kidding? Your agitation is about a ten.*

Because, yeah, cute guy sitting on *my* couch. Had never happened before. I'd never brought someone home—of any gender. That just...wasn't my thing.

My phone buzzed.

I ignored it.

It buzzed again.

Ryan's jaw tightened. "It's okay. It might be important."

"Y-you're important."

My phone buzzed again.

"Answer it." Ryan's tone waffled between panic and anger.

I put my glass on the coffee table, then hustled into my room.

Four texts. All from Nanny. All letting me know how much she would love to meet my *friend* and how she was baking lasagna because hadn't I said my friends loved her lasagna?

I called her.

"I wasn't interrupting, was I dear?"

"N-no, Nanny."

"Do you want to bring your friend up?"

"I'll ask."

"Well, the lasagna will be ready in just over an hour. I used the no-boil noodles. You know I prefer the traditional way, but I wanted it done as soon as possible."

"It's still m-morning." Like pretty early.

"Has the young man eaten?"

I thought back to the food he'd given Rainbow.

"I d-don't think so."

"Well, that's perfect. And if you just want to come up and smell tomato sauce, that works as well. Very soothing scent."

I wasn't certain about that, but I smiled. "I l-love you."

"Text me if he wants to come up. We promise to be very circumspect."

I rolled my eyes. "No t-television, okay? And maybe p-put your phones in the drawer or something?"

"Well...." She paused. "Your friend sounds peculiar, but you know I'm accommodating. I'll leave the phone by me until you text to let me know."

"O-okay. L-love you."

"You already said that." She sniffed. "We love you too. Take care." With that, she cut the line.

Debate raged within me. I just didn't know what to do.

*Leave it up to him.*

I headed back into the main living area.

To find Ryan at my desk—trailing his fingers along my closed laptop.

"My grandmother—"

"This laptop must be ten years old."

"C-closer to twelve. I use it for emailing. My g-grandfather keeps my books and p-prepares my taxes. Thank God." *But he won't be around forever.*

He pointed to the box leaning against the side of the desk. "That's a much better computer."

"I know. M-Maddox recommended it. He s-said he'd help me set it up, but he's so b-busy—"

"Did you tell him you had the computer and ask for his help?" Ryan turned that blue-eyed stare on me.

"Well...n-no."

"And you think, with everything he's got going on, that's he's going to remember?"

"W-when you put it like that? No." I'd bought the new laptop more than six months ago—and still hadn't opened it.

Ryan bit his lower lip. His hand trembled as he held his glass. "I haven't..." He hesitated.

I held myself still.

After a long time, he let out a breath. "When I heard about the war in Ukraine, and how the Russians had invaded a peaceful and sovereign country, something just...didn't sit right with me. I'm not Ukrainian. I mean, I'm Canadian way back, and like multiple generations ago, my family came from Ireland." He huffed out a laugh. "So why the battle for an eastern European country drew me in, I can't explain." Slowly he moved to the massive window facing out over the lush green backyard with the orange leaves covering patches of the ground.

*Need to rake soon.* Still, I waited.

"And...I just got on an airplane and went to Poland. From there, it didn't take much to get into Ukraine. I won't bore you with the details, but I found some people who were able to make use of my programming skills. Then my video-game prowess came up, and it turned out I had a knack for flying drones." He pressed a hand to his chest. "More than two years, and I'd begun to think I was invincible.

Other men died, but I wasn't going to be one of them. Then..." His fist, which had been by his side, sort of exploded with his fingers going wide.

*Like a bomb.*

He kept pressing his hand to his chest. "All my friends died. I *should* have died. I still can't explain why I survived. I mean, I understand how the shrapnel only nicked my heart. How medical care arrived quickly. How..." He swallowed. "They all died, Simeon. And yeah, I made my dad send money anonymously to all their families. That doesn't change the fact that I lived and they died."

I didn't know how to respond. If he'd died as well, then their families wouldn't have gotten any money. I might be conjecturing, but he hadn't said he'd done anything to cause their deaths. Just that there'd been an explosion or a bomb or something and his friends were dead and he was alive.

After what felt like the longest time, I found the courage to approach him. I tried to make as much noise as possible. Tried to telegraph my movements. Hoped he might see my reflection in the glass. Finally, I placed my hand on his shoulder.

He tensed.

I was about to pull away when he placed his hand over mine.

He didn't remove mine. Instead, he slowly turned and, very gently, leaned against me.

I might not give and receive many hugs, but I knew what to do. I let him lean on me and then, gently, I gathered him into my arms. Being aware of his injuries meant not hauling him against me like I wanted to. I could only apply the lightest of pressure. But I could show him in a way words never could that he had my unconditional support. That I'd always be here for him. That I wasn't judging him.

He trembled in my arms. Whether he was crying or not, I couldn't be certain. What I did know for sure was that I didn't ever want to let him go.

After a long moment, he pulled back. He didn't meet my gaze.

I considered for a very long time before I spoke. "Nanny and Bops h-have invited us for lunch. Lasagna." *Please make the decision for me...I don't know how to help you.*

"They want to meet me?" He met my gaze with his luminescent blue eyes shining. Not with tears, but with something else. Gratitude?

I was humbled. That he trusted me. That he felt safe with me. "Well, you're the first f-friend I've brought home."

"First friend..." His brow knit. He looked like he was about to say something, but then he smiled. "Lead the way."

# Chapter Sixteen

Ryan

*You're the first friend I've brought home.*

Those words carried me through the next few hours as I sat at Nanny's kitchen table. I hadn't known what to expect, but two nonagenarians—Simeon typed the word out for me after his grandmother used it repeatedly—with lively temperaments and tons of stories to share wasn't necessarily it.

I loved Nanny and Bops almost from the moment I laid eyes on them.

Nanny asked if she could give me a hug.

I was so surprised, I just nodded. As she gently held me, tears flooded to my eyes. I honestly couldn't remember the last time someone hugged me. Truly. That horrified me. Surely someone...but a memory didn't come to me. The couple of hookups I'd had certainly hadn't been about feelings or touchy-feely stuff.

Simeon guided his grandmother back to the stove as I'd taken a moment to compose myself. He always seemed to know the right thing to do.

His grandfather introduced himself, said we could always *hug it out later* and then proceeded to tell me how he'd worked with an architect and a builder to design the perfect house. And that he hadn't known his favorite grandson would move in, wasn't it perfect?

Only grandson, Simeon was quick to point out.

His grandfather grinned.

And so it went for hours. Nanny served lasagna, but that was almost secondary to the conversation. For an accountant, Bops had so many stories. Nanny had many of her own—mainly gossip from Mission City. She pulled out a map and gave me a tour of everything I had to do and everyone I had to meet.

I should've been taking notes.

Rainbow had arranged to deliver Simeon's truck in the early afternoon. She just showed up, handed Simeon the keys, consented to taking a tray of lasagna back to the ranch—Nanny had made three—and then she was gone. Like this was an everyday occurrence, and this was just neighbors helping neighbors. Apparently she asked after me and Simeon told her that Nanny was taking care of me.

Which was the truth.

Later, Simeon followed me as I drove home in my car. To be safe, he assured me. No big deal.

Way big deal.

The next morning, I went back to Starbucks. Tristan the barista was happy to give me my order of coffee, tea, and two lemon loaves.

This time, I popped a cassette into the console and Bon Jovi belted out "Living On A Prayer". I might've sung at the top of my lungs. I was not going to have another fucking panic attack. No way. Because

I wouldn't be lucky to have a Felix to take care of me. And certainly Simeon couldn't afford another day off work. I didn't even want to think about what I'd cost him. A coffee and a slice of lemon bread was hardly going to make up for that.

Yet I also couldn't regret yesterday.

In the end, it'd been one of the best of my life—despite the inauspicious beginning.

The next song started, and I regretted that I couldn't hit a button to skip back. Rewind on a tape deck was a pain in the ass. I'd lucked out and found a treasure trove of cassettes at Value Village when I'd went there the first week I was in town. The store was within walking distance, so I'd ventured out. After buying, like, fifty cassettes, I'd eyed the uphill walk and decided a cab would be just fine.

As I headed into the hills, I hummed along to a song I didn't recognize. And I couldn't sort out the lyrics. In my past life, I would've googled the song to figure out what the fuck they were singing. In this iteration of my life, I'd remain in ignorance.

The houses this far out of town tended to be down long driveways, so the scenery was tons of trees and a few driveways with mailboxes. Simeon's house had been barely visible from the road. I'd noticed that when I'd left. I'd also noted the street sign for Ferrars and, as I'd passed Maddox's street, been pleased I could orient myself. I kept Rainbow's map in my glove box.

The driveway to the ranch was well-marked with a huge welcoming sign I'd barely noticed the first time I'd done this trip. Now I'd ventured out almost half-a-dozen times. A kinship was building between me and this wondrous place. I wasn't healed—not by a long shot—but things that had seemed impossible two weeks were beginning to feel possible today.

Simeon had brought me to his house. To take care of me. To introduce me to his grandparents. To ensure I recovered from one of my worst panic attacks.

He'd even sent a text to Jacob, Felix's husband, to pass along to him. Like that was something neighbors just did.

Finally, just before I'd left, Simeon had insisted we exchange phone numbers. Somehow, we hadn't done that before. Because...it felt like a shift in the relationship? Simeon clearly didn't see me as anything other than a friend. So that's what friends did—exchanged phone numbers. Texting him would be a nightmare, but at least I knew how to do it on the flip phone. Those few precious texts I'd sent over the past few weeks had been worth the effort...and had also made me wish for a smart phone with a keyboard.

*Maybe one day...*

Simeon's truck, Rainbow's SUV, and another SUV I'd spotted before were in the driveway. Kennedy's? The sun had barely crested the horizon. I would've waited in the car until Simeon arrived, but I wasn't surprised to see he'd already gotten started. Between losing yesterday and the work he'd done at Maddox's, he must've been way behind schedule. Hopefully I could help him today.

I exited my car after parking next to his truck. I made my way around to the passenger side and retrieved my precious cargo.

"Woof!"

I pressed a hand to my chest and spun. "Sheesh, Tiffany, way to scare a guy."

"Sorry." Rainbow rounded the corner of the ranch house. She headed our way at a quick clip. "We weren't expecting anyone for a bit so she's running loose. She's, uh, happy to see you."

She also appeared to be eyeing my food, but that might've been my projection. I put the drink tray on the trunk. I bent forward as much as I could and held out my hand.

Tiffany sniffed, then licked.

Rainbow laughed. "I think Simeon has wipes in the cabin. Oh, wait, the water's hooked up."

"I really don't mind." I figured doggie germs were about the least of my problems these days.

"Well, I'm not great about washing my hands either, and nothing bad's ever happened to me. Kennedy's much better at remembering. Oh, and Justin and Denise. I think when you have kids, you perceive the world differently. See dangers that someone like me—happily single—would never worry about."

"Yeah...happily single..."

She cocked her head. "Sorry—"

I waved her off. "No." I forced a chuckle. "I've always been single. I was just thinking of some men I knew..." I swallowed. "Being married carries risks. Being single doesn't have the same, uh, stuff."

"Shit?"

"Yes." This time I laughed. "Yes. Married is complicated." Yet Maddox and Ravi flashed to my mind. Happy marriages *did* exist. I had no question of the love they shared. And their kids were pretty damn special too.

"That coffee's probably getting cold. Simeon can come to the house if he needs to heat it up."

"Is there not a microwave in the little house?"

She met my gaze. "I think so."

*Ah. So she's worried about me.* "I should...I mean, it's just a microwave."

"Small steps, Ryan. I can't possibly know what you've been through. But I do know everyone has their own recovery trajectory. And it's never a straight line."

"Are you certain you're not on the counseling staff?"

She shivered dramatically. "Nope. And I'm about to check on the horses. Just shout if you need something."

I wouldn't.

And she likely knew that.

But her offer was super sweet.

I scratched Tiffany behind the ears before she and Rainbow took off toward the stables. Then I snagged the drink tray with the food and headed to the little house. I didn't even know if the thing had a name.

*Knock or don't knock? I don't want to—*

The door opened.

*Problem solved.*

Simeon grinned. "You're h-here."

"I am."

He held up his thermal coffee mug. "I was j-just about to sneak over and s-steal some of Rainbow's coffee."

I gestured to the large cup on my tray. "Good timing, then."

Gently he snagged it—ensuring everything else didn't tip over.

"She said you can heat it up at the house. But then she also thinks the microwave here might be hooked up."

Simeon held the door open for me to venture into the space. Then he closed the door behind me.

"This is s-still hot. I'll p-pour it into my mug." He moved to the kitchen bar and did just that.

I considered removing my jacket, but a chill permeated the air. "Still no heat?"

"Oh, I can t-turn on the heat. The b-baseboards work just fine." He squinted. "I prefer to w-work in a slightly chillier atmosphere."

"No worries then." My coat would get some construction dust on it, but I should've thought of that *before* walking into a construction site with it. *Oh well...good lesson. You would've never thought of it before.* And I wouldn't have. That hadn't been how I rolled. "What can I do to help?"

Simeon finished pouring his coffee into his thermal mug, then moved behind the bar and into the kitchen. "There's r-recycling and garbage back here."

"Good to know. Thank you."

He eyed my tea. "Haven't done c-compost yet. On the l-list."

"You're doing everything?"

"As much as I c-can. I want it to be move-in ready."

"That's cool." I gestured to the flooring. "You ready to tackle this?"

He eyed me.

*Looking at my coat, undoubtedly.* "It's fine, Simeon. There is such a thing as dry cleaning." *Can you take wool to a dry cleaner? Surely one must be able to...*

Finally, he nodded. "L-let's get to work."

I hadn't told Simeon about speaking to my doctor earlier in the week because, at the time, it had felt inconsequential. She said a bit of physical activity was good, but to not overdo it. Marcus had basically said the same thing. So as I sorted planks of laminate to match colors and painted a bit of trim, I felt a sense of accomplishment. So what if I wasn't doing the big physical stuff? So what if Simeon could've done the work in a fraction of the time? So what if maybe he was humoring me? I was out of the house. I was helping Kennedy and Rainbow. I was making progress and doing tasks Marcus would undoubtedly feel was helping me progress to a better state of health. Certainly better than sitting at home feeling sorry for myself.

We took a break for lunch and headed over to the ranch house where Rainbow stuffed us with chicken salad and Nanny's lasagna.

Truly amazing.

Simeon and I went back to work, but at four, I headed back over to the ranch house for my appointment with Justin.

Rainbow met me as I entered and pulled me aside. "I'm so sorry."

I cocked my head.

"Justin's client ran late." She gazed around, as if trying to ensure we weren't overheard. "I can't give details, but it's bad."

Instantly, I understood. I smiled sympathetically. Clearly, she was uncomfortable. "Rainbow, I'm not in a crisis. I can see Justin later today or another day entirely. We've made progress, but..." This time, I gazed around. "I think my time with Simeon and...the others around here..." I considered. "That's helping too, you know?"

Uncertainty clouded her pale-blue eyes.

"You're thinking about yesterday."

She nodded.

"Actually, I think Justin not being available was a good thing. I had to dig deep and find a way to cope. Simeon was...amazing. And Nanny's lasagna?"

She grinned.

I smiled back. "His grandparents were so welcoming. And normal. They treated me like being over and Simeon being at home in the middle of a workday was perfectly normal. They were just...normal..."

A little laugh burst from her. "Yeah, I can see that. We try to emphasize keeping things simple. Stretching boundaries is good—when you're ready for it."

"Which I'm not."

"But you did. You chose to go somewhere unfamiliar—"

"Simeon is familiar, though. You see that, right? He's just..." *Perfect.*

"One of the best men I've ever known? Yes, I see that."

Since she appeared very much like she wanted to touch me, I reached out and touched her forearm. She'd made it clear that was fine. That she welcomed touch when it helped. I understood that she meant not in a creepy way. I got it. "I'm okay. Truly. Is there a way to let Justin know?"

She shook her head, placing her hand on mine. "If you weren't okay with this, then I had permission to knock. Truly, Justin..." She blinked. "Sometimes I feel impotent. With hurt...with rage..."

I understood. Deep in my bones, I understood. If someone was here and needed that kind of support, then the least I could do was give up a spot.

The back sliding door opened. "Hey, Rainbow." A young boy walked in.

I guessed he was about eleven or so. He had dark-brown eyes and curly dark-brown hair nicely trimmed.

Rainbow grinned. "Hey kiddo, I didn't remember you planning to come here."

"Papa's running Opal to the doctor—she's got a fever or something. Instead of trying to scoop me up from school, he texted Dad to see if I could come here. He said okay." He leaned in. "I don't understand why I can't stay home alone. I'm twelve." He rolled his eyes. "Not that here isn't amazing. I just...don't want to be underfoot."

With a smile, she wrapped her arm around his shoulder. "Feel like mucking out stalls?"

To my surprise, the boy didn't wrinkle his nose. "Sure. Can we ride as well?"

Rainbow looked outside.

Angus and I followed her gaze.

Although the boy was barely damp—there'd been a light drizzle mere moments ago—the rain now poured down. The sound of it hitting the roof permeated my consciousness.

I smiled. "Maybe not." I turned to the boy and stuck out my hand. "Ryan."

He grinned. "Angus Powers. My dads are Justin and Stanley. My foster sister is Opal. I love mucking stalls."

I blinked. "Well, okay then."

"You have a book to read?" Rainbow glanced outside. "Mucking stalls can wait. Even in your raincoat and boots, you'll get wet."

"True." He turned to me. "I get to keep spare gear here so I can always help out."

"That's great." I glanced around. "This is a pretty awesome place."

"It is."

A timer dinged. Rainbow started to move away. "You keep your-selves occupied. Angus, don't ask questions." She moved to the kitchen.

Angus grinned. "I suspect you're a client and so I won't ask any-thing. I have a book to read..." He glanced off toward the direction where Rainbow had come. "But I also got a really cool game last night. Dad wants me to play more games. So I'm not as far behind my friends."

"You don't play a lot of video games?" I arched an eyebrow.

"I prefer Tolkien. My dads say I need balance."

I snickered. "I'm pretty sure there's a Tolkien video game—"

"There are and I play them. But this new one..." He moved toward the lounge area where two couches were positioned across from each other. He'd toed off his shoes and hung up his coat while speaking with Rainbow—as if doing those things were the most natural in the world. Now he dropped his knapsack on the floor. He pulled out a handheld game console, then flopped onto the couch. He patted the seat next to him. "Since I'm not allowed to ask you about your therapy sessions, why don't you come and play a game with me."

*I think explaining the intricacies of my cognitive-behavioral therapy might be simpler.*

Still, the rain poured down. Returning to Simeon would mean getting soaked and then being chilled. Running to my car meant getting soaked and driving in less-than-ideal conditions.

Joining Rainbow in the kitchen held appeal.

Yet when this young man held out the game console—likely figuring a twenty-something guy knew how to play—I bolted.

# Chapter Seventeen

Simeon

R yan burst into the prefab on a gust of wind. Fortunately, he managed to close the door behind him before anything else blew in. Including the pounding rain.

Instantly, I knew something was wrong. I'd been installing one of the pot lights above the kitchen—because the electrician had set up all the wiring yesterday while I'd been away. I thought he'd do the lights, but he'd left them for me. He knew I could manage them, though, and he was likely trying to keep his bill as low as possible.

Nice of him.

Except now I was atop a ladder and Ryan was bent over with his hands against his thighs and breathing shallowly.

I scrambled down the ladder and headed to him. Slowly, I placed my hand on his back. *Does he feel this, through the coat? Is this the right thing to do?*

Then he arched back into my touch. Like a cat might.

So I held my hand steady as he slowly calmed.

"So stupid." He barely whispered the words—and I couldn't be certain I'd heard them correctly or if I was assuming those might be the words he was using. Still, eventually he pushed against my hand and I used it to guide him up. When he was more or less upright, his gaze caught mine.

Then he looked away.

Taking a breath—and finding courage I didn't know I had—I snagged his chin and slowly guided him to face me. I ensured the touch was feather-light so he'd know he could pull away and I'd let him go.

"B-bad session? You weren't gone long."

He shivered. "Justin was busy and then his son..." He held up his hand. "Nice kid. Asked me to play a video game with him. I ran."

"Ah." *What am I supposed to say?* "Angus is a g-good kid. Really good. H-helps me out sometimes." And that usually meant I worked slower, but I didn't care. The kid had his own trauma—including losing both parents by the time he was ten—so a kinship existed between the two of us. I'd found the courage to tell him about my parents dying and he'd shared how much he missed his parents. Then I told him how much my grandparents took care of me. And he assured me that Stanley and Justin were the best dads, aside from his first dad, of course. That he knew how lucky he was. Oh, and that he had a Shih-tzu puppy he loved named Liba and a foster sister he wished he could keep.

No doubt he had a great life. From great grief had come great happiness. But he felt guilty being happy when his parents were gone. Although I'd been relieved my father was no longer around to abuse me, I also sometimes felt guilty being happy with Nanny and Bops.

I'd mentioned all this to Justin. I didn't like going behind Angus's back, but I thought it was important Justin know what was going on.

He assured me that he was happy Angus was sharing—that it was a healthy sign. And that he'd look out for any signs of distress and if I spotted anything to come back to him if I had concerns.

If Angus asked Ryan to play a video game? That was a big deal. The kid read books all the time. I'd never seen him with a game. "Oh?" I tried to smile.

"I probably scared the kid." Ryan winced. "Yeah, I probably did. I should apologize. I mean, talk about an overreaction."

"Why don't I t-text Rainbow? You said Justin is in a s-session? I'll p-pop off a note to her that I have you and you're okay. And t-that you're sorry."

He might not be, of course, but the expression of gratitude on his face assured me I'd nailed it.

"And m-maybe get yourself a drink of water? I put a couple of bottles in the f-fridge." I offered my best reassuring smile.

After a moment, he nodded and made his way to the fridge.

*—I have Ryan with me. He's going to be okay. Apologies to Angus if he scared him. —*

*—Glad to hear he's okay. Angus is fine. I explained in a way he understands. Will text when Justin's free. —*

*—Okay. Thanks. —*

She signed off with three thumbs-up.

Ryan sipped his water. His color wasn't as hectic of a red. His pupils weren't dilated. His breathing was back to normal.

"Rainbow says she'll t-text when Justin's free."

"Uh." He drew in a deep breath. "I don't think I'm ready to examine my reaction too closely. I mean…" He scratched his beard. "In some ways, it's simple."

"B-but…" *How do I put this tactfully?* "Y-you've had two…episodes in two days."

"Yeah." He winced. "Which is what I was at before. Then, for a bit, I was doing okay." He met my gaze. "You helped with that."

I tilted my head.

"With you...I don't know." He recapped the bottle. "I can just be myself. I don't have to pretend."

"D-do you pretend with Justin? Sorry—" I shoved the word out. "—n-none of my business."

"Maybe." He smiled. "The answer is *sometimes*. I know I should be honest, but I'm struggling to admit how bad things can be. And being triggered by a video game is pretty bad."

"M-maybe."

"Yeah." He stood straighter. "What can I do to help?" He pointed to the ladder. "Need a spotter?"

I shook my head. "That was the l-last thing I'm doing today. Plan was to head out."

"Home?"

"Nah. Thursday nights my grandparents have a g-group of friends over. Anyway, they don't n-need me dropping in. I take the night to myself and head t-to Fifties."

"Best burgers in Mission City?"

I laughed. "Uh, yeah."

"Great." He winced. "Sorry, I think I just invited myself."

"Y-yes. I can't wait for you to s-see the place. D-do you want to text Rainbow or should I?"

"I'll do it. She didn't say as much, but I got the feeling things were bad—" He pressed a hand to his lips.

I nodded. "I w-won't say anything." I didn't even know who Justin's patient was, but even if I did, I'd never repeat what I might see.

As Ryan sent a text—which was going to take forever on his flip phone—I cleaned up as best I could. We were nearly finished with the flooring in here. I'd do a thorough cleaning, and finish up the little extra things. The furniture was being delivered next week. I'd be putting together the bed, bookshelves, and dresser. Fortunately, the cabinet that would contain the television was already constructed and several big guys would deliver it. The thing was massive—taking up much of one wall.

Oh, then I had to do the dining table and chairs. Rainbow had also arranged for all the accouterments to be delivered. That was the word she'd used. To describe blinds, drapes, cutlery, lamps, towels, sheets, blankets, and a bunch of other things. She might've assumed I'd leave everything up to her, but I intended the house to be show-ready when I ceremonially handed her the keys.

"I'm ready."

I glanced up from the flooring I'd been studying to face Ryan.

His eyes were bright, his coloring was back to normal, and he looked...gorgeous. Even in the crappy light of the gray day, he looked amazing.

*And he's going to dinner with me.* That was pretty cool.

He pointed outside. "The rain's eased up. I'm still damp, but I can dry off in the car."

I hadn't noticed, but he did look a little bedraggled. I'd been more focused on his emotional state than his physical one.

"Is F-Fifties on your map of Mission City? It's downtown."

"Not far from my apartment. I pass it when I drive to Dr. Raymond's office."

"G-great. So I'll follow you and we're good."

He cocked his head.

I shrugged.

After a moment, he smiled. "Okay, I get it."

I didn't, but I wasn't going to say that. I was just thinking of things from a safety perspective. Better if we went at the same time. I yanked my keys out of my pocket.

He nodded. "Okay. Uh...thank you."

This time, I cocked my head.

"For...not freaking out. Or panicking when I came barging in. I did enough for both of us, I think."

"It's f-fine. No worries." I was just so damn grateful he felt able to lose it in front of me. To have his moment where he needed comfort. And he'd sought it from me. I wanted to be his safe space.

As he was slowly becoming mine. *Having more friends is never a bad thing.*

We headed out, and I hummed Taylor Swift melodies all the way to Fifties.

Ryan stood by his car as I pulled in. He'd made the left light onto the highway and I hadn't wanted to risk it since I got the yellow. He offered me a grin when I got out of my truck. "Thought you'd never make it."

I grinned back and nudged his arm with mine as I passed him. I got to the door a fraction of a second before him and I held it open for him.

"How chivalrous." He winked, then headed inside.

The smell of grease hit me full force as I stepped in behind him. My saliva glands kicked into high gear. Memories flooded into my mind. My grandparents used to bring me here every Friday night from the time I moved in until recently. For years, my grandfather would drive us down and I'd sit crammed in the back seat. Then one day, when I realized he pretty much didn't drive anywhere else, I offered.

We piled into the Buick with Nanny in the backseat with a big grin on her face.

She patted my shoulder and called me her chauffeur.

My grandfather's face was less pinched. He never drove again.

About a year ago, Bops made an excuse for us not to come, saying something about the crowds.

Fifties? Crowds? We had always arrived late afternoon—long before the dinner rush.

I hadn't pressed.

The next week, Nanny had an excuse.

I never brought it up again. For the record, I wasn't certain the real reason, but I respected them not wanting to come anymore. I took them to their medical appointments, but pretty much did everything else. Without hesitation. I wouldn't have them forever.

"Hey Simeon." Sarabeth grinned from behind the counter. She glanced at Ryan. "And Simeon's friend?"

Ryan shot me a glance before grinning at Sarabeth. "Ryan." He pressed closer to me.

"Great." Her blue eyes flashed pleasure. Possibly because I wasn't alone? "Grab any booth you like."

Although I should rightfully sit at the counter to save booth space when I came alone, she always found a booth for me. Just...comfort.

I gestured down the aisle between two lines of booths. "B-Back okay?"

"Yep." Ryan sauntered that way and I followed, trying not to sneak a peek at his ass.

Nothing to be seen. The peacoat was too long.

*And why are you trying to ogle his ass? Curiosity?* Admittedly, I didn't spend much time checking out my friends' asses. Aside from politeness, I wasn't attracted to any of them. *Hold up. Are you...attracted to Ryan?* I was beginning to think so.

He slid into the booth so his back rested against the wall. He gazed around the restaurant, clearly taking in the ambiance. The posters from the fifties, the black-and-white photographs of Mission City back then, the newspaper article announcing the opening of the restaurant, and the jukebox painting. Oh, and the pinup waitress in the fifties outfit with the poodle skirt, blouse, and scarf around her neck.

"This is quite the place." Ryan snagged a plastic-covered menu. "Bright."

*They keep the lighting low. I think it's dim. Does he mean the wall coverings? The menu? Or do we perceive light differently?* All were entirely possible.

To be sociable, I snagged the menu. I already knew what I was having. What would be interesting was what Ryan chose.

Sarabeth arrived with two glasses of ice water. "You know what you're having?"

Ryan gestured for me to go first.

I grinned.

Sarabeth laughed. "Well, I thought you might want something else. You're mixing things up today."

*You're in here with someone other than your grandparents.* She'd never say that, though. And perhaps that wasn't what she was thinking. Maybe I was just projecting.

Ryan closed the menu. "As good as the meatloaf sounds, several people have told me that you make the best burgers in Mission City."

"All of Cedar Valley." Sarabeth winked. "Award-winning."

"Well, then, I'm definitely interested. I'll have the one with onions, tomato, lettuce, and pickles. Oh, and can I get onion rings instead of fries?"

"You bet." She grinned. "Can I start you out with a milkshake?"

"T-that might ruin his appetite. He d-doesn't know how big they are." Although now she'd brought it up, I had a hankering for one.

"We could share?" Ryan eyed me.

I nodded vigorously.

"Do you have a favorite flavor?"

Sarabeth snickered. "He likes tiger tail. You know—"

Ryan mimicked retching.

Both Sarabeth and I laughed. I couldn't be offended if someone didn't want orange cream and black licorice. Did I feel they were missing out on one of life's pleasures? Yes. Would I begrudge them their choice? No.

"B-blueberry?" I met Ryan's gaze.

His eyes lit. "I don't think I've ever had a blueberry milkshake. Sounds delicious."

Sarabeth snagged our menus. "Coming right up." She headed back to the front of the diner.

Ryan gazed around avidly, as if soaking up everything. "I've never been in a place like this."

"Not even in V-Vancouver?"

He wrinkled his nose. "I..." He sighed. "My dad didn't take me out much. We had an executive chef who prepared meals—when my father was around—and a housekeeper who took care of me when he wasn't. I'm not a complete snob, but I didn't get to go out often."

I wanted to ask about friends. Or other family members. I wanted to demand to know who had watched out for him when his father hadn't been around. *Not your place.* "Have you b-been to White Spot?"

He shook his head.

"R-really?" White Spot was a British Columbia legend. *I thought everyone who lives here has gone at least once.* I smiled. "Another n-night I get to take you. They h-have a Triple-O burger that's amazing."

"Not as good as here though, right?" He winked.

I considered. "D-different. T-they use Triple-O sauce. I l-like that too."

"Well, another night—"

An almighty crash sounded from behind me—toward the kitchen.

Instinctively, I turned—ready to hop out of the booth if Sarabeth needed help. She really was a lovely young woman with a complicated home life my grandmother had explained once. I always left an extra big tip for her.

She popped out from behind the counter and waved her hands. "Looks like we're going to have to fire the new guy." Her smile might've been rueful, but we all knew the owners wouldn't fire someone for a few broken dishes.

"You need a hand?" A guy spoke up.

Sarabeth waved him off. "All good, Rusty. If I need a computer programmer to fix the damn cash register, I'll let you know."

My chuckle mixed with other patrons'. Rusty was a computer whiz, and Fifties had an old-fashioned cash register that had been around at least since the day the place opened. How it kept working was beyond me. *How do you get parts to fix it? Oh, maybe it just never breaks. They sure don't make things the way they used to.* Smiling to myself, I turned back to Ryan.

And my heart sank.

# Chapter Eighteen

Ryan

*It's okay. It's okay. It's okay.* Even repeating the mantra didn't help. Nothing helped as I held myself as still as possible. Like any movement might give away my position.

"H-hey there."

I jerked at Simeon's speech. My gaze shot to his.

He held out his hands.

Mine were under the table. Painfully entwined. Completely frozen. I shook my head.

Instead of backing down, he lowered his hands so they rested on the table. "I'm here w-when you're ready. Because t-telling you they were just b-broken dishes—and that someone won't really lose their job—doesn't make things b-better for you. Because you're n-not really here, are you? T-that's okay. I'm here w-when you come back."

I met his gaze. Somewhere, in the back of my mind, I realized that might've been the most words he'd ever spoken to me at one time. He tended to be brief. For certain, partly because of his stutter. But I was also under the impression part was because of his taciturn nature. He didn't wax poetic because that wasn't him. Why use ten words when three would do?

Slowly, with agony, I untangled my fingers. I fought to lengthen my breaths. *Five things I can see, four things I can hear—*

Yeah, okay, maybe not that. The din of the diner was back, and I didn't find it comforting as I had earlier. Everything felt...loud. Disjointed. Disorienting.

Finally, on a huge exhalation, I yanked my hands from under the table and placed them in Simeon's open and waiting ones.

He waited for me to grab on tight before he wrapped my cold fingers in his warm ones. That warmth seeped into me almost immediately. Taking hold and clinging tight.

"Hey folks." Sarabeth appeared.

I tried to pull my hands back.

Simeon held tight.

"Shared blueberry milkshake." She placed two tall glasses on the table along with two straws. "Your dinner was not affected by the dish disaster, so it'll be out shortly."

"N-no rush."

She hesitated. "If you're not in a rush, that would be appreciated."

"N-none." He broke my gaze to meet hers. "All g-good. We're not in a hurry."

"Thanks. That'll help." Without another word, she headed back to the front of the restaurant, pausing at several tables.

With a weird detachment, I watched her. She was a pretty young woman. Early twenties? Soft curves and a lovely smile. But a sadness lurked just below the surface. Or a weariness.

Eventually, when she disappeared, I found the courage to meet Simeon's gaze.

Compassionate hazel eyes held me entranced.

Finally, after a long moment, I offered a small smile. "I'm okay."

"I know y-you are."

*How can you be so certain when I'm so uncertain? How can you keep wanting to spend time with me when I keep losing it?* I cleared my throat. "I'm sorry."

He frowned. "F-for what?"

"Well, you know..." I tried to gesture with my hands, but he still held them tight.

To my relief. Somehow he was holding me together. Grounding me. Keeping me from flying apart.

"You d-don't owe me an apology." He blinked. "We're good."

I believed him. Whether from his time on the ranch, having wonderful role model grandparents, or just being an empathetic person—he really didn't have a problem with this. Even the holding of hands. I would've bet my last dollar he didn't normally do this. Especially in public. Or maybe he did, and I'd misread him. I just couldn't be certain. Everything was shifting sand beneath my feet. "Our drink's warming."

He cocked an eyebrow.

"I'm really okay." I squeezed his hands then gently pulled mine back.

He let me go.

Part of me regretted the loss of contact. But I couldn't hold on forever. He couldn't always be the one I turned to.

*Why not?*

That thought startled me, even as I removed the wrapper from the paper straw. As much as I wanted to whine about the paper, the world wasn't going to come to an end—either from my panic attack or from me using a paper straw.

Somehow that thought, more than anything else, got me through the next two hours.

Simeon was self-effacing, a little reticent to talk about himself, and utterly charming. As we ate the delicious burgers Sarabeth delivered, we talked about our childhoods.

He didn't say he'd been raised in a verbally abusive household, but reading between the lines wasn't tough.

I didn't own up to being raised to be a complete spoiled brat, but I didn't hide the fact I'd been privileged to a level he could only begin to imagine.

He didn't specifically explain why he'd been so adamant Spring not take a job with a Surrey newspaper, but his antipathy to his hometown was clear.

I didn't talk about my time in the war, but I did talk about a few of the people I'd met in my time since returning to Canada.

By the time we finished eating, the joint was hopping and there was a line of people waiting. I patted my belly. "We should go."

He smiled. "Yeah. Okay."

As the meal progressed, he'd stuttered less. Or I hadn't noticed it as much. Conversation had flowed.

We rose, and I shrugged into the coat I'd removed earlier.

He did the same with his jacket.

Before I knew what was happening, he was at the front and paying.

When I tried to get my card out, Sarabeth waved me off. "All good. Sorry about the fuss. Have a good night."

Simeon stood by the door, waiting for me.

We exited together.

"You didn't have to pay for me." I couldn't tell if I felt grateful or angry. I was using my dad's credit card more—which annoyed the shit out of me. But he wouldn't even notice. The money wasn't even a drop in the bucket. No, that cash was a drop in the freaking ocean.

Well, maybe an Olympic-sized swimming pool.

I was getting off track.

"L-let me do something nice." Simeon offered a shy smile as we stepped into the nasty night. We huddled as we hustled to our cars. "I'm g-going to follow you home."

"It's five blocks."

He shrugged.

"Chivalrous." *Maybe a little heavy on the sarcasm?*

He held up his phone. "Or you c-could call me."

He yanked out his phone and frowned. Clearly in concentration. Then he shot me a text.

—Call or I'll worry. —

I gazed up to meet his worried expression. In an unguarded moment, I wrapped my arms around his waist.

After just a fraction of a second's hesitation—but long enough for me to question what the fuck I was thinking—he engulfed me in what I could only think of as a bear hug. Gently, though, of course. His breath on my neck, he whispered, "I've g-got you."

I believed him.

We clung on until another car pulled into the lot. Then we stepped apart.

He held up his phone as he disarmed his truck.

My car didn't have any form of alarm. And I never worried about it. The car wasn't a classic. It certainly wasn't worth stealing. I headed right, toward my apartment, while he headed left—back to the Cedar Connector and off to his home.

When I was inside, I barely had my coat off before I called him.

"Y-yep."

"I'm home safe."

"G-good."

I grinned. "What were you listening to?"

He cleared his throat.

"I won't judge." I chuckled. "Country music, right?"

He made a gagging noise. For a fraction of a second, I thought he might be choking. *Oh, he's making a joke.*

"Yeah, I hate country music too. I'm into eighties hair bands."

He laughed. "I'm a S-Swiftie."

"She's country." I knew she wasn't these days, but I had to needle him. I headed to my fridge to grab a soda. I was still pretty full from dinner, but I needed to take my meds. Mission City water might be safe, but after those years of drinking water, sometimes I just enjoyed a soda.

"N-not her new stuff." A low rumble.

"You don't have to be defensive."

"N-not."

I laughed. "You so are. That's okay, I liked her latest album." And the ones she'd released when I'd been on the front lines. This time, I cleared my throat. "Drive safe, okay? Text me when you get home?"

He chuckled. "O-okay."

Since more words wouldn't come, I disconnected the call. He'd likely taken the call through Blue Tooth, but he shouldn't be talking while driving. He had, like, deer to watch out for. Rainbow had warned me about them in the intro email she'd sent. *Deer stepping in front of car must really be a thing for Rainbow to have mentioned it, and now I'm worried about Simeon.*

Simeon's shy smile the next morning, when I showed up coffee and lemon loaf, made me happy I'd come back. We spent the morning finishing the floor. We talked more than we had previously, although I couldn't completely relax. After lunch with Rainbow and the entire Healing Horses team, I headed into Justin's office for my appointment. I plopped onto the couch while he took one of the chairs.

He held my gaze. "I'll apologize again—"

I held up my hand. "Truly no need. I mean, I feel almost good that someone needs you more than me. I mean, of course it's bad for that person." *God, you sound like an idiot.* "I'm just...glad you were here to help them."

"Well, your understanding is appreciated. We don't get emergencies often. Yesterday was..." He winced.

"Right. Well, all's good."

He cocked his head. "I'm going to be honest and say my son Angus talked to me last night about what happened."

This time, I winced. "Please tell him I'm so sorry."

"I can say he was pretty cool about it. He understands people are here to get help. He once was in that position. I'm not telling you anything he doesn't randomly tell people. The day might come when he's more circumspect, but he believes the ranch has a bit of magic about it. That we can make people feel better." He swallowed. "He wanted to know how he could make you feel better."

My throat closed up, and I blinked repeatedly. Finally, I found words. "He wants to help me? I don't even know how to help myself."

"You're here, Ryan. That's helping yourself. You're starting to open up about what's been going on in your mind. That's helping yourself. You're doing the exercises you've been taught—"

"I had, like, three panic attacks in three days."

He cocked his head. "I don't think I knew about all three..."

"Simeon helped." I could admit that much. "He was there for me."

Another smile. "That's great. Why don't you take me through what happened? Despite everything, you're okay in this moment, right?"

"Yeah." Said cautiously.

"Then that shows you have resiliency. You came back to the ranch today. You helped Simeon and then you had lunch with us. You're coming to the decorating party tonight, right?"

I'd seriously considered bailing. And yet... "Is Angus going to be here?"

Justin checked his watch. "He'll be here shortly. Stanley, my husband, is bringing Opal as well."

I drew in a deep breath and let it out slowly. "Yeah, I'm coming to the party."

# Chapter Nineteen

Simeon

"I can't thank you enough." Rainbow grinned.

"My p-pleasure." I'd cut off work a bit early to help out. I eyed the pile of plastic bins. She and I, along with Stanley and the psychiatrist on staff, Max, had hauled in about twenty bins marked *Christmas decorations* from the barn. Quickly I counted. Nope, twenty-five. I'd tried to ensure Rainbow had the lightest ones, but she'd been a little irritated at that.

To which Stanley'd quipped that, as the oldest, he deserved compassion.

In his early fifties, the guy was as fit as just about anyone I knew. I'd encountered him several times at Maddox and Ravi's.

He'd once joked he needed to stay fit, with two kids.

With Angus a very mature twelve, I figured Stanley meant Opal, their four-year-old foster daughter.

The girl was bright, vibrant, and clearly adored Angus. And could also act out in tantrums rivaling Victor and Violet.

As we stood in the great room, Max grinned. His black beard always daunted me a bit. Or perhaps the medical degree with a specialty in psychiatry did that. More than anyone else in the ranch, he intimidated me.

And that was saying something.

Stanley turned to Max. "Can you watch the kids? I'd like to have a quick tour of the other house." He turned to me. "If you don't mind."

"N-no." I was flattered.

Since Angus sat on the couch reading to Opal, we probably had a few minutes. We hustled outside, still wearing our coats, and headed to the prefab.

I unlocked the door and headed inside, then held the door for Stanley. I flipped on the lights and tried to see it through his eyes.

Those brown eyes lit. "This is fantastic. I mean, the thing was just a shell three weeks ago. So you supervised everyone coming in, right? The plumber, the electrician..."

"Y-yes. Quite a job." Our muddy boots would leave marks, but I wasn't too concerned as the furniture delivery people, even if they wore booties, would still track dirt into the house. I'd need to do a thorough cleaning.

"The place is lovely. Really cozy—in a good way. I'm sure the Dixon parents are going to love it."

*God, I hope so. Their approval means everything.* "This is a s-surprise. They don't know. A Christmas p-present of sorts."

"That's great."

"L-let me show you around." I chuckled. "The entire three r-rooms."

He grinned. "I can't wait. Should I take my boots off?"

"Thanks." I gestured to the bar. "There w-will be four stools."

And so we were off. I took him through each nook and cranny—giving him a sense of how things would be organized.

He appeared impressed. As we stood in the bathroom, he touched the sink. "So, Justin's parents are coming to stay for about a month in the summer."

"Oh?" *Where are his parents coming from? Oh, back east somewhere. Near Toronto?*

"And as much as I love my in-laws—and I do love them—I was thinking it would be nice if they had their own space. Somewhere to retreat to if our household becomes too chaotic."

"S-something like this?"

We stepped back into the main room.

"Yes. Or perhaps a wood cabin? One bedroom with a loft?"

I nodded. "Y-yes. That would fit with your property." Stanley and his family lived just down the road from Maddox and his crew. Their property also backed onto the forest. A prefab like this might be jarring to the landscape, while a cabin nestled back near the tree line would be beautiful.

"So can you build it? I'd hire the crew to do the exterior construction part, of course. Felix's husband Jacob is willing to supervise the septic system, the well drilling and construction, and so on. But I need someone to fix it up so it looks like this place." He swept his hand in the space. "To make it habitable."

"J-Jacob's a good guy. I've worked with him b-before." Not in a context like this, but definitely we could collaborate on the project. "Construction in M-March or April? Finished by M-May at the latest? If that works with Jacob."

Stanley grinned. "That's almost the exact timeline Jacob proposed. Have you spoken to him?"

I shook my head.

"Ah, so great minds—"

Someone knocked on the door.

Stanley and I exchanged a quick glance. I couldn't think of anyone on the ranch who wouldn't just wander in. I moved to the door quickly and opened it.

A tall Indian man stood in the doorway wearing a trench coat and with a messenger bag slung over his shoulder. He offered a polite smile. "Is Stanley Powers here?"

I stepped aside and gestured for him to come in.

"Arnav?" Stanley strode the few feet. "Is something wrong?"

"No...far from it." He glanced around. "The nice lady in the other house said you were here. She said Justin was dealing with an emergency."

Stanley winced. "Yes. He couldn't give me the details, but it's not a good situation. Why are you here?"

"I have something to discuss with you that's pressing. Justin mentioned the party, and I figured coming here would be simpler. Rather than you coming to the office."

"Ah, it must be important—"

"It is." He held Stanley's gaze. "Utmost importance."

"All right then." He glanced over at me.

"I c-can leave you the keys."

"Shouldn't take too long," Arnav said.

"Let's take it into the bedroom then." Stanley laughed. "That sounds really bad."

Arnav laughed. "I have visited my clients in many different places." He gave me a quick glance. "Lawyer. Jack-of-all-trades."

Since I had no idea what that mean, I merely smiled. "Nice to m-meet you." I pointed to myself. "Simeon."

He nodded. Then pulled a wallet out of his back pocket. Within moments, he was passing me a business card. "In case you ever need a lawyer. You'd be surprised at some of the clients I've cared for since passing the bar."

I tucked his card into my shirt pocket. Knowing a lawyer wouldn't be a bad thing—the one who'd helped me set up my company all those years ago had retired. "T-thank you."

Stanley gestured to the bedroom.

*Well, okay. I could just leave the keys on the bar, but he seemed to want me to stick around. I can't imagine...but what if he needs—*

The front door opened and Ryan flew in. "Guess what!? I did it! I played two rounds, and my hands were only shaking a little bit!" His blue eyes shone and his hair appeared coppery in the recessed lighting of the room.

"That's g-great." *Don't make it a big deal.* "I'm w-waiting for Stanley and, uh, Arnav." I wanted his news to be just normal. I was happy for him, but didn't think I should make it a big deal.

Ryan's brow knit. "Uh, okay."

*Was I supposed to make a bigger deal of this?* "You can t-tell me about—"

"I can't wait to tell Justin." Stanley emerged from the bedroom, clapping Arnav's back as the man kept pace. My friend met my gaze. "Uh..." He glanced at Arnav, as if asking permission.

The man gestured for him to share.

"We're adopting Opal. It's official once we sign the papers. Her mother..." He swallowed hard. "She's given up..." He blinked rapidly.

Swiftly, uncaring of who else was in the room, I approached him and held open my arms.

He fell into them. "I...was so scared. That she'd change her mind."

I was aware of Arnav and Ryan quietly slipping out of the house. I'd only met Stanley about half-a-dozen times over the last year, but I knew the man. Had witnessed his struggles to keep custody of Opal. Knew how much he, Justin, and Angus loved the little girl.

*Will Opal understand? Now, maybe not. But when she's grown? Will she feel the abandonment? The loss?* At least she wouldn't be an orphan. She'd have a family who would love her forever.

Finally, Stanley pulled back, wiping his eyes. "Sorry."

"N-nothing to be sorry for. T-this is the best Christmas p-present ever. On the party day, no less."

"A Christmas miracle?" He blinked. "Two years ago, I wouldn't have thought I was worthy. I'd hurt Maddox—"

I squeezed his arm. "All f-forgiven." Here, I could be certain because no less than Maddox himself had shared how forgiving Stanley had opened his heart to Ravi and the chance to find his true soulmate.

*Might I ever find my own soulmate?* Then I thought of the grandparents I adored. I had a damn good life and didn't have the right to ask for more. So I wouldn't. I'd take what I'd been given and treasure every moment.

I pulled the keys out of my pocket. "Let's g-go see the kids. Hopefully Justin will be available s soon."

"Yeah." He pulled me in for another quick hug. "Thank you so much."

"My p-pleasure."

He waited while I turned off all the lights and we headed back to the ranch house. The positive energy radiated off him. So did the profound relief.

Or maybe that was myself. Feeling happy because of what Ryan had shared.

When we stepped into the ranch house, Justin and Arnav stood off to one side.

Justin, spotting us, strode over and threw himself into Stanley's welcoming arms.

Tears pricked the backs of my eyes. To witness such unadulterated joy. And to have two men feel so free to express their happiness—that felt special. Hell, that *was* special.

I caught sight of Ryan—huddled with Angus on the couch. Holding a video game console.

Avery had Opal in her lap, and they were reading a book.

Kennedy and Rainbow were eyeing the fake Christmas tree.

Max, Denise, and Denise's son Adam were sorting through Christmas lights.

*I should go and help them.*

Angus whooped. "That's amazing."

Ryan gazed up as everyone in the room turned to see why Angus had shouted. That wasn't really like him. He was normally a pretty reserved kid—preferring reading to video games. Slowly, though, he was spending more time with kids his age. Justin often reported the progress to me. Somehow, he'd gleaned I was interested. That I cared.

And I did care. These kids were as close to family as I had outside my grandparents. Sure, I'd only met them a few times. But being invited in as often as had happened over the last few months felt special. *Who knew fixing Maddox's kitchen floor would lead to such friendships?*

Angus held his game console in triumph.

The door opened and a rush of cold air accompanied it.

Dean and Adam barreled in. Dean rushed to close the door. "That's blustery."

I laughed. "It's s-still above freezing."

He mock glared. "I'll have you know my Aussie ass isn't used to this cold."

Adam smacked his fiancé on the shoulder. "Language." He gestured toward the kids.

None of whom had noticed. Like, at all.

Angus barreled over, then stopped dead before Adam. "You're Adam."

He grinned. "As I've always been. Nice to see you again." Another former client who'd been open with me about his time here, in therapy.

Angus gestured toward the crew sorting Christmas lights. "That's Adam." He gestured at a younger boy in the crew sorting Christmas lights. "He's Adam too."

"Oh." Dean cocked his head. "Well, this'll be interesting." He nudged his Adam. His fiancé. "You're the second in line, right-o?"

The other man rolled his eyes. Somehow, whether in this lighting—or just because I knew him so much better than I had before—his scars weren't as noticeable.

Angus held out the controller for me to see. "Ryan got a top score. He knew a secret passage and, uh..." He trailed off.

Undoubtedly at my confused expression. I squinted.

"Do you need glasses?" He tilted his head.

Ryan came up behind him. "Hey kiddo, how about we let Simeon take his boots and coat off?"

"Right." He gazed at me sheepishly. "Sorry. I'm going to go show Adam."

Adam junior was a few years younger than Angus and clearly looked up to the older boy. With that proclamation, Angus headed across the room.

I bent to remove my boots. And to reflect on the look of happiness I'd witnessed in Ryan's eyes for just a moment. *I'd do anything to see that smile again.* After I straightened, I removed my coat and hung it on the rack.

When I turned back, Ryan offered me a steaming mug of cider. Rainbow was handing them around. "We drink first and then we hang lights." He winked. "I think she's buttering us up."

Max stopped fidgeting with the lights to accept his cider. He appeared overwhelmed, with a furrow in his brow.

"We have to h-help."

"And we will." Ryan clinked his mug with mine.

I sipped, enjoying the rich, warm flavor. "So, uh, w-what did you do with the game?" *Are you okay? What changed for you?* I couldn't ask, but I kept a close eye on his expression.

"Oh." He shifted from one foot from the other, but held his gaze on me. "There's a secret passage. I think I played that game five hundred times before I stumbled upon it." He leaned in. "But I made certain my score wasn't too high. Angus will easily be able to beat it now he knows the secret."

My heart soared. He understood. What it was like to be a young boy and to be bested at something. How often had that happened to me, and I'd been left no chance to do better?

*Too often.*

"So what's your favorite game?" Ryan asked me.

I blinked.

Ryan nodded encouragingly.

"I d-don't play. I've n-never played." Admittedly, I didn't know many guys my age or younger who didn't play.

Okay, any.

But I'd never had the inclination. Even if I'd been good at it, I worried the other kids would just make fun of me. So I never played.

"What the shit?" Ryan flinched, quickly glanced around to find we were the only ones, then beckoned me. "Come on—we're going to find Angus, and we're going to play."

And so we did.

Afterward, at Rainbow's insistence, we decorated the tree.

# Chapter Twenty

Ryan

S aturday dawned gray and bleak.

Yet I didn't feel that way.

Memories of the night before flooded back. The first thing I remembered was Stanley's unadulterated joy at discovering he and Justin were finally going to be able to adopt Opal. To make her their own. To solidify their family.

My father had never—not one single time—looked at me like that. The love in Stanley's face as he'd hugged Justin, and then as he'd hugged his little girl. The men had decided not to tell her in that moment. They figured somewhere quiet and private. Hell, she likely wouldn't understand what it meant. Or she might wonder about the mother who was giving her up.

That took bravery. Opal's mother for giving up a child for their own good. Stanley and Justin for telling Opal she was adopted and dealing with the fallout. Opal, eventually, for handling that her mother gave her up.

*Your mother gave you up.*

*Not the same thing. She left me alone with him. That wasn't bravery. That was cowardice.*

Although maybe I'd been too quick to judge all these years. Father was an impossible man to live with. As I'd witnessed for twenty-five years. I'd survived because I'd stayed out of his way. My mother might not have had that option. And I'd assumed she'd chosen not to have contact with me all this time. What if that was a lie as well? What if she'd wanted it and he had forbidden it?

I rolled out of bed, relieved to only feel a twinge in my chest.

Maybe I could write to her—

I stopped.

*Just a twinge.*

Slowly, I replayed the last few days. Sure, I'd been as protective of my chest as I always was...but I hadn't had a major pain breakthrough episode. Simeon giving me easy but meaningful tasks helped so much. I was helping, but not overdoing it. I'd carried on and, almost as if it needed to happen this way, when the psychological issues came to the fore, the physical ones receded.

*That's just silly.*

Still, I made a mental note to discuss this when I saw Marcus on Monday.

The cold of the floor was seeping through my feet, and I headed to the bathroom. After a pleasant shower, I dried off quickly and headed back into the main room. I chose a button-down and added a sweater to go with my jeans and sneakers. I tended to run cold these days. Being slender didn't help. Neither did the fact I'd been cold so often during the war. Winters were brutal, summers relatively short, and somehow I only remembered being frequently chilled.

We tried to ignore our surroundings by singing a mashup of Christmas carols. That was difficult to do with the sounds of war interrupting. My favorite song was always "Silver Bells". Something about Christmastime in the city. I missed my city. I missed my home. Our goal was just to come home and snuggle under warm blankets while it snowed outside. To rediscover the creature comforts we'd always enjoyed—and to never take them for granted again.

Deciding a decent breakfast was in order, I put on my peacoat and headed out for a stroll downtown. I could've picked Timmie's, but I had a hankering for French toast. That meant, if memory served, Fifties. I could get a waffle at White Spot, but that walk was too far, and I didn't feel like getting in the car. No, fresh air was the way to go.

The low clouds hid the mountains today, and I had this weird feeling—I knew they were there, but I couldn't see them. Just like I'd known the enemy was in a specific place, but I couldn't see them. I had to trust the intelligence and send the drone.

*Who knew all those game-playing skills would come in handy?*

I hadn't gone overseas to be a drone operator. I figured plenty of guys in Ukraine played video games. Turned out, though, I had a knack for it. Probably how I'd survived so long—I hadn't been on the combat front lines. I'd killed...but I hadn't witnessed it.

What I had seen, though... Mangled bodies. Children. Women. Soldiers.

Grandparents.

All killed by the enemy in some hellbent mission to take over another sovereign nation.

I couldn't fathom it. I couldn't see America just deciding one day to invade Canada. And maybe that was a lack of imagination on my part. The enemy said they had a prior claim. I didn't see it. Ukrainians had lived for decades in peace and as a separate country. Of course they didn't want to be invaded.

My step faltered.

*This isn't going to end well.*

No, these spiraling thoughts rarely did.

As much as I wanted to pick up the pace, I didn't want to push too hard. Instead, I tried to pay attention to the shops. Even as I had that thought, I caught sight of Lena opening the gift shop.

She spotted me and waved.

I waved back.

"One second, okay?" she called.

"Uh, sure." I hadn't intended to go in, but now I had more people I could buy presents for. I wouldn't think about the fact I was spending my father's money.

*Eventually I'll find a job. Eventually I'll be self-sufficient.* That day wasn't today, but I wasn't going to stress about it.

Lena poked her head out the door. "I shut off the alarm. Do you want to come in?"

"Uh..." *Why not?* "Yeah, I'd love that. You sure you don't need to set up?"

She shook her head as I followed her into the store. "Nah. I always leave everything organized. Clark worked last night, and he's as anal retentive as I am. Everything's perfect." She clapped her hands together. "I just got a new Tessa Carlyle. Any chance I can interest you?"

Immediately, my gaze went to the spot on the wall where my painting had hung a week ago. My breath caught. "A snowy owl?"

"Yes. Tessa alternates between erotic works, landscapes, and nature. Animals in particular. She claims she can't pick a lane and stick to it. Given how talented she is, I have no complaints."

"I'm curious about her erotic paintings. I mean, I'm absolutely buying this piece, but I'm wondering what else she might come up with."

"You didn't check out her website? Did I not give you the address? Let me find a business card..."

As she wandered back to the counter, a bead of sweat trickled down my back. *Shouldn't have worn the sweater. I'm too warm.*

*Right, because that's the real problem.*

"Uh, maybe just the painting?" I cleared my throat.

Lena stopped her hunt. "Of course." She moved out from behind the counter. "You'd like it wrapped again?"

"Do you..." *Breathe.* "It's a Christmas present for a friend."

"Oh, even better." She rubbed her hands in evident glee. "I love this time of year. Was there anything else?"

I rubbed my forehead. "A four-year-old girl? And a couple...well, they're married. He's older than his husband..." Right, because being inarticulate's going to help.

"Do you mean Maddox?"

I blinked.

She grinned. "He's not the only older married gay man in town..."

"No, uh..." *God, could you make this any worse?* "Oh, yes to something for Maddox as well. I meant Stanley and Justin—"

"Oh." She giggled. "I still can't believe Maddox and Stanley are living on the same street. After that nasty split? But Maddox forgave Stanley, and now everyone's friends."

She said these things as if gossip were a pastime. Wasn't that supposed to be Sunshine Dixon's job?

"Oh, are you getting something for Angus? I have the perfect idea for Opal—oh, unless you're getting her a book."

"I'd thought..." I considered. "I know what I'm getting Angus. I hadn't thought of a book for Opal, but that's a good idea."

Lena moved back toward the Indigenous display. "Okay, I have some ideas for the couples."

And she did. I dutifully followed her, spent plenty of my father's money, and planned to head back here after breakfast to pick up my treasured gifts.

My next stop was The Owl's Nest where Dickens was only too happy to introduce me to the children's books of a local Indigenous author, and he helped me select the perfect one for Opal.

*You can't just keep spending your father's money for the rest of your life. You need a job and self-sufficiency.*

Yeah, I did. But I wasn't there yet. In some ways, I was getting better faster than I anticipated.

Sarabeth waved me to a booth—the only empty one in the place—but I took a stool at the counter so I wouldn't take precious real estate from her. She cast me what I could only describe as a grateful look. *Does she work here all the time? That must be rough.*

I was certain Simeon had left a big tip, but I'd do the same. Every little bit helped.

As I perused the menu, my mind cycled back to the fact I was getting better. I hadn't had a twinge of pain yet today, despite the walk. I'd dealt with Lena, Dickens, and was now in a restaurant without a panic attack. I was heading to a cocktail party with a bunch of guys and a passel of kids. All this felt...hopeful.

"What can I get you, Simeon's friend?"

I grinned at Sarabeth's cheekiness. "I was thinking French toast, but I'm going with the scrambled eggs, whole wheat toast, turkey bacon, and fried tomato slices."

She nodded her approval. "Very healthy."

As she snagged the menu, I gripped it for just a moment longer. "I'm Ryan." I thought I'd introduced myself before, but she had so many people coming through the door, I couldn't expect her to remember my name.

"Ryan." She grinned. "I won't promise to remember—lots of people go through here—"

"It's okay."

"But you're staying in Mission City?"

I nodded.

"Then I'll do my best."

She headed into the kitchen to place the order, and I took a moment to reflect. Healthy food at a diner was still served *at a diner*. A step, though. I hadn't been watching what I'd been eating since eating was such a big deal. I wanted to be a healthy weight. Not scrawny and sickly...but not overweight and unhealthy. *I don't even know what that approximate weight is. Better ask Dr. Raymond or Marcus.*

*And damn, I didn't get something for Adam and Dean.*

They wouldn't be expecting anything, I was certain. But they'd been incredibly kind and welcoming to me last night—a stranger. Also, and this meant more than I could put weight into, they clearly adored Simeon. Their kindness toward him was evident. But not in a paternalistic way. No, more like good friends. Adam had hinted there was a story behind their first meeting—and I intended to tease that out of him tonight.

After a hearty, and healthy, breakfast. I headed back to The Owl's Nest to pick up Opal's book—which Dickens had lovingly wrapped. Then to the gift store where Lena had everything organized. I selected something for Dean the Aussie and Adam the former recluse—something he'd spoken freely to me about. *Had he known I'd been headed in that direction before I met Simeon? Had he sensed that was very much my life as I'd grown up?* I didn't have a good answer...but I felt certain, if Adam was interested, that we could be friends.

And Aussie Dean was a hoot.

Lena helped me select a few generic gifts and promised to wrap them as I went home and prepared for the late-afternoon festivities. As promised, she'd wrapped the Carlyle painting. I'd keep that tucked aside and give it to Simeon closer to Christmas.

*Because I'm going to be here for Christmas. And beyond. Mission City is my new home. And Simeon is...my new friend.*

Happy prospects and new possibilities indeed.

# Chapter Twenty-One

Simeon

I shouldn't have been nervous heading to Maddox and Ravi's house.

But I was.

I shouldn't have been worried about how Ryan would cope with the group—especially given how well he'd handled the decorating party.

But I was.

Finally, I shouldn't have been thinking of him as anything other than a friend in need of finding his way in a strange town and with a different life from the one he'd planned.

Again, I was.

*Ryan's just a friend*.

Yet as I double checked my new navy-blue jeans and the forest-green henley that Nanny swore brought out the green in my eyes, I tried to remember to breathe.

Ryan was just a man. A man in need of friends. And, however accidentally, I'd provided him with that opening. Perhaps these wouldn't be lasting and abiding friendships. Perhaps once he healed he wouldn't need me—or anyone else—anymore.

Also, tonight, Justin had set up some boundaries. He was still Ryan's therapist. But if their relationship veered too far into the personal, Kennedy or Avery would take over Ryan's care. That was a tough line not to cross—mostly because Justin was the friendliest guy in the world. Well, Ravi was even more gregarious. But I understood the counselor's concerns. He and Ryan had built trust with confidentiality. Losing that over any potential friendship might be detrimental to Ryan's recovery.

We'd see how the night played out. If enough people were in attendance to keep them apart, it might all be a moot point for now.

I ambled up the stairs and discovered my grandparents in the living room. The distinct smell of garlic wafted in the air. "S-smells delicious."

"Nothing fancy. There'll be leftovers when you get home." Nanny glanced up from the laptop on her lap. "Weather's going to turn nasty."

We had a weather channel, but Nanny only trusted the government site—whose information wasn't always as accurate as might be desired. Also, the station was in Abbotsford and we were over a river and much higher up in the mountains. Abby's weather station was at the airport—lower than we were.

"S-snow?"

"Yes. First of the year."

I pressed a hand to her shoulder. "Seems a little early in the y-year, or am I remembering incorrectly?"

"Climate change." She muttered the phrase as if a curse. She was very much an environmentalist. Up here on the mountain, where we had to haul our own recycling and garbage to the dump ourselves, we were far more aware of packaging and anything else we might be disposing of.

"I p-promise to be careful."

"Take the Buick." Bops hit mute on the hockey game. He'd watch hockey while Nanny would watch crafting videos on YouTube with the sound off.

And they were incredibly happy.

I left the snow tires on the Buick year-round because a bit of extra noise in the summer was well-worth not having to worry in the winter. I'd put snow tires on my truck a few weeks ago just to be safe. Winter could come any time around or after Halloween. "I think the t-truck's sturdier." This was a conversation we had often.

"You don't want to get snow in the bed."

"I can put the c-cover on. I don't think I'll be staying that l-long at the party."

Nanny wagged her finger. "You might have a good time. Don't forget the cookies I made."

Despite my protestations, Nanny had insisted on making a massive batch of cookies. Well, several batches. "The k-kids are going to get a sugar high."

She met my gaze with a devious grin. "I didn't quite use the amount in the recipe. Enough so the cookies taste good, but not so much that the kids will, as you say, *get a sugar high*."

I chuckled. "If the adults d-don't gobble them up, I'll make sure the k-kids get some." She'd made shortbread, gingerbread, and some special secret recipe cookies we called *Nanny's green jobbies*. I didn't have a clue what was in the delicious things, but any kind of icing—even green—was a winner in my book. I kissed her cheek. "I love you."

"We love you too." She blinked. "Every day, we talk about how blessed we are."

A glow of love and light settled in my chest. That warm feeling of being loved unconditionally.

Bops waved. "Canucks are down by three. Say a prayer for the boys on your way out."

Ah, Vancouver's beloved hockey team. Desperately in need of a win. The entire Canadian contingent—all six teams spread across the country—needed some big wins. Our drought for the Stanley Cup was just...pathetic. We needed to beat the Americans. "M-maybe this year."

Nanny snickered. "I don't think God will hear his prayers." She gestured to Bops. "But that doesn't stop him from trying."

I kissed her cheek, squeezed Bops's shoulder, and headed into the kitchen to retrieve the containers of cookies. Finally, I shrugged into my heavy winter coat, donned my winter boots, and headed to the garage. I'd be so warm I wouldn't need the heat in the truck as I drove—but I'd also be okay if something happened to the truck and I had to spend some time in the snow.

The first few flakes fell as I drove down the driveway. We had a snowblower and shovels capable of handling heavy snow. *Thank God you've been able to do that for them for the past almost twenty years.* Taking care of my grandparents meant everything to me. I loved my business. I loved helping people. But all that paled in comparison to the feeling of joy when I took care of the people who'd always loved me unconditionally.

I made it to the end of our street and hung a right.

I turned onto Maddox's street. Most of the houses were set back behind trees, but a few weren't. Christmas lights adorned almost every dwelling I saw. That we were nearing Christmas wasn't lost on me. Almost exactly thirty days to go.

*What's Ryan doing for Christmas? Will he see his dad? Does he ever hear from his mom? She's alive...right? God, I can't remember. But surely, after her son was injured, she reached out...*

As indifferent, and even abusive, as my father had been, he would've come to see me. Possibly berated me for doing something highly questionable...but he would've come. I didn't think I'd ever have the guts to go to war. I supposed if Canada did get involved directly in some conflict, and they needed people...

So I'd offer up a request to the universe that we not have that happen.

Maddox's driveway came into view. Parking on the street seemed prudent. Then I wouldn't get stuck on the driveway and need people to move their vehicles if I bailed. *When was the last time I went to a party this big?* Fortunately, Maddox and Ravi only tended to invite me when the party was, at the most, eight. Well, plus Victor and Violet. Which reminded me that I needed to buy Christmas presents for the twins. What did one buy as gifts for children who appeared to have everything—including love? Most especially love.

Maybe I could ask Justin or Stanley. They had Opal and... Drat. I should probably buy something for Opal and Angus. Angus liked video games, right?

After I grabbed all Nanny's cookies, I exited my truck. I locked it and set the alarm—because that's what I always did. The snowflakes were light and fluffy as I walked up the driveway. I wasn't fooled, though—the weather could turn on a dime. If I was here long enough, I'd likely be super glad I had my snow tires for the drive home.

I spotted Ryan's car in the driveway, and my insides did a little flip of nervousness. And joy. I was super happy to see him here. He'd said he was coming, but nerves could be tough. A couple of times, earlier this year, I'd nearly called my hosts to cancel. Those headaches I was going to use as an excuse had nearly become real because I could work myself into such a tizzy.

*Tizzy.*

Nanny's word.

I was about to ring the bell when the door opened.

Stanley grinned with his brown eyes sparkling. "I saw you coming with your hands full, and figured I'd make it easy for you."

His smile warmed my insides.

"Now, Opal's already on a sugar high—I blame Justin. Well, and Angus probably snuck her something as well."

I smiled back. "C-congratulations again on the a-adoption. That's..." *What's the right word?*

"The best Christmas present ever?"

"Y-yes."

He took the containers with the cookies from my hands.

"M-more sugar." I chuckled. "M-maybe just one for Opal?"

"Nanny's cookies?"

I nodded.

"Oh, yes, she'll be allowed one of those."

Chaotic noise drew his attention.

Then he turned back to me. "Thank you for yesterday. For under-standing."

"Of c-course. Best news ever."

"Yeah. Well, also the day Justin and I officially adopted Angus. That, though, was less...fraught."

"Papa." An imperious Opal appeared at her father's feet. Her eyes went wide at the cookie containers. "Yum."

Stanley laughed, "Yes, sweetheart. Yum. After dinner."

She pouted.

"Help me put them in the kitchen?"

"Yes." She held out her hand for the containers..

He took it, offered me a sheepish smile, then guided his daughter back into the fray. Judging by the noise, I'd guess lots of people were already there.

I bent to untie my laces.

Only to have my face thoroughly licked.

"H-hello Princess Sofia."

She yipped.

I eyed her. "Did Tiffany c-come?"

"We gave her the night off." Rainbow's amused voice caught my attention.

I finished with the laces, rose, braced myself, and toed off my boots. "I d-didn't realize you'd be here."

She glanced over her shoulder. From this angle, I didn't have a view of the main room. "I wanted to warn you…"

"W-warn me."

"Well, maybe not warn." Her brow knit. "Maddox just admitted to me that they've gone overboard."

"O-overboard?" That didn't sound good.

"More than twenty people."

My eyebrows shot nearly to the ceiling. "Say w-what?"

"Yeah. Apparently he invited some people, Ravi invited some people…" She snickered. "Angus invited someone, and then Ravi felt they had to invite more people…"

"S-should I leave?" I began shoving my foot back into my boot.

"No." Her firm voice had me stopping.

I pulled it back out.

She leaned in closer. "Ryan's here. I think he'd be disappointed if you left."

"O-okay."

"Now, can I get you eggnog, eggnog with rum, soda, tea, hot chocolate, coffee, or—"

"Tea w-would be lovely." I smiled. Yes, something to soothe my nerves.

"Great. I'll be right back."

She took off and before I could even breathe to center myself, Ryan appeared. "So I played another game with Angus."

He looked so damn proud of himself.

"T-that's great." *I'm proud of you too.*

"Angus says we can show you an easy game. He's got a corner staked out for us. But you say *hi* to everyone you want to. Did I hear Rainbow's getting you a tea?"

Mutely, I nodded.

"I'm going to grab an eggnog. I'll bring your tea as well." With that, he was gone.

Slowly, I stepped into the great room.

And nearly had a panic attack.

*Okay, take it one person at a time.*

Closest to me was a cluster of adults I recognized. Fortunately, the shyest member of the group caught my gaze.

Marnie, the assistant librarian, smiled. "Hello Simeon. So nice to see you in a social context." She leaned against the much-taller man beside her. "I don't think you've met my husband, Jake McGrath."

I grinned. "N-nope. But my grandparents l-love watching him." I pivoted my gaze to the handsome reporter.

He smiled back, his blue eyes shining. "Always love to hear I have fans." He leaned in. "I'm covering the anchor desk next Saturday and Sunday. Only tell your grandparents."

*Oh wow.* "Uh, t-that's exciting. I'll watch as well." Because, frankly, as depressing as the news could be sometimes, watching this gorgeous man was never a hardship.

He shook my hand.

"Oh." Marnie laughed. "This is Simeon. He's a great handyman. Fixed a leak in my basement once."

She'd been terrified to go downstairs. I'd quickly diagnosed and resolved the problem. She'd also clearly been terrified to have a man in the house. At least she'd known me from my visits to the library.

Jake nodded. "Well, I hope we have your number. After all the years I spent overseas reporting on wars, I'm not particularly handy around the house."

"C-call me whenever." I hesitated. "H-have you spoken to Ryan?"

Marnie cocked her head, then her green eyes widened. "That would be...interesting."

Jake gazed back and forth between the two of us.

"Ryan's just back from f-fighting in Ukraine. I d-don't know if he'd talk to you, but..." *What are you doing?* "He..."

"Sure. I can." Jake met my gaze. "Whatever he's up for. No pressure."

"O-okay." I wasn't certain about this, but something told me I had to try.

Jake yanked his phone from his back pocket. "Sorry, I..." His voice trailed off.

"Okay, sorry, but I have to share." He held his phone out to Marnie.

She snagged the phone and gasped.

To my surprise, she passed the phone to me.

Jake's niece sat on a couch and held the most adorable baby who had tufts of blond hair.

With a smile, I handed the phone back to Jake.

Marnie cuddled against him. "I always have a problem leaving Nate alone. I only work part-time, and he's in a great daycare, but..." She blinked.

"He's a-adorable." I blinked too. "I d-don't spend much time around b-babies." I glanced around. "W-where are Victor and Violet?"

"I think Ravi said they went down for a late nap. They'll probably be up any moment." Marnie glanced around. "How they can sleep through this noise, I have no idea."

The cacophony wasn't quite as bad as I'd expected—especially given the number of people in the room.

Then I spotted Ravi and Maddox each carrying a twin down the stairs.

Victor rubbed his eyes. Violet squirmed.

Opal toddled over to greet them while babbling somewhat incoherently, but clearly excited.

I caught Marnie grinning. "I can't wait until Nate's that age."

Jake wrapped an arm around her shoulder. "Soon enough."

"Hey, Simeon." I recognized my friend Everett's voice, and I turned.

The lawyer stood about my height and always had the broadest smile. His dark skin was a contrast to his crisp white shirt, and he wore a navy tie with...reindeers...?

"Christmas s-spirit?" I grinned. "I t-thought we were casual."

He laughed. A heartwarming sound. "This is casual. You should see me in a suit."

I didn't point out that I had. We'd attended a dinner party, and he'd just come from the office. He looked damn good in a suit.

And although he was gay as well, we'd never been attracted to each other. I considered myself lucky, though, to have him as a friend.

He gestured to the guy standing next to him. "Have you met Quinton?"

I hadn't. Although how I'd missed him before now, I wasn't certain. The adorable man wore the most garish Christmas sweater I'd ever seen—a huge Rudolph face with the nose, made of something or other, sticking out. He also wore antlers. On his head.

Slowly, I shook my head. This guy...this Quinton...was to be the first stranger tonight. To my relief, I knew everyone else.

"Great." Everett offered me his megawatt smile. "Quinton's a nurse over at the Abbotsford hospital. He works with Ravi."

"Who tried to set me up with this guy." Quinton slung his arm around Everett's shoulder.

Or tried to. In reality, the Asian man was several inches shorter and not nearly as broad as my friend.

*Oh dear.*

"Hey Simeon, how are you doing?" Adam came up on my left flank. "I see you're meeting Quinton."

Quinton radiated joy as he gestured to me. "New BFF."

Adam's smile was always a little awkward because of his facial scars, but he still managed a competent smirk. "Up to your old tricks, Quinton?"

"Moi?" The man pressed a hand to his chest. "I would never try to create mayhem and chaos."

Everett, Adam, and Adam's fiancé, Dean—who'd just joined us—all laughed uproariously.

Quinton tried for mock offense, but I couldn't have missed the glint in his eyes. He stuck out a hand. "It's nice to meet you, Simeon. I can't believe our paths haven't crossed before. Because, trust me, I would've remembered you."

"I, uh, d-don't spend much time in town."

"Well, we're just going to have to change that. Can I take you to a movie on Tuesday night? The new Hugh Jackman film is playing and, oh my God, is he not the most handsome—"

"We're here." Hillary, Maddox's sister's voice rang out as her three kids—her twin girls and younger brother Oliver—all piled into the room. Hillary's wonderful, and long-suffering, husband, Steve, brought up the rear.

Hillary's twins barreled over to their cousins, Victor and Violet, whose grins increased.

Oliver headed straight to Angus.

Huh. I'd thought Ryan said he'd be with the young man.

Suddenly, I felt someone brush against me on my right flank.

"Are you going to introduce me?" Ryan's voice, to my surprise, was tight.

I turned to find him with a smile plastered on.

*Is he in pain? He doesn't look happy. Or comfortable.* My first instinct was to guide him away from the group—to get him somewhere by himself. I couldn't, though. Not without drawing attention to him. Still uncertain, but needing to respond, I tentatively smiled. "Q-Quinton, Everett...this is my f-friend Ryan."

Ryan brushed against me. "Good friend."

Heat flushed my cheeks, and I couldn't really blame the fireplace on the other side of the room...especially since it hadn't been turned on. This room was plenty warm with just the sheer volume of people.

"Well Simeon's good friend Ryan, I'm thrilled to meet you." Quinton stuck out his hand.

After a fraction of a second, Ryan shook it. "Nice to meet you."

"And are you new in town? Because I haven't seen you around either."

Ryan shifted. "I, uh, tend to keep to myself."

"Except when you're being Simeon's BFF, right?" Quinton's megawatt smile matched Everett's.

"Oh, Simeon, there you are." Rainbow's voice broke through.

I turned to face her, finding it awkward with Adam on one side and Ryan on the other. Almost like they were flanking me. Protecting me.

From who? Quinton? I'd have pegged him as pretty innocuous.

Finally, I managed to turn.

Rainbow held out an insulated travel mug. "Hot. Be careful, okay?"

"Y-yes. Thank you so m-much."

She grinned. "My pleasure. I'm handling the drinks—which feeds my need to be useful while protecting me from all the socializing." She leaned in conspiratorially. "I love these guys, but after yesterday, I'm pretty wiped."

Ah yes, the decorating party at the ranch. Half the people here had been there yesterday as well as—plus all the Dixon sisters had joined the festivities. Healing Horses had been a bit of a madhouse. This place wasn't much better.

Rainbow met my gaze. "Did you want to help in the kitchen?"

"Oh, I was going to show him Angus's game." Ryan had turned away from the other men and now was incredibly close to me again. He didn't wear cologne, but he had a woodsy scent. Which had to be my imagination, because when would Ryan have been out in the woods?

"That's fantastic. I'm sure Angus will love more attention. Although he seems to be doing well with Oliver." Rainbow grinned. "Those two are always thick as thieves. So nice to have friends. Although I think Hillary refers to Angus and Opal as her niece and nephew, even though they're not blood."

"F-friendship can be as thick as b-blood." I might not have long and abiding friendships, but as I gazed across this sea of people, I spotted many strong connections of people who didn't have familial ties. People I'd grown closer to in the last few months.

"You w-wanted help?"

Rainbow waved me off. "You go and play games. I can rope Quinton into helping."

"Yeah, I'm sure he'd enjoy it." Ryan's voice bit.

Not a lot.

But enough for me to notice.

If Rainbow did, she didn't comment. "I'll snag him now. I've got some hors d'oeuvres coming out of the oven. I have to make sure they're not too hot. Quinton will be happy to help taste test."

I flashed to the man with the ridiculous sweater and, for just a moment, wondered what was underneath. I didn't often think of guys in terms of what they looked like...but Quinton had me curious.

Ryan slapped my shoulder, nearly jostling my arm with the tea. He winced. "Oops."

"D-do you have a drink?"

"Yeah, an eggnog that I should finish. Let's go find Angus."

I offered Rainbow a genial smile. "T-thank you."

She waved me off. "Go have fun."

"Yes."

# Chapter Twenty-Two

Ryan

*J*esus Fucking Christ.

*He's clueless.*

*Which is something I kind of love about him, but...*

Yeah, Simeon's naïveté endeared him to me. He clearly hadn't dealt with a lot of guys over the years. Without an iota of a doubt, he obviously hadn't had a clue that Quinton had been openly flirting. At first, I thought maybe Simeon was just being polite. Or even playing coy.

Pretty soon, though, his obliviousness had become clear.

As I maneuvered him through the throng of people—many of whom I had yet to meet, a guy backed up and I accidentally jostled him. "Sorry."

Because that's what Canadians said.

He turned and offered me a wide smile. "No worries. Uh, I'm Cadence." High cheekbones cut with glass, stunning eyes, and raven-black shaggy hair. Slender, but in a good way. In other words—the guy could have been a model.

"I'm Ryan. This is Simeon."

Cadence nodded. "I've referred clients to Simeon before. Amazing work, how are you doing?"

Simeon ducked his head a little. "Always a-appreciate the business."

"Oh, you might not know—I'm a realtor." He gave me a grin.

I had a moment of déjà-vu. "I've seen you before."

He cocked his head. "I don't remember meeting you. And I have to say I'm good with faces and names. Kind of have to be in my business."

I continued to stare—knowing I was staring, but unable to look away. "I'm certain..."

"Maybe in one of my ads in the newspaper? Or on a bus stop?"

"I don't take the bus."

"True...but you might've spotted my face when you were stopped at a light. I try to get my name out as much as I can. I aim to be the top realtor in Cedar Valley by the time I'm thirty."

"You'll m-make it." Simeon offered a gentle smile. "You're a n-nice guy to boot."

Cadence grinned. "I'll take that compliment."

And a memory solidified. This had been the guy I'd seen kissing my physiotherapist Marcus Branigan in his office. And while Cadence was clearly comfortable with himself—and what I perceived to be his potential queerness—Marcus certainly wasn't. Pinning down specifics on either of those two facts would be challenging...except I'd lived both in and out of the closet and found I could relate to both. And spot those characteristics within other people. I waved my hand as if swatting away a fly. "My mistake. Yeah, probably an ad." Because I sure as shit wasn't going to out either Cadence or Marcus.

Or both.

"If you ever need a realtor... Here let me get you a card."

Simeon laughed. "Yesterday a l-lawyer offered me a card. Is that a thing?"

"You saw Everett yesterday?"

My friend tilted his head. "Is he the only l-lawyer in town?"

Cadence guffawed. "Uh, no. Assumption on my part."

Grinning, Simeon said, "I m-met Arnav yesterday."

"Another excellent attorney. There are several I deal with when completing real estate transactions. Can't go wrong with either of those gentlemen." He'd yanked out his wallet while he spoke and now offered me a business card.

I snagged it and shoved it into my back pocket.

And couldn't help noticing how skinny his skinny jeans were. Practically painted on him.

He smiled, clearly having caught me looking. "I used to be a dancer. I still work out a lot to keep in shape. Although not, admittedly, as vigorously as I used to."

"Ah. I'm in physiotherapy right now—trying to rebuild my strength after an accident." *Okay, that was just shitty. It slipped out...but was still shitty.*

His grin didn't waver. "We have several great physiotherapists in town. I'm certain you're in good hands." He pointed to my eggnog. "I think I need a coffee. I've had a long day, and I don't know how long this party's going to last." He nodded toward Simeon. "Great to see you again."

"And y-you."

Then he nodded toward me. "If you're ever looking for a house..."

I didn't snicker. Nearly did, but managed to hold it in. "Not likely."

"Well, circumstances might change." Another charming grin. "See you later."

"Ryan!" Angus's voice cut through the confusion in my mind. I spun to find him holding up his controller.

A younger boy stood next to him.

"H-hello Oliver." Simeon waved.

"Hey." The boy grinned. "Angus says you don't know how to play."

Simeon arched an eyebrow and appeared to consider.

Angus nudged him.

My friend grinned.

The four of us sat on a pile of cushions in the corner. The boys were each on Simeon's side as they explained the game to him.

Sitting on the floor would make it tough for me to get up, but I figured I could ask Simeon for help. I didn't like doing that, but better to get help than risk causing further damage.

*I did this. I played the game and nothing bad happened. Now Simeon's playing the game and nothing bad is going to happen.*

Inordinately proud of myself, I leaned back to watch with amusement. I couldn't see the screen, but judging by Oliver's facial expressions, Simeon's coordination wasn't helping him. I was trying to figure out if an ability to measure something within a millimeter would be helpful playing a video game when someone crouched beside me.

I shifted my gaze to a guy I'd seen earlier, but hadn't paid much attention to, who was now approaching. Not that I determined people's suitability as friends based on their marital status or anything. But the way this guy was clearly in love with his wife, Marnie, had me giving the couple a bit of space. I didn't need to meet everyone on the first day.

He held out his hand. "Jake McGrath."

"Ryan." I returned the shake. I didn't figure my last name was important. Or, just as possibly, he might recognize it.

"Do you mind if I…" He gestured to the floor.

I grinned. "Pull up a pillow—we welcome everyone."

Simeon glanced up at my words.

The video game beeped.

Oliver sighed. "You have to focus."

Angus nodded sympathetically. "You want to try again?"

Simeon held my gaze for a long moment. He glanced at Jake, nodded, then cast me one final look before smiling at Oliver. "Yeah, I'll t-try again."

Both boys nodded their clear approval. They had a captive audience and planned to make the most of it.

"They look like they're having fun."

I pulled my gaze away from Simeon and settled it on Jake. "Yeah, I think they are. Simeon's a virgin."

Jake's eyebrows shot up.

"Oh, I meant a video game virgin."

Simeon chuckled.

*Okay, so he can hear us.*

Since I had few secrets, I wasn't worried. I was, however, intensely curious. "How can I help you, Jake?"

He hesitated. Now he'd actually planted his butt, he seemed less certain. "Do you...do you recognize me?"

Lord, what a question. Kind of arrogant, but maybe he was someone famous and, about this and most things in life, I was clueless. "I'm sorry, I don't. But...I've been out of the country for a couple years. Before that..." I floundered. "I didn't get around much."

*That doesn't sound too pathetic?*

*Right?*

*No, it does.*

Jake smiled. His bright-blue eyes lit, but also carried a trace of wariness. Or was that weariness? He rubbed his face.

"You okay?"

He blinked. "Baby at home. I didn't sleep well last night. Marnie's just amazing, but sometimes she needs a break."

I cocked my head. "I didn't realize Marnie had a baby at home. She works at the library, right?" I knew she did, but I didn't want to make it seem like I was too interested. In his wife or anyone else.

"Yeah. She's gone back part time. She loves Nate, but sometimes needs to get out of the house. The library is her happy place."

"That's evident. She found me a series of books, and I'm loving them."

"You should tell her. Things like that…" He appeared to consider. "Our family gives her meaning, so I don't want you to think that's not the case. But she's got a strong connection to books. Sharing her love of reading brings her intense joy."

"Then I'll be certain to tell her." I arched an eyebrow. "So tell me why you thought I might recognize you."

"I'm a reporter."

Involuntarily, I shifted back. Only to hit a wall of pillows.

He held up his hands. "Don't panic."

"Right. That's what everyone says to the guy who's about to panic. Let me assure you—it doesn't work."

He winced. "Sorry. That was callous of me. And I know better. I'm speaking to you off the record. If that wasn't obvious, then let me say it now. Just the two of us. Having a discussion."

"Is this about my father? Because I'll never say…"

"I don't know who your father is." Jake's brow knit. "I mean if you tell me his name, I might recognize it. I'm from Toronto. I've only been on the west coast for a couple of years. I do report in Vancouver, although I know people from Mission City as well."

"He's in Vancouver." I uttered the words, trying to keep the contempt from my voice.

Slowly, he nodded. "Okay. Well, I'm not sure that's relevant anyway. I just...I used to be a war correspondent."

My mind raced. I couldn't place the guy, but that wasn't surprising. I'd never watched the news before Russia invaded Ukraine and a couple of gaming buddies started talking about it.

And my life changed forever.

Then the penny dropped. "You know I was in Ukraine."

His gaze moved up for a moment before returning to me. "I didn't know specifically, no. But Simeon and Marnie seemed privy to information and...I might've put two and two together."

"Because you can see I'm injured." That hurt. I didn't remember specifically telling Marnie about overseas, but I might've said something. Probably had said something. She'd been...skittish...the first time I'd met her. No, not skittish. Protective. I'd needed her to see I wasn't a threat. Mentioning I was recovering from an injury had clearly put her at ease. I'd wondered how she worked in a library while being wary of men, but that so wasn't my place to ask. "What is it you want?" I didn't add the bite—but that was only because of an inordinate amount of self-control. Self-control learned after two years on the front lines.

He shifted. "Canadians are detached from the war. We've sent munitions, but we haven't sent troops."

"I know." *Duh.*

"Well, I'm suggesting that maybe we should introduce people to what it's really like. What the money is being spent on. Why winning is so critical." He eyed me. "Ukraine has slipped from the headlines—and that's wrong. Other conflicts, issues at home...but democracy is on the line and I don't think enough people realize that."

"I'm not the person to explain it to them." I pressed a hand to my chest. "Look, I can see you're a standup guy. I suspect Marnie's discerning."

Jake chuckled. "You have no idea."

*Okay, so there's a story there.*

*Maybe another time.*

"No one is interested in my story."

He shook his head. "Did you realize you made the news when you were medevacked out of Kyiv?"

My eyes widened. "What?"

"Ah." He winced. "I hope I'm not speaking out of turn. Or that I might be jeopardizing your recovery."

"How do you know it was me?"

"Well...I don't. But I'm putting pieces together—and maybe they don't fit...but I suspect they do." He scratched his scruff.

I tried not to think how much it resembled Simeon's. Although Simeon's was lighter. Then I tried not to think about how sexy I found my friend. I glanced over to find him still engrossed in the game.

"What do you know?" I turned back to Jake.

"That a young Canadian man was injured on the battlefield in Toretsk. That he nearly died, but was medevacked out of the country and, against all odds, survived until he got to Toronto. He was treated at an undisclosed location, and then..." He made a fist and then let it go dramatically. "Gone."

Despite myself, I chuckled.

"You wanted the scoop?"

"My network did. As did all the others. I'd heard through the grapevine that the guy, whoever he was, had a powerful family. Ones who spent a great deal of time and money to keep their son's name out of the news."

Again, I chuckled. But completely devoid of humor.

"Look…" He glanced over to where Marnie stood. She was laughing at something Quinton just said.

Inwardly, I growled. I didn't want the guy near Simeon. Still, I refocused on Jake. "You were saying…?"

"My wife's story was all over the news. Unfortunate, but the truth."

I blinked. "I have no idea who she is."

"Which is the way she'd prefer it stay. I'm only sharing this with you to say she comes from a well-known family. Well, her father's powerful. She stayed hidden for a very long time."

After a moment, I wagged my finger at him "You. You found her."

He winced. "Not my best moment. I had my reasons, which I won't go into. And she helped me in a way no one else could…for which I'll always be grateful. I'm just…" He rubbed his face. "I'm not sure what I'm trying to say. Except that you may still be discovered."

I snorted. "Look, Jake, I'm not hiding." *Much*. "I don't tell people what happened to me because it's a clusterfuck—"

Simeon cleared his throat.

My gaze shot to his.

Neither Angus nor Oliver appeared to have heard.

And the game beeped again.

Oliver patted Simeon's shoulder. "Again?"

Simeon grinned. "Yeah, a-again." He held my gaze for a moment later.

Whether he intended it or not, I read support. Hard for me to remain annoyed at him.

After a moment, I returned my gaze to Jake.

"Cluster," he prompted.

Laughter burst forth from me—unexpected and bringing with it relief. I smiled ruefully. "Look, I don't think coming forward will make a difference. I'm...building a life for myself here. Away from the glare of the spotlight that follows my father everywhere."

"Tough way to grow up."

*Does he know? Who I am? Or is he making a general comment?* "I wasn't deprived."

"Being rich can be as bad as being poor." He cocked his head. "But that's a leap on my part."

"That I'm rich or my dad's a shi—" I winced. "—crappy parent."

"Both." He bobbed his head. "Well, not the rich part. Serious money went into keeping your identity secret."

"But money can't forever hold that secret, can it?" I held his gaze, unblinking.

"I will never reveal I know who you are. Neither will Marnie, or anyone else I can think of. They're respectful. Small towns can be like that."

"But big city folk infiltrate, and then all bets are off." I held his gaze.

He poked his cheek out with his tongue. Then, after a long moment, spoke. "I didn't intend to reveal her. A coworker hacked my computer. So yeah, my fault. But also not something I would've ever done."

I believed him. Against all odds...I believed him.

"What are you proposing?" *Because I've completely lost my fucking mind for even considering this.*

"A sit-down interview? Is there footage of you in Ukraine?"

I wrinkled my nose in distaste. "Possibly some home stuff? I kept far away from cameras. I might've been naïve and stupid and reckless—but I still understood the ramifications for Canada if I was discovered on the battlefield. Russia was seriously pissed when they heard about me."

"You weren't the only one."

"Nah. But I would've been the highest profile."

"Ah."

I eyed him. "You really think this would make a difference?"

"Honestly? Yes, I do."

"I'm not a hero."

"And I wouldn't show you as one. Just a guy doing what he thought was right in the face of tremendous headwinds. A guy who did something greater than himself."

"You're assuming I thought I'd come back. You have no idea." I scoffed that.

Simeon's head popped up.

The video game beeped.

Jake gazed back and forth between the two of us. "Oh."

"Let me think about it?"

"Yeah, of course." He offered his hand. "Simeon knows how to reach me."

Which was several leaps more than I was able to process.

But at least the guy didn't hand me a business card.

# Chapter Twenty-Three

Simeon

J ake rose, nodded to me, nodded to Ryan, then headed back toward Marnie.

*Goddamn it.*

That hadn't gone like I thought it might.

*How did you think it would go? They'd have a kumbaya moment, and all Ryan's problems would be solved?*

Yeah...maybe not. But Marnie'd seen what I'd seen...right? That maybe Jake would be good for Ryan.

*He has Justin. Remember? His therapist?*

Right. Except Jake McGrath had seen the worst of the worst. Man's inhumanity to man. Had, if rumors were true, saved a friend's life and kept making world-changing reports. That kind of work had to leave a mark, right? Yet Jake appeared happy. Healthy.

*Appears. Do you really know what goes on behind the walls of that house? Of any house?*

Not really. People eluded me sometimes. I just didn't always understand them. But when I was plastering a wall because someone put
a fist or a foot through it? That was a side I wasn't comfortable with.

"Simeon, you're not paying attention." Oliver nudged me.

"S-sorry, buddy." I didn't look at him. My gaze met Ryan's.

He didn't appear upset. At least I hoped he wasn't. I didn't really
know him well enough to know for certain, though. Slowly, he offered
a half-hearted smile.

I wasn't as reassured as I hoped.

Quinton stepped into our little group. "Okay, these are cooled
down enough. Pigs in a blanket, beef-curry puff straight from Australia, as well as his awesome tuna-and-chickpea patties."

Oliver's eyes widened.

"Your mom said three." Quinton handed him a napkin. "Take a
selection, okay? Don't hog the pigs in a blanket."

The kid rolled his eyes. Then carefully selected one pig in the blanket and two other treats.

I took the proffered napkin and followed instructions I assumed
were meant for all of us and picked three. I really enjoyed Dean's
beef-curry puffs, so selecting those wasn't a hardship.

Angus nabbed his three.

Finally, Ryan did the same. Again he held my gaze, then saluted me
with one of them. He bit in and... His eyes opened wide.

I grinned. "Yeah, Dean r-really does make the best snacks. He
m-made me some for the road when I fixed their g-gutter a few weeks
back. I think they might've b-been able to do it themselves, but I was
really glad they called me b-because it turned out to be a bit more
complicated, and you d-didn't need to know any of that." Heat raced
to my cheeks.

He swallowed. "It's a cute story. I like your cute stories."

Oliver snickered.

Ryan's gaze narrowed.

The kid held up his hands. "You're being, like mushy. My uncle Maddox is always mushy with Uncle Ravi. Nothing wrong with that," he quickly added. "Just...I dunno...I'm never doing that."

"You might meet the right person." Ryan flicked his gaze from Oliver and then back to me.

"No. Gross. Girls have cooties and boys stink."

I couldn't help myself—I laughed. A hearty belly laugh. I was incredibly grateful he didn't feel the need to pronounce heterosexuality. At seven that would be wrong—but I'd witnessed kids doing that. Kids whose parents insisted on it. Several of those kids had come out queer later on.

Quite suddenly, Violet toddled over. She made a beeline for Ryan and grabbed a curry puff.

His eyes widened.

Quinton had moved on, after winking at me. I didn't think Ryan had witnessed the wink, and that felt like a good thing.

Ryan tried to keep hold of his food. "Can she just...?"

"She's g-got teeth." She'd chomped on me before. "She's allowed. B-but you can say no—"

He handed over his food.

She held it aloft in triumph then bit a big piece.

"Is she going to choke?"

"D-doubt it. With two nurses, a f-former search-and-rescue guy, and several people who work with the p-public, I figure we have enough medical and first aid expertise."

He eyed me.

Angus nabbed the controller. "I want to show Oliver my new game." He gazed at me. "Do you want to play this new one?"

I shook my head. "A-another time." I cast a covert look at Ryan.

He gave a subtle shake of his head. Still, I was so proud of him. He'd done so well. Several games and he'd been okay. *Is this a breakthrough?* I just didn't know.

Violet toddled off as Hillary arrived. "Okay, you've played enough. You need to...socialize."

Oliver snickered. "With who?"

Hillary bit her lower lip.

As if summoned, Marnie appeared. "I was hoping you guys could help me select some books for next year." She held out her phone.

Angus popped out of his seat, clearly eager to contribute to the library's future collection.

Oliver appeared marginally less eager, but a glare from his mom had him following Marnie and Angus over to the sofa. Hillary took off as well.

Ryan met my gaze. "So you thought Jake McGrath and I should talk."

*Am I supposed to lie? Prevaricate? Tell the truth?* "I t-think you could help each other."

He sighed dramatically. "The reporter gets his story, and I get outed...how is that helping me?"

I knew he didn't mean outed as in him being gay—but the word still had a profound impact on me. "W-when you put it l-like that...no."

"No I shouldn't do it, or no, it isn't helping me?"

"B-both."

He beckoned me over.

Taking that as a good sign, I went. Belatedly, I realized he might've been calling me over so he could get mad and we wouldn't be overheard.

Just as I plopped my butt on the ground, a little white ball of fur launched herself into my lap. The tongue licking—or kisses as Maddox called them—began immediately. My face, my neck, my hands...any exposed skin.

Ryan laughed, his eyes sparking amusement. "Well, she's no Tiffany."

"No." I rolled my eyes. "P-princess Sofia is never going to be a therapy dog."

He reached out to pet her fur.

Sensing another willing target—because she'd long figured out how pliable I was—she headed Ryan's way. Just as he was about to speak, she planted one on his lips.

His face scrunched in obvious revulsion. "Did this cute dog just give me a French kiss?"

"She does have exceptional timing that way." Quinton hovered another tray of hors d'oeuvres before us. "Eat up, guys. Remember there's no dinner. Oh, but there's dessert. Simeon, I've been eyeing those cookies your grandmother made. They look amazing."

"They a-are." I grinned at Quinton, snagged a Ritz cracker with a little square of cheese and offered him a genuine smile. "I s-should be helping."

"Oh, there are several of us." He glanced to Ryan. "What are you guys talking about? Any gossip to share?"

Ryan...growled? A sound in his chest that sounded distinctly like annoyance. *Why does he hate Quinton so much? Because the nurse is perpetual sunshine and Ryan's all grumpy?* Of course, if I'd been through what he'd been through, I likely wouldn't have been feeling magnanimous either.

I offered Quinton my best smile. "N-no gossip here."

"Too bad." He winked at me, grinned at Ryan, and took off after we'd each snagged several crackers.

"Jackass." Ryan muttered the word—loud enough for me to hear, but not with enough volume that others might.

"H-he's nice."

"He's flirting with you."

I blinked.

Twice.

"N-no he's not. Quinton d-doesn't flirt with me."

This time Ryan blinked. "Are you blind?"

I flinched.

He held up his hand. "Sorry, that was rude of me. I just—" He leaned forward. "—sometimes you seem really naïve."

I pursed my lips. "That's b-because I am." Was I going to go there? Be brutally honest? Nope. Couldn't do it. "I'm not w-worldly."

His eyes flashed with something dark. "I didn't used to be either. And after what I've seen of the world, I'd be happy to never leave my house again." He glanced around. "Okay, like, leave Mission City again."

"T-that could be arranged." I offered my best smile. "We h-have everything you could ever want." That wasn't true, of course. Mission City was a small town. For medical care alone, plenty of folks had to travel to bigger centers. But I knew what I meant...and I hoped he did as well.

"You guys mind if I join you?" Everett grinned.

Ryan offered a smile toward my friend. "Sure."

"Great. I'm going to tell you about the time Maddox and Ravi tried to set Simeon and I up."

"Oh really." Ryan's drawl was adorable. "Do tell."

And thus slipped away the next couple of hours. Just about everyone took a turn at visiting us. Whether he realized it or not, Ryan was essentially holding court, and each of my friends dropped by to get the know the stranger. To make him feel welcome. To share some innocuous tidbit about someone else—so Ryan would be in *the know* without any real gossip having been exchanged.

God, I really loved my neighbors and friends.

The last straggler was Maddox himself.

Maddox dropping to the ground wasn't as graceful as most of the others—but he managed. And grinned. "We thought a cocktail party would be simple."

"No one wants to leave?" Ryan held up his second glass of eggnog. "The hospitality here is second to none."

A chuckle came from Maddox. "Yeah, I think we did okay."

"I had f-fun." And I didn't want to leave, but surely Maddox and Ravi wanted their home back.

Maddox waved

I glanced over to find Everett, completely bundled up, waving goodbye.

Another chuckle from Maddox. "I'd have pegged Marnie and Jake as the first to leave. What with the baby—"

Everett reappeared. "Uh..." He was brushing himself off. "Has anyone looked outside recently?"

A general murmur went up within the group.

"Fuck." Maddox whispered the word—nearly under his breath. He turned to try to see outside, but the black of night only showed the reflection of the glowing inside lights.

Anticipating his next move, I rose and surreptitiously offered him a hand. With his bad knee, he probably shouldn't have sat. Or, more appropriately, Ryan and I should've moved to seating. Just...we'd been in our bubble that people occasionally joined, but never stayed within for long.

Where I expected Maddox to maybe be affronted, he took my hand with a smile and happily let me guide him up. When he moved to the window, I knelt beside Ryan. "We should probably be heading out." I placed my arm by him and held my breath.

He took it, offered the same smile Maddox had, and allowed me to help him. Very subtle. Someone would have to be watching closely to notice us.

Most people were either crowding around Everett—who was indicating a troubling high level with his hand—or they were with Maddox, trying to see outside.

"We need to be heading out as well." Jake's tone sounded more clipped than I was accustomed to. "We're parked on the road."

As Ryan and I headed into the front foyer, several people were already putting on boots.

Everett offered me a grin. "You'll be all right—with your pickup truck."

I blinked. "Did you d-drive a car up here?"

He shook his head. "Nah, I brought the SUV. I think just about everyone did." He winced. "Except there's a little car in the driveway—"

"Shit." Ryan muttered that and no one even blinked.

Maddox rounded the corner. "I'm so sorry. The forecast was for light flurries changing to heavy snow at midnight."

And we were nowhere near midnight.

Jake scrolled on his phone as Marnie donned her coat. "The app says it's snowing lightly."

Ravi, with Victor in his arms, joined the crowd. "Remember, that's taken from down the hill. The mountains have their own weather system sometimes." He nudged Maddox. "Like our first Christmas together."

Maddox frowned. "We didn't actually spend Christmas here. We were in Calgary. At your sister's—"

"Oh my God, do not remind me."

I cocked my head. I was worried about Ryan's car, but curious about Maddox's reddening cheeks. Even beneath his red beard, his skin had a ruddy color.

Stanley chuckled. "Coitus interruptus."

Several heads swiveled to him. He shrugged. "Maddox's friend Meg is also my friend, and she told me—"

"Hey. Shush." Maddox hissed. "The whole world doesn't need to know—"

"Lovely as this has been..." Jake stuck out his hand.

Maddox shook.

Marnie kissed Victor on the cheek

Hillary had scooped up Violet and had the baby on her hip.

Opal was in Justin's arms. He grinned. "I think we should all bunk here for the night."

"Hey." Hillary glared. "We'd already arranged to. Steve and I have dibs on the spare bed. You all can crash by the fireplace."

"And we'll be off." Jake held the door for Marnie.

Everett and Quinton all waved as they took off.

"Are they going to be okay?" Ryan had clearly caught sight of the swirling snow.

"They've all got SUVs. Well..." I frowned. "I'm not certain about Quinton."

"I'm sure if he didn't, he'd be begging a ride from you."

I tried to glare at Ryan, but I kind of found this side of him amusing. Quinton wasn't hitting on me. That wasn't a thing.

Stanley zipped up his coat. "I'll clear off the SUV and then you bring the kids?"

Justin nodded. "Yeah. No problem."

"We can help." Dean's Australian accent carried across the small space. "Then we'll follow you. We've got that extra climb to get up to the house.

"Sounds good." Stanley headed out with Dean hard on his heels.

Adam chuckled. "He'd never seen snow before he came to Canada."

"I think I've seen enough of it to last a lifetime." Ryan shrugged gingerly into his coat. "Australia, eh? Sounds tempting."

"Dean's got a mate—Sam. Gives tours around Sydney. He might be looking for a partner."

I cleared my throat.

Adam grinned. "Interesting response, Simeon."

"He c-can't just, like, move to Australia. Can he?"

Ryan stuck his feet into his running shoes.

"Whoa, that's not going to work." Ravi eyed the footwear.

"It'll be fine. I never wore boots in Vancouver."

"First, the mountains of Mission City are not Vancouver. Secondly..." He wrinkled his nose. "Vancouver *does* get snow. I might be from Calgary—where we get a whole hell of a lot more—but I know the city has snow days."

Why did Ryan never wear boots? Had he never left his house? That felt sad. I would've been hustling him out the door, but all the SUVs behind his car had to get out first. Another reason that, even if I was the first to arrive at a party, I always parked on the street.

*And why did he show up first?* Not that he hadn't always been prompt, but... Just another mystery.

Stanley returned a moment later with Dean. He snagged Opal from Justin. "We should be okay." He glanced over at Ryan. "As Dean would say, *sorry, mate.*"

Dean chuckled. "You almost have the accent."

"Doing my best." He met Maddox's gaze. "It's never boring."

Maddox waved.

Angus, Justin, Stanley, and Opal left.

"And that's our cue." Adam slapped Dean on the back. "I'll warm up the SUV while you clear it."

Dean eyed him. "We're going a mile. I don't think the car needs to be warmed up."

Adam offered a grin. "I'm sorry...who knows about vehicles in Canadian winters?"

Ravi chuckled. "Good luck arguing that."

Aussie Dean grinned. "We'll sort out the rest later."

Adam grinned back. "Oh yeah."

Well...no question what he was referring to.

Hillary popped her head around. "I swear it's getting worse."

Dean and Adam waved—then booted out.

I zipped up my jacket. "We'll s-see if we can dig Ryan out."

Maddox shook his head. "Past his wheels."

"And I don't have snow tires." Ryan scratched his beard. "Because it's not December yet, and I didn't think I'd need them."

"Even the r-ranch is at a higher elevation." I wasn't telling him anything he didn't already know.

"You can stay here." Hillary grinned, still gripping a twin. "Oliver will love to spend more time gaming with you."

Ryan's color changed almost before my eyes. *Ah, so he'd been putting on a show. And they're probably going to watch movies as well on Maddox and Ravi's big screen television.*

"He's g-going to come home with me." I patted his shoulder, trying to offer reassurance without spooking him.

After a moment, he gazed up at me. "I am?"

"Y-yep."

# Chapter Twenty-Four

Ryan

Simeon sometimes made very complex things sound very simple. Cutting crown molding was actually a complex process when everything was factored in. Yet as he did it, he made it appear effortless. And although I'd eyed the ceiling fan with trepidation, he explained the electrician had done the tough stuff and his only job was to attach... Yeah, I'd sort of glazed over the details. Because when, for fuck's sake, was I ever going to install a ceiling fan?

Therefore, Simeon proclaiming I was going home with him shouldn't have been really complicated. Except not only did we have to travel to his grandparents' home in a driving snowstorm, but we'd have to eventually come back for my car. Unless I left it until spring. At the moment, that felt entirely possible.

*He's going to come home with me.*

Maddox cast his gaze to me. Asking me silently, I believed, if I was okay with this. Otherwise, a space on the floor here was mine. With kids. And a television.

I couldn't think of anything less appealing.

Maybe not the kids part—although they scared the crap out of me. No, the sleeping on the floor.

Hillary wrapped her arms around her husband. "We're fine to sleep down here with the kids."

I shook my head. "Simeon's grandmother's lasagna is the best." I eyed him, hoping he'd read my meaning.

"She's probably unthawing s-some right now." Simeon grinned.

I hated asking him to make something up—because I didn't know if Nanny was unthawing lasagna—but Maddox's sister seemed like the type of person who would give up comfort for the sake of someone else.

Simeon gestured to the door. "Your feet are going to get wet."

Maddox tried to grab his coat. "I should shovel—"

"No way." Steve reached for his. "Stubborn man."

*Ah right. The knee.* Maddox had mentioned physiotherapy had done wonders but that he still had bad days. I worried today might be one of them. I hadn't witnessed anything—but perhaps others, like those who knew him well, had.

"I'm good. My own fault for wearing canvass sneakers." I gently nudged Simeon with my shoulder. "Let's go."

"Yeah."

We waved, then my savior opened the door.

And it became immediately apparent why we were in such deep shit.

The wind had blown the snow away from the door—so, in those first few steps, the path appeared deceptively clear and simple to maneuver. Soon, though, the snow was nearly to our knees. "What the hell?"

Simeon hustled—as fast as he could go in almost two feet of snow, creating a trail for me to follow. We found tire tracks, which made the trek a touch easier.

A touch.

By the time we were out on the street, he had the passenger door open.

In turn, I hustled to get into the truck. I ignored the pulling in my chest as he boosted me in. I wasn't short, but his truck felt like the damn thing was twenty feet off the ground. Which was likely a good thing on a night like tonight. As soon as I was inside, I pounded my feet to the floor—trying to dislodge the accumulated snow. Already, the shit was melting.

Simeon opened the back door, grabbed the snow brush, then slammed it shut.

I almost asked him to turn on the heater, but I figured he knew what he was doing. Maybe he wouldn't take long.

And about four minutes later, he got into the truck, tossed the brush into the foot well of the back seat, and had the truck running in mere moments. He jacked up the heat.

I held my hands before the vents.

He started fidgeting with the controls for the defroster so he could get a clear view from the windshield.

I grimaced—I would've been lost. I'd had a fancy car when I lived with my dad. Parked in our massive garage. I'd never ventured out in the snow. Why bother when everything could be delivered by someone crazy enough to go out in that weather? If I didn't go out, then I didn't have to deal with snow. Plus, Vancouver and snow didn't mix—most people didn't have snow tires and even fewer actually knew how to drive in the white stuff.

People like me.

"O-okay?"

Suddenly, I realized my butt and back were toasty. "Seat warmers?"

"F-for you. I'd be too hot."

*Well, you are hot.* Except I'd never say that out loud. "I'm appreciative." I squinted as I gazed out the windshield. "Can you see?"

"I'll keep m-my headlights on low instead of using the high-beams. Those r-reflect off the falling snow. We'll g-go slowly." As he said the words, he inched onto the road. The road that had so much snow that I could barely believe it.

"What about a plow?"

"They d-do all of downtown Mission City first. They'll b-be up in the mountains t-tomorrow."

"And if you needed to go out?"

"M-most of us have four-wheel d-drive."

"Ah."

My car had precisely none of those things. As I eyed the high-tech dashboard that ran Simeon's truck, my mind spun. Instead of focusing on all the tech keeping us safe, I kept my gaze straight ahead.

Simeon turned us onto the main road I recognized. The one that would lead to his house.

Guilt swamped me. His grandparents didn't need a house guest. Especially so close to Christmas.

I spotted something on the road. "Stop! Oh God, stop!"

We weren't traveling fast, so Simeon braked. He didn't slam on them, which wasn't a bad thing.

But I feared he wouldn't stop in time.

As soon as we were stopped, I shoved open the door and, through the knee-deep snow, made my way around to the front of the truck. The headlights illuminated a black thing right in the middle of our lane.

"Don't!" Simeon's voice carried. "You d-don't know what—"

"It's a dog."

"It c-could be a bear cub."

I'd done some reading. Bear cubs were a thing in spring. No way one could be this small in late November. "It's a dog." I knelt and held out my hand. The snow stung as it hit the exposed skin, but I didn't care.

Slowly, the dog sniffed.

"We need to get him help. I don't know if he's just cold or injured or both."

Simeon stood beside me. "We h-have to get off the road. S-someone might hit us from b-behind." Slowly he palpated the dog.

"Do you know what you're doing?"

"N-nope."

"Oh...okay." I wouldn't have been any better. At least he'd been around Tiffany and Rex. That was much more than me.

"I think she's j-just cold. At least she hasn't b-bitten me."

God, I hadn't even thought of that.

Simeon unzipped his coat.

"What the fuck are you doing?" I was freezing with my peacoat and a scarf.

"C-can you get in the truck? I c-could put her on your lap. Not the s-safest, but that might work."

Getting into the truck wouldn't be easy—but I could do it. For this poor animal, I'd do anything.

I managed to secure myself before Simeon placed the creature on my lap. As he slammed the door, she gazed up at me with the most beautiful brown eyes. I expected wariness, but when I held out my hand, she licked it. The scratchy tongue against my cold-reddened skin was almost painful, but I didn't care. "How did you get out, little one?" I tried to find a collar, but couldn't.

Simeon hopped into the truck, secured his seatbelt, and we were off again. "I c-can't believe no one came behind us."

"Maybe because no one's crazy enough to drive tonight?"

He chuckled. "Maybe."

Within about ten minutes, he maneuvered us into the left turn and then onto his street. We didn't have other tracks to follow, and that made for slow going. "What are we going to do about the dog? Can we call animal control?"

"They w-won't come. Would be d-dangerous anyway. We'll have to k-keep her safe until the plows come." He leaned forward. "I hope you d-didn't have plans."

I chuckled. "Physiotherapy on Monday. Marcus will understand if I can't make it. Or he'll just bill for a canceled appointment. That's fine as well."

"That's m-money." Still, Simeon kept us moving forward.

"Daddy's money." I hesitated. "He's paying all the medical stuff." An inward wince, thinking of all the things I'd put on my credit card.

"You okay?" He glanced over at me for a fraction of a second before returning his attention to the road.

"Yeah, I'm okay. Just thinking I need to get a job and acknowledging there probably isn't a job out there that doesn't require some tech."

"S-security guard."

I scoffed. "Okay, I couldn't run ten feet, but I suppose..."

"H-hang on."

I gripped the dog tighter.

Instead of whimpering, she licked my face.

I giggled.

"What h-happened?"

Simeon turned us into what I assumed was his driveway. I'd spotted the mailbox—same as most people had on the street—but I'd only have been able to navigate by aiming at the space between the line of trees and praying I had it right. "I can g-get us into the garage."

As he said the words, the garage door opened.

"She licked me."

Simeon smiled. For the first time since we'd heard about the snow.

He struck me as stoic. He hadn't panicked. He'd remained calm. His calm had kept me calm. I appreciated that.

He inched us forward and once we were inside, he cut the engine and let out a long sigh.

"I'm sorry," I said.

He glanced over at me. "F-for what?"

I shrugged. "I don't know. I'm Canadian. We apologize when someone just had to do something difficult, and we were partly the cause."

He cocked his head. "Y-you had nothing to do with the storm. It's not like I d-drove you home."

"Yes, but I could've stayed at Ravi and Maddox's."

A laugh burst forth from him. "Oliver would have m-monopolized your time and k-kept you up all night. The t-twins might've slept..." He sobered. "I d-didn't see the dog. I would've hit her."

I couldn't argue. "You must be cold."

He shook his head. "S-sweating."

"Ah. Well, she's cold and so am I. Do we take her into the house?"

"Have to. The g-garage isn't heated."

"Okay then."

"I'll c-come around and get her. Hang on." He exited the vehicle and came around to my side. He opened the door and gingerly took the bundle from my lap.

Our gazes met.

"You d-did good." He offered a shy smile and then stepped back.

I unbuckled my seatbelt and slipped out of the truck. I thought we might try the staircase on the outside, but was relieved when we headed into the house.

We entered a small room with a stacked washer/dryer, a sink, as well as some pegs against one of the walls.

"H-hang up your coat and scarf."

"Sure. Thanks." I draped the scarf over one peg and the soaked coat over another. I toed out of my freezing-wet sneakers. At least the color hadn't run. My pristine white socks were still clean—but waterlogged.

"T-take off those as well. How b-bad are your jeans?"

"Uh..."

Simeon laid the dog, still wrapped in his coat, on the little table.

She woofed.

He cringed.

I giggled. "They're wet."

"O-okay. You watch the d-dog and I'll get something for you to p-put on."

"Uh, Simeon...?"

Our gazes met.

"I'm much smaller than you."

"Yeah, b-but you're Bops's size. I'll figure s-something out."

I took care of the dog while he bent to untie his laces.

He struggled, and I winced. His fingers were red. Somehow neither of us had gotten frostbite. When he was out of his boots, jacket, and socks, he headed into the house.

I gazed down at the dog.

She looked up at me. Shivering.

"I know, sweetheart. We'll get this sorted."

"Did I hear a bark?" Nanny appeared at the door.

*Am I supposed to hide her? Pretend I don't know what's going on?*

The dog barked again.

Well, okay then.

Nanny stepped forward to inspect the little one. "Oh, how cute. She must be frozen. I have heated towels." She started to leave.

"I'm sure those are your good towels." Because one usually didn't heat crap towels...right?

She waved me off. "Nothing's too good for a little pooch. We haven't had one since..." She tapped her lips. "I want to say fifty-eight. Simeon's mother—my daughter—was allergic. To just about every breed. So she never could be around them, and although I told Simeon we could get a dog when he came here, he said he didn't want one."

Well, that wasn't right. He'd told me how much he'd always wanted a dog. More likely, as a scared nineteen-year-old orphan, he hadn't wanted to make waves. Hadn't wanted to disrupt the household he was moving into.

"Simeon!"

My ears rang. For a ninety-something woman, she had pipes I'd never have predicted.

Within moments, Simeon appeared. "I'm s-sorry. We'll t-take her d-downstairs." He appeared on the verge of panic.

"Nanny was just going to suggest getting the heated towels." I normally wouldn't have spoken for the woman, but I recognized panic when I saw it.

"Oh." He let out a breath. "They're your g-good ones."

His grandmother put her hands on her hips. "I have at least ten sets of *good* towels. Everybody keeps giving me more. The puppy needs warmth."

"Y-yes." He stepped into the room and handed me a pair of track pants with a sheepish look.

"Thank you." I didn't care if they were his grandfather's. I needed to get out of my wet jeans.

"B-be right back." He took off in a hurry.

"Dear boy." Nanny advanced toward me. "Is he hurt? He? She?"

"Simeon says she's a girl. He checked her over, and she seems fine. Cold and wet...but okay."

"Well, we'll get her warmed up. Do you think she's thirsty? Hungry? I could fry up some ground beef. I wish we had dog food."

"She doesn't feel emaciated. In fact, I suspect someone's worried about her. No collar, though. And we can't check for a microchip." I surveyed the dog's inner ear and didn't see a tattoo. How I knew to do that, I wasn't even certain.

Simeon returned a moment later with a pile of towels. He frowned. "You h-haven't changed."

"That would be my cue to leave." Nanny eyed me. "Glad you're here, young man. Have you had dinner?"

"Plenty of hors d'oeuvres and treats."

"Ah, but nothing of substance and not for a while. I made my baked rosemary chicken, garlic bread, and broccoli. You interested? There's cheese sauce..."

*Like I need cheese sauce as an incentive.* "That sounds delicious—but only if it's no trouble."

"None." She waved as she took off.

Simeon held the towels to his chest. "I'll take her while you get changed. Then I'll run d-downstairs and change."

Only then did I notice how soaked he was. "Yeah, okay."

He advanced into the room

Together, we got the pooch out of his coat and under a pile of warm towels.

She licked our faces.

I felt gratitude like I couldn't remember. Tonight could've been a disaster. Instead, I was safe. The dog was safe.

Simeon would take care of us.

# Chapter Twenty-Five

Simeon

"This is Constable Seth Jacobs. You've got a lost dog?"

"H-hi Seth. This is S-Simeon." *Breathe.* "S-Simeon C-Cox."

"Hey Simeon." The RCMP officer's voice softened. "How are you? You were out in this snow? I'm at the detachment. We're only going out for dire emergency calls. Haven't had any yet, thank God. Hopefully most folks are staying home."

"R-right. T-that's good."

"You told our dispatcher that you found the dog on the road?"

"Y-yes. She's n-not a stray. Too healthy for t-that."

"Are you able to take a picture and email it to me?"

"S-sure."

The dog had decided Ryan's lap was the best place to settle. I think she might've preferred Nanny's, but my grandmother was busy dishing out dinner. I'd considered putting off this call until after we'd eaten, but someone might be in distress—they needed to know their dog was okay. And well cared for. And maybe a little spoiled.

Somehow I managed to take a picture and to send it to the email Seth provided. Well, he emailed me and I hit reply and attached the photo.

"Got it." A pause. "Oh, that's Chia. She belongs to Helen Clemson. Oh, sorry, she did belong to Helen. Helen passed...I want to say a month ago. Her granddaughter's been staying at the property and getting it ready to sell. I'll get in touch with her. Although I might contact Dr. Zephyra with the photo just to be certain. But from where you said you found her—it fits. I'll also see if I can confirm the name."

I chuckled. "Yes. D-dog isn't a great name. Wait." I met the dog's gaze. "Ch-Chia."

Her ears perked.

"I t-think we might have a winner."

He laughed. "Great. I'll be in touch." He disconnected the call.

Ryan hugged the dog tighter. "So she belongs to someone."

I eyed him. "We knew she d-did." I offered a small smile. "You c-can't keep her."

He stuck out his lower lip. "I don't see why not. I can, you know, sneak her in and out of my apartment—"

"Your n-no-pets-allowed apartment." Not to put too fine a point on it.

A wince. "Yeah, that part's going to be a problem."

Bops entered the room with two plates. He handed one to me and started to hand the other to Ryan.

Who held the dog almost as a shield.

My grandfather shrugged, headed to his recliner, and within moments had his feet elevated and was digging into the most aromatically pleasing dinner ever.

I loved Nanny's rosemary chicken. "I'll eat q-quickly and then take her."

Ryan waved me off. "There's no rush. I'm certain Nanny's got some set aside for me."

"She does." Nanny entered the room, carrying her own plate. "Did you talk to someone?" She pointed to my phone.

"Seth J-Jacobs."

"Oh, such a lovely young man." Nanny sat. "Lives just down the road from your friend Maddox."

I cocked my head. "I d-didn't know that."

She nodded. "Yes. She pointed to my plate. "Eat up before it gets cold."

I smiled. That was my grandmother. I bit into the delicious chicken and moaned.

Ryan snickered. "Eat quickly. I want my turn."

Nanny pointed to the dog. "We know who she is?"

I started to speak.

Ryan glared at me, then turned his attention to Nanny. "Chia Clemson."

Nanny nodded slowly. "Helen's dog. I heard she got a new one about a year ago. I sort of wondered, what with all her health problems, but she claimed dogs made her healthier." Nanny winced. "We sent flowers to the memorial service. She was what..." She glanced at Bops. "I want to say twenty years younger than us...?"

"Closer to twenty-five." He appeared to do some mental calculations. "Her ex-boyfriend left her high and dry—" He glanced between Ryan and me. "—pregnant."

We nodded.

"Like, that was forty-some-odd years ago. Her daughter had a daughter, and that girl's..." More calculations. "I want to say twenty-one? She grew up without a father either." He met my gaze. "Nothing wrong with that. Helen and her daughter did a good job. Nice young woman. I think she works at a yoga studio...?"

"D-daughter or granddaughter?"

"Granddaughter. The daughter moved to Yellowknife last year. Got a good government job. I thought she shouldn't leave her daughter behind, but the girl was twenty. Old enough to stand on her own. I heard she was helping Helen out."

Ryan hugged Chia. "So how'd she get loose?"

No one answered.

My phone rang.

I swallowed, put the plate down on the coffee table, then swiped. "H-hello?"

"Simeon? It's Seth." He sighed. "So both Dr. Zephyra and Chloe Clemson confirmed she's Chia. She's a miniature poodle."

Yeah, I might not know much about dogs, but those curls were unmistakable.

"O-okay. What next?"

He hesitated. "Chloe lives in a no-dog apartment. And her grandmother's house just sold. In two weeks, she's going to have to surrender Chia."

Ryan gasped and clutched the dog tighter.

I narrowed my eyes at him.

"We could take her." Nanny gazed at the dog. "She doesn't look like she would be much trouble."

"Is that you, Mrs. Cox?"

"It is. Hello Seth. You always were one of the good ones."

He chuckled. "I appreciate your kind words. I, uh..." He hesitated.

"Oh, the dog would be Simeon's." Nanny met my gaze. "He's always wanted a dog. I think it's high time he considers it. *If* he wants to rescue her."

My mouth went dry. I blinked several times.

"He needs to think about it, Seth. But if you—"

"Yes." *Thank God I didn't stutter.* "I m-mean we n-need to talk, but...yes."

"Okay." Seth rustled some papers. "Why don't we talk to Chloe about whether you could arrange a foster? You try keeping Chia for a week or two and see if it's a good fit. If not, Zephyra can likely find another foster or even a permanent home."

"That's a good idea." Nanny beamed. "You always had a good head about you."

Seth chuckled. "I know you don't have dog food. She's got sensitivities, so Zephyra suggested rice and boiled vegetables. The dog will be okay without meat for a day or two. Maybe when the snow clears, you can head over to Chloe's to get Chia's things?"

"Y-yes."

Seth hesitated. "Can you take me off speaker?"

Nanny's brow knit.

I did as Seth asked.

"Y-yes?"

"Look...I love your grandmother. Adore her. But she's putting a lot of pressure on you. You rescued the dog, and if you could just look after her until the storm mess is cleaned up, I'd be grateful. We all would."

"O-okay."

"But that doesn't oblige you to keep the dog. Have you ever even discussed this with your grandparents?"

"N-no."

"Okay...maybe try to have a dispassionate discussion. Dogs are a lot of responsibility. Both Zephyra and Chloe said Chia's actually a good dog. Helen hired Torah Dixon to train her. Best of the best, right?"

I smiled. "Y-yes."

"No pressure, okay?"

"O-okay. Thank you."

"Chloe was loading her car, and she thinks Chia slipped out. The dog's been looking around—probably searching for Helen."

I blinked. "That's s-sad."

"It is. Chloe's not neglectful. She was frantic. And also had enough sense not to go out herself looking for the dog in a blizzard."

A memory of the story of Ravi chasing after Princess Sofia and them both getting lost flashed to my mind. "G-good. Seth. It's all g-good."

"Okay. I'm back on tomorrow night. Can I call and check in?"

"Y-yes. That would be great."

"Fantastic. Thanks for this, Simeon. Truly." He cut the connection.

Nanny pointed to my food. "You can nuke it."

I didn't care if the chicken was cool. I snagged the plate and dug in, careful to not shovel the food in. As soon as I was done, I headed to the kitchen.

Moments later, I had Ryan's plate.

Then I realized I hadn't heated it up. I went back to the kitchen to nuke it.

Ryan came up behind me.

I turned and cocked my head as he held two empty plates.

He grinned. "I swapped Chia for the plates. She's on Nanny's lap giving kisses."

My heart leapt. Not just that my grandmother was getting on so well with Chia, but that Ryan was comfortable calling her *Nanny*.

I pulled the plate out of the microwave.

He gestured to the kitchen table.

*Wow, he didn't flinch at the microwave. That's small, but that's awesome.* Figuring he had his reasons for pointing at the table, I sat as he did.

"W-what?"

And, of course, he'd just put food in his mouth.

I rolled my eyes.

He chewed, then swallowed. "I think she'd be good for your grand-parents." He nodded toward the family room. "They already adore her."

"I w-work all day. They can't t-take her out. She might, you know, p-pull them over."

"Could you set up a little fenced area in the yard?"

I squinted. "Sure."

He'd just put more food in his mouth.

I smiled.

He grinned back, chewed, and swallowed. "Maybe I'm wrong, but..." He cocked his head. "Maybe I'm biased. I don't want her to end up in another place. Somewhere I won't be certain she's safe."

"Zephyra w-wouldn't let that happen."

"Maybe." He wrinkled his nose. "I seem to be saying that a lot."

"You f-finish eating. I'll c-clean up the kitchen. We can take Chia out for a pee and then h-head downstairs. The hockey game's over. Nanny and Bops n-need to go to bed."

"Look at you, ordering everyone around."

I winced.

He bopped me on the biceps. "I like it." Then he ate some baby carrots.

Taking that as a cue the discussion was over, I headed to the counter and started putting the leftovers into containers.

That Nanny didn't come to supervise assured me how tired she was. I put on a pot of rice, and by the time I had everything cleared away, I had a couple cups. I pulled down a plate and gazed back and forth between the pot and the plate. *How much is too much? Or not enough? I don't want her to starve, but I also don't want her to overeat and be sick...*

"You could google it." Ryan pointed to my ass and the phone in my back pocket.

I hesitated. He'd been okay with the games tonight, and when I'd been talking to Seth. But I'd also seen him reacting badly. This could've gone either way. *He's an adult—if he says it's okay, then it's okay.* I yanked out my phone and... "How m-much does she weigh?"

Ryan blinked. "Not much. Like, maybe twelve pounds?"

She'd felt light to me as well, so I selected that option. The website spit out a number that sounded about right. I used the measuring cup to apportion the rice, added a few baby carrots, and then... "We should f-feed her in here."

He nodded, rose, and headed toward the family room.

I was about to call to him that he couldn't carry her. *He's an adult—he knows what he can and can't do.*

Sure enough, moments later he came back, Chia at his heels.

She spotted me at the counter and came straight to me.

"Chia, sit."

At Ryan's command, she plopped her butt.

And waited patiently until I put the food before her.

She didn't eat.

Ryan and I exchanged a look.

*Is she picky? What if she doesn't eat? Will she starve?*

"Chia, eat."

She dove into her food at Ryan's command.

Okay, good to know. The dog would, apparently, wait before doing things. That was great, right? Yeah, except when she escaped the house and went looking for her dead owner.

Ryan winked. He seemed to think we had this.

I wasn't so sure.

Still, I smiled back.

# Chapter Twenty-Six

Ryan

Simeon fashioned a leash and collar out of stuff he had in the garage. To my relief, he took Chia outside. He had a second jacket that wasn't soaked. My coat was still wet. Likely wouldn't be dry until morning.

As I waited for him, I wandered back into the living room. Nanny gestured for me to sit next to her.

I did as I was bade.

"You seem like a nice young man."

"Uh...I try."

"You've had some bad times."

"That's true." I'd been here three days ago, but couldn't remember what we'd talked about. I didn't think it had been anything serious, but his grandparents must've been aware why we'd come here in the middle of the day. My mind had been muddled from the remnants of the panic attack. "Uh...yeah."

"Simeon's a nice young man."

"Yes." Definitive. Strong. Unquestionable. "He's one of the best men I've ever met."

"We know he's gay."

"Okay." How was I supposed to respond to that?

"She's trying to tell you to be gentle." Bops lowered his legs and slowly used the chair remote so he was able to stand without much physical effort. "We love him, but..." He met my gaze with eyes so like Simeon's that my breath caught. "Just be gentle."

Chia barreled into the room and leapt into Nanny's lap.

The woman giggled, and the dog licked—delivering serious kisses. "Do you want to stay? I think you want to stay. Such a good girl. You'd be happy here."

Simeon entered the room and our gazes met. A small smile crossed his face. Made me wonder what the constable had wanted to say to Simeon in private. That had been a little rude, to me at least, but I had to believe the cop had everyone's best interests in mind.

"D-dogs are a lot of w-work." Simeon tried for a serious expression.

"Myrtle Windsom has a dog. A little Chihuahua. They get along great."

He didn't hide the smile this time. "M-Myrtle Windsom is seven-ty-eight."

Nanny tisked. "Are you being ageist?"

"Uh..." His eyes widened.

Bops waved him off. "Only thing I can't do is scoop poop. But there's a grabby thing you can buy, right? Or we mark it with spray paint and you scoop it when you get home. That's a humbling experience."

"I s-scooped Tiffany's poop once."

*A tad defensive?*

"Well, I've never scooped, so you're going to have to show me." I offered my brightest smile.

Simeon frowned and subtly indicated my chest.

"Oh, well, you know, grabby thing." I wanted him to keep the dog. Despite the obstacles, I felt in my bones this was the right thing. Divine providence had brought us all together on that road. Well, or Mother Nature. Someone—or something—had intervened. Of that, I was certain.

"Chia?" Simeon gently stroked her head.

She gazed up at him with adoration.

"B-bedtime."

To my surprise, she gave Nanny a quick kiss, then hopped off and gazed up expectantly at Simeon as if to say *okay, dude, what's next?*

I almost laughed.

Nanny rose.

I would've offered to help, but she managed, and I worried she might be ornery if I stepped in. Plus, Simeon knew her. If she needed help, he'd be the first to offer it.

"I'm b-buying you a recliner for Christmas." He gave her the stink eye.

"Too much money." She glared.

"I c-can afford it."

"There's no room." She gestured around the space which was, admittedly, tight.

"N-new couch. Smaller." He glared right back.

"On that note, we're off to bed." Bops met Simeon's gaze and nodded.

"Oh, you always take his side." Nanny scowled.

"When it's the right side." Bops grinned. "I love my recliner, and I think you should enjoy one as well. Good for the circulation. Night, boys. Night, Chia."

The dog perked up at her name.

Then Nanny and Bops were gone.

Simeon shook his head. He had the rope collar and leash. He caught me watching. "In c-case she needs to go out. I'm assuming s-she'll let us know."

I chuckled. "Yes, let's hope so." I headed toward the door to the basement. Funny how I'd only been here once, and I was already comfortable in the space. "Your grandparents like the dog." I headed down the steps after Simeon flipped on the lights, careful to watch my step. The last thing I needed was to injure myself.

"They d-don't understand the responsibility."

As Simeon arrived at the bottom step, Chia joined him.

*Impressive that she didn't race down or trip us.* For which I was grateful. "Uh, they used to have a dog. I think they know exactly how much work she'll be." I pointed to the general direction of his computer. "You should look for, you know, grabby things." *I'll survive. It's just a search on the internet.*

"Yeah. Except it's s-stopped working."

I frowned. "What do you mean *it's stopped working?*" That didn't sound good.

He shrugged. "I can't connect to the internet. Which is bad because Bops does my billing. He's printing out invoices, and I'm mailing them instead of emailing them."

I blinked. "Your grandfather does your accounting?" Had he already mentioned that? When I was having my panic attack? I couldn't remember. *What are you going to do when he passes?*

As if reading my thoughts, Simeon winced. "I know I h-have to learn before he dies. He's l-left instructions."

"But you'll be mired in grief." I moved toward him. "The last thing you're going to want is to be learning accounting software."

"I'll h-have to hire someone."

Which would cost him some of the precious money he worked so hard to earn.

I swallowed. Hard. I wanted to offer to learn. So that in the future I could either do the billing myself or teach him how to do it. I didn't have an accounting background, but I was a quick study. A few manuals and I'd know enough to guide him. Plus, help desks were a thing.

But I couldn't do it. Couldn't promise something I likely would never be able to deliver.

"It's f-fine. I'll b-be okay, Ryan."

His saying my name caught my attention. He didn't do it often. My father used to insist I learn and use all his associates' names. A sign of respect. *Ryan* wasn't difficult, but with how Simeon sometimes struggled on *r* words, I wouldn't have blamed him for shying away from using the name. "I...want to help." I gazed back and forth between the dog and Simeon. "Does she need water? And maybe a bed?"

She was also gazing back and forth between the two of us. Expectantly. I didn't know dog, but clearly we weren't meeting at least one of her needs.

"I c-can make a bed with spare blankets. I have l-like twenty of them."

That made me smile. "Really?"

"Nanny's friends all b-buy her blankets. As if l-living in the mountains means we don't have heat." He cocked his head. "We l-lose power more often than down in town. F-falling trees."

"So we might lose power tonight?"

He pursed his lips. "Always p-possible. We have a g-generator."

Which made sense. He might be able to do without power, but that would be hard on his grandparents. "Okay, maybe grab some blankets? Should we make a bed for her out here or in your bedroom? I mean here should be fine." I eyed the couch. "Don't forget blankets for me."

"Huh?"

I met his gaze. "Well, I have to sleep somewhere."

"You're s-sleeping in my bed." He pointed to my chest. "You c-can't sleep on the couch."

As a teenager and young adult, I'd done it many times. After sixteen hours of gaming, I often just pulled up a blanket and fell asleep where I was. Now, as a wounded adult, that wasn't so much of an option. "I can't kick you out of your bed. You rescued me."

He pursed his lips. "This isn't u-up for debate." With that, he stalked out of the room.

I eyed the couch. I could fit. He could not. Although maybe it pulled out into a bed? Some sectionals did that. I thought...

Then I gazed over at the computer. *He needs your help.* I could offer to hire a technician, but that meant spending more of Daddy's money and, more importantly, convincing Simeon to accept help. He was like me—stubborn as fuck.

After a moment, I inched toward the box holding the new laptop. *This isn't manning a drone. You're not killing anyone. No one is going to try to kill you. If you really care about Simeon, you would do this for him.* And that was the crux of this—I really cared for Simeon. Like, serious feelings. Hell, if only for the fact he'd rescued me tonight. I would've survived at Maddox and Ravi's house, of course. But here was so much better for me. Whether I took the bed or the couch, I didn't have rugrats around me. Great kids, but a little much.

"P-precious, I have a b-bed for you."

I spun. *Simeon thinks I'm precious? Oh my God, that's so sweet*— My cheeks heated as I realized he was speaking to Chia and not me.

Said pup went on her back paws as Simeon dropped a huge pile of blankets on the couch along with a pillow and what appeared to be a set of sheets. He put those aside and snagged a wool blanket. He laid it in front of the sectional.

"Does that pull out into a bed?"

With clear regret, he shook his head. "N-no one has ever needed to stay." He squinted. "You could stay in the g-guest bedroom upstairs. Nanny and Bops wouldn't—"

I held up my hand. "They've already gone to bed and don't need to be startled in the morning. I swear, Simeon, I'll be fine."

He pursed his lips as if to argue.

Both of us knew the couch was too short for him. He might not be willing to admit it aloud, but he wasn't someone who wasn't quick on the uptake. In fact, he was rapidly proving himself to be one of the smartest men I knew. Sure, my dad's associates made millions of dollars. But many lacked basic common sense. Or were incapable of social niceties. Even toward the boss's son. That being said, perhaps they perceived my father's lack of caring for me and they felt they didn't need to waste their time and energy on me.

Simeon carried on making the dog bed. On the outer edges of the blanket he'd laid on the laminate floor, he fashioned a donut of sorts with another blanket.

Chia cocked her head.

He smiled. "In a m-minute." Then he set about trying to turn the couch into a bed with sheets and blankets. Finally, he sat on the couch and gently patted Chia's bed.

Warily, she approached. She stepped over the donut, spun three times, then plopped, settled, and sighed.

Simeon did as well.

The sighing part.

As if some great weight had lifted off him.

He glanced up to meet my gaze.

In turn, I glanced at the clock on the wall. "It's only nine o'clock."

"Yeah."

"Are you tired?"

He shook his head "W-wired."

"It's been...an interesting day." I drew in a deep breath. "I want to set up your new computer. Get your data ported over, set up all the programs, and get you properly connected to the internet. I know this is a stupid question, but do you have your Wi-Fi password?"

He pointed to the desk. "H-hard-wired."

I hadn't looked closely enough to pick up on that.

Slowly, he rose—mindful of Chia. He approached me carefully. As if he worried I might break.

He wasn't entirely wrong about that.

With exquisite gentleness he grasped my right hand.

Although I'd seen it coming—because he'd telegraphed it clearly—I was still startled. I didn't touch people. That wasn't a thing. Marcus touched me in a detached clinical way. So did the doctors. But no one ever offered me physical comfort. Like Simeon was obviously doing now. Like he'd done before when I desperately needed a hug.

I blinked. Several times. "I can do this." I whispered the words fiercely. "I want to do this. For you. Because of all you've done for me."

He cocked his head.

I let out a shaky laugh. "Do you want me to start enumerating them? Because we'd be here half the night. We'd start with you calming me down after my freak-out and end with you allowing a dog into your life who you really don't need."

Where I'd expected him to laugh, his eyes flashed. "I w-want to keep her. But my grandparents d-don't need the stress."

"I..." I wracked my brains. "Aren't people with dogs healthier and happier? You saw Nanny. She was ecstatic."

"Right until Chia pulls her over, and she breaks a hip."

*Damn.* He wasn't wrong. We didn't know Chia. Or what she was capable of. I'd spotted a couple of canes and a walker by the door—but that didn't mean Nanny and Bops would actually use them. Stubborn was a word I associated with both. On the other hand, I'd seen no sign of vanity. They were logical folk. Hopefully if a cane would help, then they'd use a cane. "If I set up the internet, will you look at grabby things?"

He blinked. "You r-really want her to stay that much?"

I shook my head.

Then nodded.

"I want what's best for all of you. And if that means finding a different home for Chia, then I'll support that. But..." I flashed back to earlier. "She brings life into the house. And I remember." I used the hand he wasn't holding to gently poke his chest. "You told me how much you wanted a dog growing up." *Go for it.* "And I did too. If you adopt Chia, I'll feel responsible to make certain she's getting everything she needs."

Simeon chuckled. "You p-planning to come up here and check on h-her?"

"Absolutely. She's, like, my goddog. Or, like, my dog niece. I rescued her." *Okay, you might be overplaying your hand.*

"I c-can search for grabby things on my phone."

The phone he used to communicate when he didn't want people to know about his stutter. The stutter I didn't even notice anymore. "No. Computer."

He huffed. Then appeared to relent. He squeezed my hand. "Do you w-want something to drink?"

*Yes. Victory.* Even as I had the thought, though, my chest tightened at the thought of sitting at a keyboard. "Yeah. A tea would be great. Or hot chocolate. A bit of caffeine won't be too bad."

"Two h-hot chocolates coming up." He glanced down to Chia.

Who was fast asleep.

"She's tired after her adventures."

"W-we can maybe..." He blinked. "W-we could give it a test run. But only if Nanny and Bops b-behave." His smile turned rueful.

"I think, for you, they'd try."

He met my gaze.

I winked.

He released my hand and gestured to his mini kitchen. With a bar fridge, a sink, a microwave, and an apartment-sized dishwasher, the space ran along the back wall of this massive room.

When he headed that way, I slowly spun back to the desk. "Oh, Simeon?"

He was back at my side in an instant.

"Could you lift the box and maybe remove the laptop? I don't know how heavy it is." Probably something I could do myself, but I didn't want to touch the thing until absolutely necessary.

He nodded. Then, with little fanfare, he shifted his current laptop to the side, moved the box from the floor to the desk, and set about removing it. To my relief, he also sorted out the power cord and plugged in the new laptop. I hadn't considered that, and leaning over to figure out the power bar wouldn't have been a good idea. "D-do you want me to grab a second chair? Bops used t-to sit next to me while he showed me how to work it."

"That's a great idea."

Another quick nod and he headed upstairs. A few moments later, he returned with a kitchen chair. Not the most comfortable, but it'd do. I was to be treated to a beautiful, ergonomic chair. Probably set to Simeon's large frame...but I'd manage.

When he stepped back, I stepped forward. I swiveled the chair, gingerly sat, and slowly turned to face the two laptops. *See? Nothing bad is going to happen.*

"Ryan..."

I turned and, in just a moment, I had a ball of black fur on my lap. She licked my face, then settled on my knees. Quizzically, I gazed up at Simeon.

He held up his hands. "I d-didn't tell her that you needed her. But I think you do."

Slowly, I stroked her curly wool-like fur. "Yeah, maybe." I eyed the computers. "This is going to be awkward."

Simeon held out his hands. "I c-can take her."

Instinctively, I curled my arms around her. "We'll cope."

He grinned. "Yeah. I t-think you will."

With that, I tackled the laptops.

# Chapter Twenty-Seven

Simeon

Watching Ryan's fingers fly across the keyboard was something to behold. He'd praised me for having an external mouse—as if that was something I'd known to do. Truthfully, I struggled with the trackpad, and Bops gifted me the mouse soon after he'd witnessed the pain and extra effort required on my part. I could secure the fidgetiest screw, but trackpads were beyond me.

Go figure.

Ryan explained things as he went along. How he was porting the data. How he was setting up the programs the same way so I wouldn't have a steep learning curve. How I needed to back more things up to the cloud as well as an external hard drive. My old laptop hadn't crashed—but he said it'd only been a matter of time. I needed to be more careful with my data.

I wasn't certain I trusted something I couldn't see. I could see my laptop. I supposed I'd be able to see an external hard drive.

On the other hand, I couldn't *see* the internet.

Except I didn't really trust it either.

Ryan continued to work, occasionally stopping to pet Chia.

She always rewarded him with little kisses to his hand.

He consumed three hot chocolates while he worked. *Did he used to mainline coffee or cola during those marathon gaming sessions?* He'd mentioned them. In passing. And I couldn't fathom spending so much time at the computer in one shot. That just...felt ridiculous. Perhaps if I was working on something critical...or helping someone. But just to play a game? I would never say I thought the endeavor was a waste of time. Certainly, for me, the thirty minutes I'd spent with Angus and Oliver had been more than enough.

"Okay." He clicked something else. "If I'm still here tomorrow, I can get Bops to show me how he does your accounting. Maybe I can get things organized between the two of you. The method you have now is labor intensive. You could streamline to be more efficient."

"B-but this is the way we've always done it." I scratched my nose.

"Sometimes there are better ways." He gazed at me with those intense blue eyes. "It won't be tough for me to show you." He pointed to the laptop. "The rest will keep."

"I checked the w-weather. It's supposed to snow pretty much f-for the next twenty-four hours. D-did you need to be anywhere?"

"Just physio on Monday. I can call Marcus if I can't make it. How about you?"

"J-just the prefab at Kennedy's. I'll n-need to clear a path from the main house. Unless Rainbow's d-done it."

He arched an eyebrow. "That's a long way."

I smiled. "Rainbow enjoys physical l-labor. I don't ask. She'll also have the horses to w-worry about. That's a lot."

"What she and Kennedy have created…" I sighed. "Along with Justin and Avery. Denise and Max…"

"Yeah. S-special." I stroked Chia who'd stubbornly remained in Ryan's lap. Good thing she was so light. Otherwise his legs might've gone numb.

"Will you take her?"

"Of course." Gently, I eased her onto my lap.

She licked my chin.

I grinned.

Ryan slowly rose.

"You o-okay?"

"Too long sitting." He laughed. Not a pleasant sound. "I used to sit for hours and hours without taking a break. So unhealthy. But now that I can't, I almost miss those days." He pressed a hand to his chest. "And I need to piss like no one's business."

"Ah. You know w-where it is." He'd needed to use it when he'd come over the last time. Before we'd headed upstairs for a quiet and non-stressful meal with my grandparents.

Ryan rose and headed to the bathroom. I'd have to go myself soon.

Moments after he'd gone in, he popped his head back out. "Do you have a spare toothbrush?"

I laughed. "In a drawer."

He disappeared.

And reappeared a moment later. "That's enough toothbrushes to survive until the next millennium."

Again, I laughed. "Nanny likes to s-stock up. She found them on s-sale."

He smiled. "You could have dozens of overnight guests and never run out." With that, he disappeared again.

I stroked Chia's fur. *I don't want dozens of overnight guests. I only want you.*

That thought struck me with a force I didn't expect. I knew I was gay. Had admitted that to my grandparents a long time ago. Had basically come out of the closet with Maddox, Gio, and Ryan last week. I could've refused to answer. I could've lied. But, in that moment—with that group of men—I'd felt comfortable.

Chia nuzzled my chest.

"We n-need to get you settled. I'll be on the c-couch right next to you. You n-never have to be scared again."

Ryan cleared his throat as he stood across the room. "We had this discussion—I'm taking the couch."

"N-no." Slowly I rose and carried Chia over to her bed. Again, she turned three times and settled.

"Simeon."

"N-no."

He sighed. "How about a compromise?"

I cocked my head.

"I'm going to assume you have a big bed."

I nodded. California king. Biggest Nanny could get from the mattress store over in Abbotsford. She's been pleased it fit the bedroom.

"We could probably share the bed." He smiled ruefully. "Your virtue is safe with me."

*But what if I don't want it to be?*

*Wait.*

*Where did that thought come from?*

Ryan was injured and still healing. He'd shown zero interest in me—either romantically or sexually. And I didn't do one-night stands. Hell, I didn't do any stands. I couldn't argue with his logic, though. Two adult men. Sharing a bed.

*You could just go upstairs and sneak into the spare bedroom. Nanny wouldn't be shocked to see you in the morning.*

*Yeah, but that means being away from Ryan and Chia...they might need me.*

"I might jostle you."

"You might." Ryan tilted his head. "So I should take the couch—"

"No." *Just give in. What's the worst that can happen?*

I could think of a dozen things, but none seemed particularly realistic.

Finally, I nodded. "O-okay. We share a b-bed." My stomach clenched.

Ryan grinned. "Don't worry. This is a new experience for me." He eyed his clothes. "My jeans are in the dryer. These sweatpants are comfortable." He fingered his Henley. He'd need it tomorrow.

"I can g-give you a sweatshirt."

"That would be great."

I headed over to the bedroom.

Ryan followed.

Chia followed.

*Crap.* I halted.

Both my companions did as well.

"D-do you think we should m-move her bed? Or I c-can keep the bedroom d-door open."

Ryan eyed Chia. "I suspect she's going to follow us. Her entire world has been turned upside down today. I think having her bed in the bedroom isn't a bad thing."

I nodded. "Yeah." I entered the bedroom and opened the drawer for my sweatshirts. I had an adorable red Christmas one Nanny had bought. I hadn't had the heart to tell her the thing was too small. She'd inquired once—and I'd told her I was saving it for a special occasion. As I handed it to Ryan, I acknowledged this was a pretty special occasion. Quickly, I headed into the main room to grab Chia's bed. I didn't want Ryan to feel uncomfortable changing around me.

As I returned to the bedroom, though, I winced. I'd miscalculated. Badly.

Ryan was struggling to get out of his Henley. And his scars were on full display.

Since his face was covered, I tried to quietly back away.

And stepped on Chia's paw. Or tail. Or something.

She yipped. More of indignation, I hoped, then any actual injury.

"It's okay." Ryan's voice was muffled. "I could use help. It's been a long day, and I don't usually wear things I need to pull over my head."

I laid Chia's bed in the corner of the room, then I moved to Ryan. Figuring things out didn't take much time. Not staring at the vicious scars was another thing. Obviously they'd healed enough to not need bandages anymore. I'd cut myself badly a couple of years ago and I quickly reviewed just how long it had taken to fully heal. Even now, I had a white scar left. *Will he always be like this? The pain?* Emotional and physical.

Gently, I helped him out of the Henley.

Our gazes met.

He swallowed. "One day, like ten years from now, they'll be pale like Adam's." He blinked. "I keep telling myself that I'm lucky my face isn't scarred—but he seems to have made a happy life for himself. He said..." Another swallow. "He said going to Healing Horses really helped."

"They'll h-help you too." I snagged the sweatshirt. "N-not as garish as Quinton's sweater..." Just a Christmas tree, mistletoe, and a pile of presents. Nanny had thought it would put me in the holiday spirit one year when I'd really been missing my mom. Not my dad...just my mom.

"Quinton is bad news."

I laughed. "J-jealous?" I meant it as a joke, but his serious expression had me hesitating.

He cleared his throat. "Maybe."

I gathered the sweatshirt the way my mom used to so I could help her. "J-jealousy is a wasted emotion. Especially w-when it's not warranted." I gestured for him to put his arms out.

He obeyed. He winced...but he managed.

My heart ached. "Quinton is j-just a friend. A good guy. He t-took care of Adam. He helps people. That's r-really cool."

Our hands brushed as he put his arms in the holes. Once he'd succeeded at that, I slowly eased the sweatshirt over him, mindful to not touch him anywhere else. He didn't need that.

He popped his head out. His hair was disheveled, and I resisted the urge to smile. He looked absolutely adorable. He pulled the sweatshirt into place and then cleared his throat. "Sorry."

I blinked. "W-what for?"

"For not being capable of doing things for—"

I moved swiftly, placing my finger over his lips. I couldn't take it. Yes, I probably shouldn't be touching him. But I couldn't hear any more without losing it completely. "I d-don't care about that. If you can p-put up with my stutter, then I can help you while not judging."

This time, he blinked. "*Put up with*? What kind of next-level bullshit is that?"

I winced.

He held up his hand. "Sorry, I keep forgetting you don't swear."

Part of me was absurdly grateful, and flattered, that he'd noticed. "I c-can swear. If I hit my f-finger with a hammer? I p-promise you I can swear."

"Still, you're getting off topic."

"I d-didn't know there was a topic." A complete bald-faced lie. He wanted to talk about my stutter. Specifically, my perception of my stutter. Well, just as he didn't want to talk about his scars, I didn't want to talk about my defect either. That's what my father had always called it. *A defect.* And, of course, if Nanny heard me speaking like that, she'd have washed my mouth out with soap. Or threatened to. She'd spent the last seventeen years trying to undo the damage inflicted by my father in the first nineteen.

Ryan pointed to his scars. "They might heal, but they'll never go away." He gently laid his hand on his heart. "I'll miss my friends every day. Justin says eventually I'll reconcile the fact I lived, and they died. The fact there wasn't a damn thing I could've done to prevent it. That I wasn't responsible."

"O-okay. I think it's admirable t-that you're trying." I remembered him telling me about his friends. This must be so hard for him. Slowly, I offered my hand.

Just as slowly, he took it.

"Y-you can tell me anything. I'll always l-listen."

He pursed his lips. "Same goes. But I'll argue the hell out of you if you say that bullshit again. I don't know where it came from—"

"M-my father." I hesitated. "I c-can hear his v-voice in my h-head." *Great. Extra stuttering because I'm getting emotional.* I squeezed his hand. "I p-promise to try harder. F-for you."

"Well, I think you should try for yourself—but I'll take whatever I can get." He yawned. "I think I need to go to bed."

I smiled. "Please d-do. I'll be there in a m-moment." I still felt I should be sleeping on the couch, but I was too tired for a fight. Also, I didn't want to leave him alone. He might be by himself every night, but he was in a strange house. That had to mess with his head. At least, it would have with me. I squeezed his hand again, then gently let it go. I moved to the dresser and grabbed sleep pants and a T-shirt. I tended to sleep hot, and I'd just given him a sweatshirt. Hopefully this might balance us out.

In the bathroom, I pissed, brushed my teeth, and got undressed. In the height of the summer, I might sleep naked. The rest of the time I wore clothes—to be respectable if Nanny or Bops needed me urgently.

*I'm not going to have them forever. I need to plan accordingly. But I can't face this. Not yet.* I understood time was finite. And they were getting frailer. And having a dog wouldn't necessarily be a good thing. On the other hand, they'd always wanted a great-grandchild, and Chia could be that. God knew, I was never having kids. Because to have kids, I'd need a spouse. And God knew, again, that I had zero prospects.

After shutting off the lights, I headed back toward the bedroom. When I stepped across the threshold, Chia yipped.

I gave her *the* look. "I l-live here. P-protect us against intruders."

She huffed, then quickly resettled.

A chuckle came from the bed. "Do you think she understood you?"

"I d-don't know. I figure if I speak to her like a c-child, then she might understand me."

Another chuckle as I put away my clothes. "Simeon, I don't think *intruder* is likely part of her vocabulary. Maybe not even *protect*."

I shrugged. "We d-don't know. I'll c-call Torah tomorrow."

"Is it not tomorrow already? I feel like I've been awake for days. Like before…"

I slid into bed. I wanted to gather him into my arms—which was a weird feeling—but I couldn't. Wouldn't. Not only because I didn't have permission—although that was a big one. But because I worried about hurting him. I worried that both psychologically and physically, I might injure him. I flipped off the lamp.

Ryan gasped.

"Oh yeah. I can t-turn it off."

"No…I like it."

The room glowed with a low-purple light. Barely noticeable, but there. I wasn't going to tell him the reason. "D-dark room. I need to find my way around if something happens." *Please don't suggest I just turn on a light. Please don't judge.*

"I…I like it. I'm not in the dark anymore. I need to never be in the dark again."

I didn't know if he meant metaphorically or physically. Possibly both. "Sleep, Ryan. I'll watch over you."

He yawned again. "Yeah, I believe you will."

To my surprise, his breathing evened out shortly after that. *He must really be tired. I'll have to make sure he doesn't overdo it again.* To which I reminded myself I couldn't be telling him what to do. Or what not to do. He was an adult. A warrior. More than I'd ever done.

Eventually, I drifted off as well.

# Chapter Twenty-Eight

Ryan

A wareness came in degrees. The ache in my chest that was always present. The warmth surrounding me. The sense of comfort. Finally, of strength. Not necessarily mine...but someone's.

And then the weight on my legs registered.

*Don't panic. You're not in the war. Just...reason it out.*

I shifted.

Something shifted with me.

"Are you o-okay?"

Simeon's sleep-roughened voice washed over me.

All the events of the previous day came flooding back. I grinned. "We have company."

My bed companion sat up abruptly. "Chia?"

"Yeah, she's on my legs."

"I'll g-get her off." He was already moving.

"It's okay."

"No. She shouldn't be on the b-bed." He bent forward.

Taking the warm blankets with him.

I groaned. "It's too early." I didn't actually know the time. I'd put my phone on the nightstand, said a prayer it wouldn't run out of battery, then realized it didn't matter if it did. Who would call me anyway?

"She m-might need to go out."

"By all means." Simeon had a beautiful sandy-brown comforter with stripes of burgundy and deep green. A pee spot wouldn't match. "I should get up too."

"N-no, don't." He snagged Chia and rose. "Unless you have t-to, uh, you know..."

"Piss?"

He sucked in a breath. "Uh, yeah."

"I do need to. Too much hot chocolate."

"And eggnog."

"And eggnog." Although that had been earlier in the evening.

He rose and scooted out of the room with the pooch in his arms.

I gingerly rolled to my side and then eased off the bed. Marcus had shown me how to do this so as to cause the least amount of pain. I wandered out into the main room to find morning light hadn't even appeared. I pissed, washed my hands, and glanced in the mirror. *My beard's getting a little bushy. Will anyone care? Will Simeon?*

Because for the first time in my life, I was feeling stirrings of attraction for a man. Anyone who came before—the few hookups—had been about satisfying a physical itch. Well, not even that. They'd usually been in retaliation for something nasty my father had said. As if I could prove my manhood by hooking up with a guy and getting my cock sucked. Or, on occasion, sucking a cock. *Enough of this.* Dwelling on past decisions—pathetic as they might've been—wouldn't keep me moving forward.

Exiting the bathroom, I found Simeon toweling down Chia as she licked his face.

"Did she?"

"Yeah. I have to r-remember the spot because I didn't take a bag, and it's f-freezing out."

"How about the snow?" He'd turned off the outside light, so all I saw was darkness.

"It's b-bad. We're protected under the d-deck. Beyond that, though, it's a w-wall of snow."

"Yikes."

He nodded. "We have s-supplies."

I grinned. "I figured you might. You seem very much like a boy scout."

"Uh, no. G-group activities weren't my thing."

Of course not. Because likely kids made fun of him. I could hope not, but I knew how cruel kids could be. They'd taunted me about my weight constantly. So had my father. And apparently Simeon's father had been no better.

I yawned.

"G-go back to bed."

I tried to wave him off. Then caught sight of the clock. "It's five-thirty."

He gently eased the dog back down. "G-go back to bed."

"Will you come?"

He tilted his head. "I have to...p-piss. Then I'll come b-back."

I grinned. "See? I can corrupt you."

"You're a b-bad influence on me."

Taking that the wrong way could've been so easy. But I chose not to. If he was saying this, he likely meant it as gentle teasing—not something nasty.

Feeling a chill, I made a beeline back to bed as he headed to the bathroom.

Chia followed me and flew up onto the bed.

I gaped. How something so small could clear that height was beyond me. I eyed her. "You're going to be a bad influence on me."

She blinked.

I pointed. "Your bed."

She blinked.

I made a shooing motion.

She remained unmoving.

"You're n-not in bed?" Simeon stepped into the room. "Oh."

"Yeah. *Oh.* I asked. Nicely. I tried to shoo her." I winced. "I would've lifted her—"

"No." He stepped toward her. "S-she just needs a firm hand." He lifted her into his arms.

She licked his cheek.

He giggled.

*Oh yeah...firm hand. She's got you wrapped around her little paw.* I eyed her. *Okay, maybe both of us.*

Simeon laid her on her bed. "S-stay."

She blinked.

I laughed. "We'll see how long that lasts."

He sighed. Then gestured for me to get into bed.

I did—disappointed to discover any residual heat had dispersed. I shivered.

"You c-cold? I can turn up t-the heat."

"It's fine." I settled as best I could—ignoring the ache in my chest.

"I w-wish I could cuddle you."

"Oh?" Another thing I'd never done. Before I could think better of it, I patted the spot beside me. "You could get close."

A long moment went by. "I d-don't want to hurt you."

"I promise I'll say if it hurts. Just don't put pressure on the center of my chest." I figured he knew that much. He'd seen the scars. And he hadn't run for the hills. In retrospect, I shouldn't have ever thought he might. That just wasn't who he was.

Slowly, inch by inch, he eased toward me. Eventually, he pressed against me. "L-like this?"

I shifted so I could settle against him. "Yeah, this is nice." Awkward as fuck...but nice. I moved my hand and, after a moment, he snagged it.

A sense of well-being settled over me.

"Thank you."

"You w-welcome." He gently laid his cheek against my shoulder. "S-sleep."

Surprisingly, I did.

When I awoke, a feeling of refreshment settled over me. Different from before. A calm like I hadn't felt in a long time. I shifted.

"You o-okay?"

I nearly snapped that I didn't need him asking me that all the time. Then I remembered that, first, he'd seen my scars. Secondly, he meant nothing by it. He wasn't hovering. He was merely concerned. "Yeah, I'm okay." To my surprise, we still held hands.

Then, from nowhere, an impulse overtook me. "Simeon?"

"Uh-huh."

"Would you...?" I couldn't finish the thought.

He stiffened.

Damn.

"What's w-wrong? What d-do you need?"

*For you to kiss me. For you to prove to me that I'm still desirable. For you to remind me what life can be like.*

I hesitated. That was asking so much. Just because we held hands, didn't mean he felt *that* way toward me. Just because we shared a bed, didn't mean anything would happen. He was being solicitous. Kind. Courteous. Chivalrous.

"Ryan?"

"Kiss me?" *Holy hell. Oh well, you'll know in a moment if you've read this all wrong...*

"M-me?"

"No, the other hot guy sharing a bed with me." *Sarcastic much?*

He made a show of lifting the blankets and searching around.

I laughed.

He did too. "N-nope. No other h-hot men." Then he stilled. "You think I'm h-hot?"

I squeezed his hand. "Yeah, I do." He wasn't asking because he wanted extra flattery. He was asking because he needed reassurance. That hurt my heart.

"O-okay. I...uh..."

"You lean over me—without touching my chest—and you press your lips to mine." Might've been a stretch to assume he didn't have experience with kissing...but a pretty decent guess, if I had any idea. Not that I had much more. Suck-and-jerk sessions rarely involved kissing.

"O-okay." He released my hand so he could shift himself. Slowly, he positioned himself so he loomed over me. He laid his hand on the pillow next to my ear.

I had to turn my head.

He smiled. Barely visible in the weird purple light. *Does he have blackout blinds, or is there no window in this room?* I was trying to orient myself in relation to the main room when he brushed his lips to mine.

Feather light. Gentle. No pressure.

He pulled back.

"More."

"Yeah. O-okay."

This time, when he pressed his lips to mine, I nibbled along his lower lip.

When he opened his mouth—likely from surprise—I thrust my tongue in. I used the hand not settled between our bodies to grasp his head and to encourage him to come closer.

He hesitated before scooching closer.

Always clearly mindful of my injury.

Which left a pang of regret echoing through me. Still, I kept plundering his mouth. Hoping beyond all hope that he'd respond.

Then, quite suddenly, he did. He thrust his tongue into my mouth, then twined his tongue with mine, seeking some kind of intimacy.

Or I hoped that was what he was doing. For myself, stirrings raced through me as my blood heated. I'd never had this—a connection of mind, body, and spirit. As if that revelation freed me, something else stirred within me.

*Holy fuck.*

Something I'd never thought I'd feel again—physical desire. Something coursing through my veins. Something seeking more. I pulled back from the kiss.

Simeon's eyes were nearly black in the dark light.

"I need to ask you something." My breathing was labored, but my chest didn't hurt more than a twinge.

"Anything."

"Would you touch me?"

He cocked his head.

"Intimately. Would you be willing to put your hand on my cock?"

His eyes widened.

*Shit. I'm asking too much.*

Slowly, though, he shifted so his weight was off his hand and back onto his side. He traced his hand down my jaw to my throat.

He was about to lift it away, when I grasped his wrist.

"Gentle."

Nodding, he placed his hand back on my throat.

Slowly, and with infinite care, I guided his hand down my sternum. Down my torso. Down to my navel.

*I survived. Someone touched me and I'm still here.*

And still chubbing up.

I guided his hand farther, encouraging him to reach under the waist of the sweatpants. I held his gaze because if he was uncomfortable with any of this, I needed to know. *Should've told him he didn't have to. Should've given him a way out if he needs it.* Even as I had that thought, though, I forced it back. Simeon might be naïve about certain acts between men—but he wasn't a pushover. Peer pressure wouldn't force him to do something he didn't want to.

And as he grasped me intimately, he pulled his lower lip through his teeth.

My cock reacted to the touch. Slowly, it stiffened. Slowly, it came to life. Slowly, realization dawned. Maybe I hadn't been able to get hard before because I hadn't had a reason to. I certainly hadn't felt horny since—

*No. Don't go there. Just enjoy the moment.*

"D-do you like this?"

I nearly pointed out that of course I did. That I wouldn't be getting harder by the moment if I didn't really fucking *like this*. But those weren't the words he needed to hear. "Yes, Simeon. More, please."

Experimentally, he encircled me. He ran his thumb along my slit, as if trying to memorize me. As if trying to figure out what I liked.

*All of it.*

Then he squeezed me again.

"Yes. Like that."

He tugged.

By now, I was fully erect. "I need you. Please."

Slowly, he nodded. He often took his time with things—as if uncertain but also determined. He tugged my shaft. He twisted and applied more pressure.

I sucked in a breath.

He stilled.

"No." I nearly wailed that. "Keep going. You're making me feel *so* good." And, knowing I could've tried this myself didn't matter. *He* was doing this to me. He was making me feel good. And he was in control. Perhaps that, more than anything else, was the permission I needed. "I want to come." Words I'd never thought I'd utter again.

"Y-yes. Please." He continued with the rhythm he'd set. Maybe not as forceful as I'd expected, but just his grip on me was enough to bring me along for the ride. And, as my heart rate increased, awareness of my precarious health situation flitted through my mind. Dr. Raymond had said resuming full sexual activity might be risky, but a little excitement wasn't going to set me back. Marcus had said basically the same thing.

Then, suddenly, my balls drew up. I gave in to the pleasure that washed over me like nothing I'd ever felt before. Sure, I'd had orgasms—but not like this. I spurted cum over Simeon's hand as he gently nursed me through the climax.

And gently was the right word. He coaxed me into giving up those last few drops while clearly understanding I was sensitive. I gazed into his eyes. Blinked. Then didn't even care as tears leaked down my temples. "Thank you." I might've said that in a broken whisper.

"You're c-crying." His face crumpled.

I reached up to grasp his face, feeling the stubble of a day's beard growth in my hands. "Happy tears. Simeon, I promise you—happy tears. I..." I just couldn't find the words. Not so much that my cock wasn't broken anymore, although that was a pleasant surprise, but that I'd found joy in a physical connection. That I'd enjoyed what we'd done. It hadn't felt perfunctory. Like getting my rocks off.

*You're reading too much into this.*

Still, his expression didn't ease.

"What can I do to assure you that I'm okay?"

Simeon blinked. "I d-don't know. I d-didn't think someone would cry after, you know..."

"I would say it's not a normal reaction, but I honestly don't know." His brow knit in evident confusion.

*Make him understand.* "I've never been with someone I care about. Certainly not someone I care about as much as I care about you." *Like I think I might love you...but that's just the hormones talking...right?* I just didn't know. What I knew for certain was making him understand was important. I yanked him in for a kiss.

He responded again—in that unschooled way I found so sexy. That he didn't have experience was a turn-on for me. We could go through this together. I pulled back to meet his gaze. "Now you."

Twin spots of color appeared—so pronounced I could see them even in the low light. "Uh..." He winced. "I...uh..."

Understanding dawned. "You already came."

He winced. "You were s-so sexy and…"

"You were so primed." I grinned. "I like the idea of you coming just while giving me pleasure. But you have to promise to let me return the favor. I'd like to give you a hand job."

His mouth dropped open.

I resented having to *find the right position*, but I also loved the idea of being his first. Because, deep in my soul, I knew he'd never done any of this with anyone before. Had never let himself trust. Had never let his guard down. *Well, I'll just have to show him.* And try not to fall even harder. He hadn't made a declaration. Neither had I. But I had so little to offer that it didn't feel right.

He kissed me.

When he pulled back, I grinned.

"I accept." He slowly withdrew his hand from my track pants. "But first I need to shower, and we need to get your jeans."

Right. Clothes—easy. Not falling in love—much harder.

# Chapter Twenty-Nine

Simeon

After I showered and dressed, I headed upstairs to retrieve Ryan's jeans.

Nanny gave me a pointed look as she made waffles. "Extra this morning?"

Heat rose to my cheeks.

She made her way over to me, pressed a hand to my hot cheek, and smiled. "I like him, Simeon. You could do a lot worse."

"He's n-not mine to have."

Her smile was that knowing grin Mom used to give me. "But he might be. Keep an open mind, okay?" She pointed outside. "Snow's still falling. Hopefully the power lines don't come down."

Snow this thick could fell a weakened tree branch and easily take out a line. "We have the g-generator."

"That's true." She moved away from me so she could put the maple syrup and butter on the table. "Although I suspect you can generate your own electricity with that man downstairs."

*Oh God, does she know? Is it written on my face? I never could hide anything from her.* "N-not going to happen."

"You never know. Make sure he's been tested. Although I suppose if he's been in the hospital and not been with anyone, it should be safe." She snapped her fingers. "Should've ordered condoms with the last grocery order."

Okay, I was quite certain my cheeks matched Rudolph's nose in bright-red color. I'd gone to the store where my friend Nadia worked for years, and recently she'd switched to delivering the groceries instead of working a till. She said it got her out of the store and gave her variety in her workday. She also knew just about everyone in town.

I certainly didn't need her speculating on my sex life. Especially because my grandparents weren't likely the ones needing condoms. If Nadia knew... Well, first, that information might not stay secret for long. Secondly, I'd have to start buying groceries myself. Which I would've happily done, but Nanny felt I was too busy, and she liked using her money to ensure Nadia had work. I was pretty certain the woman had plenty of work, but I'd learned long ago not to argue with Nanny when she was in one of *those* moods.

"If I n-need them, I can b-buy them myself." I held up Ryan's jeans. "He'll be out of the s-shower and needs these."

Nanny grinned as she removed the waffles. "I think he has a fine ass."

I nearly tripped as I headed downstairs. *My ninety-something grandmother did not just make a comment about our houseguest's ass...right?* Because now all I'd be thinking about was said ass. I wasn't someone who necessarily noticed people's looks. I just wanted to be their friends and, often, after they heard my stutter, they didn't want anything to do with me. Like I was too much work or something.

Nadia had always treated me with great respect.

And now I'd associate her with Nanny's threat to get condoms on her next grocery order.

Sheesh.

Ryan stood at the floor-to-ceiling windows, wearing my bathrobe, which swamped him, gazing out over the winter wonderland.

I approached as noisily as I could. I had a strong startle reaction—especially when I was deep in thought—and I suspected he was the same way now. Maybe always had been...but was definitely now. "Jeans."

He turned with a grin on his face. "I stole your bathrobe."

"I d-don't mind."

"We, uh, have to do laundry."

*What? Oh.* "Yeah. I have w-work clothes as well. Easy enough to d-do a load."

"Great." He winced. "I sort of need my underwear washed as well. I can go commando for a bit, but I prefer having my bits...protected...from denim. But I'll be okay for a bit."

I grinned. "C-consider it done. You c-change and I'll start a load. I have m-my own machine down here."

"Great. I, uh, left everything in a pile on the floor of your bedroom."

I headed that way. Then burst out laughing.

Ryan came up behind me. And laughed as well.

Chia lay sprawled over our dirty clothes.

"She has a n-nice bed, and she does this?"

He laughed. "Yep. I think that's par for the course with a dog." He whistled.

She popped her head up.

I crouched to her level. "Are you h-hungry?"

She cocked her head.

"F-food?"

After a moment, she let out a little yip.

"I think Nanny m-made you some rice."

The dog's nose twitched.

"You'll eat it and b-be grateful. N-no going out today to get food. Sorry." I wasn't. Not really. Because I'd have an entire day with her. To find her quirks. To see how she got along with my grandparents. "I should've g-gotten Chloe's number last night."

"You said the police officer had it, right? Although he might be asleep. How about the vet? Or the trainer? Might be good to touch base with them."

"On a S-Sunday?"

"They always have the option of not answering the phone."

"T-true." I loved how logical Ryan could be. While I could be timid—especially about calling people—he appeared fearless. Or unconcerned. He was right. If Torah and/or Zephyra didn't want to speak to me, then they wouldn't answer the phone. "I'll t-text Torah after breakfast."

He gazed at me.

"W-what?"

"You haven't kissed me."

My eyes widened. Then I grinned. "You h-haven't kissed me either."

"Well, we need to rectify that." He raised his arms so he could run his fingernails through my stubble.

*Thank God there's not much of a height difference.* I didn't want him to hurt himself.

He wrapped his arms around my neck.

I bent to kiss him.

Our lips touched—soft and sweet. Then again—with a bit more pressure. Finally, he licked the seam of my lips.

Figuring that was the invitation, I opened my mouth and let him stick his tongue into my mouth. I'd always wondered about this. How it could feel so good. How it wasn't nearly as weird as I might've thought. I wound my arms around his slender waist and gently pulled him close. My cock seemed a little interested, but I gave it a stern talking to. Now wasn't the time. This was for gentleness. Tenderness. Solicitude.

Eventually, Ryan pulled back. His blue eyes were a little glazed. His smile was a little loopy.

I resisted the urge to ask him if I'd done it correctly.

His nose twitched. "Do I smell...?"

"Waffles and bacon." My grandparents didn't eat bacon, but Nanny made it for me on special occasions.

His eyes lit. "Back in a flash." Then he was gone.

*Should've told him he can get changed in here. I could leave...* Memories of helping him last night flashed in my mind. I noticed his Henley on the bed and, within just a moment, he was back—carrying the bathrobe and wearing the jeans. His nipples were hard peaks—likely because of the cold air. And his scars were clearly visible, but I didn't linger on them. Instead, I snagged the adorable sweater I'd given me last night. "Need help?"

He offered a soft grin. "I won't turn it down. Getting dressed and undressed are two of my least favorite tasks. It's why I often wear button-down shirts."

Which made sense since stretching his arms over his head seemed to cause pain. Or at least discomfort. As I helped him, I resisted the urge to ask if I could be doing anything else. He didn't need me fussing. I believed pretty strongly that if he needed something that he'd speak up.

Once he was settled, he clicked his tongue.

Chia leapt up from her spot.

I scooped up all the laundry to add to what I already had in the basket. Yep, a full load.

Ryan watched me.

I cocked my head.

"Waiting for you."

"N-no. Nanny's got fresh waffles. You g-go on up and start. I'm r-right behind you."

"Well, I wouldn't want to make the lady wait." He rubbed his belly. "I can't remember the last time I had waffles."

"Homemade."

His eyes lit. "Even better." He headed into the living room and then to the stairs. He gave me a cheeky grin before heading up with Chia by his side.

Affording me a perfect view of his truly stunning ass.

Remembering Nanny's comments had me blushing again. By the time I had the wash started and I headed upstairs, my cheeks felt cooler.

Bops waved from the kitchen table. "Thought you'd never be here. Ryan says he won't eat without you." My grandfather held up a piece of waffle. "I love you, but these are best hot off the griddle."

I grinned. "Yep." I moved to said griddle and gently nudged Nanny. "You g-go. I'll finish these up." I noticed little lines of strain on her face. That happened when she stood too long.

She pursed her lips.

I arched an eyebrow.

Silently, she moved to the table. She sat, then pointed at Ryan. "I'm here, you eat."

He gazed up at me.

I pointed to Nanny. "D-don't argue. N-not worth it."

The corners of his lips twitched upward. "Okay." With that, he buttered his waffles and loaded on the syrup.

I turned back to the griddle. *It's good to see him eating.* I didn't ever want to judge someone based on looks, but Rayn seemed skinny to me. As I'd explored him this morning, he'd felt bony. Insubstantial. *Except his dick.* Yeah, okay, except that. Heat rushed to my cheeks again as I remembered the first hand job I'd ever given. Oh, and the first kiss. Things I'd thought I'd never experience.

Ryan had to know how...innocent I truly was. I hated the word. Naïve felt just as bad. Raw. Untried. Untested. None fit. I was thirty-seven years old, for God's sake. How could I have not mustered the courage before now to ask a guy out?

Oh, because being shy with a stutter really didn't help. I also never wanted to assume either that a guy was gay or that he might be into me. Everett was gay...he wasn't into me. Quinton was gay. Or bi. Or something. He pretty clearly hadn't been into me. And I wasn't into either of them, so that wasn't a big deal.

I was into Ryan. Had been from the moment I'd seen him. Well, maybe not when he'd been scared in the bathroom. But certainly shortly thereafter. And the day he admitted he was gay? When I'd boldly told him I was as well? Well, for sure that day I'd known I was attracted to him.

Opening the griddle, I found the waffles toasted to perfection. I removed them, made certain we'd used all the batter, and shut the machine off. I never had a problem, if some batter remained, making some for later. Truly, I adored waffles.

I dropped into the chair next to Ryan, directly across from Nanny. She caught my gaze.

And winked.

*Goddamnit. The woman's going to be the death of me.*

Ryan moaned. "These are the best waffles I've ever had." He held his fork aloft.

"Really?" Nanny eyed him. "You're from fancy Vancouver."

"Well, the waffles served at brunch in The Georgian are good, but not like yours."

Nanny beamed. "Secret recipe."

"One I hope you'll share with me." Ryan cut off another piece. "Because these make me want to get my own waffle iron and learn."

"Simeon knows the secret." Nanny grinned at Ryan. "You'll just have to convince him to share that knowledge. Something tells me you can be very persuasive."

*Is dying from embarrassment a thing? I think it might be a thing.*

"I'm not certain Simeon's persuadable. He seems pretty stoic to me."

"He's ticklish." Bops grinned. "Always has been. Watch out though—he flails those arms something fierce."

Ryan grinned. "I'll watch out." He glanced down. "Thanks for making rice and veggies for Chia."

Nanny grinned. "Happy to do it. I was thinking of making some beef broth later. I could soak her rice in that to give it some flavor."

I eyed the empty dish. "S-seems to me she doesn't need help."

"Some flavor never hurt." Nanny waved her fork. "You should call Chloe today. Find out what Chia likes."

"I d-don't have her number."

"Well, unless she's disconnected Helen's landline, you should be able to reach her. I've got that number."

"Or you can call the vet or the trainer." Ryan offered me a sly grin.

I rolled my eyes.

"Simeon." My grandmother used *that* tone on me.

My cheeks heated yet again. "S-sorry."

"I think that's a very good idea. Ryan can help your grandfather clean up while you go downstairs and make those calls."

"I c-can make them up here."

Nanny gave me a not-so-subtle look with a raised eyebrow.

"No."

She glared.

Bops shrugged, trying to look all innocent.

Ryan glanced back and forth between the three of us. "I don't mind. Truly."

I warned him, "Bops is g-going to grill you."

He snickered. "I think I can handle a little interrogation. They want to know what my intentions are."

Yep. Back to Rudolph's nose again for my cheeks. Crimson was on the spectrum of red...right?

"Quite right, young man." Bops wiped his hands on his napkin, having devoured his waffles.

"All good, I promise you." Ryan met my gaze. "We're taking it slow."

*Oh we are, are we?* A hand job minutes after our first kiss didn't feel slow. On the other hand, we'd known each other for more than two weeks. Two very intense weeks. I couldn't think of anyone—aside my grandparents—who knew me this well.

I cleared my throat. "I'm g-going to try to clear the driveway."

Ryan arched an eyebrow. "It's still snowing."

"Right. B-but the more I clear, the easier it will be to get out t-tomorrow." Putting off those calls an hour was logical. Right?

Something flashed in his eyes. Then he smiled. "I can't help...but could I come out and watch?"

"You'll f-freeze. It's c-cold." I hadn't actually checked the temperature, but clearly we were below freezing.

"I've got my coat."

"Young man can wear my snow pants." Bops grinned. "He's about my size. I can gift him tons of stuff if he wants it. Well, maybe not my funeral clothes. Gotta look good when I go."

Inwardly, I winced. Outwardly, I smiled. "B-because you want pretty ashes." This was something my grandparents insisted on joking about. I was terrified of losing them—neither was afraid of death. Suffering? Yes. Death? No. They'd lived good lives. Their biggest fear was leaving me alone. But as much as I wanted to beg them to live forever, life didn't work that way. Also, both wanted to be cremated and to have their ashes spread in the forest at the back of the property. Which was so appropriate given they'd spent their entire married lives here.

"I don't want to take your clothes..." Ryan gave me a panicked look.

"Just the stuff I don't use anymore. If you don't want it, then you can donate it to the charity shop in town." He eyed Nanny. "You might consider thinning out your closet."

She gestured to Ryan. "I don't think they'll fit him. And anyway, I don't think he wears women's clothes." Then her eyes widened. "Unless you do. Which is totally fine. We're progressive here and don't judge—"

Ryan placed his hand over hers, stilling her. "I don't happen to dress in women's clothes. But I bet I'd be the best dressed in town if I did."

My grandmother actually blushed. "Well, there was that purple silk number I wore to my retirement party. I still fit in it."

That didn't surprise me. Both my grandparents were doing well for their ages. They had a few exercises they did every day. Stuff I'd asked

Marcus Branigan to show them a few years back when they stopped going out as often.

"S-snow pants?" Somehow we'd moved from me shoveling snow to them emptying closets. I eyed Ryan. "Unless you w-want to help in here." Giving him an out from the cold and wet felt right...and my grandparents shouldn't be emptying closets without assistance.

Ryan grinned. "How about Chia and I keep you company for a while, and then, when I'm too cold, I can help your grandparents organize any clothes they want to donate?" He turned to my grandfather. "I'll take a look at those clothes—if I'm not depriving you. I don't have much that fits me these days." He patted his flat stomach. "I used to be much heavier. And money's a little tight." He leaned in. "I don't like spending my father's money on myself, you know?"

"I do understand." My grandfather beamed his obvious approval. "We'll get you set up."

Four hours later, I made the difficult phone call to Chloe to get her consent for us keeping Chia. She'd been super grateful that we'd saved her dog from the storm, and although she agonized over wanting to keep her grandma's beloved pet, in the end, she decided we were Chia's best chance. I hoped we could live up to that.

I'd cleared most of the driveway and had showered, then I found Nanny in the kitchen making grilled cheese and tomato soup—with Ryan's help—and twelve bags of clothes in the garage.

Several marked Ryan.

I had no complaints about helping him try them on that evening. And the next. And helping him take them off.

Two days later, we made it to Maddox's house to retrieve his car.

We hadn't gone all the way...but we'd done just about everything else.

And although I hadn't told Nanny, I had the feeling she'd known.

Man, I was in deep.

# Chapter Thirty

Ryan

"Am I allowed to like someone. To be happy? I killed people." I held Justin's gaze as I sat in his office three days after the *epic* snowstorm. I was lucky Simeon had dug us out. Not that I hadn't enjoyed every moment in his home. His grandparents were truly some of the best people I'd ever met, and Simeon...? I tried to set aside all the good memories we'd created—but I was struggling.

"Do you see yourself as a killer?"

"I flew drones. I dropped bombs. People died."

"All that's true. But you can admit they would've killed you—given the chance."

"Well, duh. That's what soldiers do."

"And you don't see yourself as a soldier?"

This was the crux of my anguish. And he knew it. We'd done plenty of work leading up to this session. I just hadn't envisioned that Simeon, of all people, would be the impetus for this conversation. Last night, though, as I'd lain in his arms, I'd known I would have to find a way through this morass, or I could never truly enjoy the promise of what he offered.

Then he'd given me the most awkward blow job ever—and I'd gone off like a geyser because his inexperience was like an aphrodisiac to me. I *loved* being his first. To know he'd only ever done these things with me. And part of me wished I'd waited for him as well.

"Ryan?"

"Yeah?"

"Were you not also a soldier? Did you not choose to fight for freedom? For democracy? For the end of the unjust invasion of a peaceful nation?"

Justin had always been one hundred percent behind the Ukrainian cause. Or at least he'd been that way with me. And very current with the news. Whether that knowledge came from a desire to keep up with me or because he liked to have an understanding of the greater world, I wasn't certain. I'd certainly never looked beyond my father's basement.

Until the war.

"Yes, I did all those things. But I chose to be there—the other men didn't. They were defending their position. I was attacking. I thought..." I swallowed. "I don't know what I thought. I mean, I recognized I was just one person. And that one person is never the tipping point. But if I could go...and do something productive with my life...then I might be worth more than I'd been as a gamer in my father's basement."

"Just remember that's *your* characterization."

I laughed. A hollow sound. "Oh, my father felt the same way. But every time I popped my head out, I'd do something...gauche. That was the word he liked to use. I didn't know how to move in his circles—and

I didn't want to. I didn't want to be vapid and obsequious. But hiding out and playing games wasn't much better."

"You made the decision to change the trajectory of your life."

"Yes."

"Do you feel you made the wrong choice?"

"I..." Flashing to my friends who'd died, I just didn't know the answer. "I couldn't keep them alive." I'd told Justin about them. He'd sat quietly and listened. He hadn't judged.

"If you'd died, and they'd lived, would that have been better?"

"Of course."

"But life doesn't work that way."

"No." I winced. "It doesn't."

"Can you discover a way to find meaning in their deaths?"

"No."

He stilled.

Okay, maybe a little harsh. "There is no reason. It's all a waste."

"I could say you saved lives by doing what you did. I can point out you did everything in your power to keep your brothers safe. But that we don't really have a say in when our time's up."

"I don't know if I could ever go through that again." *There. That's the real issue.*

He cocked his head. "Are you thinking of going back to the war?"

"What?" I stared at him. Then replayed my words. "Oh." I waved off the notion I might go back. "No matter how desperate they might become, I'll never be allowed back. I'm a liability—in every sense of the word. I'm not fit for anything."

Before Justin could speak—as he clearly was about to do—I continued.

"I mean I don't know if I can endure that kind of loss. I mean, my mother and father will die. And that's sad. But mourning two people

I barely know is challenging. And maybe I will. Maybe their deaths will devastate me. I doubt it, though." I drew in a deep breath. "This is going to sound bizarre...but bear with me."

He nodded.

"I've met people. Here. In Mission City. People I've come to care for. Some...a lot. Simeon, for one. His grandparents for another." Since I'd dropped the *allowed to love* bomb right away, Justin didn't know this stuff yet. "I spent three days snowed in with them all. And their new dog, Chia. Sweetheart. Anyway, I... This is weird, right? That I feel more bonded to them than I ever have with my father? They're virtually strangers."

"Three days alone with people can create intense bonds. Forced proximity can have a way of compressing time. There's no room for subterfuge. You're completely reliant on each other. Given what I know of Simeon, if you'd asked to be left alone, he would've respected that."

I nodded.

"But you didn't. You asked him to include you with his family. He's spoken fondly of his grandparents."

"They're great people."

"So are you."

I waved him off.

"So are you."

I went to wave him off again...but I didn't. *Is he right? Am I a good person? I've killed. Yes, in the name of a higher purpose, but still...* Then I remembered all the atrocities committed by the enemy. All the horrible things they'd done to the innocent civilians. And maybe I hadn't killed the exact soldier who had perpetrated any one war crime—but I'd fought to ensure no other atrocities took place. I'd fought to keep the victims safe. "Is it really that easy?"

"No, it's not. I've done a lot of reading. Firsthand accounts of soldiers coming back from conflicts. Especially more recent ones—where technology has played a big part in warfare. What used to be straightforward, or at least somewhat, is now more complicated. It's never so easy as a battle against good and evil. But you were fighting for those who'd been invaded. Who'd done nothing wrong. That's powerful. I don't know if it's enough for you to forgive yourself. I'm hopeful that, in time, we can continue to work through some of this. Finding a place of peace would be good for you—but it's going to be hard-fought."

I fidgeted. I rubbed my damp palms up and down my thighs. I pressed a hand to my chest. *Oh, fuck it.* "Jake McGrath wants to interview me about my experiences for a story."

Justin blinked.

"Sorry, that sort of came out of left field, and I'm sure I could've found a better way to drop that little explosive device but I've been thinking about it, and it's been driving me nuts and—"

Justin held up his hand. "Okay, why don't we take this one step at a time. Jake McGrath, the reporter, wants to interview you."

"Yeah. I looked up his old stuff. He was a damn good journalist. Like...really good. He sure didn't do fluff pieces."

"No, he didn't." Justin scratched his beard. "I admit to not having seen much of his old stuff. I watched the other network." He smiled. "But when Marnie married Jake and he became part of the Mission City family, I admit to going down a rabbit hole one day."

"Those are dangerous." I hadn't gone too far down. The second time Simeon had gone out to clear the snow, I'd googled Jake on Simeon's computer and watched several of his award-winning stories. He and Jessica Stone were two of Canada's preeminent war correspondents. Jake was retired, but Jessica still reported from conflict zones. She'd done several pieces in Ukraine, in fact. Being on the computer had wigged me out. But not knowing what I might be getting into was more terrifying.

"Jake's good people. A true professional. I've always found his reporting fair. Not exploitative."

"So you think I should do it."

"I didn't say that." Justin cocked his head. "It's a huge leap from an ask to the decision to sit down and go on the record."

"My father won't approve."

He slowly nodded. "That's possible."

"He'll take away the credit card. I have some savings—but not much."

"That's a problem. Nothing insurmountable, though."

"I need to find a job."

"That's possible. You're still recovering, Ryan. Taking the time to do it properly is the right thing to do."

"He'll probably stop paying for me to come here."

"That would be unfortunate, but not something you have to worry about. We'll find a way for your sessions to continue. So put that worry out of your mind."

He said the words so definitively. As if this was a done deal. I'd read they had a sliding scale, but I'd never be comfortable pushing that slider down toward zero. The costs of running this place had to be phenomenal. I'd read they had grants, and generous benefactors, but surely they couldn't just...give away the counseling for free.

"Seriously, Ryan, don't worry about it. Focus on recovering. If you want to sit down with Jake—if you believe it's the right thing to do and that it might help you—then I'm fully supportive. I'll be here for you during the entire process." He appeared to consider. "You know Marnie McGrath?"

I nodded.

"Normally, I wouldn't suggest this. But if you look up Marnie Jones or Laura Derks, you'll find an interview she did with the media. Jessica Stone was the reporter on that story. Now, I would never speak for someone else...but I believe some good might have come out of that interview. At least for residents of Mission City, it gave them a better understanding of what she'd been through. People want to, generally, be supportive."

"So you think Marnie understands."

"Yes, I do. And then you might consider speaking to her. She's been open about what happened to her since that interview. She's become an advocate for victims. Quietly, though. In her own inimitable way."

"That simple?"

"No, not that simple. We'll need to prepare you."

"I...I think I'll want someone with me. Someone on my side."

"That's a great idea."

I swallowed hard. "Do you think...would it be wrong to ask Simeon?"

If he was surprised, his face didn't reveal it. "I think Simeon would be a great choice. He's a good man, Ryan. Mission City treasures him...even if he doesn't always perceive that affection."

I chuckled. "Yeah." Then I sobered. "He has his reasons for questioning."

"I have no doubt of that. I also hope him working on the ranch has given him a greater sense of community."

"Yeah, I think maybe it has." I rubbed my hands on my thighs. "Okay, I guess I have a favor to ask of Simeon and a phone call to make."

"Keep me in the loop. We've got an appointment on Friday."

I nodded.

"That's also the day of the Christmas parade. A tradition in Mission City. A bunch of us will be there with our kids."

"Sounds like it might be fun. We'll see, eh?"

"Yeah."

We rose.

"You're going to be okay, Ryan. I believe that."

For the first time in a long time, I believed him. Then I grinned. "Oh, and my cock may not be broken after all."

He stood gaping as I sauntered out of the room.

# Chapter Thirty-One

Simeon

I glanced nervously at Marnie.

After a moment, she held out her hand.

Although I didn't want to make her uncomfortable, I took the proffered comfort.

Ryan had wanted me in the room during the interview.

Jake's producer had suggested it would dilute the focus of the interview to have me present, and asked if Ryan could possibly do it just one-on-one. And of course, Ryan wanted to do the best job possible, so he'd said yes.

I'd just been so stunned that Ryan had asked me that I hadn't had the ability to form a coherent argument one way or the other.

In the end, we'd trusted the professionals. I *had* to believe Jake would take care of Ryan. I knew, without an iota of a doubt, that I'd be here for Ryan when he came out. Whether I'd be enough was an entirely different question.

"Jake's the best, Simeon." Marnie gazed at me with those stunning green eyes. "And if it's not working, he'll call it off."

"Ryan's f-father found out."

She squeezed my hand. "Ouch. My dad didn't find out until after I'd done the interview. Better to ask for forgiveness than permission?"

"D-did that work?"

She blinked a couple of times. "He said he was proud of me. And that he understood why I'd done what I'd done. I pretended I did it for myself, but I was also protecting someone else." She smiled a little shyly. "Easier to step out of my comfort zone when someone else's safety and well-being is on the line."

I believed her. I never would have chosen to be in a news bureau. Not in a million years. But for Ryan? I'd do just about anything for him. I'd even worn a button-down shirt and a nice pair of slacks in case he wanted to go out for dinner. I could smile now because he'd worn a Henley and jeans. A Henley in sky blue. That matched his eyes. I hadn't said that, though. He'd been too nervous. So I'd driven us, with eighties hair bands singing their...screechy tunes.

Ryan claimed I could pick the tunes on the ride home. Would he really want my Taylor Swift? I guess I was about to find out...

"How are you holding up?"

I met Marnie's gaze. "F-fine."

"It's a lot, you know. Jake tries to tell me it's okay. That he's fine with...everything. But he knows what I went through and that eats at him. I mean, he didn't know me back then, of course. I was just a child. But he's still angry at the man who..." She winced. "Just like he's angry at the man who hurt his niece."

Another rabbit hole I'd gone down. Ryan had shared Marnie's interview with the press from several years back. That had led to us doing some research about her and Jake's niece. My gut churned every time I thought about what they'd gone through. About how there were monsters in the world.

Ryan had faced his own monsters. Only they'd been soldiers doing what they were told to do. He felt that made them less culpable than if they'd been outright perpetrators. Then he'd recounted some of the stories he'd heard. About the war crimes. And I'd sat back in horror and listened to some of the most gruesome stories. Stuff that hadn't made the news.

And I understood his desire for vengeance on behalf of those who'd died or been maimed.

War made no sense. But when one side chose to be the aggressor, social niceties kind of went out the window.

The door to the studio opened.

Marnie gave my hand one last squeeze.

I rose.

Ryan stepped out.

He looked...beautiful. As he always did. He also looked...wrecked. As he sometimes did when he thought I wasn't looking.

I held open my arms.

He fell into them.

Marnie patted his biceps and then moved toward Jake. They headed down the hall a bit.

Ryan shook.

I grasped him tight.

"I did it."

"Y-yeah, you did. I'm so p-proud of you."

He let out a watery laugh. "You didn't see." While staying in my embrace, he pulled back so our gazes met.

"I d-didn't have to. You're h-here. That's brave. The r-rest is just icing on the cake." God, was that the right thing to say? It sounded so lame.

"Can we go? Jake said he didn't need me anymore."

"Of c-course. Do you want to go for l-lunch?" We were barely at noon. The parade, if we decided to go, wasn't until after six.

"There's a pub. Across the street. Do you think we could go there?"

"Of c-course." Great. Lame. I just didn't know what to say.

He pulled back, wiped his cheeks, then grasped my hand.

Jake stepped toward us with Marnie by his side. "You okay?"

Ryan nodded. "Yeah. Better than I thought. I'm going to talk to Justin next week. I thought I might need to talk to him today...but I sort of feel okay...?" He laughed. A little grating. "We'll see what my father has to say."

"He might surprise you." Marnie caught my gaze before looking at Ryan. "My father came around. We have a stronger relationship."

Another bitter laugh. "I'm not holding out much hope."

Jake nodded. "He got wind of this. I don't know how because we've kept it under wraps."

Ryan rolled his eyes. "He's got connections you and I can't even begin to fathom. Has he been causing problems?"

"Nothing we can't handle." Jake grinned. "We have a crack legal department. They haven't been impressed with his huffing and puffing."

"So he's not going to blow CNC's offices down?"

Jake barked out a laugh. "Oh, hell no. Don't you worry about that, okay? But I'll loop you in if things get out of hand. This story's going to air on Sunday's national news broadcast."

"Oh." Ryan squeezed my hand.

"You didn't realize?" Jake cocked his head. "I thought I made that clear."

Ryan waved him off with the hand not clutching mine. "I'm sure you did. Anyway, this was my chance to thank all the medical staff who helped me. I should do a better job tracking them down."

"If any of them step forward, I'll certainly let you know." Jake held out his hand.

As Ryan was gripping my right hand with his left, he was able to shake the man's hand. "Thank you."

Marnie smiled warmly. "You've got my number if you need to talk. I can say that I've literally been where you are now. I was lucky that my interview aired quickly, but you'll have time to prepare yourself."

"Is there such a thing?" Ryan's laugh was a little broken.

"There's healing." Marnie smiled. "And that means everything."

I believed her. Perhaps because I needed to—for Ryan's sake.

"We're heading out. Library Square Pub."

Jake grinned. "Been there quite a few times."

"Would you like to come?" Ryan gazed between Marnie and Jake.

Marnie shook her head with a bit of regret. "Olivia's watching Nate for me, and I need to get home."

My mind whirled. "D-do you need a ride?"

She grinned. "I drove in with Jake, but I'm heading home alone. He's going to take the West Coast Express after work."

Vancouver's commuter train ran from Mission City to Vancouver in the morning and back out in the evening.

"Ah."

"But thank you for the offer. You guys head to the pub." Hesitantly, she pressed a hand to Ryan's biceps.

After a moment, he relaxed into the touch.

Unsurprisingly, she'd read the room. "You'll be okay. I promise."

She probably didn't have the right to make that promise. That being said, for her to wind up where she'd started from was remarkable. If she could overcome so damn many obstacles, Ryan beating his demons into submission *was* possible.

"I'll be in touch. Sorry, I have to get to the editing suite." Jake pressed a kiss to Marnie's temple, then headed off.

Marnie pointed back the way we'd come. "Walk me to the elevator?"

Our studio escort, who'd been completely discreet until now, stepped forward.

I offered her a smile.

She returned it.

We walked Marnie to the elevator.

Ryan, to my utter shock, hugged her.

She pressed her hand to his cheek. Then, without another word, she was gone.

Moments later, our escort ushered us out onto Hamilton Street. I inhaled deeply. Snow still covered every surface with cleared paths down to the cement.

I wasn't a city boy. I might've grown up in a suburb of Vancouver, but I hadn't crossed the Fraser River often. Since I'd moved to Mission City and my grandparents' home in the country? I could probably count the number of times on one hand. In nineteen years, that was...vaguely disturbing. Except I had everything I needed in Mission City. Why come to this concrete jungle?

Ryan snagged my hand, and we walked toward West Georgia. We'd parked in the library parkade, so our car was close. He'd said the pub was at Library Square, so I assumed the place was also close. We crossed Hamilton Street at the light, and the sign for the pub came into view.

Oh, cute.

We stepped through the doorway, and a blast of warm air hit us. The snow wasn't melting outside because the temperature had yet to rise above freezing. We'd had several days of brilliant sunshine—but no warmth.

A woman approached us. "Two?"

"Yes." Ryan pointed to the far booth at the back.

She grinned. "Of course."

We followed her and then settled as she placed the menus on the table.

"Drinks?"

"W-water please."

"Me as well." Ryan unwound the scarf from his neck.

I unzipped my coat and removed it. My tendency to run hot sometimes was embarrassing, and I didn't want to be sweaty on what was, in essence, our first date.

*Wait. Is this a date?*

Ryan snagged the menu, then gazed at me. "What?"

"Is this a d-date?"

He chuckled. "Well, it's my treat. I have enough to cover it, even if Daddy's cut off the credit card. This might be my last chance to pay for a while, though, so be warned."

"I c-can pay." Not only did I make decent money, but I had a pile of it saved. Not paying rent for seventeen years had its advantages. I'd tried. At first, Nanny and Bops pointed out I was family and wasn't working. Then, when I was working, they pointed out I was just starting out. Then the excuse was that I was launching my business. Eventually they pointed out they were only really able to stay in their home because I was on the premises and doing all the work. In the end, I recognized my offers were hurting them. They wanted me to see their home as mine as well—which I did. To them, one didn't pay rent on the home one lived in.

About a decade ago, I'd stopped offering.

They'd both been much happier. Or perhaps that was just my perception.

"I know you can pay." Ryan scrunched his nose. "I didn't make any money in the army. I wasn't there to take their precious resources. My dad, to his annoyance, footed the bill for that as well."

The server paused by us. "Two glasses of water. Have you had a chance to look at the menu? Oh, I'm Lyssa, by the way." She offered a broad smile that lit her lovely dark-brown eyes. Her hair was in a ponytail and she vibrated...happiness.

Ryan eyed me.

I gestured for him to go first.

He ordered a burger with onion rings.

I ordered the same thing.

She departed with another smile.

Ryan winced. "Okay, was it me or was that an extra dose of happy?"

I grinned. "Happy is as happy d-does."

He guffawed. "You make me smile." He reached for my hand. "Thank you for that. Truly. I mean it."

I blinked. "T-that's what friends are for."

"Am I your friend?"

After a moment, I cocked my head. *Why is he asking this? Oh crap...am I assuming too much?*

He squeezed my hand. "I was kind of thinking we might be...more than friends?"

Definite question mark at the end of that sentence.

"M-more?"

*Goddamnit. For once could I not stutter on an important word?*

"Yeah." He stroked my thumb with his. "I..." He cleared his throat. "Okay, so I kind of had a revelation when I met with Justin yesterday."

He'd moved up his appointment by a day to prepare for today's interview.

"O-okay." I was always willing to listen, but part of me wondered if I was qualified to hear this.

"So, see, I thought I had a broken cock."

The water I'd been swallowing totally went down the wrong way. I yanked my hand from his, grabbed a napkin, and started coughing into it.

"Oh shit." His eyes widened. "Oops. Sorry." Except he didn't look all that contrite.

I narrowed my watery eyes.

"Are you okay?" Lyssa appeared out of nowhere. "I forgot to ask you how you wanted your burgers done. I'm still new here, and I forget the little things." She eyed me. "Let me grab you some more napkins."

Before I could say anything, she was hustling over to the bar.

Ryan held his hand over his mouth. He was enjoying my misery way too much. This was also the first time he'd truly smiled today...so if the amusement was at my expense, then I'd take my lumps and move on.

Lyssa arrived back with a pile of napkins about an inch high. She met my gaze.

I managed to nod.

"I'll take my burger medium." Ryan tipped his head at me.

I did some weird hand gesture that, fortunately, Lyssa seemed to understand as assent. Concurrence. Whatever.

By the time she was gone, Ryan was full-out laughing.

I wiped my eyes, swallowed, then smiled as well. Perhaps also shaking my head ruefully. "Y-you were saying?" I purposefully pushed my glass well out of the way.

He glanced over his shoulder. The booth next to us was still empty, a hockey game from somewhere was playing on the television behind the bar, and the music was pretty loud.

"I'll t-tell you if I see Lyssa coming this way."

"Yeah. I figured the kitchen would take time to prepare the food, and we'd have privacy." Unrepentantly, he grinned. "Do you think she heard me?"

"N-no idea." My breathing had finally returned to normal. "B-broken..." I was capable of saying the word. I just wasn't going to.

"Cock." He waggled his eyebrows.

*How can he joke about this? This sounds serious. Well...roll with it.* "Yeah."

"So. I never thought I had a particularly high sex drive. TMI, I know, but I need to be honest—and not just because Justin says so."

I nodded.

"I had sex a few times. Random hookups. I just figured...you know...that's what guys do. I didn't want to be the loser in the basement who never got any action."

*Ouch.* Of course, in a real sense, I was the loser in the basement who never got any action. I understood, though, that I wasn't who he meant.

"Then Ukraine and all that, and when I come back, I have zero interest in sex. Okay, fine. Eventually, though, as I'm healing, I'm thinking...like I should jerk off or something, right? Just to make sure it works."

I wanted to point out he'd been recovering from life-altering injuries...but now didn't seem the time.

"And I couldn't do it. So then I figured something was wrong with my head and that's why my cock was broken."

Still, I wasn't certain if I liked the way he said *broken cock*. Vulgar words never bothered me—I worked on construction crews, for crying out loud. But when someone spoke derisively of themselves? That hurt my soul.

"Then I'm kissing you, and…" He reached for my hand.

I offered it gladly.

"And, like, I got hard."

*I was there. I noticed. I did as well.*

"So I asked Justin about it." He laughed. "No, I told him on Tuesday I didn't think it was broken anymore. When I went back yesterday, he insisted we talk about it after I'd prepped for my interview."

"And?"

Ryan's expression turned thoughtful, with one eye sort of squinting. "He asked me if I'd ever considered that I might be demisexual."

I blinked. Then wracked my brain for that term. I'd done a bit of internet research a while back, but hadn't found anything that might help me out of my predicament of being too damn shy and embarrassed about my stutter. So I'd powered down the laptop and read a book instead. "D-demisexual?"

"Yeah. Like, that I have to have an emotional connection with someone before I can move into the physical with them. That yeah, sure, I could have sex with random hookups but that was only after a hell of a lot of effort."

"O-okay." *Just act cool and let him explain it. Don't panic.*

"But like, with you, I have a connection. I mean, I hope you feel it too—"

"I d-do."

"Right. So Justin explained that if I was successful at making an emotional connection with someone, and the physical attraction followed, that I might be demi."

That sounded deceptively easy.

"W-what does that mean?"

"I..." He waved the hand not clutching mine. "I thought that something was wrong with me. I didn't look at attractive people and think *I want to bang that.*"

I frowned. I didn't feel that way either. I liked people, but I didn't see them in a sexual way. Perhaps because I was just so grateful they wanted to be my friends? Then I considered. I found Maddox attractive. But he was taken. Everett was handsome—but he wasn't the right guy for me. We didn't fit. Quinton was super cute, and very flirty, but he hadn't ever indicated he wanted more. And even if he had, I wasn't certain he was the one.

But Ryan?

Yeah...he was my one.

*How do I tell him? What if he doesn't feel the same way? Wait. What if he's trying to tell me he does feel the same way? I'm so confused.*

"What I'm trying to do, in my awkward way, is to thank you."

I frowned. I was so confused.

"For bringing me home that night. For sharing a bed. For kissing me."

"Two burgers with onion rings." At least this time, Lyssa spoke from several feet away instead of coming up and scaring us. She placed the plates before us. "Ketchup?"

We shook our heads.

"Anything else I can get you?"

We shook our heads again.

She leaned in. "You two are just the cutest." With that, she took off.

Ryan met my gaze. "Big tip."

Yeah, I'd say so.

# Chapter Thirty-Two

Ryan

The parade was fun—watching the kids interact with all the people participating.

Loriana, Marnie, Mitch, and Jake represented the library. Well, the men pulled the wagon while the women distributed pencils with fuzzy heads and the library's name on them. Opal's reaction upon being gifted hers was priceless and, if only briefly, derailed her from her mission to see Santa Claus. Angus kept her enthusiasm up, even though he'd confided in Simeon and me that he'd never actually believed in Santa. His parents had raised him to be pragmatic—his word, not ours.

Victor and Violet weren't all that impressed with the goings on. In fact, eventually Violet just decided to take a nap.

Ravi gazed at me ruefully. "She's going to be up all night and very cranky tomorrow while we're on our flight. In retrospect, flying to

Calgary the day after the parade isn't such a good idea." Then he smiled. "You're sure you don't mind house-sitting?"

"Are you kidding? Getting out of my studio and into a mansion?"

My new friend guffawed. "I don't think a cabin with three bedrooms, two bathrooms, a recalcitrant dog, and stuffed with baby paraphernalia counts as a mansion."

He was right, of course. And having grown up in one of the biggest houses in all of Vancouver meant I knew the difference. Still, Ravi and Maddox's home was the perfect size. Simeon's home was the perfect size. One didn't need nearly twenty-five rooms for just two people. I'd always assumed my father would remarry—but he never had.

I checked my phone.

Jake's people had sent me the rough cut of the interview—to Simeon's phone. I hadn't watched it. I couldn't change anything...but I could be prepared.

Jake had also read his people the riot act and that if he discovered my father had early access that heads would roll.

Given how much money my father had, I wouldn't be surprised if he managed to buy access between now and Sunday anyhow.

"Santa! Santa, Santa, Santa!" Opal jumped up and down with enthusiasm.

Violet woke up, scrunched her face and started to wail.

Undaunted, Opal tried to get out onto the street.

Justin had a firm grip on her.

Maddox had Violet in his arms by the time Opal had her candy from Santa and he'd moved on.

"Daddy? Papa? Want to say *hi*."

Justin winced. "We'll go to the mall on Sunday, okay sweetheart? Santa will be there."

"Mall?" She squinted.

Stanley and Justin exchanged looks.

Internally, I smiled. I didn't do malls. Never had and never would. Apparently these two weren't big fans either.

"Santa's hanging out near the ice cream store." Angus glanced at his fathers.

With evident relief, Justin smiled. "Yes, ice cream."

"Yay! Go now." Opal grabbed Stanley's hand and tried to drag him down the street. Assumedly toward their vehicle.

"Santa's still busy." Stanley crouched. "But we can have a scoop of ice cream at home before bedtime. Two more sleeps and then we'll try to see Santa at the mall." He glanced over at Justin with a bit of trepidation in his eyes.

Justin leaned toward me. "Last year she had a meltdown and cried before, during, and after the Santa visit. Whoever has that job is a true saint."

A job I would never, not in a million years, take.

Simeon, who stood quietly beside me, grasped my hand. "G-good luck."

"Oh, we're going to need it." Justin rolled his eyes. Then, as if catching himself, smiled. "I love them."

Angus snagged his hand. "We love you. Opal wants her ice cream."

Opal was, in fact, trying to drag Stanley down the street.

Justin wrapped his arm around Angus's shoulder. "You want some too?"

Angus grinned. "I won't say *no*."

"Yeah, I suspected not."

The family took off.

I pivoted my attention back to Maddox and his family. "I'll be there tomorrow morning at ten."

"Great." Maddox jiggled Violet. "And Chia's welcome, okay? As long as she gets along with other dogs. Don't worry about anything. The house is dog proofed."

Simeon squeezed my hand.

Chia was home with Nanny and Bops tonight. Getting plenty of love and spoiling. She was, though, in all the ways that mattered, Simeon's dog.

And since I'd sort of been staying over every night, she was quite accepting of me. We'd collected all her paraphernalia from a grateful Chloe who'd tearfully thanked us about a million times for taking her grandmother's beloved dog.

A dog who'd certainly wormed her way into my heart.

Sort of like the man who'd taken the mantle as her owner. Although he preferred *companion* since he didn't like the concept of ownership.

Standing here with Simeon watching the parade was fun, but in a way, I wasn't looking forward to the next five days. Simeon needed to stick close to home because of his grandparents, and I'd committed to staying at Ravi and Maddox's. Oh well, after those five days at Maddox's, I had plenty of time to focus on my man.

The snow had halted much of the work on the prefab house, as Simeon had mostly finished the interior. Crazy man now thought he could have one of the Dixon sisters' bathrooms finished before Christmas.

Gio was eager for the work, so they had their marching orders.

*I wish I could help.* With the bathrooms as small as they were, I would be an impediment, not a help.

Beyond that, I wasn't really looking forward to all the tech in Maddox and Ravi's home...but I was finding myself less panicked. Plus, I didn't *have* to turn on the television. Thank God, Simeon didn't mind just sitting around and talking when we were home.

Once most of the parade goers had moved on, we made our way back to his truck.

"D-do you need to pick up anything at your apartment?" He bit his lip. "I mean, you're c-coming home with me tonight...right?"

I pressed a kiss to his lips. "I wouldn't have it any other way."

His relief—and happiness—were palpable.

We did snag more clothes from my apartment—including a nifty sweater Bops had gifted me. I figured he'd get a kick out of me wearing it. I'd never cared about fashion. In fact, I didn't even really know if the clothes were in or out of style. Moreover, I didn't give a fuck.

After sharing a quick chat with Nanny and Bops, Simeon ran Chia out and then we headed downstairs while his grandparents headed to bed. They'd clearly accepted I was going to be hanging around, and they appeared happy about this change in circumstance.

After a seriously amazing hand job—Simeon's hand was big enough to encircle both our dicks, and he jerked us to climax—we snuggled under the blankets. When we awoke in the morning, Chia demonstrated her new trick.

She could jump on the bed.

I frowned. "How can something so small jump so high?"

Simeon rubbed his face. "D-don't know. But Nanny's making pancakes as a sendoff for you."

"Uh, she realizes I'll literally be one street over?"

"Yep."

"Okay."

"S-she's going to miss you." He nuzzled my neck. "I'm going to m-miss you."

I tipped his chin up so our gazes met. "Not as much as I'm going to miss you."

To my delight, he rolled his eyes.

I pressed my lips to his.

We were late for pancakes, but Nanny gave us *that* look and Bops commented on the warming weather and how we might give Chia more freedom since she clearly knew who her *fathers* were.

I nearly choked.

Simeon just grinned.

Two hours later, after possibly the most chaotic handoff ever, Ravi, Maddox, and the kids were on their way.

Chia and Princess Sofia were curled up in front of the fireplace—even though it wasn't on.

I'd have sworn they were even more exhausted than I felt.

Simeon pulled me under a blanket on the couch, and we spent the next few hours reading. I'd convinced him to try the series about the female police detective set in the future and he was loving it. He swore he'd thank Marnie the next time he saw her.

Lunch was simple soup and sandwiches and then we walked the dogs all the way to the end of the street and the cul-de-sac where Adam and Dean lived.

Who just happened to be heading out for a walk with Chip, their retriever.

Sofia pulled on the leash as hard as a ten-pound dog could, to see her friend. Chia was guarded at first, since she was smaller than Chip's head, but when he played gently with Sofia, she allowed herself a careful nose-sniff.

Dean waved enthusiastically. "Great. You're saving us a stamp or two."

Simeon and I exchanged glances.

Adam smiled. "What he's trying to say is, we're inviting you to our wedding at Healing Horses on Christmas Eve."

I blinked. "You want us?" I didn't question their sanity—but it was a near thing.

Dean grinned. "You thought you'd get out of it? We're basically having everyone who was at the cocktail party last weekend. Maybe without the snowstorm, but we'll see."

"You w-want a snowstorm?" Simeon gawked.

"Well, I'd like a Canadian wedding." Dean snagged Adam's hand. "What's more Canadian than snow? I asked my friend Sam, but he can't make it from Australia. Too busy with his tourist business. But he's coming in the winter. Their winter." His quick clarification had me remembering the seasons were reversed down under. "Or we'll go there."

Adam blinked. "We will?"

Dean glanced at him. "We talked about this?"

His fiancé scowled.

"When I was, uh…" Dean glanced over at us, his cheeks turning a nice pink that had nothing to do with the still-chilly temperatures.

"Blowing me." Adam apparently didn't have a problem filling in the blank. He glared. "We'll talk."

Dean pressed a kiss to his lips. "And I'll convince you."

"Yeah, I probably will allow myself to be convinced."

Adam's rueful smile made my heart sing. I barely knew the guy, but Simeon had filled in some blanks. Terrible car crash. Twin brother killed. Burn scars. Guilt. In some ways, he felt like a kindred spirit. Someone I wanted to get to know better. Even if we didn't exchange our trauma stories, I hoped he might be someone who would see me clearly. See my pain and how I worked to get past it.

Dean turned his attention back to us. "Two in the afternoon. Dress warmly. Well, the actual ceremony is inside, but we're planning winter fun."

"If there's snow and not rain." Adam rolled his eyes. "This wasn't my idea."

"We'd talked about a long engagement, but..." Dean gazed at his fiancé. "We decided we didn't want to wait."

I nearly asked if that had something to do with Dean not being a citizen, but I remembered something about permanent residence status and a secure job and...did it really matter? I was under the distinct impression that if Dean had to return to Australia for some reason, Adam would simply follow.

"We'll be there." I glanced at Simeon. "Sorry, I shouldn't speak for you. You might—"

He pressed a chilled finger to my lips. Then he turned to the happy couple. "We'll b-be there."

"Great." Dean appeared to be nearly vibrating with excitement. Or wanting to jump up and down.

As if tired of just standing around, Chip bopped Sofia on the head.

Sofia lowered on her front paws and then lunged.

The big mutt lunged in return. Clearly not in an aggressive way. In a *let's have fun* way.

Chia slowly backed away.

"Okay, on that note." Adam tugged Chip's leash.

The beautiful dog immediately came to his side.

Sofia yipped.

I gently guided her to my side.

"Oh, no gifts." Adam met both our gazes. "If you're in a position to make a donation to the ranch, that's great, but totally voluntary. We just want you to come, okay?"

"Perfect." I smiled at the men. "Thank you."

"No, thank you." Adam held my gaze. He seemed to be saying *I get it. I really do.*

I appreciated that.

Simeon and I headed off to finish our walk while Adam and Dean turned along the road in the opposite direction.

"M-maybe one day you'll see their home." He grinned. "They l-live in a castle."

I halted. "A castle?"

He grinned. "Y-yep. It's up the hill and behind the trees. You come out from the forest, and it's truly awesome to see."

*Okay, didn't see that coming.* I should've known better—Mission City was this magical place where people smiled, problems didn't feel as brutal, and where cute dogs showed up at unexpected times.

I couldn't have been happier.

# Chapter Thirty-Three

Simeon

"We have something to discuss with you." Nanny sat on her spot on the couch, with her knitting needles clacking away. She knit little hats for preemie babies in the hospitals in Abbotsford, Chilliwack, and Maple Ridge. Mission City didn't have a maternity ward. I'd discovered this while driving Nanny to the various hospitals to drop off the hats. All our births were in Abbotsford, and high-risk cases were sometimes sent to either New Westminster or the women's hospital in Vancouver. That brought home the small-town nature of Mission City. I worried a bit about other specialty care, but hopefully none of us would need it, and Abbotsford was close.

I was also grateful Nanny's arthritis was mild and she could continue knitting.

Bops shut off the television.

Curious, I sat a little straighter.

Nanny eyed me. "We got a phone call today from the retirement village on 7$^{th}$ Avenue."

I blinked.

Bops grinned. "This is great news."

My grandmother laid her knitting on her lap.

My gaze caught on her work. *That doesn't look like a baby's hat.* But then what did I know?

Nanny caught my gaze. "Oh, this is a scarf for Ryan."

Tears pricked my eyes. She said it so casually. As if she expected Ryan to be around at Christmas. Which was still just over two weeks away.

"R-retirement village?" I couldn't think of which one. There were several large buildings on the street—including a school—but I couldn't place this.

Nanny nodded. "We've been on the waiting list for almost four years."

My mouth opened as I tried to find words. When I couldn't, I shut it. I'd assumed they'd be staying here until they died. That eventually I'd move upstairs to care for them. This was their home...how could they not want to stay?

"We've surprised you." Nanny laid her hand over mine.

"S-shocked. I d-don't understand."

"It's simple, my boy." Bops grinned. "We miss our friends. We love you, okay? Don't ever doubt that. But we're isolated up here. Several people we know have moved into the village, and they love it. Nanny and I put our names on the waiting list. We had a specific request, though. Two rooms next to each other with a shared door. There are only a couple of those." He eyed me. "You know we don't sleep in the same room anymore."

I did, and so I nodded. Bops' snoring had worsened, and since it wasn't apnea that could be treated, the solution for Nanny to get any sleep was separate rooms. And so they slept in different rooms. But still loved each other fiercely.

I cleared my throat. "When?"

"In the new year. We'll have one last Christmas here and start the new year in our new home."

"Oh." I sought fortitude. "I g-guess we s-should call Cadence."

Nanny's brow knit. "Whatever for?"

"You'll w-want to sell the house, right? Or need to? Retirement v-villages must be expensive." I had no idea the cost, but I saw plenty of dollar signs.

Bops and Nanny exchanged a look.

She tilted her head.

He nodded.

She squeezed my hand. "We're going to tell you two important things, but we have something very important to ask. Do you promise to answer truthfully?"

I nodded. "Of c-course." I couldn't fathom was she was about to ask. I also couldn't consider lying.

"Do you want to stay in this house? Even if we're gone?"

I blinked. I'd always thought I'd stay here, even after they passed. This was my home. Had been for seventeen long years. Almost as long as my home in Surrey had been. Again, I cleared my throat. "It'll b-be empty without you. B-but yes, I'd stay. I love it h-here. This is m-my home."

"That's what we hoped." She squeezed my hand yet again. She understood, even if I couldn't articulate it, how much I needed her reassurances right now. The forthcoming upheaval sort of blew my mind. "And you'll move into the primary bedroom? And live in this house as if it's yours? Because it will be."

"Uh..." *Did you think you were going to continue sleeping in a windowless room in the basement?* Yeah...perhaps I had. I loathed change. As I gazed into my grandmother's expectant look, though, the answer came to me clearly. "Of c-course." Then I had to be honest again. "I c-can't afford to buy the house."

Nanny and Bops exchanged another look I couldn't decipher.

"W-what?"

Bops fidgeted. "We're going to tell you something and it's likely to upset you."

I winced. I didn't like bad things. Most of my time was spent avoiding bad things.

Nanny patted my hand. "Your mother paid back the money we'd given her."

I blinked. I didn't understand.

Nanny winced. "We don't think she married your father for money...but she probably stayed in the relationship because of it. In the early days, we tried to warn her. Then, when your trouble became clear, we asked her to move home with you. That we'd take care of you both. Your father..."

"Yeah. My f-father." The less said, the better. "Okay. So h-how much do you have. Or is t-that a bad question to ask?"

My grandparents exchanged yet another look.

"Almost a million." Nanny shrugged. "The money paid back plus seventeen years of interest. Some years have been better than others. The past two have been remarkable. We didn't put the money into anything other than GICs and bonds. Nothing that would ever lose its value. Nothing risky."

"A million dollars?" I might've squeaked that.

In unison, they nodded.

"And you have this house." I ran through the listings I'd seen recently. For fun, I perused listings of properties for sale. Partly out of genuine curiosity and partly to see what the realtor was up to. From the number of houses he was trying to sell at any given time, I'd say pretty damn busy. "I should c-call Cadence."

"Why?" Nanny cocked her head. "I thought you just said you want to stay." Another look between my grandparents. *Why can't they just say everything at once and let me sort it out? These dribs and drabs is driving me nuts.* But, of course, I wasn't going to say anything.

"We have that money." Bops held my gaze. "Also, when I sold my accounting practice, I got a decent amount of money. Which I've also invested. Your grandmother has a pension from the school board for having worked so long. We have our Canada Pension Plan and our Old Age Security."

I shook my head.

"What he's trying to say, dear, is we're just fine. We're gifting you the house. It will be your primary residence. It's yours, my dear. Everett is preparing the paperwork, and it'll be done by the time we move. He'll explain all that to you when we transfer the house to you. There are papers you have to file with the government for that. Carrie, the nice young woman who bought your father's accounting firm, files all those taxes."

I frowned. "I k-know her. She d-does my business tax returns." And my personal ones. *Young* was very relative. She was almost a decade older than me. I drew in a deep breath. "Are there any o-other surprises?" I hadn't taken in all that had just been dropped on me, but I preferred to know now instead of later.

"Well, there is one thing..." My grandmother gave me her brightest smile.

An hour later, as I sifted through all the paperwork my grandparents had given me—even knowing much more awaited me after I saw Everett and Carrie—my head spun at their last *suggestion*.

*We think you should ask that nice young man, Ryan, to move in. He's always here. Seems silly for him to be paying rent for an apartment downtown, doesn't it?*

Chia sat on the end of my bed and watched me as she licked her paw.

"You're g-going to have to learn to b-be alone during the day."

She blinked and continue to lick her paw. As if saying, *yeah...so what?*

I'd have to speak to her trainer, Torah, about what the protocol would be. I certainly didn't want to crate Chia, but if that was the best way, then I needed to consider it seriously. I jotted a note on the pad of paper I'd snagged. My to-do list was growing.

My grandparents were at least letting me organize their move. I'd already emailed a company I'd worked with before, and they'd sent me a quote that felt reasonable.

*I'm a millionaire.* Between the money in the trust and this house, plus my small savings, I was really in a good spot. Nothing was to change, though, as far as I was concerned. Except I couldn't work until all hours on projects. Nope. Chia needed me.

*Ryan.*

Nanny's suggestion kept circling in my mind. I'd considered asking him to move in a week ago for a hot minute, then rejected the idea. I essentially lived in a one-bedroom basement apartment. We had a storage room I could probably clear out for him, but it didn't have a window either. And yeah, he was welcome upstairs at any time—in fact, my grandparents adored him, but the basement wasn't a great place. I'd glimpsed his studio apartment. For all the industrial feel to the older building, he had huge windows that faced due west. He got tons of sunlight. Down here, I never got direct light.

But Nanny and Bops had suggested that I move into the master suite. With Ryan, no less. I blinked again, trying to take this all in.

Chia huffed and put her chin on her paws as she gazed up at me with those puppy-dog eyes.

"W-what?"

She blinked. As if conveying, *I didn't say anything...*

To my relief, Helen hadn't maintained a fancy *poodle* haircut. We'd need to give Chia trims from time to time, but otherwise, she was fine. I'd have done the fancy stuff if I'd had to, but I'd googled poodles and the pictures of those dogs in their poofs and puffs...I'd managed not to laugh. But barely.

*You're off track.*

Because I didn't want to think about Ryan moving in.

Well, maybe I did. The idea of him living with me made my heart want to dance. Was like a blast of sunshine in the windowless room. There were obstacles, though. Emotional and practical ones. He'd need, at the very least, snow tires. Better yet, an SUV. But stuff like that was way out of his reach, and if I knew one thing for certain about Ryan, it was that he didn't want money, gifts, or praise. He wouldn't let me just pay for stuff. He wanted to live humbly—both physically and emotionally.

His story had aired Sunday night and, as Jake promised, the interview had been gentle. Probing, but respectful. Informative, but not gratuitous. My heart had ached, watching Ryan keep his composure as he talked about his losses. *Such a strong man, even though he doesn't recognize that.*

To the best of my knowledge, Ryan's dad hadn't called. Apparently the man was in Macau on some business jaunt.

My phone rang.

*Ryan.*

"H-hey."

"I miss you."

I grinned. "I m-miss you too. B-but we had dinner together." Chia and I had run over to Maddox's house and had enjoyed fried chicken that Ryan had picked up in town after his physio appointment. The dogs devoured their kibble and then had watched us balefully as we'd indulged in fast food. Because of my grandparents' health, we never ate fried chicken here anymore. Nothing fried at all. And since they were still going strong in their nineties, I planned to keep my indulgences to the minimum. I hoped to get their longevity and their health.

"I know...but that was hours ago." Ryan's tone was a playful whine.

"Y-you're silly." And I loved it.

"Because I have something serious to say."

"Oh? W-well, I do too...although mine can wait until w-we see each other again."

"Mine..." He sighed. "My dad called."

I held myself still. I'd put him on speaker phone and had laid the phone on my bed, and I didn't want him to hear me react. When he didn't speak, however, I ventured, "Oh?"

He blew out a breath. "He..." Another pause. "He said he was proud of me. Like, really proud. And that he might not understand my choices, but he had to respect them."

"W-wow."

"Right? So fucking unexpected. Just...out of the blue." He sighed. "It gets more complicated."

"Oh?" *Better to stick to one-syllable words and let him come to you.*

"He says he's set up a trust. And I'll get a set amount of money each month for the rest of my life. Like a pension or something. Like I would've gotten if I'd been a soldier in the Canadian armed forces and had gotten injured and was forced to retire."

"T-that's great."

"I don't want it."

"I know." I didn't have an iota of doubt that he wanted nothing to do with the money. "B-but you can do whatever you w-want with it."

"Huh?"

*Am I doing the right thing, or am I suggesting he do what I would do?* I drew in a deep breath. "You c-could donate it. Find somewhere to be g-generous. P-plenty of good causes." He could also keep enough to survive on, but that might feel like blood money to him—something I certainly wasn't going to say.

"You mean like Ukraine?"

"S-sure. I think that's a great idea." *Is that the right thing to say?* "Or H-Healing Horses. Or a d-dog-rescue place."

He chuckled. "Sofia's curled against me. I'm on the bed in the spare room."

"She's a g-great dog. Chia's on my b-bed with me."

Another chuckle. "And here I was about to suggest phone sex."

"R-really?" I might've squeaked that. We'd made out a couple of times at Maddox's house, but we hadn't actually climaxed. A bit of frotting and blue balls had been fine. Jizzing in someone else's house felt weird.

"Nah. I'm just..." He blew out a breath. "He called, Simeon. I just...didn't expect that. Well, I figured he might, but that he'd be derisive. Cruel."

My heart ached. We hadn't spoken much of our lives *before.* Before he'd gone to Ukraine. Before my parents died.

Ryan said in a much brisker tone, "So, what's your news?"

I was suddenly unsure, shy about asking him something so vital over the phone. And if I shared one part of the news, I wouldn't be able to stop. I gathered up the papers and dropped them off the side of the bed.

"What was that?"

"M-me getting ready for bed. I w-want you to talk to me while I f-fall asleep. I can share my n-news later." I scooted under the covers, making myself comfortable while not disturbing Chia.

In the end, she moved up and plopped onto Ryan's pillow. Her favorite spot.

I made a mental note to wash the pillowcase before he returned.

"What do you want me to talk about as I bore you to sleep?"

"Well..." I yawned. I'd worked bloody hard today on Kennedy's bathroom. I wanted to have both bathrooms in the ranch house done by Christmas Eve. For Dean and Adam's wedding. "T-tell me again how you think Quinton's hitting on m-me."

A low rumble. "Yeah, okay. So I know you think he's all innocent, but he's not..."

Yeah, Ryan's favorite delusion. Within moments, I was out like a light.

# Chapter Thirty-Four

Ryan

Christmas Eve dawned bright, beautiful, and with a massive snow dump from the day before.

Simeon had plowed continuously yesterday. Hopefully he'd maintained a way for us to get out of the house because today was the wedding day, and I was super excited. Funny, because I'd never been to a wedding before. I'd always thought of them as perfunctory and boring. But the joining of two men whom I considered friends? That sounded awesome.

My boyfriend stirred beside me and gently tugged me into his arms. He was always so careful of my chest. The one thing I'd noticed over this past week now we were back to sleeping together was how little pain I was actually in. I'd thought I'd learned to live with it—but being without the fucking thing was pretty damn sweet. "It's Adam and Dean's day," I reminded Simeon.

"Mmm." He was still super sleepy. He'd worked like a dog the past two weeks, and when he'd sent the pictures of the completed bathrooms, I'd been thrilled for him. And so damn proud. Oh, he and Gio had stripped down to skivvies and worn nothing but a towel in some of the photos. Those snaps would *not* be on Simeon's website. He'd shown me on his phone, and I'd been okay with both the eye candy and the electronics. Slowly, I was becoming more and more comfortable with little bits of tech.

One day, when I'd finished an appointment with Justin out at the ranch, Angus had approached me with a serious-eyed preteen at his side. "This is my friend Kyleigh. She's, like, one of my best friends in the world. And she reckons she can beat you at the video game."

So I'd battled an eleven-year-old for supremacy. I'd lost—and not for lack of effort on my part. That girl had been tough to beat. I knew plenty of women gamers—some of whom put up with a lot of shit. I suggested a site to Kyleigh that she might want to check out. One I knew used to be kid-friendly and generally free of misogyny. And after I'd done that, though, I'd considered going on the site to make sure the thing was still safe for young women.

But I hadn't. I'd eyed Simeon's laptop all night, but hadn't found the courage.

Nor had I found the courage to answer the question he'd asked two weeks ago. The first night I'd stayed over after finishing my rather un-eventful stint as a house sitter and doggie servant. God knew, Princess Sofia lived up to her name. Friendly, playful, and a little prima donna who did *not* like it when I left her alone. But I knew for a fact she was *abandoned* regularly and survived. Such dramatics...

*"I'd like you to move in with me."*

Said after he'd dropped the bombshell that his grandparents were moving to a retirement village near downtown Mission City.

I'd driven past the place to check it out. As if I could somehow divine by looking at it whether or not it was good enough for two of my favorite people in the world.

I might've also used the drive to buy a Tessa Carlyle painting for the happy grooms that I'd give to them later. They'd invited us over a week ago, and by the end of the evening, I considered them friends.

Although the men had some amazing artwork, I'd spotted a bare spot on the wall where they might consider hanging the stunning painting of a mother deer and her fawn in the forest. A forest I'd come to associate with the hills north of Mission City.

I'd also stocked up on gifts for just about everyone I'd met. So yeah, I'd dipped into the first pension payment my father had sent. I'd been hesitant...but the idea of sharing my good fortune made spending the money sting less. Plus...my father was rich. And for all his...nastiness with me...he did things aboveboard. He wasn't a slumlord. He didn't take advantage of vulnerable people. He just knew a good deal when he saw one and made shrewd business decisions. He couldn't possibly spend all his wealth. If I spent a minute fraction of it bringing happiness, what was wrong with that? And I hadn't bought extravagant gifts. Just little thoughtful things to show people how grateful I was.

Grateful they were in my life.

Grateful I might one day lead a somewhat normal life.

Grateful I was alive.

"You're t-thinking too hard."

I scooched back against Simeon so that his morning wood brushed my ass. "You want me to do something about your hardness?"

He chuckled. "I'm o-okay. We need to g-get up."

"I checked. The snow's stopped and the sun's out."

"O-okay. But I still need to g-get up."

"Let me give you a blow job?"

He growled as he nibbled on my neck. "N-never going to turn that down."

We'd worked out a weird position that didn't put stress on my chest, but still allowed me to go down on him in a way that brought us both pleasure.

After I finished him off, he snagged my cock and gave me a couple of firm tugs before I tumbled over the edge with him.

Justin's theory about demi made so much sense that I kind of felt stupid for not seeing it earlier. But then why would I? I'd never let anyone get close enough to me. And, if I had my way, I'd never have to worry about getting close to someone else ever again.

Simeon was my person. He was the one I wanted to grow old with. To spend my life with. To hold my hand into the uncertain future before me.

I still wasn't healed—either physically or emotionally. But even Justin was pleased with home much progress I'd made in just six weeks.

"Shower." Simeon stroked my chin. "L-love this."

I returned the favor, scratching his stubble. "I like this."

He scrunched his nose. "N-no. Not for the w-wedding." I loved the scruffy look, but I knew he felt it looked a bit unkempt. He'd been working so hard that he hadn't taken the time to shave for the past week or so.

I'd done everything I could to support him. Which included practically moving in, taking care of Chia, and watching out for Nanny and Bops. And, because I spent so much time here, I'd nearly finished reading the series Marnie suggested. Now she was on the hunt for a couple of police procedural novels from gay authors with gay protagonists. Something I hadn't even known existed.

Lack of imagination on my part.

"W-will you shower with m-me?" Simeon asked this question each day. And each day I politely declined. He'd seen my scars when he'd helped me change a Henley or sweater, a dozen limited glimpses, but I still wore a shirt in bed. He didn't touch me there, didn't focus on them. In the shower, being full naked had felt too vulnerable.

*Carpe diem.*

A favorite expression of one of my comrades-in-arms. Apparently there'd been an American movie with an English teacher, and the instructor had taught the line to his students, and...I'd lost the thread at that point. I kept meaning to look up which movie. But that would mean getting on a computer to search. Or I could ask Marnie. Anyway, and then I might want to watch the movie. Which would involve watching television. And reminding me of my friend. My dead friend.

None of that appealed to me.

*Carpe diem.*

"Yeah, I'd love it."

Simeon's eyes widened in evident surprise. He swept in for a hard kiss. "T-thank you."

"It's just a shower. With my scrawny—"

He cut me off with another kiss. A request, I supposed, that I not put myself down. He was big about that. Asking quietly I not be so negative about myself. Well, I'd turned the tables on him more than once. I was certain he hadn't realized how easily he denigrated himself either.

Something we both had to work on.

In the shower, though, I sort of lost my nerve. Turning to keep my chest out of view, I handed him the loofah. "Wash my back?" I knew he wouldn't touch anywhere he wasn't invited to.

He grinned. "You b-bet." And he did. With thoroughness. And he might've felt it necessary to clean my crack as well.

We had yet to discuss whether we were going to move beyond *suck and jerk sessions* as we called them.

I certainly wanted to...but I'd never push him. If things remained exactly as they were for the rest of our lives, I'd be fine with that. This relationship truly wasn't about sex. Our time together was a celebration of a meeting of the minds. Of shared goals. Mutual respect. Any sex was just a bonus. Although an awesome bonus I wouldn't mind expanding.

He pressed a kiss to my shoulder as the water cascaded down from the waterfall low-flow showerhead he'd installed a couple of years ago. "C-can I jerk you?"

I chuckled. "Like I'd ever say *no* to that."

And within moments I forgot about my discomfort with my scars as he jacked me off to completion.

Then, of course, I had to return the favor.

I was big on equality.

Somehow we managed to get clean, dry, dressed, and upstairs for Nanny's waffles.

She pointed to the clock.

Simeon blushed.

I guffawed. "We were busy in the shower."

His blush deepened.

Nanny beamed.

Bops chuckled.

We ate delicious waffles.

Near the end of the meal, Nanny cocked her head. "I thought you were going to a wedding today."

Simeon nodded. "W-we are."

"Dean and Adam's." My contribution.

Another nod. Apparently Simeon had brought the couple around in early fall to meet his grandparents. Pretty much at his grandparents' insistence.

He'd thought they were maybe being nosy.

I now could see they were just concerned he might be lonely when they left. Having friends just a stone's throw away—in relative North Mission City terms—was important to them.

"Then why are you wearing plaid?" Bops glanced back and forth between the two of us. "What's wrong with dress shirts?"

"And you're wearing jeans." Nanny tisked. "Really. What are you thinking?"

Simeon grinned.

I laughed. "That we're having a lumberjack contest. Dean's idea, so don't go thinking Ravi was up to something nefarious." I smoothed down the fabric. "I asked Simeon not to shave. Thought that might give him a better chance."

Nanny laughed. "Oh, my dear. Simeon doesn't like a beard."

I grinned back. "I know."

She scrutinized us both, turning to me first. "I like your red-and-blue stripes—that works." She stared at Simeon. "Golden-rod? Seriously?"

He glared at me.

I blinked, then batted my eyelashes—trying for innocent and likely failing miserably. "I think it matches his hair."

Simeon feathered his hair in just *that* way. He really had no idea how fucking sexy I found it.

Bops chuckled. "Simeon and vanity are two words that don't go together."

"No, they don't." My love was across the table from me. Otherwise, I would've pecked his cheek, or grabbed his hand under the table.

Twin spots of color appeared on his cheeks. "No f-fair."

Nanny snagged his hand. "We only tease the ones we love." She eyed me. "I suspect he's the same."

"I am." Easy assurance. I'd never said mean things about people growing up—because I'd been the butt of so many cruel jokes and comments.

"Well, the wedding photos should be interesting." She nudged Simeon. "Take a few snaps for me. Especially one of the grooms. Two handsome men."

That she spoke of Adam being handsome was a reminder that beauty was more than skin deep. Some people might find his scars hideous. Nanny didn't even factor them into her calculations of his character. He was a good man. He loved his fiancé. He was kind to Simeon. Those were the attributes that made him attractive.

And she'd raised Simeon the same way. To have those same beliefs.

He met my gaze. "Y-yes, Nanny, I will take photos."

"Oh, let's do one of the two of you before you go. Like your first date."

"Oh, our first date was at Library Square Pub. After my interview with Jake."

Nanny and Bops had watched the interview when it aired, later telling me how moving they'd found it.

Those two spots of color reappeared on Simeon's cheeks, and he wouldn't meet my gaze.

*Probably recalling the* broken cock *discussion.* I grinned unrepentantly because if anyone should be embarrassed it was me, and fuck that noise.

He continued to blush.

"Well, sounds like you had a lovely time. I can't say I've ever been to Library Square. The last time we went to the opera, we ate at Brown's

Social House. On the plaza at the Queen Elizabeth Theatre? I miss the opera."

"If I can swing tickets, would you let Simeon and me escort you?"

Nanny blinked. "Well... We stopped going because driving into Vancouver because such a chore."

"I d-didn't know that." Simeon frowned. "I would have d-driven you."

I pointed to his phone. "When's the next show?"

He whipped it out, and within a minute was showing the screen to Nanny.

She grinned. "Oh, I love that one."

"Then you shall have tickets." Heedless of how tactless this was, I yanked out my credit card and shoved it across the table.

Simeon gawked.

I shrugged. "I wanted to get them something they'd like, but I had no idea. She's just told me what she wants. Can you find four seats? If not together then two pairs?"

"Uh..." Simeon frowned.

*Oh shit. He's never bought tickets. Goddamn I'm such an asshole.*

I snagged the credit card back and held out my hand.

Slowly, Simeon handed the phone over.

Pushing down the panic, I checked the website. "Oh, I used to have an account with these guys. I wonder if it'll accept my password or if it will require two-factor authentication." Which would mean resurrecting my email and the thousands of unread messages. But for Nanny and Bops, I'd do it. "Oh, great, I'm in." I tapped a few times. "How is the twentieth of January? That's a Friday. Oh, wait. If we go on the Thursday night, I can get us four seats together in the dress circle. Only two steps."

Could Nanny and Bops do steps? They never left this floor, so I had no idea.

Bops guffawed. "We can do the stairs all the way down to Simeon's if we have to." He held up his arms in a muscle man pose. "We're strong."

Nanny chuckled. "Well, maybe more in mind than body. Yes, dear, we can do a few steps. Oh, I love the idea of us all going together. We'll need to rest up, but what a wonderful night that will be."

I didn't wonder out loud how many more of those there might be. Nanny and Bops hardly left the house, and a night in Vancouver would be taxing for them. But hopefully a night they'd remember. "We can park at the theatre, and I bet if we go early enough, we can have dinner at Brown's."

"Oh, lovely." Nanny beamed. "I won't ask about cost because that would be gauche of me, but Bops and I can buy dinner."

*Gauche.* But dad wasn't saying it about me. No, Nanny was saying she wouldn't be that way by asking. She was using it in a teasing manner. Which took the sting out of hearing the word that so had the power to wound me.

I entered my credit card information then stopped. "Oh, damn."

Bops straightened. "What?"

"I should change the account address so nothing ever goes to my dad's place." I smacked my forehead. "Do you know, I can't remember the street number of my apartment building?" I tried to remember how to open another tab to search.

"Oh, just use here." Nanny rhymed off the address.

For a full ten seconds I just sat with that.

To her, this was simple. This was my home.

Simeon confided his grandparents hoped I'd move in.

I hadn't really absorbed that, though. I thought maybe they worried he might be lonely. Or they hoped I could contribute to rent. Or something else in the abstract.

But no. She was saying I was home.

I blinked back the tears as my eyes blurred.

Bops handed me a napkin. "Don't you have to finish that transaction in a set period of time or you lose the tickets?"

"Uh, yeah." I sniffed as I wiped my eyes.

"Well damn, man, you don't want to lose the tickets."

His quiet way of letting me know no one had an issue with me nearly bawling like a baby at the kitchen table on one ordinary Christmas Eve morning.

And, in that instant, I saw my future. Nanny and Bops wouldn't always be here, of course. Chia wouldn't always be on her bed in the kitchen that she haunted when Nanny was cooking and liable to sneak her a little treat.

Simeon might not always be young and blond. I might have a few white hairs of my own.

But I was home.

"Yeah, I'll nab those tickets."

And perhaps finally embrace my future.

# Chapter Thirty-Five

Simeon

The grooms wore plaid.

Seriously.

That sounded like a title of a romantic comedy, but that was how things went. Oh, for the actual ceremony they wore white shirts and navy wool trousers. They posed for six photographs, then each hustled upstairs to the renovated bathrooms.

Phew. I'd finished them off yesterday. All sparkling clean and ready for today.

Ten minutes later, they'd reappeared.

Dean in fuchsia-pink plaid and Adam in emerald green.

I hadn't known those colors existed in the plaid universe. Possibly because once Ryan had settled on goldenrod for me, I'd ceased my search. The deep blue in his shirt nicely matched his eyes. I did *not* believe the goldenrod matched my hair.

Looking around the room, though, I was glad Ryan had chosen outlandish for me.

Ravi stunned in purple. Violet and Victor wore matching lilac shirts with black corduroy pants.

Stanley had opted for a conservative gray with burgundy accents.

Everett had chosen baby blue to complement Quinton's baby pink. They weren't here as a couple per se, but they'd come together.

Kennedy and Rainbow wore matching cream with taupe accents.

Maddox and Justin had both opted for the traditional red and black They were giving each other a run in the stereotypical lumberjack category. While Maddox actually wielded an axe on his property—he'd shown me—Justin had chosen to let his beard grow bushier than usual.

We had secret balloting, and the winner was to be announced after the sleigh rides.

Yep...sleigh rides.

Kennedy knew a guy up the road who had a working ranch and who offered sleigh rides during the winter when it snowed. When the forecaster had promised the white stuff for today, she'd had him bring down the sleigh along with a couple of his horses. We'd each only get about ten minutes, but I was about to get my first real sleigh ride.

Ryan's first as well.

He gripped my hand.

I pulled him into my side. "S-selfie for Nanny and Bops?" I held out my phone.

"Oh, let me take it." Quinton snagged the phone before I could say anything.

Then he held it up to my face.

Ryan sighed. He'd explained about cybersecurity and how cops could open my phone without my permission by holding it up to my face—just as Quinton had just done.

I pointed out I didn't really have anything incriminating on my phone because, as he knew, I wasn't actually a criminal.

He'd huffed.

And said something about being more secure when he upgraded his phone.

Which I took as a big win. He didn't *have* to have a smart phone. But living up in the semi-wilderness area north of Mission City meant having a good, reliable cell phone was critical. When the power went down, if the generator didn't kick in, at least I'd have data and a way to communicate.

He'd huffed that landlines were a thing.

We still had one at the house. An expense I was happy to keep up.

I pulled Ryan close as Quinton grinned.

"Oh, I want one with you kissing."

I blinked at Quinton's seeming command.

Ryan slowly turned me so we faced each other. He put his hands on my clean-shaven cheeks and tugged me toward him.

Our lips touched.

That feeling of rightness that I was so accustomed to settled over me.

"I want some tongue."

"There *are* children." Maddox's amused voice had me pulling away from Ryan.

"Oh, like they haven't seen you and Ravi going at it." Quinton playfully swatted Maddox's biceps.

Ryan snagged me around the neck and dragged me down for a full-on kiss.

Surprised, I opened my mouth.

He thrust his tongue in.

My brain sort of short-circuited as he pressed himself flush against me. Memories of his tears this morning hit me again. In that moment, I'd witnessed quiet acceptance he'd be moving in. He'd be starting a new life with me. We could put the past behind us. Not forget...no, our world wariness came from long-experience. But we could now forge a path of our own choosing. Write our own destinies.

Wolf whistles and cheers brought me back into the present.

Ryan grinned against my lips.

We pulled apart and slowly faced the crowd of about twenty on-lookers who were all smiles.

I'd known I had acquaintances in Mission City. After I'd fixed Maddox and Ravi's kitchen floor—and they'd started inviting me to their place quite often—I felt I had friends. Now, though? Everyone here felt like extended family. Hell, Dean and Adam had invited us to their wedding. And yeah, neither had any family still alive...but to look at me and say *yeah, he's so important to us that we want him to share our sacred day* meant everything. And to include Ryan because they understood how much he meant to me? Words escaped me.

Adam came over to us. "Guys, don't steal my thunder."

I ducked my head.

He smacked me lightly on the chest. "Kidding. You know I hate being the center of attention."

I knew he did. Even though he'd been a former model, that had changed in an instant. Today, though, he'd put himself out front and center because he loved Dean more than anything in the world.

Unbidden, I pulled him in for a hug. Emotion washed over me. The gratitude for friendship. The pride in him. Happiness of being with

Ryan...it just overwhelmed me and hugging Adam felt like a safe thing to do.

"We love you, man." Adam whispered in my ear. "We're so glad you're here. And we're thrilled you seem happy."

"I am h-happy." I sniffed as I pulled back from the embrace.

"Good. Who knew that dinner all those months ago would lead to this?"

We looked at the gathered group.

"Yeah. W-what a different six months makes."

"Right?" He grinned. "I didn't know I'd fall for Dean. You hadn't met Everett. Stanley and Justin hadn't known they'd be able to adopt Opal. All these amazing things."

"That's l-life."

"True." He gestured to Dean, who made his way over.

They kissed.

That warm, happy feeling sank deep into my bones. I didn't know I could be this happy.

Ryan tucked himself against my side as Dean and Adam moved toward Stanley and Justin.

Quinton returned my phone. "I might've snapped a whole pile of pics. For Nanny and Bops." He hadn't actually met my grandparents, but he knew how important they were to me and, to Quinton, that made them part of his life. He just...had an expansive view of the world. The more people in it—the happier he was.

"Thank you. T-they'll appreciate it."

He waved and then darted to catch Violet who was headed toward the kitchen.

Kennedy stepped into the room and shut the sliding-glass door. "The sleigh fits four or so. You can squeeze in a couple of kids as well.

For the first ride, though, I think the grooms should have some alone time."

Everett hooted. "Oh, yeah."

Dean grinned as he snagged Adam's hand. "I like the sound of alone time." They snagged their coats and headed outside.

Kennedy made her way around the room, clearly allocating space. She arrived at Ryan and me last.

"So you'll be the last ride. Just the two of you."

"Oh." That sounded almost too good to be true.

"Well, I could split you up and—"

Ryan pressed his hand to my chest. "Alone is perfect."

She grinned. "I thought it might be. Helps that you don't have children."

And, by my calculations, she'd split up Quinton and Everett to make the numbers work—so that Ryan and I would have some alone time.

Ryan gripped my arm. "This is lovely. Thank you."

"M-me? I didn't d-do anything."

"You know all these amazing people." He squeezed my hand. "You asked me to come home with you first."

I smiled. "You d-didn't want to camp out on the floor with Alexa, Alannah, and Oliver?"

He shuddered. "Uh, no. My own kids, maybe. Someone else's? Less enthusiastic."

I stilled. "Your k-kids?" *He doesn't have kids. Is he talking about some hypothetical future or is he trying to tell me he wants kids? How am I supposed to respond? What if I say the wrong thing?*

"Simeon?"

After a moment, I gazed into his eyes. "I w-want kids, Ryan. If you d-don't, then that's totally fine, but I w-want kids."

Slowly, he smiled. "I do too. There are so many orphans out there. Kids in foster care. Kids who need our help. We have a house. A beautiful, amazing house. A house we could fill with kids."

"So you'll m-move in?"

He laughed. "I figured after I told the ticket place where to find me, that was a given."

"I d-don't want to assume."

"I'll give notice on my apartment. I signed a lease, but the manager said they've got a waiting list. She'll let me out of the agreement." He pressed a hand to my cheek. "I don't ever want us to sleep apart again, okay?"

"F-fine by me."

We kissed.

"Damn." Maddox eyed his phone. He glanced up and hotfooted over to Justin. "Can I borrow your computer?"

"Sure, it's in my office. Follow me."

The two men headed down the hallway.

Ravi sighed.

Ryan darted to catch Violet who was again heading toward the kitchen. He snagged her around the waist. "Not so fast, monster."

"Thanks." Ravi held out his arms and Ryan dropped her into them.

"What's wrong?"

Ravi appeared to consider. "Maddox has worked for this company for years. They just merged with two other companies whose cybersecurity sucks. Maddox has been struggling to get everyone aligned and where they need to be so there aren't breaches. Apparently there's a lot of highly classified information that would be really easy to hack into." He drew in a breath. "I don't care if Maddox has to work more...but this is really stressing him out. He needs to hire someone, but he keeps saying he doesn't have the time to look through all the résumés."

"Cybersecurity?" Ryan scratched his beard.

"Yeah." Ravi laughed. "Way over my pay grade. I can manage the computer at work to do my job, but I want to care for my patients, not do all that data-entry crap."

"When would he want someone to start?" Ryan continued to scratch his beard.

"Like, yesterday. He warned me he's likely going to need to work tomorrow. Now, I'm not a traditionalist per se, but Christmas Day means a lot to me. To both of us. I support him, though. And the twins don't understand yet. They won't care when we actually open presents."

Ryan snagged my hand and tugged me close. He cleared his throat. "I...I have a degree in cybersecurity. I didn't just fly drones in Ukraine—I did computer stuff as well. A lot of it."

Ravi nodded. "Okay. But I thought..." He didn't finish the thought.

We all knew what he meant. Ryan could barely tolerate being around a cell phone.

*But he set up my laptop. He bought the tickets. He's been in therapy for over a month and he says it's been helping.*

I squeezed his hand, offering unspoken support. Whatever he wanted, I was all in. I'd have his back.

Again, he cleared his throat.

Justin reappeared. He headed our way. "All good. He says fifteen minutes tops. Stanley and I will take the kids on our sleigh ride and if Maddox isn't back, one of us will go with you and the twins."

"Uh, Justin?" Ryan's voice was a little strained.

"Yeah?" Justin cocked his head. "Are you okay?"

"I think..." For the third time, Ryan cleared his throat. "I think I might want to ask Maddox for a job."

Justin slowly nodded. "I think that's a great idea. I think you might be ready."

Ryan stood a little taller. "Yeah, I am." Then he tucked himself into my side.

I held him even as he trembled. Well, either Maddox or myself would be with him for the next few days as I was off work until after Nanny and Bops moved into the retirement village. I pressed a kiss to Ryan's temple. "You'll b-be okay. I'll take care of you."

Again, he met my gaze with luminous blue eyes. "Yeah, I think I will be."

# Chapter Thirty-Six

Ryan

Sleigh rides were possibly the most romantic thing ever. As I snuggled against Simeon, with a blanket on our laps, a sense of rightness sank deep into me. The clouds had appeared earlier, and now the first flakes of snow fell. This was an out-of-body experience. Like I was watching a romantic movie being filmed.

Simeon was the perfect hero. Tall, blond, handsome, and with a kind heart. I was sort of the other hero—damaged and needing aid. But not in a helpless way. No, I'd asked for help and then accepted it when it had arrived. Justin, Marcus, and Dr. Raymond were part of the team. Today I didn't have any physical pain. And the emotional felt manageable for the first time in a long while.

As if reading my thoughts, Simeon put his arm around me.

Which was perfect because sometimes I put my arms around him. Whoever needed the hug, got one. We had that kind of relationship.

"Is this r-real?"

I gazed up at him. "What do you mean?"

"C-can someone be this happy and it's all g-going to work out?"

"Yes, it can." I considered my words carefully. "It won't always be perfect. I mean..." I flailed a little.

"P-people die."

"Yes." Exactly what I'd been trying to say but couldn't.

"D-dogs die."

"True. But she's just a year old. If we manage to keep her out of trouble, we might get a long life."

"I saw Torah y-yesterday."

Torah... "Oh, the dog trainer."

"Yep. She said she t-thinks Chia would be a perfect therapy dog. She asked m-me to consider taking her for training in the new year."

My ears perked. "Really? That would be amazing. She's right, Chia's got the right temperament. I met several therapy dogs while in the medical wing once I was out of the intensive care. Those visits perked me up. Made me want my own dog."

"And n-now you have one."

"Yes, now I do." I blinked. "And I have a man I love."

He blinked. "L-love? Fuck."

"Are you okay?" I straightened. Simeon never swore. Like, ever.

He winced. "I wanted to say the word l-love without stuttering. The most important w-word ever."

I placed my gloved hand against his cheek. "You know I don't care. I really fucking don't. I don't even notice it, Simeon. Okay? Do you understand?"

Slowly, he nodded.

"Now, do you love me?" *Oh God, please say* yes. *Please don't let this be one-sided.*

"Of c-course I love you." He grinned. "I d-didn't stutter on the word."

"Nope, you didn't." I pressed a kiss to his lips.

The sleigh bells rang, and the driver turned to us. "Time's up guys." I grinned. "Thanks."

He grinned back. "You two are almost as cute as the grooms."

I almost asked him if he'd do this again sometime. Like maybe when I proposed to Simeon. Because that would be super romantic. But also way too soon.

We folded the blanket, then stepped out of the sleigh. We made our way back to the ranch house and entered via the sliding-glass door.

Rainbow was there to greet us. "Take your coats off, and I've got sparkling cider in flutes. We're about to toast the grooms."

"And to announce the winner of the plaid contest." Quinton ran his hand up and down his shirt. "I'm a shoo-in."

I laughed. How had I ever seen him as a rival for Simeon's affection? He wasn't like that. He was friendly, helpful, an incorrigible flirt, and just a great guy. Someone I hoped to eventually call friend.

When Simeon and I had our coats off, Rainbow handed us the glasses.

Adam and Dean stood together and the rest of us gathered around in a circle.

Dean pressed his hand to his chest. "I didn't know I could be so happy. With our friends as witness, I got to pledge myself to the best man I've ever known. Now, don't tell my mate Sam that." He winked.

"We should call Sam." Adam met Dean's gaze.

"Uh…" Dean bit his lower lip. "I haven't told him any of this. When we go down to see him, I want it to be a big surprise. Plus, he told me he's got a new guy. Named Levi. So I can't wait to hear all about that."

Adam chuckled. "Something you haven't told Sam? I'm shocked."

Kennedy raised her glass. "To the happy couple. May you have a long and loving marriage."

"Like your parents, eh?" Dean grinned.

Rainbow snickered. "Yes, I'd say our parents are a good example. Although I'm not certain you want to raise eight daughters. But, hey, I might—"

"Cheers." Adam raised his glass.

Okay, so he probably didn't want eight daughters. I didn't blame him. I linked my arm with Simeon's. I wanted kids. I never would have predicted that, but after seeing the carnage of war, I wanted to help. Maybe an orphan of the war. I spoke Ukrainian. Might that help? Or might there be a child here in Mission City who needed us? In good time, though. I still had more healing to do. I still had to find a way to propose to the man I wanted to be with for the rest of my life.

We raised our glasses in toast.

When that was finished, Kennedy handed Dean a folded piece of paper. "I did the count myself. The winner was clear."

Adam snorted. "This was Dean's idea, so he gets to announce the winner."

"And then I want a photo with everyone." He pointed to the gentleman in the back of the room. The sleigh driver. Ah, so he'd take the photo and then everyone would be in it.

Dean made a big show of opening the paper and grinning from ear to ear. "And the winner is..."

*Seriously? Just announce it.*

"Simeon."

My man gripped me tightly. "W-what?"

Cheers rose from the small crowd.

Rainbow came over to us and handed Simeon the gaudiest statue I'd ever seen.

Clearly Dean had put a lot of thought into this crazy scheme.

Simeon grasped it and blinked rapidly.

Truly, I wasn't surprised. He looked amazing in the shirt and, more importantly, his friends wanted him to feel welcomed.

"Picture." Adam beckoned us in. "On the stairs, I think."

And so we did. We surrounded the happy couple and the nice driver took about two dozen photographs with a fancy SLR camera.

Dean promised everyone photos as he and Adam made their way through the throng to say their farewells. To no one's surprise, they were just heading home to have a quiet Christmas with Chip and Maurice the cat.

Perfect for them.

Just like I'd spend Christmas with Nanny, Bops, and Simeon. Oh, and Chia, of course.

Perfect for us.

With Rainbow's help, I'd snuck the painting into the back of Adam's SUV so they'd find it when they got home. I wasn't surprised to find several other gifts there as well, despite the no-gifts rule. I'd also overheard Kennedy mention the ranch had received a slew of donations, including several large anonymous ones.

Dad had asked me what I wanted for Christmas. Something he hadn't done in about a dozen years.

I said a donation to Healing Horses.

He'd made it happen. He'd also arranged for me to have my own credit card that he didn't pay off each month. That modicum of independence. And now I might have a job. Something I could be really good at.

"I watch that movie every Christmas." Rainbow's voice carried to me as chatter resumed now the grooms were gone.

I turned toward her. "Which movie?"

"*It's a Wonderful Life.* I watch it every Christmas."

"Oh. I've never heard of it."

Simeon turned to gape at me. "N-never?"

I shook my head.

"W-we should..."

*Watch it. He wants me to watch a movie with him.*

*Fuck it. If I can set up a laptop and play a game with Kyleigh, then I can watch a movie.*

"Can we watch it tonight?"

"I h-have the Blu-ray. Nanny and Bops w-watch it every Christmas Eve. I can text them and ask them to w-wait."

"That would be great."

And watching the movie was an amazing experience.

I was cuddled between Nanny and Simeon on the couch and when I cried, my boyfriend held me.

We'd settled that we were boyfriends on the drive from Healing Horses back to our house. Well, Simeon's house. But I'd live in it. At some point we needed to talk finances, but I figured that would be tacky to do before Nanny and Bops were settled. I wanted to contribute.

Like buying tissue because I used half the box watching a movie that had a fucking happy ending.

By that ending, I was done in. Simeon made our excuses, and we headed downstairs. He undressed me and after brushing my teeth and pissing, I crawled into bed.

He wasn't far behind me and sleep pulled me under quickly.

So much for celebrating our upgrade in relationship status.

In the morning, though, when I awoke refreshed and alert, Simeon still snoozed. He was a morning person—when he was working and on the clock. On weekends he slept until Nanny hollered that breakfast was on the table. Part of me thought that was a little odd, but the rest of me found it adorable. The love in this house was immeasurable. Every gesture, word, and thought was for the others. Not a selfish bone in anyone's body.

That blew my mind and, in fact, I'd discussed it with Justin. He'd said to embrace the love and give it back as best I knew how. That loving might be a challenge because of my upbringing. But that I should work toward being an equal partner. Not just financially, but emotionally as well.

Lying in Simeon's arms, the sense of rightness was everywhere.

I scooted back so my ass brushed his cock.

He groaned.

*Oh good. Morning wood.*

Matching my own.

"Simeon?"

"Mmm?"

"I'd like to, you know…"

He nuzzled my neck. "We always y-you know…"

"But I want more."

He stilled. "R-really?" Then chuckled nervously.

Carefully, I turned in his arms so I faced him. I pressed a finger to his frown line. "Simeon, we're about to have a really serious conversation."

In turn, he slowly nodded. His eyes were so dark with just the purple light in the room. The light I was so accustomed to.

"First. You can say *no*. You can *always* say no. And then we don't. There are no hard feelings on my end. No recriminations and no judgements Just an understanding that now isn't the time."

He opened his mouth.

I gave a short shake of my head.

He closed it.

"If today isn't the time, that's okay. If there's never a time, that's okay too. Plenty of gay couples don't have anal sex. For many different reasons—none of which they have to justify with the world. What we do or don't do in our room is entirely our business. For instance, you might not feel comfortable with your grandparents in the house."

He gave a small smile.

I cocked my head.

"I've b-been masturbating for years, and we've b-been loud already. I've been celibate, n-not incapable. I just..." He drew in a deep breath. "I d-didn't see you coming. I'll never regret you...but I d-didn't see you coming. And you're r-right. It's o-okay if we don't. I'm w-worried."

"Worried?" I tried to imagine what might concern him. I'd assumed his grandparents were the biggest impediment. If I hadn't known how early it was at the moment, with them still asleep upstairs, I wouldn't have ventured this. Nothing like Nanny yelling *waffles* to end a make-out session. Truly epic.

"You w-were injured, Ryan. Badly. I w-worry about you all the time."

"Oh." I frowned. "But you don't need to. The pain's mostly gone—unless I do something stupid."

"L-like having sex?"

I pursed my lips. "I've done some research. There are positions. And we need to keep it lower key."

"L-lower key?" He arched an eyebrow.

"Languid. Slow. Look, I'd prefer that way for the first few times anyway. There's something to be said for all-in heart-pounding cocks-drilling sex, of course."

His eyes got even wider.

"And that's what I used to do. The few times I hooked up with people." I almost kept the rest of that thought to myself, but I'd promised complete honesty. "I did it that way because I thought I had to. I just wanted to go in, have sex, and get out. I mean, I only had anal a couple of times. And that was fine."

"F-fine?"

"Okay, I didn't necessarily enjoy myself. But, with Justin's help, I've realized the lack of pleasure came from the fact I had zero emotional connection to those guys."

"B-broken cock..." Those two spots of color high on his cheeks appeared.

I pressed a quick kiss to his mouth. "Not a problem between the two of us. Back then, I wanted to prove I wasn't just a loser in his dad's basement. They didn't mean anything. Which makes me sound horrible."

He shook his head. A quick jerk. "L-lots of guys have anonymous sex. You h-had something to prove. Well, n-not with me. N-never with me." His expression was so earnest. Like he needed me to understand how important this was to him.

"Just like you have nothing to prove with me." My chest felt lighter now I'd shared my entire truth. Not exactly the conversation I'd envisioned—but one that was completely necessary if we were going to move forward. "Do we understand each other?"

He caressed my cheek. Then lightly trailed his hand down my neck. And lower. He stopped right above where my scars were. He'd seen them enough to know the precise location.

I nodded, biting my lower lip.

With the gentlest of touches, his continued to trail his hand down my body. My sternum, my chest, my stomach, and lower still. He did something he did frequently—he slid his fingers into my sleep pants.

Some nights, when we were frisky, I might not wear them. I always wore my shirt, though. Last evening, I'd been so exhausted that I'd undressed, put on both halves of my pajamas, and had dropped into bed. A day of revelry, fresh air, friends, and plaid contests had plumb worn me out.

Simeon, for all his embarrassment about his stutter, was less so with his body. He'd sought permission, early on, to sleep naked.

I'd been over the moon with joy.

So there he was, perfect and bare. And here I was. Time to make things equal this morning, with him tugging on my waistband. "Take them off." A request I made frequently.

He did so, sliding the pants off my hips as I twisted so he could do it.

He eased them over my legs. Gently. Always so exquisitely gently.

When he went to grasp my shaft, though, I stilled his hand. "My shirt too."

"Yeah. O-okay."

He guided me to sit up and then, again with the gentlest of hands, he helped me out of the shirt. He tossed it over the side of the bed.

Chia yelped.

"I'm sure you're fine," I told her. Likely more surprise than anything else, since Simeon's toss was nowhere near her bed.

She huffed.

Simeon and I chuckled.

"W-will you lie on your back. I know w-we can't, uh, that way. B-but..." He gestured to my chest.

I understood the request. A denial was on the tip of my tongue. *If I don't let him do this, he'll never trust I'm really okay. And weren't you saying just the other day how much you craved touch?* I'd had so much from him—but I never tired of it. It was never enough. And

I didn't know how to ask for more without seeming greedy. So I lay on my back, placed my hands by my sides, and tried to be open both physically and emotionally. I'd never been so vulnerable. I understood that.

Judging by his expression—he understood that as well.

He started at my clavicle. Tracing his fingers along the delicate bones. Prominent bones. To Marcus's pleasure, I'd gained a couple of pounds. Mostly muscle, he maintained. He said it'd be okay to gain a little bit more. I'd never go back to the way I was...but something other than scrawny would be nice. My physiotherapist suggested I ask Dr. Raymond for a referral to a dietician. On my ever-growing list of people to ask for help.

The scarred skin was darker and ridged.

He hesitated.

I grasped his hand and gently touched his fingers to my chest. Some parts were supersensitive while for others I had almost no sensation. Those contradictions meant his touch disconcerted. And, in the same breath, reassured. He'd never judge me. Never look at me in disgust. He'd simply accept me as I was, and if this was as good as it ever got, he'd be okay with that as well.

As he traced the scars, something within me broke open. Tears pricked my eyes, but I fought them. At any other time, I wouldn't have. Simeon would never judge me. Now though, in this moment, he might misinterpret them. Instead of tears of joy, he might see them as tears of pain.

Later.

I'd find the words later to tell him what this meant to me.

He eased his fingers along the lowest ones, then continued his trail downward, as if he did this every day.

My cock plumped a bit at the first light touch of his fingers.

He started to pull away.

"What's wrong?"

"You're n-not...you know..."

I grinned. "Deep conversations might make me a little less hard. Keep touching me and I promise I'll perk up."

He continued to frown.

I pressed a hand to the furrow in his brow. "What is it?" I nearly said *sweetheart*, but we hadn't had that conversation. No one had certainly ever used an endearment with me. If I wasn't certain how I felt about it, it would be legit that Simeon might not know either—or might feel uncomfortable. "Simeon?" I also nearly said that we could stop. But he knew that and he hadn't pulled away.

He cleared his throat. "Uh...w-who does what?"

For a long moment, I simply stared into his beautiful face that was so dear to me. "Oh."

"Yeah. O-oh."

"Have you thought about it? About how you might like it?"

"W-what did you do with the other m-men?"

I blinked. *Okay, we're going there. Only fair given I'm the one with the experience.* "I topped. I didn't feel comfortable letting some guy fuck me when I'd met him ten minutes earlier. Now...one guy stuck around for a few hours and we switched. With him, I sort of enjoyed myself. He was...funny. Easy-going. I think he, more than anyone else, saw my vulnerability."

"Are you a s-switch?"

"Uh..." I rubbed my face. "Sure...?"

"Ryan." Part exasperation, part amusement, part...annoyance.

*How have we not had this conversation before now? Oh, right. Because I wasn't ready, and I didn't want to spook him.* He didn't appear spooked now...more uncertain. And that was on me. I smiled. "Not really. Well, maybe. I enjoyed bottoming...with him. Perhaps I might with you. Because we definitely have to try both ways. I mean, if you want. You should have the opportunity to figure out what makes you happy. Because that's what I want—to make you happy."

He rolled his eyes. "If w-we keep circling around this, Nanny's g-going to call us for breakfast."

It was barely six. We had time. "I suspect she'll let us sleep in—given it's Christmas morning."

His eyes widened, then he moved in for a kiss.

One I returned with joy.

"Merry Christmas." He grinned. "I l-love you. You're the best p-present I could ever have."

I pretended to pout. "But you haven't seen my gift."

He frowned.

"Oh, don't worry. Just a little something I bought." He didn't need to know how much it cost. Or that my dad had essentially paid for it. I was supporting a local artist. That assuaged some of the guilt.

"Why d-don't I trust you?"

For an instant, I panicked. Then I reminded myself he was only speaking in this specific gifty context. He trusted me. We were discussing sexual positions. For a virgin, that had to be tough territory. I drew in a deep breath and let it out. "I'd like to top. This first time. If you're okay with it. Because legit cool if you don't want to because, you know, it will be your first time, and bottoming is a very vulnerable—"

He placed his finger to my lips. Not in a judgmental way. Or a way of shutting me up. But in his way of letting me know that I'd made my point, and he'd heard all of it. "I'm okay with b-bottoming. I l-like the idea of you taking the l-lead. And y-yes, I'd like to try both."

Relief flooded me. Not that we'd reached a consensus. Well, that was pretty sweet. But that he was on the same page with me. He needed to explore. He needed to know what made him feel good. The quickest way to that was trying various things. And I loved the idea of being the first to do these things to him. With him. That we could explore together. "Are you ready?"

He nodded enthusiastically.

"Crap."

He arched an eyebrow.

"Well, lube and condoms."

"You t-think Nanny didn't stock me up?" He rolled his eyes. "I d-did as well. B-but I found extra supplies in the b-bathroom that I didn't put there. I'm not sure I l-like the idea of her climbing the stairs, but the thought was sweet." He ducked his head before meeting my gaze. "M-maybe, if we're m-monogamous, we might...?"

I nodded. "I've been tested. Standard practice given everything."

"And I'm d-definitely a virgin." He grinned.

"Okay. A conversation for another time." Because the level of trust involved in going bareback was phenomenal. I'd certainly never done it. I was neg. No question about it. But if he wanted me to get tested again, I'd happily do it. "Um, now?"

He pressed a kiss to my lips. "L-lube is in my nightstand." He pressed his hand to my cheek. "So yeah. N-now."

# Chapter Thirty-Seven

Simeon

*I*'m going to have sex. Like real honest-to-goodness penetrative sex. Because blow jobs and hand jobs definitely counted...but they weren't the same. I rolled over to snag the lube. I turned back to find Ryan lowering the blankets. In the dim light, his erect cock definitely stood out. *He let me touch his scars. He trusts me.*

As I trusted him. I handed him the condom and then fingered the lube bottle. Was I supposed to do something with this? Now I regretted all the times I'd considered exploring myself but hadn't. What had I been thinking? Oh, that since I was never going to have sex, that it just didn't matter. I wasn't repulsed...just resigned that it was pointless.

Ryan grinned. "Do you want me to prep you?"

I glanced down at his decent sized erection. "Y-yes."

"Cool. I love this part. Okay, lie in the middle of the bed. On your back."

I kind of liked bossy Ryan. I needed him to take control of this situation. And I might've also had a long conversation with Ravi a couple of weeks ago, in his capacity as a medical professional, about how to handle things with Ryan if we ever got this far. Ravi had given me a few tips. Then reminded me that my partner had a pretty good head on his shoulders and likely understood his own limitations. Still, as a nurse, he'd given me a list of things to watch out for. And none of them appeared to be an issue at the moment.

Lying on my back, I spread my legs. I'd never felt so exposed but, as I gazed into Ryan's dark eyes, never felt so cherished.

He donned the condom. "Easier than trying to do it with lubed fingers. Because we're using a lot."

That he understood meant everything. Clearly my inexperience showed. Instead of ridiculing me, though, he was making me feel like waiting for the right person had been the right choice.

He coated his finger with lube, then positioned himself between my thighs. He gently lifted my balls, then rubbed his hand around my rim.

Okay, kind of chilly.

Then he slowly worked one finger inside.

My body, clearly confused, felt odd. Like this wasn't how things were supposed to be.

He wiggled his finger with a grin.

I smiled.

"Yeah, you'll get used to it. I promise you, it's going to feel so fucking good."

"I b-believe you." And I did. He was that kind of man. The one who would take care of me. Would ensure my bliss was as intense as his.

He added a second finger and slowly sank deeper.

I drew in a deep breath as I adjusted.

"You're amazing. I don't think I say that enough. I'm in awe of you." He scissored his fingers, gently coaxing me to relax.

Still weird, but I was getting used to it.

Then he sank his fingers even deeper—almost like he was questing for something. Searching for a way to increase our connection. *Prostate.*

I wouldn't have thought that possible right up until the moment he hit that sensitive spot inside me. My already intensely interested cock jerked and a drop of precum dripped onto my belly. My eyes widened.

He grinned. "I promise you that we can have all kinds of fun with that."

"R-really?"

That unrepentant grin continued. "You bet. Just wait until I introduce you to butt plugs." He winked.

Which, a few minutes ago, might've freaked me out. Now I was intrigued.

Slowly, he withdrew his fingers.

I missed the contact.

He slathered more lube on his cock. He appeared to consider, with pulling his lower lip through his teeth.

"W-what? Is s-something wrong?" I'd tell him to stop if that was what he needed. This had to be up to him. Just as, he'd said, I could call a halt at any time.

"I was thinking maybe I should lie down."

I started to rise.

"But I think this'll be okay." He met my gaze. "We'll play it by ear?"

"Of c-course." Again, I almost pointed out we didn't *have* to do this. That nothing was riding on actual intercourse. That my love for him wasn't dependent on any particular act. That if I only got to hold him for the rest of my life, that would be pretty okay by me.

"Pull your knees up and out of the way."

I did as he suggested.

He positioned himself between my thighs and guided himself to me. "This might hurt."

"I'm okay." I assumed it wouldn't hurt as much as the time I'd sliced myself with the knife...so I figured we were good.

Slowly, he nudged himself into me.

I breathed.

He continued.

A strange fullness filled me. A stretch that turned into a burn. I *could* handle it, but I also struggled with it.

"You okay?"

"Yeah."

"Great. My head's in. That's the worse of it."

"O-oh. That's not so b-bad."

He laughed. "Only you would put it like that."

His words weren't meant cruelly, so I laughed.

Centimeter by centimeter, he pressed farther and farther inside me.

To my relief, I acclimated. I welcomed him. My body adjusted and the intimacy of the connection brought tears to my eyes.

Wordlessly, he brushed the tears away.

He truly understood.

"I'm seated. You okay?"

"G-great." I nodded.

"Now I'm going to move."

"O-okay."

And he did—sliding nearly out, then pushing back in. Again, and again, and again. Maintaining a steady rhythm that had me panting.

He was working hard to go slow and smooth, hold himself up, keep things easy for me.

In the back of my mind, I worried about him. But he truly seemed okay. No wincing. No jagged breathing.

I pressed my hand to his brow, wiping away a sheen of sweat.

He grinned. "I need you to jerk yourself. I would, but I'm a little busy." He said that on a hard thrust.

*Like yeah. Of course.* I took myself in hand and did exactly what he suggested. I tugged. I twisted. I ran my hand over the slit and my index finger rubbed the precum. If possible, I got even harder.

"Same time. Get yourself off, sweetheart."

Oh. That made sense. I jerked each time he thrust. Slowly, inexorably, I moved toward the climax I chased. The one I needed so very badly. Then, suddenly, a feeling overwhelmed me. "I'm c-coming."

"Thank fuck." He continued to thrust.

My cock jerked and cum erupted over my hand.

Ryan thrust a couple more times as I nursed myself through what was, quite possibly, the best orgasm ever. He held himself still, blinked, then stared right into my eyes.

I held that gaze as I tried to decipher his message. Clearly he was climaxing. Emptying himself into the condom that was inside me. *We had full-on sex. A man came inside my body.*

So yay, for checking another thing off my bucket list. Except...this was so much more than that. I'd waited so many years, avoiding this moment, knowing I wasn't ready. I just hadn't realized I'd been waiting for him. For this one, special, caring, gentle man.

But I was so freaking glad I had.

"Uh..." His arms shook.

"What d-do you need?"

"To pull out and to lie down."

"Of c-course."

He pulled out.

I held in the yip. Wow, I was sensitive down there now. Then I helped ease him to his side. I turned so I faced him. Once he was settled with his head on the pillow, I again wiped his brow. "N-now I'm going to ask if you're o-okay."

He closed his eyes for a moment, then opened them. "Yeah, I'm really superbly amazingly okay."

"You s-seem relieved."

"Well." He cleared his throat. "You weren't sure you'd ever have sex?"

I nodded—appreciative he understood.

"Well...I was never sure I'd have sex again." He pressed his hand to his chest. "Or that I'd be able to have it without being in pain."

I grasped that hand. "Are you in p-pain?"

He shook his head. "A twinge."

I frowned.

After a moment, he pressed his hand to my furrowed brow. "I'm fine, Simeon. Just being honest. Like, for now, let's stick to once a day."

I laughed. "That s-sounds like a lot."

He joined me in the laughter. "Maybe? I have no idea."

"S-so we do what feels right for us."

"Right. Will you kiss me?"

"With p-pleasure." Careful not to touch anything that might be sensitive, I leaned in for a kiss. The *twinge* comment worried me, but he was capable of making his own decisions. Of figuring out what he could and couldn't do.

Our lips touched in what felt like the most important and most poignant kiss we'd ever shared.

When we pulled back, I gazed into his eyes. "I love y-you." I grinned. I'd said *love* without stuttering.

"I love you too. This is..." He cleared his throat. "A forever thing, right? Like I don't have to set up another app on my phone?"

I frowned. "I don't think you c-can put apps on your flip phone."

"Right. Boxing Day, I'm going to brave the crowds and get myself a real phone."

"Or y-you can just open your present from me." I ducked my head.

He put his index finger under my chin and guided my gaze back to his. "You bought me a smart phone?"

"Well..." I winced. "If you're g-going to live up here, you really need one. I figured w-we could leave it in your car attached to a charger. F-for emergencies only."

"Or I could reacquaint myself with the technology so I can practice that game. I really do want to beat Kyleigh." He winced. "That sounded bad."

I laughed. "If she's anything like Angus, s-she'll probably be thrilled. Those kids like a g-good competition."

"I guess I have my marching orders." He stroked my cheek. "Shower then more sleep? Sleep and then shower?"

"Shower then we m-make waffles and pancakes for Nanny and Bops for a change. It's a Christmas t-tradition. I might be c-crap at it, but they always pretend I'm the best c-cook ever."

Ryan smiled, kissed me, then pulled back. "Shower together?"

I smiled. "I w-wouldn't have it any other way."

# Chapter Thirty-Eight

Ryan

S imeon was *not* the worse cook in the world. I'd be in the running for that title. Even with the lessons I'd gotten, I still could barely crack an egg.

Which was why I took Chia for her morning constitutional while Simeon did the honors. I'd have to learn, of course. I wanted to be an equal partner in our...relationship. Today, however, wasn't the day for me to try to learn. My brain was too full of sex, kisses, shower hand jobs, and trying to figure out the next step.

Maddox had texted Simeon, asking him to ask me if I was serious about the job.

I told Simeon to text back a yes and then confirmed he'd bought me a smart phone for Christmas.

He had. He just hadn't been certain if he was going to give it to me, or if it was going to wind up being a first-anniversary gift. Which warmed my heart because it meant both that he saw us staying together for a long time and that he was willing to respect my boundaries when it came to technology.

I'd never fly a drone again. But answering a text? Composing an email? Ensuring against a breach? Those were things I could manage. Thanks to Justin. Thanks to Angus. Mostly, thanks to Simeon. He hadn't charged in and rescued me. Instead, he'd stood by me, held my hand, and had offered unconditional support. I might not have made it if he, or anyone else, had pushed. Instead, everyone gave me the space I needed. If I never relinquished the flip phone, that would've been okay with the folks who cared about me.

Simeon mentioned a shelter, Lissa's House, that took in abuse victims. Apparently they were always looking for phones that could anonymously given to people so they could communicate without the chance of being traced.

I made a note to contact them in the new year. Donating a flip phone felt so insignificant. Maybe I could convince Dad to make a donation as well—he was always looking for worthy charities so he could ease his tax burden. Which might've annoyed me before. Now I saw what a difference the donation he'd given anonymously to Healing Horses would make. They could see clients who didn't have funds. They could do more good.

That meant something.

Chia shook herself.

Hell, I hadn't even noticed the snow starting to fall. *Where'd the sun go? Sheesh. Too much in my head.* That used to be a place I hated being. Now being alone with my thoughts didn't scare me nearly as much as it used to.

I clicked my tongue.

Chia turned, and we headed home.

Home.

When I'd been overseas, in the middle of a war, I'd realized I could never go home. At least not back to my father's house. Not just because it had all the latest technology—which I'd come to hate. No, because I couldn't abide by the extravagant lifestyle. The absolute excess. The grotesque shows of wealth.

Now, though, I could stomach the idea of perhaps going to my father's home for dinner. With Simeon, of course. I'd mentioned him to my dad...just so we were absolutely clear on where my allegiances lay. And that I was unquestioningly gay. I'd hidden the hookups from him. Had never shared my secret.

He'd assured me he didn't care.

I'd believed him. He'd changed. I'd changed. Our relationship would, thank God, never be the same again.

The break in the trees let me know we'd made it back to the house.

Without being instructed, Chia turned up the driveway and guided me to the first place in my life where I'd felt true acceptance. True love. And there'd been others now. The ranch. Maddox and Ravi's home. Adam and Dean's castle. Eventually, Justin would release me from his care. He'd carefully kept that barrier up when we socialized. Perhaps we should've terminated the relationship, and I should've moved to Kennedy or Avery's care. I hadn't wanted to. Justin had respected that. When we ended the professional and therapeutic relationship, though, I planned to invite him, Stanley, and the kids over. Maybe I'd buy a wicked gaming system and teach Angus a new game. I'd have to figure out what Opal might like. Probably a book. Whatever toys we bought would need to be good quality because the twins would have a go at them shortly.

*And maybe your own kids?*

We entered the front door. I grabbed the doggie towel and tried to dry Chia off as best I could. She made a beeline for the kitchen—undoubtedly to check to see if Simeon had dropped anything.

With care, I removed my coat and boots. My chest didn't hurt, but I wasn't taking any chances. If something did happen, it might curtail our sex life. Simeon wouldn't mind, of course, but I might. Now we'd actually had sex, I was looking forward to more. Marcus suggested, if I wanted to bottom, that I ride Simeon. That wouldn't put pressure on my chest.

I kind of liked that suggestion.

He poked his head out of the kitchen. "You o-okay? You're flushed."

I grinned. "No, that's rosy cheeks from the biting wind that's picked up. And it's snowing."

"Yeah, I n-noticed. Come into the t-toasty kitchen and get warm."

He didn't need to extend that invitation a second time. I slid my feet into a pair of Bops' old slippers he'd loaned me and headed to the kitchen. "Can I help?" The heavenly smell of cooked waffles tickled my nose.

"You can c-cut oranges into sections. And one grapefruit. D-doesn't mix with Nanny's meds, but Bops c-can have one."

I winced. I'd tried a grapefruit in the hospital. Because I'd been bored? I couldn't remember the reason. The damn thing had been gross. Just...gross. I sat at the table with the cutting board, a knife, and a pile of citrus fruit. With a grin, I got to work.

Chia dropped herself onto my feet.

"We should call Torah. See about getting Chia into therapy dog training."

Simeon grinned. "I t-texted yesterday. She said she's got a new c-class in January and a spot w-with Chia's name on it."

"Oh, perfect." I smiled. We really were on the same wavelength on so many things.

"She's f-fixed, so we don't need to worry about that. Dr. Zephyra emailed her m-medical records, so I've got them. We'll keep seeing the vet, of course."

"Another Dixon sister." I laughed. "I think I could almost name them all."

Simeon laughed. "See? You're a t-true Mission City resident. H-home." He gestured around the room.

"Home." I echoed the word. And had a flash of our future. Sitting here and doing this with kids. Our kids? Foster kids? Didn't matter. I'd have to attend parenting classes, or watch videos, or whatever. Because I only knew about what not to do.

*Something to ask Justin about.* He and Stanley had become guardians of Angus when the kid had been ten. Steep learning curve as the boy had been grieving losing both parents within a short span of time. He'd lucked out with an uncle who loved him and a counselor willing to relinquish that role and move into parent. An adoption later, and they'd been a family. Then fostering Opal and another adoption, and suddenly their family was full of love.

I flashed to the kind lawyer who'd gently delivered the news to Stanley. Arnav? Someone whose path I hoped to cross. "Hey, are we going to Quinton's New Year's party?"

Simeon snorted. "It's g-going to be s-something."

"Is that a yes?"

He nodded.

"Great."

"What's great?" Nanny asked as she and Bops entered the kitchen.

Simeon kissed each on their cheeks as they made their way to the kitchen table.

"Oh, this is such a treat." Nanny made a big production of sitting.

"Great is having you here to enjoy the labors of your grandson's hard work." I passed a plate of fruit. "Well, I helped."

Bops winked as he snagged a wedge of grapefruit. "We can see."

"Trust me—you don't want me anywhere near a griddle."

"I'm g-going to teach him." Simeon shot me a look. "W-within a month, he'll be w-whipping up gourmet meals."

Nanny laughed. Then pressed a hand to her lips. "Sorry." She managed to get that around her hand.

"Are you saying you don't think I can learn?" I pretended affront, all the while loving the sparkle in her eyes.

"Well, maybe with Simeon showing you. He's the best teacher."

Simeon placed a plate of waffles on the table. "B-because I learned from the best." He blinked. "I love y-you both."

Bops snagged his hand. "Same goes, young man. Don't think we're not going to miss you terribly. We expect regular visits. When you're not too busy with work," he quickly added.

Because he would never heap guilt on a grandson who had given so much—and received so much in return. The love in this room was palpable. Like a physical entity. A welcome guest.

*Will I ever be like that with my dad? Maybe not. But I can be like that with whatever kids I'm blessed to have.* I wanted to ask Nanny and Bops to make sure they stuck around for any potential great-grandchildren, but that wasn't fair. It might take years for Simeon and me to have kids. His grandparents might not have that much time. Or knowing what perhaps could come might be an incentive to keep them going.

Simeon met my gaze. He took a deep breath. "Uh… Ryan's s-staying. And we, uh, t-told each other that we l-love each other." He squinted. "I d-didn't say that right."

I rose and moved to him swiftly. I caught him around the waist.

He moved his hand, holding the spatula, out of the way.

I kissed him soundly on the mouth. "You said that perfectly. You always have just the right words."

"Boy reads a lot." Nanny eyed a slice of orange. "Gives him a good vocabulary."

"Oh." I nearly smacked myself on the forehead.

"O-oh?" Simeon frowned.

"I left something in my car. I have to go get it."

He pointed to the pancakes. "R-right now?"

"I might forget."

"We can always remind you." Bops grinned and tapped his noggin. "Still got it. Whip-smart. Sharp as a tack." He wrinkled his nose. "Did I get that right?"

I didn't stick around to assure him one way or the other. I darted to the front hall, removed the slippers, and shoved my feet into my boots. Yeah, I could wait until we formally exchanged gifts, but this was too damn important. I scooted out to the car, removed the package, then headed back inside. I swapped out boots for slippers and was back in the kitchen in no time.

Simeon sat at the table, with his grandparents, forking a pancake onto his plate. He eyed me. "T-this can't wait?"

"Nope." I gestured for him to rise and take the parcel.

He did. Clearly confused, but always willing to follow my weird and chaotic lead.

"Open it."

Gently, he untied the rope. When that was freed, and he'd dropped it on the counter, he tackled the brown wrap.

"I daresay it's a print or a painting." Nanny beamed. "I like the idea because we'll be taking a few of our favorites with us."

"Hear, hear. Charming idea." Bops pressed a hand to my forearm. "Well done."

Simeon gasped as the last of the paper fell away.

"Oh, show us." Nanny might've demanded that.

"It's s-stunning." Slowly, Simeon turned the painting to show his grandparents.

"Now, I know there aren't grizzlies in Mission City. So a bit of license is being taken. But bears live here, and this painting was just so—"

"Majestic." Nanny pressed a hand to her chest.

"Realistic." Bops' contribution.

"Over the couch," Nanny added. "Pride of place."

"Or over the bed," Bops added. "Also pride of place."

She swatted at him.

Simeon strode from the room.

I gazed back and forth between the two people who knew him best.

"Nowhere in here for him to put it down." Nanny nabbed the butter. "He's going to come racing back in here and give you a hug."

Which Simeon promptly did. He appeared to be ready to give me a wild hug when he glanced down at my chest and slowed his movements. He held open his arms, leaving the decision to me.

I stepped into them. Knowing he'd care for me. Knowing I'd be okay.

We stood like that for several long moments.

Bops cleared his throat. "You're going to have to microwave the food to heat it up."

Simeon laughed. A little damply. "W-we'll manage."

Yeah, we would.

We were going to be okay.

# Epilogue

Simeon

As Chia strode purposefully into the Cedar Valley Retirement Village, she clearly believed she owned the place.

With her newly minted scarf denoting her as an official therapy dog, she sort of did.

That being said, Ryan and I had met with the administrator of the facility first, and we'd obtained permission, and we'd met with a good portion of the staff so they'd know what to expect. Chia wasn't their first therapy dog, but the last one had retired in September. Now, in April, residents were apparently abuzz with news of the newly arriving visitor.

Nanny and Bops didn't know. This was to be a surprise.

They'd seen Chia a number of times since they'd moved in. At least once a month they came out to the house for brunch. Nanny was absolutely tickled at the redecorating we'd done. Bops had commented on the *big bed* in the primary bedroom.

As Ryan liked to remind me...I'd turned puce.

Nanny and Bops sat at a table on the patio, basking in the warm spring air. A heat wave of sorts was hitting Cedar Valley. A nod to climate change, or so I thought. Nanny remembered the temperatures being this hot in sixty-eight. Or maybe that had been seventy-two. Regardless, she'd assured me during last night's video call, this wasn't unprecedented.

She spotted us first, smacking Bops on the chest.

He jolted, as if he'd been snoozing. He did that more and more.

We'd managed our night at the opera, but he'd needed three days to fully recover. So we weren't likely to go again.

"What? Oh, hi, boys." He waved.

I smiled because I'd always be his *boy*. I'd asked Ryan if he minded being called boy. He'd said he was honored. That had made me smile.

Nanny nearly bounced in her seat. "Chia!"

Our dog kept her cool and delicately made her way over to my grandmother.

"Oh, what a pretty kerchief. Does that mean you're an official therapy dog?"

Ryan grinned. "Yep."

Nanny clapped. "Oh, I'm so very proud of you." She patted Chia. "Is she allowed on my lap?"

"As long as she's nowhere near where food is, she has permission." Again, Ryan grinned.

The list of rules was extensive for here, and we intended to follow every one.

"P-pat your lap and say *up*."

Nanny patted her lap. "Up."

Chia checked with Ryan.

He indicated she could jump.

She leapt into Nanny's lap.

Nanny giggled. Bops guffawed. Several other people pointed.

"Will we get our turn?" A gentleman with a walker stood nearby.

"Everyone who wants to." Ryan stroked Chia's fur. "I mean until you all tire her out."

Several people laughed.

"We'll wait our turn. A few hours until dinner." The guy headed off to a table where two women sat.

"That's Ernesto." Bops leaned closer. "He's got Alzheimer's. If he meets you tomorrow, he'll have completely forgotten. He lives in the high-care wing."

Thus far, Nanny and Bops were in the lower level of care. I liked that they would be able to move up as their needs progressed. Unless something catastrophic happened, they'd likely be able to stay here until they passed. Given how happy they were, that was a true blessing.

Ryan pressed a kiss to Nanny's cheek.

She giggled.

Ryan laughed. "I know where your priorities lie." He moved to Bops for a hug as I kissed Nanny as well.

"H-happy anniversary."

She blinked. "You remembered." Then she waved her hand. "You always remember."

"W-we worked hard to make sure Chia was qualified for today."

Nanny hugged the dog. "Best anniversary present ever."

"Well, we have another one." Ryan offered his trademark grin.

I cocked an eyebrow. We had agreed my grandparents truly had everything and that Chia being here today was enough.

Ryan gazed at Bops.

Bops nodded back.

After a moment, Ryan stepped before me. Then dropped to one knee.

Nanny gasped.

He fished something out of his pocket. Before I knew what was happening, he held a ring box out to me. He gestured for me to take it.

I did. I didn't open it. I just stared at him.

He cleared his throat. "Okay...so I had this grand speech rehearsed."

"Even passed it by me." Bops beamed. "Asked my permission as well." He turned to Ryan. "I warned you that you might forget it all."

Ryan forced out a laugh. "You did warn me. I just..." He gazed up at me. "You're the best thing that ever happened to me. And I didn't know this much love was possible." He gestured to my grandparents with his chin.

"An added bonus." Bops again. Clearly enjoying himself.

Nanny pressed a hand to her heart. "Oh, this is so lovely." Then she turned to Bops. "You knew?"

He laughed. "I love you, my dear. Have you ever, in your entire life, been able to keep a secret."

"I'm certain..." She trailed off. "Okay, perhaps not."

We all laughed.

My attention returned to Ryan.

"Open the box, sweetheart."

His name for me. He used it all the time when we were alone. Well, and my name. But mostly sweetheart. Because he thought I was the nicest man he'd ever met. I tried to argue that some of our friends were even more awesome—but he wouldn't hear of it.

And since he was the best man I'd ever met, I called him my love. Usually without stuttering. Because, around him, I had a sense of calm. A calm similar to that which I felt around my grandparents. That I didn't have to try so hard. That no one was judging me.

I opened the box.

A simple gold band. I removed it and set the box on the table. I squinted and found the inscription. *My sweetheart. My love.* Good thing I didn't need reading glasses yet, because the typeface was tiny.

I held out my hand.

He put his in mine and let me tug him up and into my arms.

We kissed.

Then he placed the ring on my finger.

I stared down as he slid it into place. "H-hey. It fits."

He laughed. "I might've measured with a piece of string one night while you were dead to the world."

I cocked my head.

"The day you finished the extension at Maddox and Ravi's. You couldn't even stay upright."

That had been a week ago. I'd worked with Jacob's construction company to get the rooms finished. The extension had an office for Maddox where he and Ryan could work when they needed to collaborate, as well as a huge playroom for the twins. Maddox's old office had been converted into a spare children's room as he and Ravi had put their names forward and they'd been approved as foster parents. Like having twin terrors in their terrible twos wasn't enough...they were willing to take in children in need.

Ryan and I had spoken to social services. They were happy to take our application and to begin the process of running background checks, but the fact we'd been together for such a short amount of time had been a concern. I'd also noticed the worker checking for wedding rings when we'd first met with him. Well, we were about to rectify that.

"A M-May wedding?" I gazed hopefully into Ryan's eyes. Now he had a ring on my finger, I knew he was all-in.

"You haven't even accepted." Nanny tisked. "And September would be much better. More time for me to plan."

"June." Ryan held my gaze. "Something simple. I asked Kennedy, and she's willing to host us at the ranch."

I laughed. "They're g-going to become known as a wedding venue."

Ryan laughed. "Oh God, don't say that to her. I pointed out we met there. She's nothing if not sentimental."

Nanny chuckled. "Those Dixon sisters are good women."

"T-they are." I gazed into Ryan's eyes. "We're really d-doing this?"

"You're my heart."

I eyed him. "And your d-dad?"

"He's paying for the wedding."

Which sort of meant everything. Between Ryan's amazing salary working in cybersecurity and my income with the handiwork, we did just fine. A wedding at the ranch wouldn't stretch our budget much.

But for him to have come this far with his father? That he'd let the man pay for our wedding?

I blinked back tears.

"Sweetheart." His voice caught.

"I'm j-just so happy."

Bops cleared his throat.

We glanced over to find everyone watching.

"Nice proposal. We want the dog." Ernesto grinned.

Ryan and I sealed the proposal with a kiss.

And toured Chia around the patio where she was the star of the show.

As it should be.

Want more Gabbi Grey?
Everett's story is coming up next in her Love in Mission City series.
Check out *Rayne's Return* (Love in Mission City Book 4).


Other Love in Mission City stories available:
Ginger Snapping All the Way (Love in Mission City Book 1)
Stanley's Christmas Redemption (Love in Mission City Book 2)
The Beauty of the Beast(Love in Mission City Book 2.5)
Sleigh Bells and Second Chances (Love in Mission City Book 3)
Rayne's Return (Love in Mission City Book 4)
Gideon's Gratitude (Love in Mission City Book 5)
Quinton's Quest (Love in Mission City Book 6)
Ulysses's Ultimatum (Love in Mission City Book 7)
Love in Mission City: The Boyfriend Gamble
Love in Mission City: The Four Seasons
Love in Mission City: The Boyfriends Duet
Love in Mission City: The Shorts
Love in Mission City: The Wedding Duet
A Daddy for Christmas 2: Foster
Puppy Pride
A Daddy for Christmas 3: Lorcan
Pup, Pup, and Away
A Daddy for Christmas 4: Raphael
Anderson's Reinvention
Rayne Check
Archer's Awakening
Leo's Lust
Finn's Find

Styx's Storm

Thought You Were the One

Love Without Reservations

Page Against the Machine

The Lightkeeper's Love Affair

Ace's Place

Marcus's Cadence

Not in it for the Money


Also:

Edging Coach (co-written with L.A. Witt)

Hugh (Single Dads of Gaynor Beach)

Anthony (Single Dads of Gaynor Beach)

Xavier (Single Dads of Gaynor Beach)

Love Furever (Friends of Gaynor Beach Animal Rescue)

Husky Love (Friends of Gaynor Beach Animal Rescue)

Yorkie to My Heart (Friends of Gaynor Beach Animal Rescue)

A Furever Home (co-written with Kaje Harper – Friends of Gaynor Beach Animal Rescue)

Axe to Grind(Road to Rocktoberfest 2023)

Grindstone's Edge(Road to Rocktoberfest 2024)

Voice to Raise (Road to Rocktoberfest 2025)

Drums and Lullabies (Road to Rocktoberfest 2026)

My Past, Your Future

If Only for Today

Catch a Tiger by the Tail

Solstice Surprise

Valentino in Vancouver

You See Me

Sun, Surf, and Surprises

Ginger in the City

Caressa's Homecoming (Bound by Love Book 1)

Cole's Reckoning (Bound by Love Book 2)

Donovan's Men (Bound by Love Book 3)

A Little Christmas: Tobias

Sizzling Sydney Nights

An Uncommon Gentleman

A Sensible Gentleman

A Wounded Gentleman

Didn't See You Coming (The Haunting of Pinedale High – YA)

Finding Noah (Foggy Basin Season 2)

Noah's Holiday (A Foggy Basin Short Story)

Dancing Through Pride (A Foggy Basin Short Story)

Keystrokes and Kittens (Foggy Basin Season 3)

Hot Rucking Canadian

Big Rucking Disaster

Unlocked and Unlost


Audiobooks


Ginger Snapping All the Way

Stanley's Christmas Redemption

Sleigh Bells and Second Chances

Rayne's Return

Gideon's Gratitude

Quinton's Quest

Ulysses's Ultimatum

Rayne Check

Archer's Awakening

Leo's Lust

Finn's Find

A Daddy for Christmas 2: Foster

Puppy Pride

A Daddy for Christmas 3: Lorcan

Thought You Were the One

Love in Mission City: The Shorts

Page Against the Machine

The Lightkeeper's Love Affair

Ace's Place

Marcus's Cadence

Not in it for the Money

Hugh (Single Dads of Gaynor Beach)

Anthony (Single Dads of Gaynor Beach)

Love Furever (Friends of Gaynor Beach Animal Rescue)

Husky Love (Friends of Gaynor Beach Animal Rescue)

A Furever Home (co-written with Kaje Harper – Friends of Gaynor Beach Animal Rescue)

My Past, Your Future

If Only for Today

Catch a Tiger by the Tail

Solstice Surprise

An Uncommon Gentleman

A Sensible Gentleman

A Wounded Gentleman

Didn't See You Coming

Unlocked and Unlost

Want a free short story? The story is set in Gaynor Beach, California where there are plenty of single dads and puppy rescues! You can sign up for my newsletter so you can keep up with all the great stuff I'm doing as well as pictures of my own pooches, Ally and Finnegan.

Hemingway's Happy Day

Love contemporary MF romances? What's better than love in the beautiful Cedar Valley in British Columbia, Canada? Find small town romances with a touch of angst, a bit of heat, and a lot of heart...

The Absolution of Abigail Reardon (prequel)
The Luminosity of Loriana Harper (Book 1)
The Making of Marnie Jones (Book 2)
The Redemption of Remy St. Claire (Book 3)

# Interested in knowing more about Gabbi?

USA Today Bestselling author Gabbi Grey lives in beautiful British Columbia where her fur baby chin-poo keeps her safe from the nasty neighborhood squirrels. Working for the government by day, she spends her early mornings writing contemporary, gay, sweet, and dark erotic BDSM romances. While she firmly believes in happy endings, she also believes in making her characters suffer before finding their true love. She also writes m/f romances as Gabbi Black and Gabbi Powell.